Praise for Anna DeStefano

"Anna DeStefano is a treasure!"

—Teresa Medeiros, *New York Times* bestselling author

"A completely captivating story."

—The Reading Café for *Let Me Love You Again*

"One of the most powerful novellas I've ever had the fortune to read and review."

—Fresh Fiction for *Here in My Heart*

"You won't want to put it down."

—Night Owl Reviews for *Love on Mimosa Lane*

"Anna DeStefano is a rare talent."

—Brenda Novak, *New York Times* bestselling author

"Celebrates the resilience of not only the holiday spirit, but the human spirit as well."

—*USA Today* for *Christmas on Mimosa Lane*

"One of the best books I've read all year."

—Kristan Higgins, *New York Times* bestselling author, for *Three Days on Mimosa Lane*

His Darling Bride

Also by Anna DeStefano

Echoes of the Heart Series

Here in My Heart: A Novella

Let Me Love You Again

Seasons of the Heart Series

Christmas on Mimosa Lane

Three Days on Mimosa Lane

Love on Mimosa Lane

Daughter Series

The Unknown Daughter

The Runaway Daughter

The Perfect Daughter

Atlanta Heroes Series

Because of a Boy

To Protect the Child

To Save a Family

The Firefighter's Secret Baby

Other Contemporary Romance

A Sweetbrook Family

All-American Father

The Prodigal's Return

Romantic Suspense

Shattered Witness

Science Fiction/Fantasy

Secret Legacy

Dark Legacy

Novellas/Anthologies

"Weekend Meltdown" in *Winter Heat*

"Baby Steps" in *Mother of the Year*

"A Small-Town Sheriff" (Daughter series)

ANNA DeSTEFANO

His Darling Bride

ECHOES OF THE HEART

Montlake Romance

This is a work of fiction. Names, characters, organizations, places, events, and incidents are either products of the author's imagination or are used fictitiously.

Published by Montlake Romance, Seattle

www.apub.com

ISBN-13: 9781503951426
ISBN-10: 1503951421

Cover design by Mumtaz Mustafa

Printed in the United States of America

To the family we hope to be.

To the love we're born to give.

To the dream.

Community.

Chapter One

"Come on, Law," said the older man behind the bar of McC's Tavern. "Don't leave me in the lurch."

"I can't cover tomorrow night, Rick," the bartender said to what appeared to Mike Taylor to be the pub's owner.

Rick plunked a pint of ripe strawberries onto the bar. "I got no one else to cover second shift."

"And that sucks," Law commiserated. "But my last final's Monday morning. And I have a wife and daughter who'd like to get to know me again, once I'm not chained to campus and my course work every hour I'm not hauling ass here. I can't blow my shot to finish my undergraduate degree 'cause Paisley crated her cat, strapped it on the back of her Harley, and went trailing after some dude."

Mike's full attention lifted from the local paper he'd been reading at the bar. He pushed away his half-eaten lunch and nudged up the brim of his Stetson. The other men's conversation had officially become too entertaining to tune out.

It was an early-August Thursday in the small community of Chandlerville, Georgia. McC's was midafternoon empty. He'd been the place's only customer for the last half hour while he'd lingered over a cheeseburger, sweet potato fries, and a draft. The bartender and owner had mostly ignored him since Law pulled Mike's beer and Rick ran his food out from the back. The two were prepping for their evening shift, making numerous trips to wherever they stored supplies. Replenishing booze and napkins and swizzle sticks, and the menagerie of condiments that mixing popular drinks demanded.

"If you have to study for exams," Rick said, the shorter, rounder of the two men, "do it here."

"During Friday-night rush?" Law maneuvered a fresh keg of Guinness under the dark oak counter.

Rick pulled glasses from the compact dishwasher and slid them into their overhead runners. "It'll be a slow night."

"Then cover the shift yourself."

"It's not gonna be *that* slow."

"No kidding."

"So don't bail on me." Rick jammed his hands to his waist, a midlife paunch spilling over his jeans' belt.

"It's the only time I've asked off in two weeks."

"Hell, I know you got other priorities. I'm just in a bind."

"And I sympathize." The rangy bartender sounded more like a commiserating friend than a pressured employee. He wiped down the counter with a soft cloth, his attention stalling on Mike before returning to his boss. "Things have been in a bind since the recession nearly dragged you under. But you and Kristie kept the place open. Business is growing. Train another second-shift bar back."

"Next week, I promise." Rick nailed Mike's eavesdropping with a *WTF* stare. "In the meantime, Friday-night baseball will be on the flat-screens. We'll have a packed crowd from six till last call. You'll make a week's worth of tips in one easy shot."

Law shook his head. "I'm pulling all-nighters straight through the weekend."

"I've got nothing going on until early next week," Mike said.

He eased back on his stool, as stunned by the offer he'd blurted out as the other two seemed to be.

Needing to clear his head, he'd hit town early with a few necessities loaded in his Jeep and a powerful hankering to drift for several days. A new contract was on the horizon. It would be a much-needed distraction from the business he'd left behind in Atlanta. And from the other realities of his life that clung like a second skin no matter how far or how fast he moved. Especially this time of year.

Tending bar for these guys would kiss off some of the free time he'd carved out. But he liked to get the lay of the land when he rolled into a new place. Ease into the flow of things. And McC's was a local hangout, according to the guy Mike was subleasing his furnished apartment from—and the kid behind the gas station register, and the elderly checkout clerk at Sweetie's Fairway, a cross between a mom-and-pop general store and a full-service butcher shop.

"If you need someone to fill in for a day or two," he reasoned, "I could—"

"Don't reckon we've met," Rick interrupted.

"Mike Taylor." He held out his hand. "I'm new in town."

Rick eyed Mike's worn Stetson and wrinkled clothes.

The bartender shook Mike's hand.

"Law Beaumont," he said. "You have any experience tending bar?"

"Worked my way around the country and back a few times doing it. Paying the bills. Meeting interesting people. I've got something steady lined up starting next week. But I could give you a few nights if you need a stand-in for Flora or whatever her name is—the one with the cat and the Harley."

"Paisley." Rick crossed his arms over a belly that could have seemed jolly on a less cranky man. "My wife's niece. She's flighty, but she's the second-best bartender in the county."

"*Was* the second-best," Law reminded him.

"That would make you number one?" Mike nodded at the bartender and pushed the brim of his hat higher. "And me nobody from nowhere. I get it."

"You're a drifter." Rick glanced through the bar's open-paned windows at Mike's mud-encrusted Jeep. "Just waltzed into town. Already nosing into people's business. Probably blow right back out whenever the mood strikes you."

"Probably." It had been close to a decade since Mike had been a sticking-around kind of guy.

Law went from studying him to grabbing more of the glasses sitting in the dishwasher. He wiped them and hung them overhead with the rest. "I don't expect his mood will change before tomorrow night."

"So I should sign him right up?" Rick asked. "To take care of my best customers during my busiest rush?"

Mike recognized the distrust, the cynicism. And he'd typically steer clear of the vibe.

But there was something about the place, the town itself. He'd arrived only last night, but he'd spent the morning walking picturesque streets warmed by a sluggishly rising sun. Everywhere he'd turned, people and homes and small businesses had invited him closer with smiles and waves and introductions. Chandlerville seemed spun from the kind of charm you wanted to capture in a postcard image, to keep in a memory box instead of mailing. He couldn't help but want to burrow in for a spell.

"I'll be out of your hair in a couple of days," he said. "I don't mind pitching in."

"Why?" Less confrontational, Rick seemed to be debating whether Mike was just plain nuts.

"I like helping where I can." Wasn't making a difference what taking this break was about? Maybe this one more than all the rest? "I like places where good people do the best they can for each other. Being part of something like that for a couple of nights wouldn't be a hardship."

"No, I don't suppose it would be." Law gave Mike a more thorough once-over. "I could work with Cowboy here tonight. See how he fits in with the staff."

Rick threw his hands in the air.

"What the hell." He headed out from behind the bar and stalked past Mike. "Show Law what you're worth, *before* the afternoon rush starts. If you know one end of a mixed drink from another, you're on tonight while he's around to pick up after you. Handle the happy hour and dinner food orders folks make at the bar, and we'll talk about tomorrow."

Rick stalled out a few feet away.

"And . . . thank you, I guess." He dug his hands into his jeans' pockets. "I'll go find the paperwork you gotta fill out. Even if we all end up regretting this by sundown, Kristie will have my ass come payroll if I don't make it official."

The man headed down the same strip of a hallway that led to the kitchen and wherever McC's stored its supplies.

"Kristie?" Mike asked Law.

"His wife. Rick's CPA. His conscience. He'll tell ya she's the real reason he kept this place going a few years back when businesses all over were tanking. The woman's a genius at investments and taxes, strangling the last gasp of oxygen from every dime."

Mike joined him on the other side of the bar. "You know them pretty well?"

"They've been good to me since I moved to town."

Mike took the absence of details in stride. Lots of people kept the nuts and bolts of their lives close, for a lot of reasons they didn't discuss. "So folks around here don't automatically distrust every newcomer on sight?"

"I didn't say that." Law tossed him an apron identical to the one wrapped around his hips. "But helping out a neighbor who's got nowhere else to turn should earn you some cred."

"It's really no big deal." Mike relaxed deeper into the right-place, right-time moment. "Where do we start?"

Law waved a hand at the bar's shelves and cabinets, the bottles and glasses and equipment and other flotsam. "Make me a seven and seven. A lemon drop. A frozen margarita. A manhattan. Then we'll move on to the complicated stuff."

"After you taste what I mix?"

"I'm a recovering alcoholic," the guy said with the same emphasis Mike would have given to announcing that he was left-handed. "But I'll know you've got game when you don't have to cheat with a mixology app on your phone. Ready to rumble, Cowboy?"

Mike lifted his hat, smoothed back his hair, and resettled his Stetson. Nuts or not, this was going to be fun. He reached for a highball and twirled the glass in his hand.

"Guess we're about to find out."

"Benjie's not seriously here," Nicole said to Bethany Darling, taking the words right out of Bethany's mouth.

She'd been thinking it ever since her louse of an ex had slinked back into town the end of May, and kept popping up on her radar with disturbing regularity.

"Maybe he just wants a beer?" Bethany begged the universe at large.

"Honey." Nic crossed her supermodel-long legs. She was perched on the stool to Bethany's left. "Richie Rich wouldn't be slumming in a place like this for anyone else but you. I'm sure Mummy's wondering why he's not holding court with her at their family table at the country club. You gotta nip this one in the bud."

"Put that dirty dog down," Clair insisted from Bethany's right, *really* needing a mute button. "He's been panting after you for too long. You've ignored him. Your family's ignored him. Even we've ignored how he did you wrong, because it's what you wanted. If the guy had a clue to catch, he would have by now."

Bethany snuck a glance around at the half dozen or more people casually listening in. Most of them were dressed in jeans and Braves shirts, a lot of the guys and more than a few of the women wore team ball caps. As she caught their attention, several smiled. Some in support. Others in commiseration.

It was nearly eight o'clock. McC's Thursday-night happy hour had been a crazy swarm of friends and neighbors clustering around nearby tables. Now the dining room that doglegged off to the right brimmed with patrons, too. Standing room at the bar was maxed out, with more regulars pouring in by the minute—most recently, Benjie Carrington.

Thankfully, he'd stopped to talk with an elderly couple sipping wine and waiting near the hostess stand.

"It's time to be brutal." Clair's sage wisdom came with a side hug.

Bethany shrugged off her bestie. "We don't all do brutal as effortlessly as you do. You have a revolving door of hotties—including one of my brothers—perfectly happy to be loved and left anytime you crook your finger at them."

Nic, not the hugging type, nudged Bethany with a sharp elbow. "Smack him across the nose with a rolled newspaper. Can you think of a better place to finally be done with the jerk?"

"So, basically, make a spectacle of myself?" Bethany toasted the overfull room with her nearly empty glass of wine. "I don't think so."

Her days of embarrassing herself over guys were behind her. She'd lost it after she'd dumped Benjie the end of their senior year of high school. Then she'd compounded her misery by attaching herself to a steady stream of emotionally unavailable men—so sure with each new love that she'd finally found *the* one who'd be everything her heart desired. Now her heart was firmly focused on more important things. Permanent things, like friends and family and the community she'd come back to.

"To hell with anything Benjie or any man wants from me," she told her friends and herself.

"Like that guy has ever cared about what *you* want," Clair warned. "In his warped view of reality, you two are back to ground zero."

"While the whole town watches the show?"

"You're a Dixon, honey." Nic shook her head. "Your family should have its own Facebook page, the way people keep track of your comings and goings. Everyone's weighing in on him panting after you again."

"He's kinda pitiful these days," Clair said. "Folks are shunning him for the lying, cheating dog he was to you. Meanwhile he's running his sainted daddy's dry cleaning business into the ground."

Bethany winced. "His father died, C."

"Ralph Carrington was a crank," Nic reminded her, "and he's been gone for two years."

"And Benny had no problem," Clair added, "leaving his mom to sink or swim handling things on her own—until he skidded out of art school, with no one interested in commissioning or showing his no-good sculpture."

Bethany shrugged.

"His family's money could have bought him *some* kind of apprenticeship in New York." She'd refused to follow Benjie to Manhattan after high school. It had meant giving up her scholarship, but it wasn't like she'd been able to paint anymore anyway. "It was his father's donation that finally got him a spot in art school."

"Your talent's the main reason Benjie got into Pratt, and you know it." Clair tossed her long blonde hair over the nearly bare shoulder of her micro-mini sundress. "Make this a smackdown to remember."

Nic wiggled her smartphone in Bethany's face. She was constantly tweeting, sharing, tumbling, gramming, or whatever else she did with her legion of virtual playmates.

"You'll be trending on social media by midnight," she promised.

"My dream come true."

"Hashtag, *DirtyDogGetsHis.*"

"Hashtag, *HellNo.*" Bethany yanked the phone away and smacked it to the bar.

Clair pouted. "The guy deserves it."

"My family doesn't."

Bethany had put them through enough. Her dreams of being a painter dashed, she'd run off to Atlanta after aging out of foster care. She'd no longer trusted anyone or anything she knew. Wanting a totally new life, she'd been desperate to start over again. And again. And then again.

She'd wised up a year ago, making her way back to Chandlerville with half a dozen failed fresh starts in her rearview mirror. But even then she'd kept her distance from her foster family, mortified by the way she'd cut them out of her life. She'd been unsure of her welcome no matter how many ways her parents and older siblings had tried to reach out to her, or how hurt they must have been at her reticence.

Now, settling back into the family was the only dream she was chasing—even if the Dixon clan still loved all-in, like a tidal wave of unconditional acceptance that left her close to sobbing in gratitude one minute and nearly breaking out in hives the next.

"I don't want a fight," she told her friends.

Clair's side-glance labeled Bethany a liar.

"He'll get the idea," Bethany insisted, "if I keep ignoring him."

"Disappearing, you mean," Nic corrected. "While you use steering clear of Benjie as your excuse."

"I'm doing no such thing."

Bethany had reconnected only this past January with the people she should have trusted from the start. Her foster family had a wedding and Marsha and Joe's thirty-fifth anniversary on the horizon. And Bethany was going to be there for every moment of it. The planning and celebration. Helping any way she could. Soaking up how lucky she was to have a place in their crazy, zany world.

"I don't care what Benjie does anymore." So what if his unwanted advances were jumping up and down on her last nerve? "I told him to get lost last week when he showed up drunk on Dru and Brad's doorstep. I'll tell him again if he really comes all the way over here. Pitching a public fit will only cause more gossip and get my family involved. My brothers have been chomping at the bit all summer to measure out some Southern justice."

"You could snag yourself another guy to hang out with," Nic suggested. She laughed at Bethany's rude hand gesture in response. "I know you've sworn off men. But I'm just saying. That would get the point across to *BenBotheringYouLongEnough*, without raising a caution flag with your bad-boy bros."

Bethany wasn't so sure about that. Her parents and older foster siblings knew enough about her life in Atlanta to say a time or two or twenty that they were happy to see her settling down.

She drained her pinot gri, her attention wandering to the one person in McC's who seemed oblivious to her dilemma. Rick's newest employee, working his first night behind the bar, had been attentive, efficient. But he'd yet to chat her and Nic and Clair up the way he had other patrons clustered around the horseshoe-shaped counter. Not that Bethany had noticed. Much. Except for wondering who he was and where he'd come from. And why what was clearly about to go down with Benjie should feel even more mortifying with this gorgeous stranger there to witness it.

Bethany watched him bend over to pull something from the minifridge beside the sink.

Clair sipped her beer. She caught Bethany staring at the guy's assets. "I've seen you look at a box of Dan's strawberry cupcakes that way. Right before you inhaled a half dozen of them."

Bethany fluffed the spiked, purple-tinged bangs of her close-cropped auburn hair.

"I don't know why I let you two talk me into girls' night," she complained.

Benjie had worked his way deeper into the crowd, stopping to talk to a table of Braves fans who were being polite. But they were clearly wanting to get back to the game they kept glancing around him to watch.

"I mean," Bethany said, "what were the chances he *wouldn't* show up? I could have stayed put in Atlanta. Pitched in at the youth center after teaching my class."

"Or headed straight to Dru's as soon as you hit Chandlerville?" Nic tsk-tsked with a shake of her head.

"I need all the painting time I can get." And her peaceful, makeshift studio at the house that her foster sister shared with her fiancé was Bethany's haven.

"You *need* a social life," Clair corrected. "Pronto. Which doesn't include volunteering teaching children how to be creative, pulling all-nighters in your painting cave, or covering odd shifts for your sister at the Dream Whip. All so you can steer clear of Mr. Wonderful over there."

Nic was now keeping a closer eye on Bethany than on Benjie. "Not that he's the only reason we're seeing less and less of you by the day. Your family is ramped up to an extreme state of togetherness. Even for them. It was freaking you out long before this new thing of yours started up in the city."

Bethany smiled. The same way she did each time she remembered that beginning next month, she'd be working a few days a week as an artist in residence at a Midtown Atlanta co-op.

"Now you have an even better reason to ditch us," Nic griped. "We practically had to drag you out tonight like—"

"Some kind of *friend-tervention*?" Clair tugged at the mid-thigh hem of her dress. The thirty-something guy sitting on her other side nearly fell off his bar stool. "You need to lighten up, B, before you crack. Date a little. Have a good time. Stop letting your family get to you. Stop worrying about getting your heart stomped by another Mr. Wrong. Have a little fun with—"

"Mr. Right Now?" Bethany's gaze returned to the sexy cowboy behind the bar.

He sported the kind of neatly trimmed beard stubble that would have made him her type . . . if she was allowing herself to have a type these days. The faded Stetson he wore might have been overkill on a less rugged man. His jeans were worn in delicious places. His soft chambray shirt elicited fantasies about smoothing her fingers across the muscles that rippled beneath as he and Law worked in fluid tandem.

She shook her head, appreciating the view and her friends' concern. But the kind of flirty hookups Nic and Clair thrived on weren't for Bethany anymore. Her heart, she'd learned the hard way, hadn't come with the necessary off switch. She fell too hard, too fast. And she'd already loved enough men in her life.

She glanced out McC's windows to the gently falling night, longing to be back at Dru's fighting to make something happen with her paints and canvases. Instead, she was at a bar, watching Benjie Carrington's latest descent into public intoxication.

"Is he actually wearing jeans?" she asked.

Nic snorted. "Who knew it would take half a decade in New York City to yank the stick out of his uptight butt."

Benjie made eye contact with Bethany finally, as if he'd just realized she was there. His smile went all intimate and *How you doin'?* The room seemed to shrink, everyone between them zeroing in on Bethany's eye roll. The fury she hadn't shaken in five years bubbled higher. Like an overheated pot of soup, threatening to soak everything.

Clair finished her Stella and motioned for another, flashing the new bartender a smile. "Too bad Papa Carrington's check to that fancy school couldn't buy Benny some actual talent."

Nic drained her vodka cranberry. "I hear he's thinking he can get his work into a local gallery. He's been flashing a lot of green around, donating serious bank to the Atlanta art community."

Bethany had peeked at the sculpture samples he'd pinned to various social media boards—both school projects and freelance attempts. They were as flat and uninspired as the sketches and paintings she'd tried to help him bring to life when they'd dated. But in high-end art circles, money often trumped talent.

And money—unlike inspiration—was something Benjie had never lacked.

"His pieces have a better shot getting placed somewhere prominent in the city than mine ever will," she admitted.

"Fraud," Clair said.

"You're a hundred times the artist he'll ever be," Nic reminded Bethany.

"Except I'm not making art anymore."

"Not since he—"

"Screwed me?" Bethany's gaze locked with the gorgeous brown eyes of Law's new colleague.

The guy gave her a slow smile and a fresh glass of pinot. A jolt of adrenaline sizzled through her. She went to look away and couldn't. Neither could he, evidently, his eyes widening as their fingers grazed. His touch lingered. His easy wink said he'd meant it to.

"Stop avoiding the inevitable," Nic said.

"Inevitable?" Bethany mumbled, sizing up the six-foot-tall-and-then-some bartender who'd caught her attention as soon as she'd walked into McC's.

Nic poked her with another elbow.

"Ouch!" Bethany yelped.

"You're drooling." Her friend pulled Bethany's hand and glass toward their side of the bar. She handed Bethany a napkin.

The cowboy winked again before walking away. His backside had Bethany spilling her wine as she gulped it. She wiped her mouth. Her attention wandered lower, snagging on obscenely scuffed boots that looked to be for hiking, not riding.

"Earth to Bethany," Clair called.

"I . . ." Bethany said. "What?"

Her friend hitched a thumb over her shoulder. "*Ben-Stalkin'YouBaby*'s here." She grinned at the running massacre she and Nicole insisted on making out of Benjie's name. "Pull yourself together."

Their bartender had returned with a cold Stella for Clair, who preferred her fancy Belgian beer out of the bottle. He passed Nic a fresh cocktail, then propped a brawny arm on the counter and settled in for the show.

Who *was* this guy? And what the hell was wrong with Bethany, sitting there thinking that if the only way to teach Benjie a lesson was to get her *Girls Gone Wild* on one last time . . . Wouldn't it be fun to do it with an easy-smiling cowboy?

She cocked her head at him. Not that she was seriously considering hooking up with a total stranger who was studying her as if he were sorting through the first pieces of a complicated puzzle. Not when just the sight of the man left her desperate to find out whether he felt and smelled and kissed as good as he looked.

But Benjie didn't have to know that, right?

"We've never met . . ." she heard herself saying to Rick's new hire. "But would you consider maybe helping me out of a bind with my—"

"Hello, gorgeous." Benjie invaded her personal space, sliding between her and Nicole.

"Back away slowly," she warned him, "and no one gets hurt."

He'd always been James Bond handsome. Pierce Brosnan's Bond—tall and lanky, almost effeminate. The most strenuous physical activity Benjie had ever embraced was lifting his arm to ask his parents for a handout.

"I was hoping you'd be here tonight," he said, meaningful and sincere and fake beyond bearing. "I guess destiny has taken a hand."

Nicole mimed a gag at his *Casablanca* misquote. "Or you're destined to step outside and stand in front of Bethany's truck."

"While she runs you down," Clair offered.

"In overdrive," Bethany concurred.

The bartender chuckled his approval.

When Benjie slashed the guy a killing glare, the cowboy—why hadn't she bothered to even ask him his name?—tipped back his weathered hat and casually checked the flat-screen overhead. The Braves were in the bottom of the sixth. His brown eyes twinkled when he glanced back to Bethany, and Bethany only, as if Benjie didn't exist.

It felt as if the guy had hugged her.

Then Benjie and his bourbon breath crowded Bethany even closer.

"Let's get a table," he cajoled, "so we can talk privately."

"I believe the lady asked you to back off," said the hunk she'd invited into her problems.

"I did," Bethany told her ex.

"I know we have a lot to work through." Benjie's words kept slurring around the edges. "But I—"

"I get that you're a miserable failure," Nicole interrupted, "running back home with your tail between your legs. What I *don't* understand is how you think it'll make things better getting your drunk on and trying to hit on our girl after the way you used her."

"Go home and lick your wounds, Benny," Clair told him, purring the nickname he despised. "You're just making yourself look silly."

"As opposed to you walking through the center of town herding a dozen dogs at one time?" Benjie glared down his nose at Clair the way all bullies did when they meant to puff themselves up by beating away at someone else.

Clair had cornered the concierge pet care market in Chandlerville and three adjoining communities. The suburbs north of Atlanta were becoming bedroom communities for young, dual-income, affluent families. Caring for their pampered pooches, felines, exotic birds, and fish (and even snakes, hamsters, and once a potbellied pig named Princess) had flourished from Clair's part-time high school gig into a growing empire that required a full-time staff of four to meet the growing demand for her services.

"Do you need someone to scoop up after the next boom-boom you drop on the curb?" Nicole asked before Clair could sink her gel-polished talons into Benjie's jugular. "Maybe we can fit you for one of those doggie diapers."

"They make unfortunate potty training accidents a cinch to handle," Clair offered, ever so helpful.

"I need the two of you"—he cupped Bethany's elbow and sneered at her friends—"to stop pointing your bony fingers at my and Bethany's relationship, just because we all shared the same air in high school."

"Relationship?" Bethany's wine rebounded up the back of her throat.

She jerked away and pushed off her stool, swallowing the sickening burn.

Annihilation. That was what it had been. Her very public comeuppance for believing Benjie Carrington was where she'd find the love and security, the *forever* she'd always craved. They were going to take the art world by storm, he'd said. And she'd left her heart wide open to him, when she hadn't been able to with anyone before that, not since she was a little girl.

"You never gave me a chance to explain, sugar," he insisted. "To really apologize. It was a long time ago. And I know I made a mistake. But I can make it right now. We could still be good together. Let's meet for lunch. Dinner? There's Dru's wedding next month. I'll escort you. It would be a great way for me to break the ice with your whole family. Surely—"

"*Surely* you've lost your mind." Bethany was in his face, fists clenched. Shaking. "Make it right? I loved you! You said you loved me . . ."

To hell with what anyone else heard. Screw him, and screw not letting things get back to her family. Long-buried rage was bubbling over, choking her, fueling the need to do something, anything, to make him understand. He'd been her first but by no means her last mistake of the heart, and she'd never forgive him. She'd never forgive herself for being so stupid.

Her friends were right.

Enough was enough.

"I dare you to show up at Dru's wedding," she said. "I've been patient. I've even felt a little sorry for you. But if you get anywhere near me or my friends or my family on my sister's big day, I'll—"

"Bethany?" Clair gripped her arm.

Bethany shrugged her off and silently wished for the several inches of additional height it would take to put her eye-to-eye with the dirty dog in front of her.

"You actually think," she said to Benjie, "that I'd—"

"Bethany . . ." Nicole said, a split second before McC's cowboy bartender appeared from out of nowhere and eased Bethany to his side.

"Is there a problem, darlin'?" he asked.

Chapter Two

Bethany stiffened against the strong arm curled around her waist.

She told herself to call off the gorgeous bartender, right then and there. That she could handle Benjie herself. Then the cowboy looked down at her with his dark-chocolate gaze and a quizzical eyebrow that his hat hid from everyone else. And *OMG* did he smell good.

But he'd also called her *darlin'*. And nothing good could come of that. Not when she was liking his lazy amusement on her behalf, and his touch, and his hand on her arm—despite how badly she wanted to scratch Benjie's eyes out. She tried to step away and failed. She worried her bottom lip between her teeth, causing the cowboy's attention to refocus on her mouth.

The immediate connection between them was stronger than anything she'd ever felt. And that was saying something, considering she'd once had the tendency to lose her heart between *Hello* and *What's your name?* And then the bartender tucked one of the longer strands of her grape-tinged bangs behind her ear. The sexy, gentle gesture made her feel protected.

Lord help her.

"I'm happy to do whatever you need," he said. "Just give me the word."

And then he was pressing her back against his front, and the two of them faced Benjie together. The bartender shot her ex a smile laced with menace. Bethany knew, because she was gaping up at him. So were Clair and Nicole.

"You seem to be upsetting the lady," he said.

"*You* seem to be looking to get fired," Benjie lobbed back. "My parents have known Rick Harper for years. What's your boss gonna say when he hears you're harassing female customers instead of sticking to serving drinks?"

"He'll think it's my first day on the job, and I decided to bounce a bad-news jerk who's causing a scene."

Nicole's shock melted into an approving smile. A quick lift of her chin egged Bethany on. *End this,* she mouthed silently.

"Rick'll understand my guy standing up for me," Bethany blurted out. "Especially when I'm being harassed by a dirty dog like you."

She was rewarded with a chuckle from the man who literally had her back.

"I might not have known my boss since I was in diapers," he said to Benjie. "But I'd bet my tips tonight that Rick will see things my way, not yours."

"I'd like a piece of that bet," Clair weighed in.

"Your guy?" Benjie croaked at Bethany. "Since when?"

"Since we met in Atlanta," Bethany's partner in crime fibbed. He'd obviously been paying more attention than he'd let on to her conversation with her girlfriends.

Bethany nestled her head against his chest, starting to enjoy herself. "Friends of friends introduced us."

"I don't have to tell you how irresistible she can be," the cowboy said without a smidge of a Texas drawl. "We sat up the rest of the night talking . . . and so forth."

Benjie's eyes narrowed. "And so forth?"

"*My* so forth," Bethany spat out, while a fresh wave of awareness arced between her and the towering stranger proclaiming how irresistible he found her. "As in my business, not yours."

Her rescuer snuggled his cheek against the side of her head, as if they cuddled all the time. She glanced up. Her lips brushed the yummy-smelling stubble along his jawline. Totally by accident. But what on earth was that scent he was wearing? And where could she buy like a dozen bottles of the stuff?

She realized she was running her hands up the soft sleeves covering his arms. And she was enjoying the tactile sensation way too much, making the dizziness of being close to him worse. She didn't even know his name, and she was pawing at him, falling down a familiar rabbit hole.

Any rational man would be sprinting back around the bar. This one gifted her with another playful wink. Meanwhile, her ex was seething.

"Whatever I do." She refocused on Benjie before she succumbed to licking the cowboy like a lollipop. "Whoever I do it with, nothing about me has anything to do with you anymore."

"I heard you'd started chasing whatever warm body crossed your path," Benjie mocked, a drunken ass through and through. "I thought maybe since you were back in Chandlerville, you might be ready to settle down."

"With you?" Bethany sputtered.

"You want me to make him go away?" The cowboy sounded like he'd relish the task. His muscular arms tightened around her.

She shook her head. "He's not worth it."

The humiliation of the spectacle they were making was already bad enough. As was the truth in what Benjie had said. She *had* chased after emotionally unavailable guys—empty relationships that had flamed out fast and furious. And what did she have to show for it? An even more battered heart than when she'd first come to live with her foster family at fifteen, and even more shell-shocked instincts about people.

She wouldn't recognize real love if it hauled off and slapped her in the face.

She leaned into the stranger holding her. For a second she indulged in his heat, his strength. She wrapped herself in the harmless dream of them really being a couple. Of what it would mean to be part of something lasting that could feel good for more than a moment.

"You've got to be kidding." Benjie looked Bethany up and down. "Why the hell are you wasting your life on nobodies like him? You deserve—"

"You?" Bethany asked.

Tears welled. Not because of the long-ago hurt he'd caused. But because she'd let herself still care. She'd avoided dealing with this, and him, for so long. She wanted to go back and confront her teenage self. She wanted to shake herself now.

How could she have tangled up her life with someone who clearly only cared about himself? How could she have kept making the same mistake for so many years after she'd booted Benjie's ass to the curb?

"You think I deserve *you*?" she asked.

The cowboy turned her to face him, his features no longer teasing. He was quietly furious.

"Not on your life," he said. "That's why you invited me to your sister's wedding. Right, darlin'?"

"What?" Bethany and Benjie said in unison.

She blinked to clear her thoughts. And she would have managed it, too, if the bartender hadn't pressed her body closer, making everything inside her burst to life with vibrant streaks of inspiration, freedom, anticipation. Emotions that hadn't consumed her in a very long time. And before now, they'd only come when she was painting.

She framed his face with her hands, trying to understand when she should be pushing him away.

"You deserve so much more, darlin'," he whispered as their lips inched closer. "Anybody can see that."

Careening down a slippery slope of her own making, she lost herself in a kiss she wasn't sure she'd started. Maybe he had. But who cared? He tasted her, and her ears rang. Her body strained closer, and he groaned. His soft, firm lips coaxed, and she was on the tips of her toes, demanding more.

Faintly, from somewhere far away, she heard Benjie curse. Clair and Nicole cheered. Bar patrons clapped. Bethany ignored it all, reveling in the wonder of being wanted. A current of need swept her away. She'd been here countless times, falling with no bottom in sight and no solid place to stop and wonder if she was making a mistake. But it had never felt like this—this gentlest, most bad-ass kiss of her life.

Her cowboy was tender while he crushed her closer. He was patient, letting her take the lead, sliding her hands up his chest, linking them around his neck, her fingers running through silky, shaggy hair, knocking his hat away. She gave herself to the freedom of it feeling like . . . painting. This was the way she'd *once* felt when her art had seemed as easy and natural as breathing. When every time a brush was in her hand, she'd escaped into the rush of being completely herself—the *Bethany* she'd never been able to be with people.

This stranger's touch and kiss were consuming her with the same kind of inspiration, a bewitching spark of perfection she wanted to cling to, claim as her own, make forever real.

"You two ever gonna come up for air?" Benjie snapped. "Or should I book you a room at the EZ Sleep?"

The cowboy broke off first. His lips caressed Bethany's flushed temple while her body trembled. *Trembled.* And she didn't do weak. Not anymore, not with men. She stayed plastered against him, not sure yet if her legs would hold on their own.

He pressed his forehead against hers.

"Hi," he said, panting for air.

She inhaled, feeling people's attention glued to them. "Hi, yourself . . ."

"You okay?"

"I . . . I'm not sure." Of anything at the moment. Including the answering confusion in the guy's gaze as his attention dropped to her lips.

"I hear ya'." His smile was easy, charming, dangerously addictive. "Your lip gloss. It's—"

"Bubble gum." Her favorite flavor for years. Benjie had hated it.

"Yum," said the stranger holding her.

Bethany peered at him through her Technicolor bangs, gathering herself to apologize and come clean to everyone about their charade. Things were getting entirely out of hand.

But the guy's gaze was swirling with desire, his brown eyes nearly black, like rich clouds casting about a stormy sky. His pulse was having a tantrum at the base of his throat. What on earth was she supposed to do about how badly she *didn't* want to let him go?

"Your cologne," she whispered. "It's . . . nice."

He thumbed her bottom lip. "Some men *are* nice, darlin'."

"Nice or not, you're going to be in a world of hurt," said an all-too-familiar masculine voice that most definitely didn't belong to Benjie, "if you don't take your hands off our sister."

Mike settled the delightful darlin' against his side. Her petite body had gone rigid. The sweet softness that had melted into his kiss had frozen up, brittle enough to shatter. He hadn't a clue what he'd gotten himself into. But he had no intention of getting himself out until he knew she was going to be okay.

He studied the mountain of a man who'd spoken.

The guy stood, arms crossed, next to the jerk whose mouthing off had been Mike's excuse for diving headfirst into helping the auburn-haired, purple-banged pixie he'd had his eyes on since she'd claimed a corner of the bar with her girlfriends. Two equally large and angry guys flanked the mountain—all of them looking to be the same age and shaped from the same *Don't make me angry, you wouldn't like me when I'm angry* . . . mold.

Mike's protective instincts kicked up a notch. He edged in front of the woman her friends had called Bethany, partially shielding her. She stepped right back around him—not so much rejecting his support as not wanting to need it.

"Bethie?" The mountain wore a navy pinstriped suit, a ruthlessly starched white shirt, and a loosened maroon tie.

All of it was Armani, if Mike didn't miss his guess. But the guy's street fighter's stance and the cold glint in his blue eyes hinted that the road to becoming whatever success he was had been neither straight nor narrow.

"Who the hell is this?" Armani demanded.

The dirty dog—Did a grown man really allow himself to be called *Benjie*?—had puffed up again.

"He's the jerk who just had his tongue down your sister's throat," Benjie slurred, well on his way to being blackout drunk. "He's probably in her pants, too. Says he's her plus one to Dru's wedding. I heard Bethany'd lowered her standards since I left for college." He directed the last bit of verbal poison at the woman standing proud and tall between Mike and the others. "Must be exhausting," he said to Bethany, "panting around Atlanta for lowlifes to hook up with."

"You son of a bitch," Armani said as Mike's hand clenched. "You need to shut up before I—"

"Don't," Bethany told her brother. She glanced back at Mike, then down at his fist. "Both of you back off."

"Listen to her." Benjie's next slimy smile was for Mike. "You'll do your time for assault, and then I'll come after you in civil court. My parents' lawyers are sharks. You'll be bartending the rest of your life to cover my settlement. That's an awful lot to put on the line for a cheap piece of country ass."

Armani flattened him with one lightning-fast punch.

Benjie dropped like a stone.

A whoop went up around the bar.

"Oliver!" Bethany shouted over the commotion.

Benjie pushed himself up, rolled over, and flopped back down on his ass. Armani braced to take another swing. The other brothers, none of them looking anything alike except for their size, appeared to be just as pissed and ready to wade in. Benjie shook his head, his bell clearly rung.

"I'll have your ass," he slurred at all of them.

Armani reached into his suit jacket's inside pocket. He pulled a card from a small leather folio and tossed it to the ground.

"Have your mommy and daddy's legal team call me," he said. "A half-dozen witnesses will vouch that you took the first swing."

"I'm in." Bethany's blonde girlfriend took a long pull of her Stella.

One of the brothers stepped to her side and kissed her soundly. "My kind of woman."

"That's the story as I saw it." The brunette who'd been sitting to Bethany's right stirred her cocktail with her finger.

Heads nodded all over. Including Law's, behind the bar.

Law had been friendly enough to Mike all shift, but he wasn't looking entirely pleased with the current turn of events. Mike was right there with him. There was a fine line between helping and causing more harm than good. And his involvement in whatever this situation was had most definitely tipped into the latter category.

"Get out of here," Armani told Bethany's ex. "Stay clear of my sister if you know what's good for you. My family's been patient. My sister's been more than reasonable putting up with you after what you pulled in high school. Now I'm telling you to get. And stay gone."

"This is between Bethany and me." Benjie used his Braves jersey to wipe at the mess the mountain had made of his nose.

Armani cracked his knuckles.

The gutless wonder inched closer to the door.

"Our family's a package deal, Carrington," advised the blond guy cuddling with Bethany's friend.

"You nip at one Dixon," the third brother weighed in, "we all bite back. That glass jaw of yours'll stay intact a whole lot longer if you remember that."

Benjie stormed out the door.

"I can fight my own battles, Oliver." Bethany looked regal as a queen as she confronted the posse of male disapproval that was now being directed toward Mike. She was all of five-foot-nothing. And she wore what looked like a vintage dress that she'd thrown on over a pair of paint-splattered jeans, frayed down to holes in both knees.

Mike would have recognized her as a kindred artistic soul, even if he hadn't overheard her and her girlfriends talking about her painting. She was vibrant, vivacious, with an uncontainable energy he'd felt instantly drawn to. So when she'd outright asked him for his help, and then kissed him senseless to sweeten the deal, and *then* had gone along with his lie about them dating in Atlanta . . . Was it any wonder that he'd lost his mind and dove headfirst into bedlam?

He caught himself grinning down at her like a besotted ass.

"Nice boots," he teased.

They were red leather and coated with the same misting of vermillion and fuchsia as her Levi's. When she scowled at his smirk, and then the heel of those audacious Justin ropers came down on his instep, he bit back a curse that was part pain, part admiration at her gumption.

"You've invited a stranger to the wedding?" the blond brother asked.

The man's curve of a smile suggested that he might be enjoying himself more than he was letting on. He and the bad boy still standing beside Oliver sported identical navy T-shirts with what looked to be a sheriff's department insignia stenciled over their hearts.

"Dru said you'd RSVP'd stag." The third guy's Southern accent ran the deepest.

Bethany inclined her head toward the room full of avid spectators. "My dating life isn't fodder for public discussion."

"Does your dating life have a name?" Oliver asked. "Who is this guy, Bethie?"

"Mike Taylor." Mike didn't bother offering his hand, mostly for fear that he'd pull back a bloody stump.

"He and I were . . ." She searched Mike's features, as if asking if he was sure he wanted to do this.

"Bethie and I"—he shot her a disbelieving smirk at the adorable nickname—"have been dating off and on in Atlanta."

"Right." She looked more than a little shell-shocked by the story they'd concocted on the fly.

"I've just moved to Chandlerville temporarily," Mike added, keeping his end of things neutral.

"Only family calls her Bethie," the blond cop said. "And except when our parents do it, she hates it."

"Which is exactly why you oafs keep at it." Bethany ran her fingers through the spiky bangs that looked just right on her.

She studied Mike again, long and hard, as if measuring him for a suit.

Or a coffin.

If she told him to get, he'd head around the bar and be grateful for the hot-as-sin diversion of having her in his arms for a few minutes. Which wasn't to say that he wouldn't mind pretending for a little while longer. Long enough for her brothers to stand down and give her and Mike a few minutes alone. His mouth was watering for another of those bubble gum–flavored kisses.

Her cheeks flushed bright pink, as if she'd read his mind. Then she took his hand and stared down her family.

"Leave Mike be while he's in town. Stop acting like a pack of redneck yokels seeing to their little woman."

"Does Mom know he's coming to the wedding?" asked the lighter-haired guy.

"You're my brother, Travis, not our dad."

"I didn't see a plus one for you on the guest list," said the other cop. "Dru's been driving me crazy with it."

"And you, Brad Douglas, aren't officially my brother for another month."

Her grit and sass outshone her sprite-like stature all to hell and back. And damn, Mike liked sass in a woman. He licked his bottom lip. Then he locked gazes with the brother in the two-thousand-dollar suit, who appeared to be as good at reading minds as Bethany was. Oliver looked ready to throw another punch.

"Look," Mike said, "I didn't mean to make trouble."

He didn't do this kind of thing at all.

Gorgeous, spirited women who kissed like sex bombs were great. But he sensed this one was different, and for the life of him he couldn't say why. Except that Bethany had had him on the ropes with one look. With one hesitant request for help, she'd laid claim to protective instincts that Mike had buried deep. Which was the biggest red flag of all *not* to get involved.

There was a reason bartending had become an escape for him whenever he cobbled together the time to indulge. The easy flow of the lifestyle, listening to customers, harmlessly flirting with women, talking sports with the guys, and serving everyone with an anonymous smile . . . It made Mike happy. Mostly *because* people forgot about him between one sip of their beer and the next.

For a couple of years after he'd left home, he'd worked in whatever bar job he could snag. Cutting ties with his old life, he'd traipsed all over mixing just enough drinks to pay his way to wherever he wanted to go next. Living a drifter's life had cleared his mind, slain the worst of his demons, and given him perspective. It had saved his sanity and taught him how to leave personal drama to other people.

These days, he'd rebuilt enough structure and connection in his life to be good again to someone besides himself. He couldn't come and go as often as he liked, but he was once more making a difference in the world. Most days he even managed to find a way to like himself. But complicated family dynamics like the one playing out around him were never going to be his scene again.

"I never meant to—" he started to say.

Oliver held up his hand. "This is a private matter. And considering that my brothers and I have never set eyes on you, and you just had your hands all over our sister, this would be a good time for you to find somewhere else to be."

Lawyer, Mike guessed.

Lethal was the next word that came to mind.

Bethany pressed her body back against him. "I said leave Mike alone."

His fingers curled around the lithe muscles that nipped in at her waist. She relaxed a tiny bit more, tempting him to stroke. Instead, he glanced at her increasingly concerned girlfriends and beyond to their avid audience.

"Humiliating your sister in public isn't what I had in mind," he said to Bethany's siblings. "I doubt it's what you do for kicks on a Thursday night."

The Brothers Grimm exchanged uneasy glances.

"Bethie." Oliver's expression looked too soft suddenly, for such a hard-edged man. "We didn't mean . . ."

"To treat me like I can't handle my life," she asked, "and whomever I invite to be in it?"

Mike felt her tremble and hated it. His thumb rubbed reassuring circles against her palm. She absently squeezed his fingers back. He wasn't certain she realized what she was doing, but three sets of male eyes took in the intimate gesture, and her brothers' granite jaws tightened to the breaking point.

Bethany looked down at her and Mike's intertwined fingers.

"Oh, for God's sake." She wrenched her touch away and dashed tears from the corners of her eyes. Then she pushed through the crowd, heading straight out the door to the parking lot.

Her girlfriends slid from their stools in a wave of exotic-smelling perfume. They each slipped an arm through one of Mike's.

"Why don't you go see if she's okay?" Vodka Cranberry said.

"We'll take care of these boys," purred the blonde who preferred Belgian beer.

They smiled and turned their attention to the other three men.

"Thursdays aren't usually your scene," the blonde said to Travis. "Is it some kind of early bachelor party?"

The police officer nodded, doing a double take at the beauty's classily displayed bosom, which she'd pressed against his arm.

"Everyone's slammed with work," Travis explained. "It's the last night we could all get the time off."

All three men glanced toward the door that had swung shut behind Bethany. To their credit, they looked like they wanted to kick their own asses for upsetting her.

"Let's order another round at your table then." The brunette led Oliver and Brad away from the bar, her friend and Travis following, the friendly group ignoring Mike now as if he'd never been there.

Instead of being relieved and getting back to proving his bartending chops to Law, Mike battled the impulse to trail after the woman who'd just publically written him off.

"You two really dating?" Law poured bright green liquid out of a shaker into two long-stemmed glasses, their rims coated in sugar. "It's been a long time since I've seen Bethany Darling that genuinely into a guy."

I heard you'd started chasing whatever warm body crossed your path . . .

Benjie's description of Bethany's love life hadn't rung true to Mike, even before Law's insight. There was something about the woman's sweetness, the innocence of her reaction to Mike's kiss, that had warned he was holding the kind of woman a man cherished forever and always.

His heartbeat stuttered at the memory, halted altogether. Then it was trying to beat its way out of his chest as the rest of Law's revelation sank in.

"What did you say?" Mike asked.

Law handed the drinks to a waitress. "I've only been in town for a few years, but I've never—"

"Her name." Mike couldn't process anything else. He pushed his way between the couple who'd claimed the girls' seats at the bar. "What did you say Bethany's full name was?"

Law rinsed the shaker in the sink and reached for the vodka to start the next drink. "Bethany Darling? She's a real sweetheart. You'd be crazy to let her get away without—"

Mike raced for the door, past Rick, who'd finally made an appearance, wearing an apron stained with whatever mishaps were plaguing the kitchen.

"What the hell's going on out here?" Rick demanded as Mike blew by him. "Someone said you took on the Dixon boys and lived to tell about it."

"Nah," Mike heard Law say while Mike threw open the door to the parking lot. "He helped put Benjie Carrington in his place. Oliver and Travis will thank him for it, once . . ."

Mike ran outside, leaving Law to deal with Rick's recap.

Bethany Darling?

He scanned the parking lot, coming up empty. He was the only one there.

The powerful grumble of a well-tuned engine caught his ear. A flash of color streaked by. A pixie-sized pickup fishtailed out of the lot. The thing was painted in a pink-and-white camouflage pattern. And sitting behind the wheel as it took off down Main Street was a still-pissed redhead.

A cluster of early twenty-somethings walked past Mike, staring after the truck. He shoved his hands into his pockets and rocked onto the heels of his hiking boots. Snagging another minute before heading back inside, he tried to make sense of what had just happened.

He'd kissed himself and a woman senseless, that's *all* that had happened. Except she was a woman clearly dug into her close-knit community and her family. And an artist who'd talked with her girlfriends about her painting, while they'd complained about her work taking up even more of her life lately—and about her spending too much time in Atlanta. How was he supposed to have put two and two together and known that sticking his nose into this particular artistic vixen's life was the very *last* thing on earth he needed to be doing?

He scratched the side of his head, realizing only then that his Stetson had fallen off somewhere inside.

Bethany Darling lived in Chandlerville?

Well, wasn't that a kick in the pants.

Chapter Three

It was just after noon on Sunday, and Bethany was late.

Late made her crazy. Which meant most days she was more than a little nuts, because late had a perpetual hold on her life. She'd tried to master a better sense of the kind of time other people moved in. The kind where she'd turn up where she said she'd be, when she'd promised to be there.

But as a little girl, living first with her mother and then her grand, the world had been a reality she'd desperately needed to escape. Time had become her sanctuary, where she could disappear and resurface occasionally, only to discover that no one really cared that she was back. So losing herself had become a peaceful, fluid stream where her reality could stretch and reshape itself, relinquishing its hold on her to the dreams about things and places and experiences that no one else could spoil.

When she'd learned in high school that she could paint those dreams into being, she'd thought she'd truly found heaven. She'd disappeared into her art then, losing herself in her own world for even longer stretches of time. Only by then, she'd been shutting herself away from a foster family that was desperately trying to reach her.

From the start, Marsha and Joe Dixon had wanted her for themselves. For always. She understood that finally. But at fifteen, the only safety she'd really known had been those long, sweet flights of imagination. Then that world crashed around her, too, along with her relationship with Benjie. Leaving her eighteen, aged out of foster care, unable to paint, and refusing to go to art school.

So she'd run for years after that, desperate to avoid anything else she could lose simply by letting herself want it.

When she'd finally come home, everyone had welcomed her back as if she hadn't tried to forget them. The very least she could do now was not worry people with having to wait on her, wondering if she'd show for something she'd said she'd do, and if she didn't, how long it would be before she resurfaced.

She and time remained a work in progress. But she couldn't believe she'd let herself be late today of all days. She'd promised to make extra time for Shandra. One-on-one girl time that was supposed to have started fifteen minutes ago. Which might not have seemed a big deal to most people. But to a kid like Shandra, who was trying to believe in her own place with Marsha and Joe, fifteen minutes of wondering whether or not you mattered to someone you wanted to matter to might as well be an hour.

Bethany rushed through her foster parents' home, barely registering the kids sprawled in the living room and the racket of a video game war filtering down from an upstairs bedroom. She didn't see Joe, her foster father, and she'd meant to get there early enough to check on him. But she didn't dare stop until she found her sister and made some serious amends.

Bethany and Shandra had clicked instantly. Bethany didn't know the high school junior's whole story. Probably no one at the Dixon house ever would. But like Bethany, Shandra had fended for herself, at least emotionally, for most of her young life. And Bethany knew better than most how hard that could make it to open up and let anyone else in.

Meanwhile there Bethany was, looking like a no-show for grabbing lunch with her sister who, before coming to Marsha and Joe two years ago, had been dumped from two other group homes—for underage drinking and her willingness to do whatever her friends wanted, as long as it sounded like a good time. The two of them had connected over their compulsion to escape, as well as the guilt that came with never really meaning to hurt anyone in the process.

Bethany had wanted to show her younger sister an alternative to chasing empty relationships that would never be enough. She, along with Marsha and Joe, wanted to help Shandra put the broken pieces of her self-confidence back together. They were determined to prove to her that she could trust people—before *Shandra* was in her twenties, with her own avalanche of regrets crashing down on her, not certain what it really looked like to dream free and happy in the real world.

One of those pockets of happiness Bethany had found, thanks to a suggestion from her older foster sister Dru Hampton, had been the volunteer work Bethany did several days a week at the Midtown Youth Center in Atlanta, teaching art classes to inner-city kids. And on Sundays over the last couple of months Shandra had become her eager assistant, falling as in love as Bethany was with the students and their excitement for art.

It had become their thing, an easy, effortless connection Bethany treasured. And on their way into Atlanta they always grabbed brunch at Grapes & Beans, Nicole's bistro. It was a little extra girl time just for Shandra, where they could talk about her crazy love for fashion and her hopes to get into a design school when she graduated from Chandler High. But last night—for the last three nights—Bethany had stayed up late painting. She'd kept at it most of this morning, too. And by the time she'd surfaced long enough to realize what day it was, it had been a few minutes before noon.

She hadn't bothered with more than washing her hands and face before peeling out of Dru and Brad's driveway and heading for Bellevue Lane, knowing she'd be late. She rushed into the kitchen now, her Army surplus boots skidding to a guilty stop at the sight of Shandra eating a sandwich at the center island.

"Hey," she said to their foster mother, who was pouring a glass of lemonade.

Marsha's worried expression brightened. "Thank heavens you made it. How's the painting going?" she asked, while Shandra ignored them both. "Dru won't say a word about what you're doing, and none of us are allowed to peek into your studio when we go over to the Douglas house. When do we get to see what you're up to?"

Bethany bypassed the question she had no answer for and dropped onto the high-backed kitchen stool beside Shandra. "I'm so sorry I'm late."

The girl's clothes were a trendy explosion of color and unique craftsmanship, testimony to her ever-expanding sewing skills. Marsha and Joe's budget didn't stretch far enough to cater to Shandra's lust for something new to wear every day. So the teenager had gotten a part-time job at the Dream Whip, helping prep when she could for Brad and Dru's busier shifts. And when she wasn't spending every cent she made on fabric and patterns, she was repurposing clothes she already had, turning them into a constantly evolving wardrobe that was the envy of the richest girls her age in town.

"I totally blew it," Bethany admitted. "I forgot to set my alarm last night. Actually, I never went to bed . . ."

She shook her head.

Excuses were a gateway drug to believing she couldn't stop making the mistakes that kept shaping her life. She'd been hiding the last three nights from the debacle she'd made out of girls' night at McC's—secretly obsessing over the cowboy she'd *debacled* with. And she'd used her art as an excuse for not talking to anyone yet about Mike and Benjie, not even Nic and Clair. *Certainly* not her family.

She'd lost track of time, because that was exactly where she'd wanted to be—lost again, in a world of her own.

"I should have been here on time, regardless," she said. "I let myself get too caught up in trying to figure out how to paint . . ."

She clammed up again.

The new art pieces plaguing her were supposed to be a surprise for Marsha and Joe's thirty-fifth wedding anniversary. Which, not by accident, coincided with Dru and Brad's wedding day.

"I shouldn't have worked until the morning was nearly gone," she said to her sister. "I'm sorry. Really. I didn't forget about you."

Shandra shrugged. "Whatever."

Marsha pulled another tumbler from the cabinet beside the sink, poured, and gave Bethany and Shandra both some lemonade.

"Are we going to get to see whatever you're trying to figure out this time?" she asked Bethany. "It can't be easy, painting after taking so much time away from it. Your father and I admire you so much, the way you keep fighting to get your art back on track."

Bethany nodded. She didn't want to worry her mother with the truth that the creativity that had once given Bethany so much pleasure felt more like a crucible these days. A frustrating battle of wills, when painting had once been as easy as breathing.

The last thing her parents needed was to be even more worried about her. They were already dealing with enough. Of course her parents had sensed, regardless, that something was off with her art. They'd most likely ferreted out whatever Dru thought she knew. Marsha and Joe were like nurturing ninjas—their hearts ambushed yours before you had a chance to duck and cover, understanding and caring you into submission.

"I appreciate the vote of confidence," Bethany said. Her foster parents' unflinching support never ceased to amaze her. "It's no big deal. Painting's . . . just not like it was before."

"Maybe this new residency you landed will do the trick. You must be so excited."

Marsha and Joe had been over-the-moon thrilled for her when Bethany broke the news a few weeks back that she'd have professional studio space at her disposal in Atlanta come September, thanks to a grant program she'd applied for—using her high school paintings as her portfolio.

"It's exciting." Bethany would never forget opening the acceptance email that she'd weaned herself down now to rereading only about ten times a day. "And terrifying."

"This Artist Co-op. It's near Midtown, too, right?" Marsha glanced at Shandra, who hadn't looked up yet from the sandwich she'd barely touched.

"Near the youth center, yeah." Bethany wanted to pull her sister into a hug.

But the fifteen-year-old was skittish when it came to physical displays of affection that she didn't initiate. It had taken Bethany a long time, too. Some foster kids never warmed up to casual touching. It was one of the many things that made kids in the system different. Marsha and Joe made clear at the start of each placement that whatever one of their kids was comfortable with was perfectly okay with them. And they expected everyone else in the community to follow suit.

"I can take you by the loft after we finish class," Bethany told her sister. "Show you around for a few minutes, unless you need to get back before I do Dru's thing tonight."

Marsha consulted the enormous whiteboard beside the laundry room. She used it as a family calendar. She could teach a Fortune 500 corporation a few things about team planning and managing a labyrinth of conflicting commitments.

"There's nothing much going on this afternoon," she said. "Just homework and chores. You girls go enjoy your day."

Shandra stared at Marsha through the sweep of braids framing her oval face and exotic features.

Marsha nodded encouragingly. She switched her smile to Bethany. "How long's the new residency? Is it really covering all your expenses?"

"As long as I meet the requirement for volunteer hours." Bethany's insides flipped at the once-in-a-lifetime chance she was being given. It still didn't seem real. "Which I already am, teaching my classes at the youth center. And any supplies the artists use while they're on site are provided. We just have to email the business manager a list of what we need. The co-op raises money through corporate grants and from art shows the first Friday of every month."

"Maybe you'll have something to show in a few months," Marsha said, while Shandra came out of her funk a little more—enough to listen for Bethany's answer.

They'd been texting back and forth since the news broke,

Shandra excitedly saying that one day she wanted to be a real artist, too, like Bethany. Only with clothes, maybe working for a designer in New York or Paris or somewhere fabulous.

"I'm going to do my best," Bethany promised over a knot of panic.

Everyone pulling their weight with fund-raising was crucial to the community of artists she was joining. She'd no longer have the luxury of floundering in the obscurity of her makeshift studio at Dru's.

"Joe and I know you will." Marsha patted Bethany's hand. "Don't let wanting something as badly as I know you did this opportunity spook you into thinking you can't do what you were born to do. This is your chance to prove to yourself that you can."

This was Bethany's *new* chance, her mother didn't say, not to let what had happened to her in the past define the rest of her life. Not that Marsha would push Bethany to talk about her past unless she wanted to. Just like Bethany's mother had no doubt heard about Thursday night's scene at Rick Harper's bar, but would wait for Bethany bring it up. Another of her parents' superpowers was letting people come to terms with difficult things in their own time.

And today's time, Bethany reminded herself, was about her kids in the city—and her afternoon with Shandra.

"Give me a chance to make being late up to you." Bethany inched her stool closer to her sister's. "Even if you've already eaten, there's time to grab some of Nic's dessert. The kids at the center have been asking about you all week. Especially Darby. She'll *die* over this outfit you have on. And you care about her, I know you do. Don't give up on your friend and today because of me."

A lot of foster kids turned feeling that the world was always letting them down into an excuse to bail on the things and people they loved. Bethany didn't want her sister making that mistake the way she had.

She realized Shandra was staring at her.

"What the hell are you wearing?" her sister asked.

"Language," Marsha warned.

"What the *heck*," Shandra corrected with attitude, "are you wearing?"

Marsha set Shandra's plate and glass in the battered farm sink.

"It's a painting outfit." These days there was oil paint on pretty much all of Bethany's things, even fresh out of the laundry. But she usually took the time to at least change out of her grungy work clothes. "We'll be doing a ton of painting with the kids today, so I figured what's the harm?"

"Or maybe"—Shandra's expression was a caricature of teenage disdain—"you figured looking like a cartoon bag lady again would get some random hot cowboy guy to do another face-plant on your lips in front of half the town."

Marsha laughed.

Bethany glared at her charge for the day.

She handed their mother her glass. "We've got to go."

"Sounds like Thursday was a girls' night out to remember," Marsha said.

Bethany grabbed Shandra's arm and dragged her toward the front of the house. "Tight schedule. Running late. Don't want Shandra to miss her cheesecake on the way into the city."

"Is he really your date for the wedding?" their mom called after them. "Dru said she hadn't spoken to you about it yet, but that she didn't know anything—"

"Gotta go!" Bethany shoved a smiling Shandra out the Dixon front door. "I'll have her back tonight by eight. Tell Dad I hope he's feeling better today . . ."

Shandra giggled as they made their way across the freshly mowed lawn to Bethany's crazy-colored truck, parked at the curb near the brick mailbox. Birds singsonged in the trees overhead. Fall wouldn't arrive in even the northernmost parts of Georgia for at least another month.

Bethany pointed her finger at her sister, secretly relishing Shandra's happy laughter. "You're not to be trusted."

"And you're so *busted*."

Shandra propped her flip-flopped feet on the dash while Bethany pulled away from the house. The girl's long, dark legs caught the attention of a couple of teenage boys riding by on bikes. Shandra waved at them.

"Everyone's saying you've been seeing this guy in Atlanta," she said, "and that's maybe why you haven't been around the house much the last few weeks."

"Everyone who? And there is no guy in Atlanta. Thursday night was the first I've seen him."

And Bethany *wasn't* talking about Mike Taylor with her little sister. Nothing had happened with him that she or her family needed to talk about or think about . . . or dream about ever again.

"Bethany Darling swapping spit with a total stranger in the middle of a bar . . ." Shandra unwound a bright blue bandanna from around her wrist and reshaped it into a fun do-rag that she tied around her hair. "*Sure*. Cowboy Bob's just some dude who walked in off the street."

Bethany screeched to a halt at the corner of Baxter and Main. "Cowboy who?"

"That's what everyone at the house calls him. Boris and Fin played cowboys and Indians last night. Cowboy Bob was Woody from *Toy Story*." Shandra snickered. She'd used air quotes for the name *Woody*. "Bad news. Things got a little bloody. Your guy didn't survive the shootout."

"He's not my guy. Would you stop it? I . . ."

A horn beeped. The light had changed. Bethany let off the brake. She told herself that getting to Nic's as fast as she could so she could fill her sister's mouth with cake instead of gossip wasn't an excuse to speed.

"Stop talking about Mike like that," she told Shandra, trying to sound like she didn't really care. "Stop talking about him, period. I don't know the guy. How did the boys even hear about him?"

"Selena and Oliver and Camille were over for dinner Friday night. Oliver was pretty steamed. He's the one who called him Cowboy Bob first."

"Oliver knows Mike's name. They talked at McC's."

"Our brother and the guy you don't know at all? Except that his name is Mike, not Bob. And he's your date to Dru and Brad's wedding."

"He's not my anything."

"That's not what I heard. Marsha and Joe, too. And—"

"All the kids at dinner Friday night. I get it. I'm going to kill Oliver."

Shandra dug a stick of gum from the pocket of the five-dollar jeans she'd picked up thrift store shopping with Bethany. The teenager had frayed them by hand to look like something straight off a runway.

"Some of my friends' parents were at McC's," she said, grinning even wider.

"Oh my God."

Why had Bethany assumed that if she laid low for a few days, things would blow over?

She pulled into Grapes & Beans. Her stomach plummeted at the packed parking lot. Had every local in the place heard the rumors, too? Was it too late to floor it out of the lot and head straight to the city?

"Cheesecake!" Shandra bounded out of the truck.

"Woo-hoo." Bethany's stomach growled. She hadn't eaten since sometime yesterday. "Right behind you, kiddo."

And she was.

Even after she caught sight of the handsome, Stetson-wearing man watching her and Shandra make their way across the parking lot.

Mike watched the woman who'd monopolized his dreams for the last three nights enter Grapes & Beans with a teenage girl dressed like he'd imagine Bethany might have in high school. All color and bold accessories and complete disregard for what anyone else might think of what she was wearing. Pretty much the same way Bethany was dressed again. Otherwise, the two of them couldn't look more different.

But they had their heads together, whispering loudly as they approached the hostess, their affection for each other clear. This was no doubt another foster sibling. He'd heard an earful about Bethany and the Dixon family from people who'd introduced themselves to him at the bar or around town. More than willing to part with a little light gossip, folks had also pumped Mike for details about Thursday night. He'd begged off sharing. Which in such a close-knit community evidently made neighbors even friendlier.

He'd waved at a few familiar faces today, before settling into a two-top table at the local sandwich, coffee, and wine hub that had come highly recommended. Grapes & Beans was bustling with an enthusiastic Sunday crowd. Its farm-to-table menu options rivaled anything he'd found in Atlanta. The couples and families seated around him clearly agreed, lingering well into the start of their afternoons. There wasn't an empty table in the bistro's two dining rooms.

Tucked away in a corner by the front windows, he'd just turned his attention to a bowl of rustic red pepper and tomato bisque. A pulled pork lettuce wrap would arrive any minute. He'd hoped to be on the road in about half an hour—heading back to Atlanta to grab more of his personal things, and to take care of some business that he'd originally planned to put off while he was in Chandlerville.

Bethany was pretending she hadn't seen him. She and her young friend had left the hostess stand behind and were aiming for the coffee bar, wading through the crowd drinking espresso or lattes or a glass or two or three of wine. Friendly hellos greeted them. Bethany responded but didn't stop until she'd reached the pastry case and waved at the woman sitting behind it, whom Mike had already recognized as one of her girlfriends from the other night.

The brunette beauty was wearing the same uniform as the rest of the staff—black pants and a deep purple Grapes & Beans T-shirt. She'd been seated at a dinette table since Mike had arrived, absorbed in a phone conversation while her employees—at least, she appeared to be the one in charge—took orders and hustled out food and drinks to the hungry hordes. *Nicole*, his waitress had said the woman's name was. The waitress had added that *Nic* was working on plans for an upcoming catering job.

Nic smiled at her newly arrived friends, said a few more words into the phone, rolled her eyes, and hung up. She waved the waiter working behind the pastry case toward other customers and dealt with Bethany herself.

Bethany kept her back to Mike, when she'd clearly noticed him sitting by the window—after she'd driven up in the outlandish pickup that he wanted to snap a few shots of for his Instagram feed. Her young sidekick kept sneaking glances Mike's way and smiling. So did several nearby tables of diners. Bethany caught the teenager in the act and hustled the kid behind the counter.

"But it's Cowboy Bob," he heard the girl say.

Subdued laughter followed and lots more stares—people's attention shifting back and forth between him and Bethany.

Suddenly the woman he'd been schooling himself not to pester was marching his way, wearing paint-spattered overalls cut off above the knee to create shorts that she hadn't bothered cuffing. The hems were frayed in long tendrils of cotton that swayed each time she moved, and her curvy legs were accentuated by opaque tights patterned like a checkerboard. They disappeared into chunky combat boots.

Mike let his gaze slide all the way down. She was like one of the savory dishes being served up around him, tempting him beyond bearing to sample something he shouldn't. He took his time tracing her body, all the way back up until their gazes collided. Hers was icy, set off beguilingly by the purple she'd washed into her bangs. It knifed through him—the memory of those same eyes smoldering after they'd kissed.

They were the kind of bottomless gray that could cut a man to ribbons one minute, then melt him into a puddle of need the next.

He unfolded his long legs from under the table and stood. She stopped inches away. He reached out his hand to shake, which was lame. Her incredulous expression agreed.

"We're not dating," she announced loud enough for everyone to hear. "We never met in Atlanta. We were total strangers until the other night when you . . ."

Her tirade fizzled.

Self-conscious silence followed.

"When we kissed?" he offered. "Because you asked me to help you fake out your ex?"

She bristled on cue. No independent woman wanted to need a guy's help. This one less than most, he suspected.

She crossed her arms beneath delightfully rounded breasts. He tipped up the brim of his hat, wondering whether nature had hit the jackpot, or if she worked out to keep her petite frame so toned.

"I asked you to help," she conceded. "But you didn't have to take it so far."

"*You* kissed me first." But he couldn't say that if she hadn't, he wouldn't have done the deed himself.

"You invited yourself to my sister's wedding."

"I didn't hear you contradicting me after your brothers showed up."

"I was doing you a favor. They were already pissed enough. I figured I'd wait for a better time to tell them I found out your name at the same time they did. Meanwhile, the entire town and my family are gossiping about us. Whoever you are, whatever you're doing in Chandlerville, this stops now."

"You're breaking up with me before we even have our first date?" He manufactured a look of shock. "I feel a little tawdry. Used. Were my make-out moves that rusty?"

"We didn't make out!" She glanced around. People had the decency to look down at their food. "It was just . . ."

"It was just what?"

He'd been wondering that very thing, while he'd lain awake at night telling himself that it had only been a kiss. A great kiss, but a fake one. He'd been helping a beautiful stranger give a loser a much-deserved public flogging. That was all.

Mike had had no intention of hunting down *this* beautiful stranger in particular, to ask her if those fake, endless moments in each other's arms had felt as shockingly real to her as they had him. But he hadn't been able to stop thinking about her. Worrying about her. Hoping to meet her as he continued to explore Chandlerville and worked Friday night's shift at McC's.

"You're crazy," she said. "You know that? Taking on my foster brothers the way you did, your first day in town."

"Because two of them are cops?"

"Chandlerville's finest," she confirmed with pride. "You'd have run across Travis and my almost-brother-in-law sooner rather than later. Oliver, too. And they'd have—"

"Threatened to rearrange my nose like he did the mongrel's?"

"Mongrel?"

"Benjie. Your dirty dog."

"He's not *my* anyth . . ." She pressed her thumbs to her beautiful, tired eyes. "Never mind."

"You looked like you were gonna toss up your wine when that jerk showed up. Then you were practically spitting in his face. Whatever he did, however long ago he did it, I was happy to help send him on his way."

"You did more than that."

"*We* did more than that."

He should let it go, he told himself. They'd gotten the chance to talk it out, in public. It was exactly the kind of closure she seemed to have needed, just as he did. He was fine slamming the book closed on their encounter. But he wasn't going to pretend that it wasn't the best damn read he'd ever had.

"Don't tell me I'm the first guy who's lost his head over kissing you. What was a cowboy to do, ma'am?"

"You're no cowboy." She studied him the way he'd felt her eyeing him the other night—before she'd gotten around to acknowledging that he existed. A whisper of a smile transformed her heart-shaped features into the timeless beauty of a pocket Venus. "That was . . . the lamest line I've heard in a long time."

"So now we've established that I'm nice and lame?" He ticked the two words off on his fingers.

And she smiled.

Damn, he was a goner if she didn't stop doing that. Bowing out of this mess would be the best thing for both of them. He knew that. He knew who she was now, and that he should leave well enough alone. Sure, flirting with her was fun. But it was risky fun, and he didn't do risky.

"I'm sorry people are talking." He really was. "I didn't mean to make trouble for you." Not when she seemed to have more than enough of it already. "I haven't said a word to people about Thursday night. I wouldn't do that, when you made it the best first shift of any job I've ever worked."

She rewarded him with a rueful head shake and a soft laugh, making today the best Sunday brunch of his life.

"I don't know why . . ." she said, sounding mystified. "But I believe you. I should have thanked you the other night. It was sweet, what you tried to do. Sweet, if misguided."

She had no idea.

"You're welcome." He ignored the impulse to keep her there talking, even if she only kept telling him how crazy he was. "And no worries. Tell your brothers I'll stay out of your way while I'm—"

"Wow!" Her young friend rushed over with two plates of cheesecake, handing one to Bethany. She grinned at Mike. "You really are a cowboy."

"I'm not." He touched his finger to the brim of his Stetson in a clichéd greeting. "The hat just comes in handy. I do a lot of outdoor work and hiking."

Bethany's attention dropped to his scuffed hiking boots. "Well, that explains that."

It didn't explain anything important, to Mike's way of thinking. He knew a lot more about her than a stranger should. And he didn't know how to tell her that without disrupting her life even more. But he didn't know nearly enough about Bethany to satisfy his curiosity. He could stand there talking to her the rest of the day, and he doubted it would be long enough.

Which was a definite cue for him to be on his way.

He reached into his back pocket for his money clip, pulling out enough bills to cover whatever the check would be plus a healthy tip.

"Wow." The teenager snatched away the clip for a closer inspection. "That's cool. It looks like an oversized paper clip. Where did you get it?"

"Shandra . . ." Bethany handed it back to Mike, her fingers brushing his palm, his entire body responding. "Don't grab other people's things."

"It's no big deal," he mumbled.

He dropped his money and bent to pick it up, his ears buzzing the whole time while he wondered if Bethany's skin was just as soft everywhere.

"It's something I've had for a long time," he said to the teenager she'd called Shandra. "My . . . someone important gave it to me."

It was a Tiffany piece. Sterling silver. His brother had left it to Mike in his will, along with another priceless possession that their Park Avenue parents would have likely thought was meaningless and thrown away.

Nicole showed up, delivering the rest of Mike's lunch.

"Welcome to Grapes & Beans," she said, eyeing Bethany. "Fancy you two hooking up again in my place."

"Accidentally," Bethany corrected.

"The way you *accidentally* made out with him Thursday night?" Her friend smiled between Bethany and Mike. "Did you trip and fall?"

"He was lurking in the corner," Bethany insisted.

"I was eating soup," Mike corrected. Soup that was now cold. He'd have someone pack up the rest of his food to go.

"I wanted to settle things," Bethany said. "And I guess we have."

"Once you two finish talking"—Nic directed a mockery of a sultry smile at Mike—"maybe I'll *settle* a few things myself."

"Don't you have a business to run?" Bethany snapped. "Customers to schmooze?"

Nicole gave Mike a schmoozy smile. "How's your lunch, Cowboy?"

"You make soup"—Mike checked out the lettuce wraps she'd placed on the table—"and sandwich magic."

"Nic's brunch is the yummiest in town." Shandra beamed at Bethany's friend. "The best cheesecake in three counties."

"I'm sure it is."

"I'll send you over some," Nic offered. "On the house."

"I appreciate it, but I'll have to pass. Dessert and I aren't a good fit."

"You mean like food allergies?" The teenager glanced to Bethany. "Like Camille?"

The house phone rang over the voices and brunch sounds around them.

"It's for you, Nic," a male voice shouted from the other side of the place.

Nicole's chin dropped to her chest.

"If that's your sister-in-law again," she said to Bethany, "I'm going to drive over to her and Oliver's new house and beat her senseless with her lesson planner. I know helping with Dru and Brad's wedding is her first official contribution to the Dixon family, but—"

"Besides Camille," Shandra corrected.

"But," Nicole said, "Selena's obsessing. All over town. And the event's a month out. Everything with the catering is on track, including her special orders. She needs to give it a rest, but she keeps checking the plans, rethinking them. Maybe we'll do lemonade. Or should it be just iced tea? What about hot tea and coffee? It might be chilly after sunset, even in early September . . ."

Nicole's rounded eyes and *OMG* expression made Bethany laugh.

"She just wants Dru and Brad's day to be perfect." Bethany swiped off a piece of her cake with her finger and licked it clean, torturing Mike. "We all do."

"It will be perfect," Nicole insisted. "I have all the sub-vendors lined up. I'm personally doing the project management on this one. It'll be frickin' incredible. Even if I have to shoot Mrs. Selena Rosenthal Bowman with a tranquilizer dart."

Nicole took the edge off her threat by circling an arm around Shandra.

"You come eat your dessert with me while I take this call," she said to the teen. "Then you can learn how the barista machine works."

"We're supposed to be having girl time." Bethany looked guiltily from Mike to her sister. "I didn't mean to throw another wrench in that."

"I don't mind," the kid insisted.

"Good," Nicole said. "That way when I steal you away from the Dream Whip, you'll already have started your training." She steered the teenager toward the coffee bar, glancing back over her shoulder. "You two sit, so everyone else can get back to their food."

Bethany surveyed the roomful of people waiting to see what she'd do next. The flash of vulnerability in her bright eyes blasted away at Mike's best intentions. He shoved the wad of money he'd meant to toss onto the table back into his pocket along with his money clip. He palmed her elbow and eased her toward the chair across from the one he'd vacated, letting her go almost as soon as he'd touched her.

She stared daggers at him in a way that he found perversely enticing.

"You could cut and run." He planted himself in his own chair. "But that's not your style, is it, Bethie?"

"I'll stay for a few more minutes." Her spine ramrod straight, her plate of cheesecake clutched in her hands, she eased down until she was sitting, too. "As long as you promise never to call me that again."

He placed his unused fork in front of her and then spooned up a mouthful of surprisingly tasty cold soup. "Eat your dessert. We'll keep things light and friendly. It'll stop everyone from thinking that each time you've headed into Atlanta, I've been your big-city boy toy. People will look their fill, get tired of eavesdropping, and move on to juicer gossip."

"And then?" she asked uneasily. As if she wanted to believe he was genuinely trying to help, but she just couldn't get there.

"Then we go our separate ways." After he'd snagged a few more minutes with her. Just a few. "It's a big town. I won't be here all that long. No harm, no foul."

Because who did walking away clean from places and people better than him?

Chapter Four

Bethany let the mini backpack she carried instead of a purse slide off her shoulder. It thudded to the ground, mocking her plan to zip in and out G&Bs with Shandra, ordering their cheesecake for the road.

That would have meant Bethany not needing to shut down the rumors about her and Mike. Or not starting any rumors in the first place Thursday night, by running from her brothers and a guy who'd been really, really good at making her want to stay. She could remember the panicked shock of looking down at McC's and finding her fingers tangled up with Mike's, even though she'd been just as furious with him at that point as she'd been with herself and her brothers.

That funny, gorgeous, infuriating guy was now sitting across the table from her, haloed in the daylight streaming through Nicole's sparkling windows. While Bethany was so hungry she could dive headfirst into the slab of cheesecake Nic had sliced up for her.

Begrudgingly, she picked up his fork while Mike took a long swallow of his iced tea. He wiped his lips with one of the cloth napkins Nicole insisted on using instead of paper ones, even though it dipped into her anemic profit margin. Bethany suddenly found herself fantasizing about being that napkin. Feeling Mike's soft mouth on hers. The strength of his hands on her body. His hard muscles bunching and rolling and steadying her as he eased her into his lap, too—

Oh, good grief!

"Eat." He finished his soup and wrapped a helping of pork in a crisp leaf of iceberg lettuce. "At least stop looking like you're going to stake me with my own utensil."

"What?" She was holding the fork the way she would a butcher knife. "Oh . . ."

She shoveled in a heaping portion of cheesecake. Groaning, she closed her eyes, her taste buds oozing with sugary goodness.

"So good," she murmured through her next bite.

She blinked, realizing that Mike's focus on her had intensified. And not in a *let's silence all those crazy rumors* way. He was staring as if she were a decadent treat he wanted to gobble up.

She brandished the fork again. "No dessert for you, remember?"

He cleared his throat with a teasing wink. "Doesn't mean I don't crave something sweet every once in a while."

He bit into his lettuce wrap. The man even chewed sexy. A metal bracelet glimmered at the cuff of another long-sleeved shirt.

"MedicAlert?" She recognized the symbol. Oliver's daughter, Camille, wore something similar. The little girl never left the house without it. Not since she'd had an allergic reaction in the spring that had landed her in the ER and scared everyone to death. "Is that what the sugar's about?"

"I can have a little." He didn't seem to mind her nosiness. It had been his idea to sit and chat like buddies. "As long as it's in careful combination with other foods. It's easier to lay off the stuff entirely when I eat out, though. I don't feel deprived, not these days. When I get sick of cooking and cleaning for myself, farm-to-table places like your friend's are great."

"Farm-to-table? Cooking and cleaning? That makes you, what, a citified cowboy?"

"I'm not a cowboy, remember?"

She wiped her own mouth, telling herself to stop teasing him.

He smiled every time she did, making her think far too seriously about how easy it would be to chat away the afternoon. She had a class of kids in Atlanta she and her sister needed to get to. And she was already enjoying herself way too much for flirting to be a good idea under any circumstances.

"So, Grapes & Beans is great." Mike polished off another wrap.

She nodded. "I usually stumble in here for breakfast after I've been—"

"Up all night painting?"

"How did you . . . ?"

She followed his glance to the gossamer peasant blouse she'd thrown on yesterday under her cut-off overalls. Paint was blotched here and there on all of it. She crossed her legs, her boots clunking into the café table's center leg. A wedge of her super-short hair slid in her eyes. She waved it back and discovered a smudge of oil paint at her temple, where she often tucked a smaller brush behind her ear.

She'd been working with shades of reds and pinks and oranges. Which one had made it to her face? She hadn't even bothered to check her reflection in the bathroom mirror.

"Everyone's used to me like this," she admitted, not caring if he understood. Really. What did it matter?

"Everyone?"

"Nic's staff. Customers who know I eat here because my friend lets me mooch on whatever she's made too much of."

"So you stumble in here most mornings . . ." He checked his watch. "Afternoons. And you wield your cake fork like a lethal weapon at whoever snags your attention?"

"No." She took a less-outrageous bite of her cake. "Evidently you bring out the worst in me."

"Or your painting is making you cranky, hence the all-night grudge match." He smiled, as if he approved.

"I couldn't get something . . . right."

"Something?"

"The canvas I'm working on. The light, the way it's reflecting off everything. The dimensions. The depth. The heart of it. It won't come to life. At least not the way I'm used to painting. It's been that way for a long time. I . . ."

She realized she was rambling and he was listening and that she was telling him things she hadn't yet worked up the courage to even discuss with her parents. And he'd been right: no one was paying them any attention anymore. Well, almost no one. She glanced toward the pastry case, where Nicole was on the phone still. She and Shandra both smiled, Shandra giving Bethany a campy thumbs-up.

The kid would be chattering about Mike all the way to Midtown. And Bethany would have to indulge her—this was Shandra's day. All while the things Bethany didn't understand about the guy or her reaction to him would continue to swirl inside her, distracting, agitating, refusing to take shape, just like her painting.

"I'm working on a piece for my foster parents," she explained, cautioning herself that Mike was simply listening to be polite. That his seemingly genuine interest in what she was saying was a figment of her imagination.

Her paintings meant nothing to a total stranger. And maybe that's why it felt so easy to vent to him—someone, unlike her family and friends, who wouldn't be trying so earnestly to help, who'd just let her talk so she could figure things out for herself.

"It's important to get it right, you know?" she asked him.

He nodded, as if he did. "For your foster parents?"

"They come with the foster brothers who welcomed you to town the other night. And another foster sister, Dru, who's half-owner of the Dream Whip, in case you're hankering for the best burger, fries, and shake around. Just please . . . try not to make another scene if I'm on the clock."

"You work there?"

"I help out when they need me, which has been a lot lately. Dru and Brad are pretty distracted."

"By the wedding? Your sister's marrying one of the angry guys from the bar, right?"

"Brad's usually more laid-back than that. But with a baby on the way and a wedding next month, he's a little on edge."

"Then maybe he should have been the one to deck Benjie."

She snorted. "Oliver did enough damage on his own."

Mike refolded his napkin beside his empty plate. "This wedding I invited myself to sounds pretty important to everyone."

The cake Bethany had polished off without realizing it began to curdle in her stomach.

"You couldn't have known it would set my brothers off like that." She'd already given Mike a pass a dozen times in her mind, while she'd made a point of not fantasizing about what he would look like decked out in a suit, his face cleanly shaven, no hat shadowing his features. Or maybe he could keep the sexy hat. She wouldn't quibble over a technicality. "But it's a big deal. An even bigger day than usual. Dru and Brad have waited a long time to do this right. And my dad . . ." Joe deserved a perfect memory almost as much as the bride and groom. "My foster family's been through a lot lately."

"Is that why this Selena is driving your friend crazy about the catering?"

"Yeah."

"And Selena is . . . ?"

"Oliver's wife." He'd married his high school sweetheart in June, in a simple civil ceremony at the county courthouse, with just close family there as witnesses. His and Selena's seven-year-old daughter, Camille, had been beaming ear-to-ear, reigning supreme as Selena's maid of honor and one-girl wedding party.

"And the lesson planner?" Mike asked.

Bethany frowned. It took a minute for Nic's rant to come back to her. "Selena's a teacher at Chandler Elementary."

"Armani married a schoolteacher?" Mike sounded genuinely confused for the first time. "So what, exactly, does all of that have to do with your painting yourself into a stupor to finish something for your parents?"

She blinked at his intuition, caught off guard by how carefully he'd kept track of the scattershot details of her story. "You know all that stuff I mentioned my family going through?"

He nodded, not rushing her, not jumping back into the conversation, not looking around for an exit as if he didn't really want to know the answer to his question.

"A chunk of it's been about me," she said. "At least recently it has. I've been a wild card for years, no matter how hard my parents tried to help me settle in around here."

Mike ran his thumb along his chin. He'd let his beard grow in even thicker. "I know how that goes. I get it."

Did he?

"I just want them to know . . ." She braced her arms on the table. "How much it all meant to me, even if it's taken me years to realize it. Their support and the way they've always been here, waiting for me to come to my senses. I want them to see it hasn't been a total waste."

He'd propped his elbow on the table, his chin on his hand. His soft gaze brushed hers like velvety brown suede, his expression brimming with . . . something indescribable.

"I'm sure"—he reached across the table for her hand, the gesture easygoing, natural as could be—"that the last thing your foster parents think you've done is waste the fresh start they've helped you make."

Her fingers tangled with his, making her ache to feel his body supporting hers again, the way he had when they'd faced down Benjie.

"How do you do that?" she asked.

His thumb stroked her wrist. "Do what?"

"How do you understand . . ."

Me, she couldn't bring herself to say.

"I don't." He let her go and brushed the streak of paint on her temple. His hand retreated to his side of the table. "Not really. But I've done my own kind of searching for years. From one drifter to another, it looks like you've finally landed where you want to be."

She shivered, desperate to believe him.

"Do any of those wild cards of yours," he asked, "have anything to do with *BenALoserAllHisLife*?"

She laughed at his hijacking Nic and Clair's running joke. She slapped her hand over her mouth when she realized people were staring again.

"Only the part," she told him, "where five years ago he passed off several of my paintings as his to get himself accepted to the New York art school we were going to together."

Mike's expression hardened with the kind of swift fury she'd seen on her brother's face just before Oliver punched Benjie.

"He stole your work—plagiarized it—while he was dating you?"

"I'm pretty sure," she conceded, "that painting was the *only* reason he was dating me."

"He wanted you to teach him how to do what you did?"

"As if I knew. And when I couldn't . . ."

"He outright took credit for something you created."

"Several somethings. Flattering, huh? And I'd thought it was true love. It took me a while to sort myself out after that."

"And now he's sniffing around again? The guy's lucky Armani didn't take him apart before Thursday night."

"It was a long time ago." Years of wrong men and wrong turns. She slid to the edge of her chair. "My mistakes with him are a distant blip on the radar."

"Then why invest so much energy into avoiding him?" Mike asked, putting two and two together and coming up with far more than he should have.

She smiled and got to her feet. "I'm not avoiding him anymore. Thanks in no small part to you. And now you know the story behind the story. So, thank you again."

"You're welcome again. But—"

"No worries about the wedding, of course. I'll make sure my family knows the truth. They won't bother you about Thursday anymore."

"No worries." He rose, too. The buzz of countless conversations quieted as diners tuned in for the big finish. "Helping someone should always be this much fun. I hope I haven't added to the issues with your family. And in case we don't get the chance to talk again, I—"

Shandra rushed back over. She crashed into Bethany, nearly toppling her with a hug that wasn't really a hug, but it felt like the best hug Bethany had ever gotten. Because her carelessness that morning hadn't dimmed her sister's enthusiasm for the day.

"We're going to be late," Shandra said. "Class starts in forty-five minutes."

"Another foster sister?" Mike asked, letting go of whatever he'd been about to say.

"Twin sister," Shandra quipped.

Bethany nodded. "This is—"

"Shandra." Mike touched the brim of his hat in another greeting. "I heard. And it's Cowboy Mike, not Bob."

"She's my forever sister," Bethany clarified. Today of all days, Shandra needed to know Bethany was in for the long haul. "Once a Dixon, always a Dixon."

Her sister beamed.

Mike did, too, as if their very personal moment had touched him. He held his hand out to Shandra. "It's a pleasure to meet you."

Shandra shook. "Wow. Oliver didn't say you were a hottie. No wonder Bethany's been keeping you to herself all this time."

"Gotta go." Bethany shook his hand as well, purely for the benefit of their audience. "Thanks again, Mike."

His grip held firm, as if he regretted saying goodbye as much as she did. He lifted her fingers to his mouth for a kiss. "The pleasure's been all mine."

"I . . ." She pulled free. "I guess I'll see you around town sometime."

"Sure," he said. "See ya around."

Bethany practically dragged a gaping Shandra through the riveted G&Bs crowd, to the door, and then outside to her truck. Bethany should have locked herself inside the thing in the first place and sent Shandra to pick up their cheesecake. Because as hopeless as Bethany was at being on time, she was evidently even less skilled at ignoring the reckless things men like Mike Taylor made her feel.

Drifting men. *I'm not going to be around for long* guys. But while they *were* around, did they have to know how to push all the right buttons?

She fired the truck's engine and groaned at the dashboard clock. "We're going to be late."

"Mike's really cute," Shandra gushed.

He really, *really* was. Cute, and a passel of other surprising things beneath all of his easy-on-the-eyes charm.

"You sure you can't make Mike an exception to your no-dating rule?" her sister asked.

Bethany didn't trust herself to answer as she flipped her blinker and turned onto Main Street.

"Thought you'd pulled up roots and headed out for another contract gig," Mateo said.

Mike's transgender Atlanta neighbor ran the tattoo parlor around the corner from Mike's building. He was out for an afternoon stroll with his two Chihuahuas, Areeba and Undalay, and his Chiweenie, Paco.

"I'm wrapping up a few loose ends." Mike locked up his Jeep where he'd parked it at the curb. "George will be on point while I'm away. You boys look sassy."

The three-hundred-pound former bodybuilder was in mid-transition and wearing one of his favorite turbans, a colorful scarf he wrapped around his bald head as often as he did his neck. Befitting the warm August afternoon, the rest of him was decked out in cargo shorts, flip-flops, and a fuchsia tank top. Each dog wore a vest in an identical hue.

"Not all of us can pull off impoverished cowboy chic, love." Mateo and his entourage breezed down the road. "Get yourself a little somethin'-somethin' while you're gone this time. This isn't a good look for you."

"What look?" Mike took stock of his standard uniform when he wasn't working: clean shirt, reasonably clean jeans.

"All work and no play." Mateo waved over his shoulder. "Giddyup, cowboy. I expect to see you smilin' next time."

Chuckling, Mike headed down the building's alley to his entrance. He typed a code into the electronic keypad to bypass the security system, while an image of another brightly dressed beauty filled his mind. The lock reengaged as he took the steep steps two at a time, reaching the top and typing a second code to access his apartment. He was greeted with the glare from the overhead skylights, and a not entirely unexpected growl of annoyance.

"Morning, sunshine." He dropped his backpack onto the edge of his battered, aircraft carrier–sized desk.

Georgina Spenser, his business manager, was typing away on Mike's keyboard, files and folders, papers and highlighters and Post-its strewn across his desk. Her hair, curling madly, mocked the headband she'd slid on to control it.

"Aren't you supposed to be settling down in Small Town, USA?" she asked. "Filling up your wandering well. Staying out of my hair for at least a couple of weeks."

"I'm just back for—"

She pointed a fluorescent green highlighter at him like a switchblade.

"*Don't* tell me you've already bailed on your gig and have some project in mind you need me to drop everything and help you make happen. Not unless you're hankering for an IRS audit, because I haven't gotten enough done yet to even file an extension. I put off dealing with taxes until I knew you were good and gone."

"I'm gone." He headed into his small bedroom in the back corner of his studio. Not much was there except a twin bed, a closet for his meager wardrobe, and an enormous flat-panel TV that covered most of one of the walls. He plucked a three-ring binder from the rumpled bedclothes. "Just as soon as I get my mother to stop texting about this donation she won't take no for an answer about."

"She hasn't been taking no for an answer about it for weeks. Why not keep on ignoring her for a while?" George was the youngest of five children, the rest boys—a tomboy to the core. She snatched the binder from Mike when he returned to the desk. "I've been looking for that. You never put your toys away when you're done playing with them."

She slid the notebook into the row of identical binders that spanned the top shelf of the long, low bookcase behind the desk.

"This is *my* apartment," Mike reminded her, removing the book, double-checking the label George had printed up for the binding, making certain he had the right one. "You're not the boss of me. You haven't been since we were kids. Remember, I can fire you anytime I want and find someone who doesn't commandeer my space every time I step away from it, or nag me about what I do with my own stuff."

"You told me to crash here while you're gone. I've got the rest of your year to sort out once the taxes are done, and a ton of scheduling to finalize. It's enough to keep me busy for a month, and I can spread out better here. Don't even think about popping in over and over like you're peeing on trees to mark your territory. This is *my* tree for the foreseeable future."

"Yes, ma'am." Mike smiled and flipped through the book.

"Seriously," George said, her tone losing some of its playfulness. "Do you really think this is the right time of the year to be dealing with your mother? I can read the calendar. The anniversary is always hard on you. I figured it was mostly why you suddenly decided to get away from things here. Why dive back into family drama now?"

Mike scanned the images he'd been staring at most of the night before he'd left for the suburbs, ignoring the childhood friend who'd helped keep him sane since he'd bolted from New York an angry, nineteen-year-old young man. He couldn't help thinking about Bethany and her drama. And how she and her siblings and friends seemed to weather things together.

"I'll be gone before you know it," he said, "and stay gone this time."

"Uh-huh," was George's reply to his non-answer. "How are you settling into nirvana?"

"The locals are loving me. Eating out of my hands. I'm probably the most well-known *new* guy who's ever rolled into Chandlerville."

"Well-known or notorious?" George leaned back in Mike's desk chair. "Is it possible you've pissed someone off already?"

"Not exactly." He flipped through more of the low-resolution digital proofs George had painstakingly organized into binders by years taken and series and subjects.

He consoled himself that Bethany had gotten around to enjoying their conversation at Grapes & Beans almost as much as he had. She'd let him make her laugh while he got to know her better, while he'd held and kissed her hand . . . The attraction between them had been as unmistakable as her compulsion to bolt from him—and as real as his knowing that he should let her go.

"I need to get a look at August's and September's schedules," he said to George. "You were working on them when I left."

She plucked one of the color-coded folders from the stand at the edge of the desk and laid it in front of him. He stared at it as if it might bite.

"What's going on with you?" she asked when he went back to flipping through the binder. "Getting something printed and framed is a week's work. Plus riding herd on our vendors because you'll want everything perfect. Then there's the hassle of packaging and shipping it all up to New York. Neither one of us has time for that right now."

"We're just talking one image." He reconsidered the project. "Maybe two. At the most a small series. No rush. I'll pick the proofs and make notes for cropping the group. We'll talk mat and framing options later. But it's got to be the right set of shots. I'm thinking opposites, sunrise and sunset, same scene. It should say something about exploring and finding your way . . ."

Home, he finished silently.

A home he'd never know again.

He always thought about the past more in August. But there was something about being in Chandlerville the last few days that had made looking back less painful than usual. And if sending his mother the framed prints she'd been harping for was a harmless way to be close to her and the memories—why not go ahead and get it done?

When he surfaced from his thoughts, George was watching, waiting. It seemed sometimes as if she'd been holding her breath for ten years. She tossed her highlighter on the desk and folded her hands.

"You're taking a break from all of this, remember?" she asked. "You're caught up on orders. You don't owe anyone anything. Your mother won't stop calling, but she never wants to actually talk. You needed to be out of touch, but not as long as it would take to go hiking somewhere so remote you'll start talking to the wildlife and expect something furry to answer back. I don't recall your getaway plan including locking yourself away in your darkroom, mumbling over capture and contrast and exposure. You wanted to be with people who don't know anything about photographers who specialize in obscure mediums. You wanted to blend in, mind your own business, kick back and cruise for a while."

"Yeah . . ." He yanked off his hat and threw it onto the other guest chair. "That was the plan."

He'd dabbled in everything since he was a kid, as surprised as anyone at how quickly he'd mastered whatever form of photography he'd studied. Large-format, infrared, underwater, macro, panoramic. He used an array of processing techniques and papers when he developed film, mostly specialized treatments for high-resolution digital images. His prints were in more demand every year, while his pseudonym kept his private life private.

In the fine-art circles where his work was well-known, his limited output was seen as a selling point rather than a limitation. So he set his own hours, chose subject matter that appealed to him, and hand-selected the patrons he sold to and galleries that represented him. And when he was off the grid, needing a real-life fix to keep him going before he dug back into a creative vein, he was typically gone, no exception.

"This isn't about your mother wanting what she wants when she wants it." George had never been a fan of Olivia's, though she regularly ran polite and professional interference between Mike and his mother. "Cruella's always on your case about putting your work in a gallery she's partnered with, or some art show one of her cronies is curating. And you're always ignoring her." George read the label on the binder's spine. "This time it's about Jeremy, right?"

Mike slipped his hat back on and met the gaze of the only piece of his childhood he'd hung on to.

It was always about Jeremy.

George motioned with her chin toward the binder. "Those are the images from the last trip you took for him just before he died."

It had been the August Mike had broken with his parents, needing to get the hell out of New York for good once his brother was gone. Mike's fiancée at the time had seen her life going a different direction. She'd expected marrying him to be her entrée into his family's money and position in Manhattan society. So that was the August he'd left her behind, too.

George, more Jeremy's friend at first and closer to his age, had been the only person Mike had kept in touch with regularly when he'd first struck out on his own—causing his mother's dislike for her neighbor's youngest child to grow exponentially. By the time Mike had begun to take his work seriously, George's double major in business and art history had made her a perfect fit to manage the things he didn't have the patience to.

These days she was a cross between a brutally honest friend, a meddling big sister, and a demanding business partner. Wherever he wandered now, George helped him set up shop. She helped keep the work—and occasionally Mike's demons—from overwhelming him.

He studied the series of images he'd selected. He'd promised never to tap into them commercially. When he looked at them, he only wanted to picture the joy on his older brother's face when Jeremy had first seen them. They'd shared a love of the outdoors, and Mike's passion had become bringing the world back to Jeremy long after his brother could no longer explore nature himself. It was a bond their mother had been more than a little jealous of toward the end. But maybe now would be the right time to finally share these particular memories with her.

Mike flashed back to Bethany's hug with her forever sister. Her brothers' well-intentioned overprotectiveness. Her wacky but loyal friends. Her obvious affection for all of them was as beautiful as the woman herself.

"These would be for the foundation's holiday gala?" George asked. "The silent auction your mother's chairing?"

"I always have you send a few prints."

"Not images this personal."

"They'll show people Jeremy's joy for life." Mike felt the theme expand. "The way he lived the hell out of every day, despite the odds he faced."

"Thanks to you." George smiled through her worry. "Are you really ready to hand Livy a piece of your private world? So she can make money from something you did just for your brother?"

"The money's not the point." It had never been the point. "And it's for the foundation. Research and grants and scholarships. Jeremy wouldn't mind supporting that."

George held out her hand for the binder. She scanned the two pages of proofs Mike had settled on. "This has nothing to do with whatever you landed in the middle of in Chandlerville?"

"I didn't say that." Mike scowled, sidestepping her curiosity.

He could never BS anything past George for long. But he wasn't ready to talk about it yet.

How it wasn't settling well that ten years had passed since he'd had Jeremy in his life. How it suddenly didn't feel like enough of a distraction, losing himself for a few nights at McC's and then in the job that had called him to Chandlerville in the first place. Not after stumbling into Bethany Darling. Not when Mike couldn't stop thinking about her and wondering what Jeremy would think, too.

"Help me pick a handful of shots." He pointed at the notebook. "Then you can get on with your orgy of tax planning. You can send me high-res proofs when you've got a minute, and I'll think through the rest. Send digital copies of the schedules, too. My being out of sync if I pop back over this way won't do anybody any good."

Neither would his breaking his promise to steer clear of Bethany from here on out.

"And while you're at it," he said, making it sound like an afterthought, and wishing it truly was, "there's a number in New York I need you to track down for me."

Chapter Five

"This one's for virgin daiquiris," Dru Hampton said just before seven that night. The mother- and bride-to-be handed Bethany one of the two blenders she'd dragged from her kitchen cabinet.

Dru and Brad were transforming Vivian Douglas's turn-of-the-century Victorian into their own space, with Bethany helping them every spare minute she had. The plan was to be done before the New Year, in time to welcome home the beautiful baby girl they were naming Vivi, after Brad's grandmother.

"And this one is for everyone else." Dru shoved a matching blender at Bethany. "Don't worry about me. The bunch of you have a blast getting boozy at *my* bachelorette party."

Bethany juggled the appliances and set them on the worn Formica countertop. "The wedding's nearly a month off. Are you sure this rates as a bachelorette party?"

Her foster sister patted her gently rounded belly, adorably accentuated by one of the body-hugging sundresses Dru wore pretty much all the time these days.

"I'm finally not feeling like rot," she said. "I'll take my party now, thank you very much, in case the morning sickness makes an encore appearance."

"You're the one who decided to plan a big wedding in the midst of all of this."

Bethany admired how effortlessly feminine her sister looked, despite Dru's expanding baby bump. Bethany's wardrobe—dressing most mornings while rushing out the door blinking sleep from her eyes—resembled the tattered aftermath of an exploded box of crayons.

"You and Brad could have done things quick and dirty," she said, "like Oliver and Selena."

"I want the big day." Dru gave a dreamy sigh. "With the family there, the whole town. Music and flowers and photographs to look at forever, and Brad and me feeling like the luckiest people on the planet."

"Or the sickest, if that little princess growing inside you is feeling ornery."

"Weddings take time to plan, and we didn't want to wait to start a family."

"You play, you pay. Besides, if drinking virgin daiquiris at home with the girls is bugging you, go gripe at your bar-crawling fiancé."

"Done and done." Dru yanked the freezer door open. "I hit my breaking point when he rolled in Thursday night drunk off his protect-and-serve butt. We had a heart-to-heart over the pot of coffee he needed to pry his eyes open the next morning."

"At least the boys got it out of the way early, too. No one'll be hurling on your wedding video."

"Whatever." Dru massaged her belly, rooting through the freezer with her free hand. "Brad's officially dry until this little bundle shoves its way into the world. He'll be drinking sparkling cider with me after we say our I-dos."

Bethany plugged in the blenders and took the tubs of premade daiquiri mix from her sister. Trays of ice came next. The vintage aluminum kind. Bethany pulled the levers to pop the cubes free, loving the honest, straightforward way her sister and Brad loved. They'd fought hard to get to this place.

"If it makes any difference," Bethany said, "Clair and Nic said that after I left, the guys' partying was pretty tame. Travis and Brad might have been a little overserved, but they had Oliver as their designated driver."

"Overserved by your cowboy?" Dru grabbed a bottle of rum from the pantry. "The guy you now say means nothing, only he would have decked your ex if Oliver hadn't? I hear your clinch at McC's drew quite a crowd."

"It was just a kiss." Bethany fed mix, fruit, ice, and booze into the first blender. And Mike kissing her hand earlier today had *just* been a goodbye. "I've already explained why."

She'd talked to Marsha and Joe when she'd dropped Shandra off an hour ago. To Dru and Selena when she'd returned to the Douglas house—where she'd moved in after the first of the year, when Dru and Brad had offered her their guest bedroom. She had Oliver and Travis and Brad to track down next. Of course they'd hear an earful on their own.

"Everyone needs to let it go now," Bethany insisted, including her.

"Good luck with that. You're helping me over at Mom and Dad's tomorrow afternoon, right? So we can pretend to do wedding stuff while we check on Joe? You know Mom or someone else will bring up your Cowboy Bob."

"His name is Mike." Bethany stabbed the switch to transform the first mixture into frozen perfection. She licked stickiness from her thumb and met her sister's steady gaze. "And he's nobody to me."

"He has you spinning. While the family's been watching you slowly come unglued the last month or so."

"I am not." Bethany absolutely refused to be. "I'm fine."

Her sister didn't look convinced. "If you spend any more time painting, Brad and I are going to move your bed into the sitting room. And now you have a creative space to disappear into in Atlanta, on top of the kids you're already teaching three days a week down there."

"I love it here," Bethany insisted. "With you and Brad. With everybody."

"I know you do, kiddo. You never would have stayed so close, even when you were on your own in Atlanta, if you didn't want to be with the family. But you're spending more time by yourself every week. Don't ask me of all people to believe that's by chance. Is it too much, the wedding and the things you're doing to help Brad and me around here and at the Whip?"

"Of course not."

Dru had had her own problems adjusting to aging out of foster care. She hadn't hesitated to share all the gory details when she and Bethany had started talking again in January—after Dru and Brad had reconnected. Before long, Dru had taken Bethany under her wing, the way Bethany was trying to pay that kindness forward with Shandra.

Her older sister had made a place for Bethany in her home so Bethany could stop working odd jobs around town to make ends meet—including doing the majority of the cleaning at Dan's

Doughnuts, in exchange for living in the postage-stamp-sized studio apartment Dan and Leigh Hastings owned above their bakery. Dru had smoothed the way for Bethany to reconnect with their family, too.

There was nothing Bethany wouldn't do to repay her sister or any of the people who'd always been there for her, no matter what.

"This family means everything to me," she insisted.

"I know it does." Dru's expression resembled Marsha's when their mother was being supportive but ruthlessly realistic. "But your art means almost as much to you. And even though I've kept everyone else out, I can't help peeking into your studio every now and then."

Bethany stared at the floor, dread prickling at the back of her throat at the coming conversation. It was a wonder it had taken her sister this long to say something.

"I've seen all the unfinished canvases," Dru said. "All those nights, all the work you've been doing. You're so determined to have something to give Mom and Dad at the wedding. And now you're pursuing this residency in Midtown. But is any of it making you happy?"

Dru waited for Bethany to look up.

"How long has it been," Bethany's sister asked, "since you've finished a canvas? Including last year, when you lived and painted in that tiny place over Dan's."

Bethany swallowed. "Since high school."

It was the thousand-pound gorilla on her shoulders. It was the secret she'd been keeping from everyone—even from herself, as often as she could make herself forget. Because if she just kept painting and thinking that the next canvas would be *the one* to dream its way into the world, then she could keep believing she was happily settling into her old life, and that things were finally working out.

Dru handed her a worn dish towel trimmed in a crazy green-and-orange pattern that looked like something straight off the *Brady Bunch* set. Bethany wiped her fingers, squinting against her stinging eyes so she didn't have to wipe them, too.

"Is it still because of some guy in high school?" her sister asked. "Because Benjie made swiss cheese out of your heart and your ability to create?"

Bethany shook her head, swamped with the memory of Mike's steamy kisses Thursday night instead of her run-in with Benjie. "Of course not."

"Is it all the wedding planning and craziness?" her sister asked. "Because we—"

"I need to be close to everyone again." Even if Bethany didn't know how to hold on to them yet. "Especially now that . . ."

"Dad's sick?"

Joe's heart attack in the spring had been a blow to everyone. For Bethany, it had been the shock she'd needed to get that there were no guarantees. That the time to finally get things right in her life, to learn how to be with the people who'd always loved and accepted her, was now. And as nerve-rattling as the last few months with the family had been, she'd relished every second of being back with them.

"It's okay," her sister said, "if you've been seeing this guy Mike in Atlanta. If that's why you're not interested in dating guys around here, it's—"

"I'm not dating *anyone*." Bethany set up Dru's mommy cocktail in the second blender. "I'm dealing with enough baggage already. There's too much else on my mind."

"Then clear your mind and hang with someone who makes you feel good, if that's what this guy does for you."

"Now you're channeling Nic and Clair instead of Mom."

"Dating just for fun isn't a personality flaw, Bethany."

"It is when you've landed as many losers as I have."

"Then stick to kissing hunky guys in bars, if that feels safer."

Bethany snorted at the idea that anything she might do with Mike would feel safe. She started the second blender while she portioned the frothy pink confection from the first one into four martini glasses. The delicate gilded-rimmed stemware had been Vivian Douglas's.

"Just don't think you have to hide a guy or anything else from the family," her sister said.

"Now, why would I hide anything from the clan, after the boys were so laid-back about meeting Mike the other night?"

The guy would be an absolute blast to date, no doubt. He was funny, charming, and sweet. His interest in Bethany's art earlier today, genuine or not, had made her feel incredible. Each time she was near him, the knotted-up things inside her felt as if they might finally slip loose. Each glimpse of Mike made her want to capture his rugged profile in paint.

She poured the bride-to-be's alcohol-free drink and handed Dru the glass, intending to push through the butler's door into the living room where the other women were waiting.

Dru blocked Bethany's escape, sipping her mocktail. "You know that whatever you do, whatever you're going through, whatever you need is okay with me, right?"

"Of course I know that."

Her foster sister ambushed her with a hug. "You can't give up on love, Bethany. Remember that. Maybe some people can. Maybe sometimes you want to. But you're not made that way, or when you aged out of the system, you wouldn't have stopped running when you got to Atlanta."

The kitchen door swung open from the living room. Selena poked her head inside, glorious dark curls framing classic features and almond-shaped eyes.

"No fair," she said as Bethany and Dru slid apart. "You two are bogarting the libations, while Ginger and Leigh and me are exiled with Vivian's cuckoo clocks." She cocked her head at Dru. "Exactly *why* haven't you tossed them out yet? They'd make great kindling for a bonfire."

Dru helped Bethany stage the tray with three rum-doused daiquiris. She handed the final one to their sister-in-law.

"Brad's grandmother's favorite things belong here," Dru said. "They've belonged here a lot longer than I have, so they're staying. Now, let's kick this bash into high gear." She disappeared into the other room with the tray, leaving Selena to hold the door open for Bethany to follow with Dru's drink. "I need you ladies' help to get Bethany dishing about Chandlerville's newest bartender!"

"Rick's not talking," Selena said half an hour later, the party conversation stuck firmly on the subject of Mike. She'd snuggled into the corner of Vi Douglas's weathered brocade couch. "I didn't get any more out of him and Law than what Oliver reported. Or maybe they don't know any more about Thursday night than the meltdown the rest of the bar saw. Your man of mystery," she said to Bethany, "sure knows how to make an entrance. *Give.*"

Bethany tossed popcorn at her. "You've been pestering Rick Harper for gossip?"

"Hey"—Selena tossed Cheetos back, each of her fingernails

polished with a different color Bethany suspected perfectly matched her niece's manicure—"my husband finally got his chance to defend his baby sister's honor. The whole family's been waiting for half a decade for that Carrington louse to eat a face full of somebody's knuckles. And to add insult to injury, some new-in-town guy was necking with you before my man and his sidekicks got there. And you say it was just to piss Benjie off? I'm rooting around for whatever details I can dig up."

"Oliver would have asked Rick if Selena hadn't," Dru said. "He's always been overprotective where his baby sister is concerned."

"He told me once," Selena said to Bethany, "that when family services first placed you with Marsha and Joe in the midst of your *I don't need no stinkin' home* phase, that it was like looking in a mirror."

It had been the same for Bethany.

When you came from a life so fractured you wish you'd come from nowhere, you learned not to want wherever you wound up next. She and Oliver—and she and Shandra now—had recognized that about each other, without having to know the details about their very different journeys to foster care.

"He's still steaming about whatever he thought he saw when the boys walked up to you," Selena said. "To hear Oliver bluster, you would have thought Rick's new bartender was taking advantage of you."

Ginger Reed Jenkins released an exaggerated sigh. "Why doesn't some gorgeous cowboy ever take advantage of me?"

"Because *your* husband," Dru answered, "would knock any man who tried clear to the next county."

"No one was *taking advantage* of anyone at McC's," Bethany insisted.

“Which only makes inquiring minds want to know more,” Dru quipped. “Especially after you and Cowboy Bob were getting chummy at brunch.”

“I wanted to apologize and clear the air.”

“Travis stopped by the bakery for his coffee and cruller this morning,” Leigh Hastings said to Bethany, “and asked Dan what he knew. I guess your brother figured since you lived over the bakery for a year, maybe we were in the vault. My husband told him we didn’t have the scoop on whatever you’re hiding about the guy. And that even if we did, we wouldn’t be sharing the deets unless you said it was cool.”

“Thanks,” Bethany said. “But I’m not hiding anything.”

“Come on.” Dru waggled her eyebrows. “We need some juicy gossip to liven things up.”

She yawned and propped her bunny-slippered feet on the coffee table. She had a fuzzy slipper collection that rivaled Bethany’s obsession with patterned tights.

“I’ve arranged for a stripper,” Leigh offered.

“I brought the *No Boys Allowed* movie.” Bethany raised her glass in another toast, hoping to nudge the conversation along to a different topic.

“We’re stocked up on your drug of choice.” Selena checked with Ginger, who patted the shopping bag she’d dropped onto Vi’s threadbare oriental carpet.

“Then it’s a hootenanny.” Dru pulled a throw pillow into her lap, smiling slyly. “But first . . . more dish.”

“He sure is easy on the eyes,” Ginger purred.

“I hear he’s a hunk of burning love.” Leigh relaxed into the cushions behind her.

“He turned heads just eating soup at G&Bs,” Dru noted.

Bethany drank too much daiquiri too fast, thinking about just how easily he'd turned *her* head again.

Brain freeze!

She winced.

"What I don't understand," Selena said, "is why you seem so bent on letting this guy slip away, even if Thursday night was just a fluke. There's clearly plenty of chemistry there."

"Maybe too much chemistry?" Dru asked.

While everyone waited for Bethany to answer, the out-of-rhythm ticking of close to a dozen wall-mounted cuckoo clocks filled the room. She inhaled and reminded herself that none of them meant any harm. Ginger and Leigh were good friends of Bethany's, not just Dru's and more recently Selena's. They were great women, wonderful people, and they'd been around Chandlerville long enough to know Bethany's history, at least since she'd been placed with the Dixons.

So why was Bethany fighting the itch to leave the party early?

"I'm having a hard enough time dealing with everything," she confessed, "without worrying about whether what I'm feeling for a new guy is going to get me into as much trouble as falling for all the other guys I have."

Selena and Dru exchanged a long look.

"So you are falling for him?" Dru asked.

The doorbell rang, sparing Bethany.

"I thought our stripper would never get here!" Leigh glided across the room, her drink in hand. She sipped as she opened the door. "Hey, Peter. How's your night going?"

"Busy Sunday." Peter Forino was the eldest son of one of the families that frequented the Dream Whip. "You're the third house I've been to just on this street."

"And it used to be such a nice neighborhood."

"What?" His cheeks reddened beneath his adorable freckles and teen acne.

"Nothing." Leigh brushed a reassuring hand down his arm as Bethany and the rest of the party animals giggled. "Just set the pizzas on the coffee table. How much do we owe you?"

"For two large pies?" He stepped inside, dropped off the boxes, and checked the ticket taped to the one on top. "Extra toppings. Deep dish. That's twenty-five fifty. My dad heard what tonight was for." He grinned at Dru, his expression slipping to confusion when he caught sight of her slippers. "He threw in breadsticks and marinara sauce for dipping, and told me to tell you to have a great time."

"Make sure you thank him for me," Dru said.

Selena stood and dug a wad of bills from her tote bag, passing them over.

"That covers your tip, too," she said. "Thank Vinnie for all of us."

Peter counted what she'd handed him and grinned. "Thanks! I will."

He jogged back to the door and outside to the compact car his folks had bought him for his eighteenth birthday—with the understanding that he'd be delivering for Little Vincent's Pizza more nights and weekends than he'd be cruising with his friends.

Bethany slipped into the kitchen for the paper plates and napkins Dru had insisted on. No decorations, no fuss, no cleanup. Her pre-wedding bash was either going to be a fun, easy break for everyone, or it wasn't happening. By the time Bethany returned to the living room, Selena had flipped open the box of cheese and pepperoni, extra mushrooms, and was pulling out the first steaming slice.

She plated it and handed the bounty to Dru. "Vincent and Betsy Forino make the cutest kids. Their youngest, Bella, is the reigning princess of my second-grade class."

"Peter just came in for dress shoes to wear to the Chandler High Homecoming Dance." Ginger ran a local shoe boutique, Neat Feet, that her parents had started ages ago. "He's up for homecoming king."

"A hunk of burning love in the making." Leigh grabbed a plate and a slice from the veggie box. She nibbled daintily, crust first.

"Let's hope his parents teach him to benevolently wield his power over women." Dru glanced Bethany's way, her understanding clear for how confusing love and belonging could be. How Bethany's instinct might always be to distrust where her heart wanted to lead her. "The world is full of enough men only interested in what they can get out of a woman, never in what they could give."

"Not your man." Bethany took her first mouthful of the best pizza on the east side of Atlanta. She closed her eyes in reverence, savoring the spicy, cheesy goodness. "Brad lost his heart to you when we were all kids. The same way Selena was Oliver's one and only from the second they set eyes on each other. I'm glad I'm here to see the four of you finally wising up and figuring things out."

It was that kind of life-changing wisdom Bethany desperately wanted for herself.

"To Dru and Brad." Selena raised her slice in a toast.

"To the bride and groom," everyone chimed in, eyes misty with their hopes and dreams for their friend and sister's future.

Dru sniffled. "I think I need a handful of those pills." She wiped her eyes and patted her rounded belly. "The second trimester's supposed to be calmer than the first. But I keep watering up about absolutely nothing at all. I'm happy, I'm sad, I'm excited, I'm a total brat . . . Whatever I'm feeling, I always wind up crying. It's infuriating."

Bethany's never-let-the-world-get-her-down sister looked radiant, not furious. And so much in love with the life she and Brad were starting together, it was impossible every time Bethany saw Dru not to believe that the same could happen for her if she wanted it badly enough.

Ginger plucked a bag of assorted Jelly Bellies from her tote and handed them to Dru. "Heavy on the buttered popcorn and cotton candy."

"Another mommy-friendly cocktail coming up," Bethany said. "Selena, you fire up the porn."

"Score!" Dru dug into her candy while Leigh snagged the bride her second slice of pizza.

Bethany headed to the kitchen. The opening music to *An Affair to Remember* kicked off on the DVD player. She smiled, reminding herself how lucky she was. And that, especially tonight, she had no business worrying about Mike and how sparks flew every time they saw each other.

You sure you can't make Mike an exception to your no-dating rule?

"Forget the sparks," she scolded herself as she made Dru's drink.

Sure, their instant connection had come out of nowhere. But why *was* she making such a big deal about it? He was a nice guy, having some fun his first few days in town. If he'd wanted to have fun with her, fine. If the goodbyes they'd said today meant the fun was over, fine. It was no big f-ing deal.

She had to stop overthinking things and people, as if the entire world were a threat she had to constantly be on guard against. She finally had happiness within her grasp. Warm, close nights like tonight, with people who cared about her laughing in the other room, waiting for her to join them. What did it matter whether some cowboy she'd kissed had felt the same things she did?

Tonight was the magic she'd been searching for all her life. She had the family she'd fought so hard to get back to. It was time to finally, completely, let them all the way in.

You can't give up on love, Bethany. Remember that.

"I'm not sure how long I'm staying this time, Mom," Mike said over his cell phone. "A few weeks. Maybe a month. My service is replacing someone last-minute who had an unexpected family emergency. The guy already had a furnished apartment in town lined up to rent and a preliminary site visit scheduled for today."

"Can't someone else do it?" A resigned sigh said that Livy Taylor already knew the answer.

"I'm happy to help."

"As long as it's not your family you're helping."

"I help a lot of families, Mom." Mike was years past engaging in Olivia Taylor's passive-aggressive insistence that he move back to New York permanently. "Including you and Dad."

"But the foundation's charity gala—"

"Isn't until Christmas. And—"

"It will take months to cultivate the interest and donations we're needing for a silent auction this important."

"George and I are already looking into which pieces to send."

"That's wonderful, darling," his mother fake-praised, turning up the charm—ignoring his mention of the family friend who'd been with them at Jeremy's bedside the day he passed. "But you know we'll need details and images as soon as you can get them to us, and—"

"You'll have them."

"*And* this would be the perfect time for you to take a public role in a foundation event. Get your feet wet working with the board directly on the auction. Your brother would be so proud if he knew you were pitching in personally to help other families who've—"

"Been through what ours has," Mike finished for her.

Nudging up the brim of his hat with his knuckles, he turned off Main Street onto Maple, heading for Bellevue Lane.

"I'll frame something high-dollar donors can't refuse." Even if the only people who'd appreciate the significance of the grouping would be him and George. "We'll email high-res images once they're framed and matted. The grouping will bring the donations you need. But you know that's all I can do."

It wasn't Mike's first contribution to the family business—to honor his brother, not to please his parents. Years ago he'd made his position clear to Olivia and Harrison Grover Taylor III. If they ever reneged on keeping his involvement anonymous, he'd sever his final ties to their posh, status-obsessed Manhattan lives.

"But we could get so much more interest in your donation if people finally knew—"

"You won't need more interest. If the city was embroiled in a natural disaster, you'd manage to charm press coverage for one of your shindigs."

"But putting a face and a name to the mysterious fine-art photographer HMT? We'd have super donors eating out of our hands. It could fund years' worth of programs and scholarships and projects in honor of your brother's battle. We'd earmark some of the money for the initiatives you've insisted we start. Revealing the identity of a celebrated contemporary photographer would turn this year's gala into the event of the—"

"You and Dad turned my brother's disease and his death into a crusade that consumed the last of his and my childhoods. You were at it even after he died, trying to orchestrate a press interview bedside. He was a twenty-five-year-old man. My brother. *Your* son. Not a photo op. And I'm not sacrificing any more of my life to your obsession."

"We're fighting for a cure." His mother's tone slipped closer to tears—or fury, with Livy it was impossible to tell the difference—as the fight she and Mike had had countless times took its nastiest turn. Her vowels had reclaimed the Brooklyn accent she'd shed when she married into her husband's moneyed world. "We're fighting just as hard as Jeremy did."

"And I've supported you financially whenever you've asked." Through JHTF, the Jeremy Harrison Taylor Foundation. "But this philanthropic carnival you and Dad have been on for decades isn't right. Half the money you raise goes back out the door to pay for your next glitzy event. Not to fund research or testing trials or legislation that would stop cystic fibrosis from taking more kids and young men and women away from their families."

His mother grew silent.

A different son—a younger him—might have worried he'd hurt her feelings. Mike knew better. Livy was an unrelenting, competitive survivor, wrapped up in the luxurious trappings of a socialite's beauty and breeding. His disappointment in what JHTF had become couldn't make a dent in her drive to do and have more than her contemporaries.

"So we'll see you whenever we see you," she finally said, "same as always. Why did you call, then? Georgina could have contacted us about this year's donation. She usually does, after you've disappeared somewhere, lugging your cameras to godforsaken places where no one can reach you. Or because you're working odd jobs in a medical specialty you insisted on pursuing but hardly ever practice. You spent three years earning a four-year degree and more time getting your certification. But you can't stay in one place long enough to even devote yourself to that seriously. It's all so disappointing. You have so much potential, Michael. There's no limit to what you could become if you'd stop blaming your father and me for everything and get on with living your life instead of avoiding it."

"I don't blame anyone."

Not even his parents, for seeing him as a vagabond squandering his *potential* to give them a prestigious career or job title to brag about at parties.

"And I called because . . ." Mike wasn't up to coming straight out and mentioning that today was the anniversary of Jeremy's death. "I guess I wanted to hear your voice."

There was no point in him returning to New York full-time. Forging an adult relationship with his parents had never been in the cards. But he'd missed them—or at least the family he wished he and his parents and brother had been—every day since Mike had left, the morning after Jeremy's funeral.

"It's good to hear your voice, too." The real emotion behind Livy's admission gutted Mike.

He looked around him as he drove, at the peaceful, everyday normalcy of Chandlerville. Jeremy, sick and all, would have loved growing up in a community like this.

"If your service got you to move to Podunk last minute," his mother cajoled, "can't they replace you? Come up here for a while if you need a break. You can always go back to this hobby of yours later."

"Helping people rehab isn't a hobby for me, Mom."

Of all the things he'd done since moving away from his parents' elite, superficial lives, he was most proud of becoming a physical therapist. Getting his PT degree, training for his certification in cardiovascular and pulmonary rehabilitation, had quite simply saved him after he'd helplessly watched his big brother suffer for so long. He only took a couple of clients a year, working a few months at a time. But each placement was a priceless opportunity. A reminder that he could make a difference, even if staying in one place for long had never worked out for him.

"I can do good things here," he told his mother.

"Good things"—Livy's voice grew cold, the way it did at some point during each call—"that keep you as far away from your father and me and your brother's memory as you can get."

"I keep Jeremy's memory alive my way." Grieving his brother was the one thing left that Mike and his parents had in common. "You and Dad focus on keeping the foundation going."

"I hear you're showing an interest in JHTF's Developing Artist grant," his mother said, confirming his suspicion that she would catch wind of the information he'd asked for. "I'm confused, though, about what George wants from the grant director."

Mike braked at a stop sign and thumped his head against the back of his seat.

"Just some information about the scholarship program." He pulled to the curb of a sprawling two-story home set back from the street beneath a cluster of live oaks. "It's no big deal."

Now, *this* yard—he looked around and smiled—this yard was a big deal. The trees' limbs and leaves shaded the front yard and the home's roof, dappling everything with drops of sunlight. Who would have thought that something as . . . charming as this and the other houses on the street could exist only twenty miles from bustling, ever-expanding Atlanta.

"Let me go," he said. "I'm at my appointment."

"I don't suppose I have a choice."

No, I don't suppose you do. "Once we have the prints for you, George'll get a patron newsletter out to drive bidders to the auction. I'm sure the gala will be another fabulous page-six success."

"Yes . . ." Livy said, her tone distant, lifeless. "Just promise me . . ."

Mike braced himself for more of her litany of complaints.

Promise me you won't settle down somewhere away from us for good. Promise you'll get all this nonsense you're doing out of your system one day, and you'll come back to your life here. Don't make a mess of what you could become, because you can't let go of your brother.

"Just promise me that you're making yourself happy," she said instead. "We haven't heard you truly happy in so long, even after that last crazy trip of yours to photograph an active volcano."

Mike gripped the steering wheel.

A parent's concern wasn't supposed to sting, because you couldn't trust it to be genuine.

"I am happy, Mom," he said out of habit. "Why don't you and Dad plan to come down after the gala? For New Year's, maybe. I'll be done with this contract by then. You can see up close what I've started in the city. Understand what I do a little better. Maybe we can head out somewhere beautiful after that. There are a couple of spots in the North Georgia mountains Jeremy would have loved. We could—"

"Darling, your father and I couldn't possibly. You know how it is. There are too many people depending on us here. Things get more hectic every year."

Mike knew exactly how it was.

He rubbed at the pulse throbbing like an ice pick behind his temple.

"I'll let George know she'll be hearing back from the grant director," he said as several kids raced through the front yard of the house he'd parked in front of.

They headed around the corner toward the back of the place—three boys and a girl, laughing and chasing one another, not a care in the world, effortlessly active in a way Mike's brother had never known.

"Of course, darling," his mother said. "We're happy to give you whatever you need."

Right.

"I love you, Mom. I'll touch base once the pieces are ready to ship. I'm sorry I missed Dad. Tell him I love him, too."

"I will." The line dropped without Livy returning the sentiment.

Mike tossed his cell onto his Jeep's dash.

The kids ran back around to the front yard, kicking a soccer ball now. The young slip of a girl, maybe twelve or thirteen, stole the ball and then trapped it, darting away, giving the guys a run for their money, making them hustle before she passed it over. And then she stole it again.

Mike chuckled, feeling the tension of talking with his mother ease. The kids' good-natured grudge match could likely be heard through open windows up and down the block, while parents and neighbors smiled at the happy sounds of childhood and sunshine and free time. The moment made him think of Bethany and her friends and family.

He'd bet the lot of them squabbled often, just like the kids playing on the lawn. Getting into one another's way. Causing unfiltered mayhem and loving every second of it. Meanwhile, George was the closest thing to real family that Mike could call his own now.

He sincerely believed in the work his parents were doing—the parts of it that actually resulted in helping people. But he wouldn't call their strained, long-distance connection or his brief pilgrimages back to New York each year a real relationship. He'd filled his life instead with the things and places he'd promised Jeremy he'd keep discovering. And he was lucky to have the chance. To have had his brother's inspiration in his life for as long as he had.

Nodding, smiling at the idyllic scene beyond his windshield, he put New York out of his mind. He slipped off his hat and refocused on the rewarding afternoon of work ahead. Walking around to the curb side of his Jeep, he dragged out the duffel that was large enough to carry all he'd need for a preliminary site visit.

Beyond taking a blood pressure reading and checking basic vital signs, a lot of what he'd do today would be asking questions and getting the lay of the land. Deciding where it would be best to hold sessions. Getting to know the patient and his environment and immediate family enough to be sure Mike was a fit, and for him to formulate a high-level rehab plan before his next visit. Next time they'd delve more deeply into analyzing the patient's physical and mental state, beyond the medical history Mike had received from MedCare. This was a get-to-know-you visit, a baseline that every other session would build on.

The kids' roving scrimmage blocked his path to the house. He dropped his duffel, content to watch. Instinct had him digging the cell he'd reclaimed from the dash out of the pocket of the loose exercise pants he'd worn instead of jeans. He snapped a picture or two or ten. He made a mental note to ask for permission from the adults inside and to offer to share his shots. Then he framed and reframed the evolving scene some more, capturing the carefree childhood spectacle, the shady front porch behind the kids, the changing leaves overhead that were egging fall on, while refusing to relinquish the last of summer.

He adjusted angles and focus, the capacity of his latest smartphone's camera ridiculously advanced compared with what had been available even a year ago. The kids kept playing. He continued to shoot, maxing out the features of the photo app, lost in the richness and innocence of their world. He finally looked up, blown away anew.

He'd been walking the streets of Chandlerville for days, capturing random images, visiting local businesses, and striking up conversations with people who'd been more than welcoming. While he enjoyed the urban vibe of the Midtown Atlanta area where he'd lived for the last several years, he preferred open spaces. Nature. Beauty in all its complex simplicity. Chandlerville seemed to exist in rarified limbo between the homespun farmland being worked not five miles away, and the urban bustle of the South's most industrial city.

"Whatcha doin'?" a young voice asked.

A girl with bright green eyes, an infectious smile, and a head of dark curls gazed up at him. She was maybe six or seven and wore pink jeans and a Hello Kitty T-shirt, clearly not dressed for soccer.

"Where did you come from?" he asked.

"Next door."

She pointed at the bushy hedge covered in massive pink and purple blooms that made him think of cotton candy. The yard beyond looked like a cameo of a botanical garden.

"Because my sisters just got here," she explained. "Well, my other sisters, the ones that don't live with my grandparents anymore. Well, my other grandparents, not the Grammy I live with next door."

She looked a little lost as she stopped speaking, as if her rambling details had confused even her.

"Well"—she shrugged—"my mom and me used to live next door with Grammy. Now we have a house down the street. And a dog. Bud. After flowers, because Blossom would have made him sound like a girl. But I'm here almost every day. And I still have my own room. My grammy says I always will as long as she lives there. And my mommy said it was okay if I came down while my sisters and my other grammy talk . . ."

The little magpie flashed a megawatt smile while she gulped in air. One of her eyeteeth was missing. Her attention shifted to his phone.

"Whatcha doin'?" she asked again.

"Making memories." He knelt and showed her his last photo.

"Of my grandparents' house?"

She swiped through his recent images, manipulating the gallery app with the ease of a millennial who'd been using smart devices since she was in diapers.

"You make it look so pretty," she praised. "How did you do that?"

"I just played with what the camera saw, until it saw what I wanted it to."

She scrolled her way back through the photos he'd taken in town. "They're all so pretty!"

"Want to try?"

She snatched the phone out of his hands, nodding. "Can I do it on my mom and dad's phones, too?"

"Anyone can do it." He helped her take her first shot, showed her how to turn the phone to get a landscape view, how to zoom in for the next snap. Then he stood while she continued playing on her own.

She finally looked up, wonder in her expression. "Wow."

He couldn't have said it better himself.

"Let's see what you got." He crouched beside her and switched back to the gallery, selecting the first of her shots from the thumbnails.

She frowned as he studied more of what she'd done. "My pictures aren't the same as yours."

"It just takes a little practice. Every camera's different. Get used to the one on your mom or dad's phone, and you'll be a pro in no time."

"That's so cool!" She gave him another smile, each one improving his afternoon by leaps and bounds.

"Camille?" a soft voice called from the porch.

An attractive, middle-aged woman stood there, the front door open. She was dressed in khakis and a green knit blouse that was covered in a dusting of what looked to be flour. Her hair had once been a vibrant red, he'd guess. It was a tousled, shoulder-cropped wave of auburn now, shot through with silver.

"Who's your new friend?" the woman asked.

"Grandma Marsha!" The little girl sprinted up the steps, taking Mike's camera with her. She shoved it at the woman. "Look what I did."

Dutifully inspecting each picture, the woman smiled at both the photos and the child.

"Beautiful," she praised. She hugged her granddaughter to her side and straightened. "Can we help you?"

Mike headed toward them. "I'm from MedCare, ma'am. I have a site visit scheduled with Joe Dixon. My name is—"

"Mike?" Bethany was suddenly in the doorway, too.

Her appearance—the effect seeing her had on him every time—knocked him back down a step.

"Mike?" Another woman—a blonde who was just a little older than Bethany, maybe—appeared from inside. "*The* Michael Taylor? You're Cowboy Bob?"

The older woman chuckled. Then a very tall man with a thick crop of gray hair walked stiffly up to the ladies from the depth of the house.

"So, Bethie," the man said, looking Mike up and down while he hugged Bethany to his side. "We finally get to meet your non-date to Dru's wedding?"

Chapter Six

"I'm Mike Taylor, sir." The young man moved his duffel bag to his left shoulder so he could shake Joe's hand with his right. "And the other day was a . . ." He glanced at Bethany, and Joe watched the guy's expression melt. "It was a crazy misunderstanding. I'm actually a rehab tech from MedCare. I'm here for your preliminary site evaluation before we begin our work together."

"He showed me how to take these, Grandpa!" Camille piped up while Bethany stared at their visitor as if he might disappear if she blinked.

Camille handed Joe a smartphone.

"What do we have here?" Joe bent so they could look at the display together, wincing at the sharp stab of stiffness in his back.

"Pictures I took." His granddaughter scrolled through the photos. "And these are Mike's. His are better, but he says mine are good, too, and I just need practice on Mommy and Daddy's phones. And he was showing me how, and look at what I did. Isn't that cool?"

"They're beautiful." Joe pressed a hand to his lower back so he could straighten, earning himself the attention of every adult on the porch—including his new physical therapist. "It's very cool."

"You're going to help my grandpa?" Camille asked the young man.

"I am . . ." Their visitor's gaze flicked back to Bethany, whose attention had dropped to the motorcycle boots she'd worn today, along with a flowing, ankle-grazing sundress. "As long as that's not a problem."

Bethany blinked at Mike through her bangs. "You're a nurse?"

"A physical therapist. My specialization is advanced cardiovascular and pulmonary cases like your father's." He smiled hesitantly at Bethany, as if he couldn't stop himself. "This is your foster family?"

"Mine, too," Camille said.

"Mine, too." Dru grinned, like a Cheshire cat lapping up her sister's awkward moment.

"They have lots of foster kids, like my dad," Camille added. She'd been more excited than Joe and Marsha—who'd been thrilled—when she became an official part of their sprawling brood. "And now they have me, too, because me and Mommy came back to Chandlerville to visit my other grammy. And my mommy and my daddy made up, and now I have two grammies and a grandpa and lots of uncles and aunts, right?"

"Right." Marsha nodded enthusiastically. Then she gasped as Selena and Oliver's angel snuggled against Joe's legs, too, and Joe staggered.

Damn his balance. It came and went for no reason.

He gripped the door frame. "No sense in sorting this out on the porch. Let's take the conversation inside."

He and Marsha hadn't put too much stock in the rumors about whatever had gone down at McC's last week, even after their son's griping at Friday night's dinner. Bethany had denied that anything of real interest had gone on at all. Joe and Marsha had figured they'd give her the benefit of the doubt until they saw differently with their own eyes.

They'd hoped to get a chance to talk with her more this afternoon, when Bethany and Dru stopped by to cart away a new batch of the wedding gifts he and Marsha kept accumulating, as neighbors and friends dropped them off. Which of course had been a ruse by the girls, who'd thought they needed to be there to support Joe's finally agreeing to look into physical therapy.

Bethany led the way into the house, looking closed up again, the way Joe had seen her too many times in the years he and Marsha had had her as a teenager—and more and more often in the months since they'd gotten her back with the family. Her young man, or whoever this guy was, looked to be considering beating a path back out the door. Except of course for the way he couldn't keep his eyes off Joe's little girl.

Legs shaking, Joe trailed his family into the living room. He'd been reading the paper there when the doorbell rang. The kids were either playing outside, upstairs, or making themselves scarce—for fear they'd be assigned one of the random chores Joe and Marsha made sure popped up if someone dared to look bored.

Marsha hooked her arm around Joe's, casually supporting more of his weight than she should have to, two months after his open-heart surgery. She waited until he was settled in his recliner before taking a seat on the end of the couch closest to him. Dru joined her, Camille scampering into her lap, leaving the remaining two upholstered chairs for Bethany and the guy who wasn't her guy. Evidently this was *Joe's* guy, if Joe wanted his mobility, stamina, and respiration to improve enough for him to keep working full-time. And to do more than sit on the sidelines of his daughter's upcoming wedding.

Bethany claimed the chair farthest from everyone. Joe's new rehab aide dropped his duffel to the floor. Mike remained standing, linking his hands behind him, clearly unsure of his welcome.

"Would you like to have a seat?" Marsha asked the young man.

Mike checked with Bethany, who wouldn't make eye contact. His attention dropped to the hand Joe hadn't realized he'd clenched on the arm of his recliner. It took Joe a while these days to find a sitting position that would ease the stiffness that had become chronic in his back. He loosened his grip and reached behind him for the pillow he wouldn't have needed before, using it like a bolster. Like an old man.

Mike withdrew a folder from his duffel and settled in the chair next to Bethany's.

"Thank you, ma'am," he said to Marsha.

"I understand that you and my daughter have gotten to know each other a bit already," Joe ventured.

No sense avoiding the obvious. And, okay, he conceded to his wife with a raised eyebrow, maybe he was delaying the inevitable questions to come about his derailed recovery.

"I . . ." Their guest hesitated. "I wouldn't say we know each other well."

"Well enough to have the whole town buzzing," Dru offered.

"This is a nightmare . . ." Bethany finally looked at the guy. "I'm so sorry. I—"

"Don't worry about it," Mike assured her.

"But . . ." Bethany started to say, her voice trailing off the way she used to stop speaking midsentence as a teenager—back when she'd been afraid that something she'd say could make them stop wanting her.

Joe studied the reaction of the quiet, respectful young man he'd heard had stood up for Bethany with as much conviction as her brothers. Mike reached toward her. He hesitated and pulled his touch back, as if not wanting to add to her distress.

"If my working with Mike is going to make you this uncomfortable, sweetheart"—Joe waited until he had Bethany's attention—"I can postpone doing rehab until MedCare finds someone else."

"No," his wife and two daughters said in unison.

"Dad," Bethany insisted. "You're not putting this off again because of me."

"You don't want to get better, Grandpa?" Camille asked.

"Of course he wants to get better." Marsha reached for Joe's fingers and squeezed. "Your grandpa knows not doing what his doctors have been recommending for months is no longer an option."

Joe did, even if he didn't want the expense and the added fuss of at-home rehabilitation. But he was still too weak. He hurt too much. Too much of his life was slipping away. He had too many people depending on him, for him to rationalize not doing whatever he had to do to get better. And the kids always came first.

It was the promise he and Marsha had made to each other a long time ago, and it had never steered them wrong.

He patted his wife's hand.

"What have you got there?" He nodded toward Mike's folder.

"Your preliminary files." Mike placed the paperwork on the coffee table. "Nothing that you haven't already seen. Records from the hospital and follow-up visits with your doctors. Some notes from your insurance agency. Bare-bones details that I'll want to discuss with you as we customize your rehab plan together. But none of that's important right now, sir."

"What is important right now?" Marsha asked.

"In my experience," the young man said to Joe, "your commitment to the process is all that matters at this stage. As your wife pointed out, you've repeatedly delayed this step that your doctors prescribed for you when you returned from the post-surgery rehab center. And unless a patient is fully on board with the benefits of home therapy, committed to our program and to additional exercises between visits, there'll be very little long-term benefit from our working together."

"Let's not overdramatize things, young man." Joe strummed his fingers on the arm of his chair. "I need a little help stretching and getting my strength back. That's all. There have been some bumps settling back in at my job. But I'm a claims adjuster for an insurance company. It's not like I'm going to be running marathons."

"But you're not sleeping through the night, either," his wife said, "or eating much of anything that I don't pester you to eat."

"Or doing most of the things you usually do around here, Dad," Dru added.

"Like playing with me and the other kids." Camille nodded for emphasis when Joe looked her way.

"Limited stamina and mobility," Mike said, "and loss of interest in everyday activities are common obstacles to recovering from bypass. Dealing with the side effects of some of the medications you've been taking post-op adds to the problem. There can be debilitating mood swings and bouts of uncharacteristic anger and frustration and the sense of wanting your life back to normal. Which can make it even more difficult for you to commit to the work it's going to take to get us there."

"Us?" Joe barked. He felt his wife flinch and then relax.

Marsha smiled encouragingly, as if telling him everything would be fine.

She'd been his rock to lean on since his heart attack, making sure everyone else in the family was okay, too, especially with Dru and Brad's impending wedding and Bethany's return. Meanwhile, all the kids Joe and his wife were currently fostering needed to be looked after. And there was only so much his older, "aged-out" children could pitch in to help with. Their lives were getting busier by the day.

Joe was becoming a burden to his family. He was watching his wife grow more tired and worried by the day. And there didn't seem to be a damn thing he could do to stop it.

"I think I can help you, sir," Mike said. "If you're ready to fully commit to your recovery, it would be my privilege to assist you. You have an excellent chance to regain the quality of life a man your age should have, particularly with this kind of support network in your corner."

Marsha smiled, the sparkle in her beautiful blue eyes telling Joe that Mike had won her over. And her instincts about people were as good as money in the bank. If she thought this man was worth keeping around, then who was Joe to argue? Except he wasn't the only one needing to face a few difficult truths if this was going to work.

Bethany kept staring at their guest, smiling when Joe doubted she realized it. Almost flinching when Mike looked her way. She was a bundle of nerves around the guy.

"I'll agree to rehab," Joe said. He pointed at his daughter and then Mike. "But only if whatever's going on between you two stops being a problem."

"It's not a problem, Dad," Bethany said. "Really. It's just—"

"It's just that my child who has finally made her way back to this family was already having a hard enough time settling in. And today she looks even more like she wants to find somewhere else to be." Joe levered himself out of his chair with a groan, facing Mike. "I suspect that has something to do with you, sir. Which means you two are going to figure whatever this is out, and Bethany's going to be okay with you coming around. Or you're not setting foot in my house again."

Joe headed slowly for the kitchen, motioning for everyone else to follow so Bethany and Mike could talk.

Bethany shot out of her chair.

Mike stood, too. He towered over her, wearing gym pants today, pristine white sneakers instead of grungy hiking books, and a relaxed-fit golf shirt. He'd shaved. There was no hat in sight. His hair, a bit too long still, was neatly combed. There wasn't a whiff of the cowboy she'd met, until she lost herself in those eyes that weakened her knees.

"I thought you were a bartender," she said, silently pleading with her sister and mother not to desert her. The other women followed Joe into the kitchen with Camille.

"I'm a lot of things," Mike said.

"And you're telling me you really didn't—"

"Know that I would be your dad's physical therapy aide when I kissed you until we were both senseless?"

Bethany felt her body heating at the memory.

"No," he insisted. "I didn't."

"What on earth where you doing bartending at McC's?"

"Law and Rick needed help Friday night. Thursday was my tryout. I'm a decent bar back. It sounded like fun, and I like to get to know a place I'm going to stay in for a while. Unless Rick's in another bind, I doubt he'll need me anymore. But you never know."

"You never know?"

The corners of Mike's mouth ticked up into a smile that he seemed to be trying to control. Bethany realized how close she was to him. Practically pressed against him while they talked softly in comically loud whispers that she was certain her sister at least could hear—Dru's ear smashed against the now-closed kitchen door.

"Are you okay with this?" Mike asked.

Okay with it? This was a guy she'd embarrassed herself with, whom she'd consoled herself with probably never seeing again. And even if she did, it wouldn't mean anything. Only there he was, standing in front of her in her parents' living room. And the needle on her hunky-guy radar was pinned to the red zone. Now Mike was going to be in and out of her parents' house on a regular basis—unless Bethany put the brakes on her foster father's rehab.

"Why wouldn't I be okay with it?" She put several inches between them. "I don't know what my dad thinks is wrong. I've told my family about Thursday night, and that we're not dating. Why would it be a problem for you to help Joe if you can?"

"Well . . ." Mike caught her hand. He lifted her fingers for a kiss like the one he'd given them at Nic's, making Bethany's sensitive skin there—everywhere—tingle. "There's the fact that you can't seem to stop wanting to be next to me, but every time we get close, you keep—"

"Stop that." She yanked her hand free.

"Shoving me away." He backed out of her personal space, the way he would from a frightened, cornered animal. "What *did* you wind up telling your family about me?"

"The truth. That I asked you to help me with Benjie at the bar. And that I was . . ."

"Grateful?"

"Momentarily confused."

"About liking having a total stranger kiss you? Or about trusting me to help in the first place?"

She inched even farther away. He *had* been a stranger. She'd been in a room full of friends and neighbors, and eventually family once her brothers showed up. But with Benjie zeroing in, when the pressure was on and she'd accepted that she needed help, her subconscious had run once more toward the unknown—straight into Mike's arms.

"So what if we kissed?" she reminded Mike. "We agreed it was no big deal when we said goodbye to each other at Grapes & Beans."

"Well, I guess this is hello again."

He made a motion with his hand that she suspected would have had something to do with his hat. He rubbed his fingers through his shaggy haircut instead, tugging at the ends.

"I don't think your father's trying to throw us together as a couple or anything," he said.

"Good, because Joe has no business trying to."

Mike grew more serious. "I think he's looking for a legitimate reason to back out of physical therapy. He doesn't want to admit that on his own he might not recover any better than he has. But on some level, he's probably also thinking that no matter what he and I do together, things might stay the same or maybe get worse. That kind of circular logic, a sense of hopelessness, can trip up a lot of patients. Ones who haven't waited nearly as long as your dad has to get started."

"Do . . ."

Every heartbeat and breath and instinct was screaming for Bethany to be next to Mike. For comfort. To touch him. To demand that he say *yes* to her next question.

"Do you really think he can get better?" she asked.

"I know he can." Mike smiled. "And as far as what's happened between us, I wouldn't mind Joe or anyone else in your family giving me a hard time about it while he and I work together. But your dad cares about you, and he's seen and heard enough about us to question whether I should be here."

"Because of me?"

"Because we started off on the wrong foot. Joe doesn't need that kind of distraction. Or another excuse to rough out his recovery on his own. If the two of us agreeing to reboot things gives me the next hour with him and the PT sessions we'll hopefully schedule, what's the harm?"

"Reboot?"

"Me not being your worst nightmare," he pressed, "every time we wind up in the same place. Us getting to know each other in real time, the way we would have if I hadn't manhandled you at first sight."

Bethany raised her hands to stall his hard sell.

"I asked you for help at the bar." And she hadn't minded one bit of the way he'd handled himself or her. "I kissed you. And I seriously doubt you could ever be a woman's worst nightmare."

Mike looked skeptical. "I have an ex-fiancée who might disagree with you."

"She dumped you?" Bethany couldn't fathom it.

"It's a long story."

One that had ended with Mike being single, gorgeous, unattached, and saying he wanted to get to know Bethany better. Her stomach did a crazy flip.

"How often has Joe backed out of physical therapy," he asked, "since the rehab center released him?"

"Every other time he's gotten close to making this decision."

Mike brushed a comforting touch down her arm. "I know how difficult that can be for a patient's family. This first step is the hardest for your dad—admitting he needs help. Followed by our first few sessions that he will probably feel are a waste of time. Some patients call therapy off even then, before they give themselves a chance to make sustainable improvements."

"My foster father's not a quitter. He doesn't just need to get back to work for my family's sake. He wants to walk Dru down the aisle, be an active part of her wedding, and have enough energy to dance with her at the reception. He's loved her like his own flesh-and-blood daughter since the day he and Marsha brought Dru home, and he doesn't want to miss a second of her big day."

But on a difficult morning now, Joe was exhausted just from walking down the stairs and sitting through family breakfast—barely eating a few bites of whatever Marsha had made to tempt his nonexistent appetite.

"The wedding's not even a month away," she reminded Mike. "Will he be ready for that?"

Mike dug his hand into his pocket. "I can't make any promises, even if that means I'm talking you out of putting up with me."

"You're not. And I'm not trying to make you think you have to."

What she was, was terrified for her parents and their fresh crop of foster kids—including Shandra—and what would happen to all of them if Joe couldn't recover fully.

"Your father's challenges," Mike said, "are more than physical at this stage. Men like Joe aren't used to feeling weak and out of control and unable to pull themselves together by muscling through a problem. It's going to take time to relearn how to listen to his body. To accept new limitations and adjust to what normal is going to feel like post-bypass. The sooner we can get him thinking in that direction the better."

We.

Bethany peered up at the guy.

"You're worried about him, too," she said in wonder. "You really are a good man, Michael Taylor."

"Stranger things have happened. But is that a strike in my favor, or against me? Don't you like good men?"

She exhaled, choosing her words carefully. "Let's just say I wasn't looking for a man at all at this point in my life. Let alone one who . . . makes me feel as good as you do."

"Because feeling good is so overrated?"

What had Bethany ever known about getting feelings and relationships right? Even feeling good could hurt, when feeling pretty much of anything made you need to disappear.

Mike crossed his arms when she didn't answer him, his legs braced as if he were readying for battle.

"Let's start small," he suggested. "Can you at least stop looking like you're going to bolt for the door every time we see each other and you have a powerful hankering for more of my manhandling?"

He was teasing her, she realized.

And of course she was liking it.

"Could you not be such an adorable ass," she said, "about understanding me better than a guy should, considering we've only fake-dated so far?"

He considered her terms. "I can work with that. Can *you* put up with the rumors around town if we actually do make some time for that first date? At least from your friends and neighbors. I'm assuming your family would leave you alone now if we spent time together."

Bethany snorted. "Clearly you haven't been around families as large and nosy as mine."

"That's true enough."

There was something wistful about the way he scanned Marsha's comfortably decorated, cluttered living room. Bethany tried to imagine what it would look like to someone else.

It was the hub of the house. Where Marsha or Joe helped with homework and distributed chores, bandaged scrapes and bruises, and refereed skirmishes that ranged from halfhearted bickering to the domestic equivalent of World War III. Later on, most evenings—at least before Joe's heart attack—Bethany's foster parents could often be caught cuddling on the couch or in Joe's recliner.

"Can you put up with me decking the mongrel," Mike asked, intruding on Bethany's memories, "if Benny makes another play for you?"

"I'm sure Joe wouldn't expect you to cause bodily harm on my behalf just to prove we've made peace."

Mike tipped the invisible brim of the cowboy hat he hadn't worn. "Consider it a bonus, ma'am."

An intriguing bonus.

All of him was.

"Just friends?" she asked. "Going on a first date?"

He was the one who stepped closer this time. "I didn't say I didn't want to be more than friends."

And she didn't say how every time he popped onto her horizon, it felt as if she were free-falling into him. It was exactly the way she'd locked into her paintings in high school, obsessed from even the tiniest first brushstroke, not able to stop herself until what she was creating was finished.

"Bethany," Mike said. "Congress doesn't take this long to pass legislation."

She realized the last of her doubts were gone, like storm clouds beaten back by a vivid blue sky. "If you're this skilled at putting your patients at ease, my father's in excellent hands. You're good at making people believe that you care about them."

"Maybe that's because I do care." Mike's gaze narrowed. "I don't take on a lot of patients. This work is very personal for me. I'm in for the duration, no matter how much time it takes from the rest of my life. For the record, I don't hook up with a lot of women, either. And when I bartend, I never hit on customers."

"And I . . ." It was important to her that he knew, after what he'd heard at McC's. "I don't sleep around. Not the way Benjie made it sound."

Mike tipped up her chin. "I don't have any problem believing that."

"That"—she gestured between them—"you and me at McC's . . . that was my first kiss in a long time."

"Mine, too. I'd say we both remember how to do it just fine."

"Except it felt . . ."

She let him ease her into his arms, his body solid against her softer one.

"How did it feel?" he asked.

She didn't know how to describe it.

So she kissed him again instead, his lips a soft, lingering question, a gentle request. Until the excitement grabbed them, a powerful surge, an all-in wave of need making his body shiver along with hers.

Bethany wanted. It was a visceral, edgy, beyond-reason type of want that streaked color behind her closed eyes. Heat coursed through her clinging body, consuming everything as Mike's hands turned gentle, comforting, calming the both of them. His restraint brought Bethany back to the reality of her parents' den, and him easing her away.

"It felt risky," she panted, trying to understand.

Mike nodded, searching her face for his own answers.

She could step back from him, she told herself. And she did. But she couldn't make herself stop wanting to know him better. To understand why he had such an intoxicating, undeniable effect on her.

"So." He braced his hands on his hips while he caught his own breath. "We'll take things slow. No pressure. More talking, less kissing until we get to know each other better."

"No strings attached," she instructed herself and Mike. "No expectations. And I assure you that when we get around to that first date, it'll be a just-friends night."

"Agreed." He reached out his hand and waited for her to shake. "I need to get back to your dad. But I . . . really do want us to talk, Bethany. To get to know each other the right way. I'm . . . I wish we had more time now. I mean, I'm glad about working with Joe. But you and me. There's something . . ."

"Whatever it is will keep," she reassured him, finding his sudden bout of insecurity endearing. "And I've been thinking about you, too. A lot more than I wanted to. Talking with you yesterday at Nic's was . . ."

Nerve-racking. Exciting. She shrugged off the impulse to believe that it had been anything more than chemistry.

Dating just for fun isn't a personality flaw, Bethany.

"I'm glad," she finally said, "that we're giving it another shot."

"Risky it is then." His sexy cowboy's smile was back. "Don't make me wait too long for that date now, darlin'."

He hoisted his duffel over one shoulder and walked toward the kitchen to help her father . . . while Bethany rubbed her fingers over her lips, tasting Mike's kisses and wondering what the hell she'd just gotten herself into.

Chapter Seven

"You're not hiding out down here all night," Clair said to Bethany almost a week later.

Bethany didn't know what time it was. She never did when she worked on a new piece. And since new pieces were all she was working on these days, it was no small accomplishment that she knew it was Saturday again.

Clair and Nicole had shown up at the Artist Co-op's loft a few minutes ago, wanting Bethany—who'd turned her phone off, so she hadn't gotten any of their texts—to join them for drinks at some trendy Midtown place Nic loved. They'd been trying to corner her ever since her run-in with Mike at her parents' house. And, yes, technically Bethany had been hiding from them.

But it wasn't personal. She'd been avoiding everyone since she and Mike had *worked things out* the way her dad had needed them to. Which had been code, evidently, for Bethany drowning in second thoughts ever since, and she didn't know how to explain to herself or anyone else.

Mike had started therapy sessions with Joe. Marsha had called Bethany a couple of times to say things were going well enough—and to ask if Bethany and Mike had gone out yet. Dru kept Bethany filled in, too, on whatever she'd heard about Joe and Mike's every-other-day work. It sounded as if their father's recovery was progressing at a slow pace, though Joe seemed to be wanting to do his best. So far his lagging energy level and outlook continued to be a challenge.

And, oh, by the way, Dru managed to slip in after each report, *when were Bethany and Mike going out?*

And Bethany's friends . . .

Nic and Clair were just as curious in their own supportive way. Never pestering her or asking outright what was going on. But her friends' just-checking-in texts and IMs had become increasingly persistent. And *someone* had given Mike the phone number to the Douglas house. No one in her family would have done that.

Now he was trying to reach her at Dru and Brad's, leaving his own messages, asking Bethany to call him back, and adding to the mounting pressure for her to make good on her commitment to see him again. But to be fair, when Bethany had gone hunting for a last-minute sub to cover today's shift at the Dream Whip, it hadn't *entirely* been because she'd needed somewhere to hide.

A work slot had suddenly opened up at the Artist Co-op, and she'd jumped at the chance to get on the schedule sooner than her September start date. The co-op used a website calendar system to track free-of-charge work times for its artists. August's schedule had already been booked when Bethany's residency was accepted. The loft's office manager had said to keep checking the system in case a cancellation came up. That morning Bethany had struck gold. Back-to-back day and evening slots were hers if she'd wanted them. So she'd been on her way into the city in under an hour, relieved to be twenty-five miles away from Chandlerville for the day and blissfully working on a new project.

Ten hours later, her new canvas, like all the ones she'd abandoned before it, was mocking her from its easel. Almost making it seem like a blessing when her friends snuck into the loft through the street-level entrance behind another artist heading home for the night.

Almost.

"It's late," Nicole reasoned. "Take a break for something to eat at least."

Bethany shook her head. "The next resident working in this space isn't due in until morning. I'm going to figure this piece out by then if it kills me."

"All you're going to do is keep staring at what you've already painted, until you nix it and start over and stare some more."

"You don't know that."

"I know it's what you've been doing for months at your sister's house. Dru said so."

"Now you're doing it here," Clair chimed in.

"This painting doesn't stand a chance any more than the others," Nic said. "You're obsessed with painting something perfect for your parents."

"An obsession I could live with." Bethany eyed the canvas she'd been tinkering with since before noon.

Her friends had told her that it was after nine. She'd been staring at her barely begun landscape for she didn't know how long now. Trying to listen to it. Needing it to speak to her. Needing to feel . . . something from it, besides a void of creativity refusing to inspire her.

"Obsession I could work with. But this . . ." She pointed her brush at her painting. "This is just . . ."

Her work made her feel nothing at all.

And she had absolutely no idea how to get back what she'd once had.

"It's gorgeous." Clair flinched at whatever reaction flashed across Bethany's face. "It's a gorgeous beginning at least. Come out with us and loosen up. Go home and indulge in that sexy cowboy who's waiting to woo you. Do *something* besides spending more and more time not liking anything you're painting."

"Really," Nic said. "People are getting worried. Your dad already was, before you cut yourself off from everyone entirely. Now look at you."

"What?" Bethany glanced down at the floral sundress she'd layered over daisy-patterned tights and her hot-pink high-top Converse sneakers.

Clair took stock of her, too. "Things are getting a little *Night of the Living Dead*, B. Dru said you've been on a painting tear since last weekend. Let's get you in a shower. Get some food into you. Maybe you could sleep a few hours? Let this canvas go for a while."

"I can't."

Bethany couldn't let another idea—her favorite so far, for her parents' anniversary—slip away from her.

"What about Mike?" Nicole asked. "How long do you think he's going to wait for you to stop running yourself ragged, obsessing over whether or not to go out with him?"

"That's not what I'm doing," Bethany snapped at her friend. "And he said he wouldn't pressure me."

"Why would a guy like Mike have to pressure you?" Nic ignored Bethany's temper and turned her away from her canvas. "He seems really nice. You said so yourself, after you saw how much he wants to help Joe."

"Enjoy the bounty." Clair plucked a compact from her purse, opened it, and held the mirror in front of Bethany. "Once your eyes aren't so bloodshot you can barely keep them open."

Bethany turned back to her misfit painting. "What's it going to take to get rid of you two?"

"Don't bother trying to piss us off by being rude." Clair pried the paintbrush from Bethany's hand and tossed it onto the worktable that was covered in tubes of oil paint and the other items Bethany had checked out of the co-op's supply closet. "We built up an immunity to your brush-offs in high school."

She rubbed at the aching muscles in Bethany's hand, the ones that always cramped when she was in the middle of a creative binge.

"Don't stop," Bethany groaned, willing to endure her girlfriends' pushing their way into her current creative crisis, as long as Clair didn't stop.

"I doubt you're going to scare your cowboy away, either." Clair tended to the pressure point in Bethany's hand, until Bethany wanted to scream in relief.

"The next time you see him," Nicole said, "do you really want to be sporting the dark circles and six-feet-under skin tone of a zombie? How long do you think you can keep this up?"

"As long as it takes . . ." Bethany sighed, too worn out to keep fighting with her friends. They were just trying to help. And it was entirely possible they knew Bethany better than she knew herself. She winced as Clair hit a particularly tender spot. "Whatever it takes, to show my parents what I see every time I look at the world they gave me, when they agreed to take on the mess that I was at fifteen."

She didn't need to sleep. She didn't need thoughts of Mike distracting her. She didn't need to be worrying about what would happen when they finally went out for real. She *needed* this painting to make sense.

How did she explain the emptiness inside her where her imagination used to dream in effortless abandon? Or the panic she felt each time it seemed her art would never come back. How did she tell people that if they wanted to worry about something, to worry about who and what she'd become if she lost her creativity for good?

"If I get too tired later," she said with renewed determination, "I can crash on one of the cots down the hall for a couple of hours."

The loft was equipped with small sleeping areas for residents, alcoves that were little more than dorm rooms. But they were magical havens with blackout curtains and white-noise machines. Artists who needed to recharge could lock the door and grab a few winks whenever they needed to.

"I have to figure this painting out," she insisted.

The three of them studied what she'd done so far.

Bethany reclaimed her brush from the cluster of rags she used to mix colors on a palette board, thinning hues out, creating custom tints and textures. She'd wanted to capture the Dixon house this time, instead of leaning into another portrait of the family.

Over the last few months she'd tried and failed to paint her siblings, one by one, and then their parents. She'd also attempted several family groupings—Oliver and Selena and Camille, Dru and Brad, Marsha and Joe and the younger kids. All from photos Marsha had collected over the years. Bethany had wanted to capture each detail. But the perfect reflection of her family that she'd been going for had refused to materialize. Then she'd watched Mike gaze around Marsha and Joe's living room for the first time . . . and a new idea had sparked to life.

In her latest canvas she'd gone for an interpretation of the Dixon house, instead of painting an exact replica of the home she loved. From memory alone, she'd create her impression of the magical world that had been her fresh start. She'd wanted viewers to feel what she'd watched Mike take in.

She'd wanted to capture the love seeping out of every inch of the place, palpable to anyone who entered Marsha and Joe's home. The acceptance and belonging, and the way her foster parents had made Bethany and her siblings feel instantly welcome. The second chance Marsha and Joe had tirelessly offered to broken lives that were desperate to become whole.

Bethany had wanted her parents to know what that meant to her, what *they* meant to her and all of her siblings. Even if she still needed to keep her distance sometimes, the world her foster parents had given to her was absolutely everything she'd dreamed family could be. *That* was what she'd hoped to bring to life when she'd started painting this morning.

"I thought you liked things to look more . . ." Clair hesitated.

"Realistic?" Nic ventured.

"Yeah." Bethany's gift had always been photorealistic painting. "Not so much anymore."

Her use of light had come so easily once. As had the pure, simple lines that had emerged so effortlessly. She'd had a natural gift, according to her high school art teacher, for drawing the eye into the very heart of an image—whatever image she'd loved so much, she'd had to capture it—making the viewer believe they were looking at a photograph instead of thousands of brushstrokes. She could remember losing herself in the escape of capturing each of those early moments, never once questioning whether an image would come to life.

For over a year now she'd been fighting to get the technique back, ever since moving to the apartment above Dan's. She'd thought setting up her studio at Dru's in January would be the turning point that would seduce her creativity into playing nice. Now she was counting on her residency to kick-start things.

She'd been so excited when she'd hauled a fresh canvas out of the supply closet this morning. She'd picked her paints, going by feel alone. Committed to doing something different with the house and the yard surrounding it, she'd let herself be drawn to less realistic colors. Lighter, brighter, more whimsical hues. The result, once she'd started working, had rendered an almost surreal composition, like nothing she'd ever produced with a landscape. It was as if you could look through the walls and roof of the house, even the trees and shrubbery. The effect was ghostly in a welcoming way she'd hoped would draw the viewer in, the same as her more "accurate" paintings.

She'd started with a deft wash of green against a bright white canvas. Trees and grass and sky had taken ethereal shape in different hues of the same base color, mixed with creams and light pinks. She'd framed the area where a hint of the house currently existed, waiting to take clearer shape once she focused on it. *If* she got around to focusing on it. But every time she tried to execute more of the building itself, amid her otherworldly reflection of the yard surrounding it . . . the perfectly imperfect foster home that had saved her, was *still* saving her, wouldn't appear.

"It's going to be pretty," Clair proclaimed in an overly optimistic way that had Bethany wanting to crawl under her worktable.

"You know," Nicole amended, "once you're finished doing whatever you're doing."

"I don't *know* what I'm doing."

Except it felt as if Bethany were suffocating.

She looked around her, really seeing the loft for the first time since she'd started working. The other artists scheduled to work second shift in the cubicles around her either hadn't arrived yet or were taking a break for dinner. She vaguely remembered day shift people coming and going, conversations up and down the hallway outside the alcove she'd reserved. She'd waved at their friendly remarks as they'd passed, mumbled a hello or goodbye.

She'd been so jazzed to be there. So sure another change in creative scenery would do the trick. She'd actually been psyched about finally calling Mike back when she was done, to tell him what he'd inspired her to paint, and that she'd finally finished something.

"I'm starting over." She dabbed her brush into the darkest, rawest green on her palette board and confronted her canvas, ready to cross a gigantic *X* through it.

"No!" Nicole stepped between Bethany and the painting, her arms spread wide. "It's too beautiful. Seriously"—she blocked Bethany from stepping around her—"girl, I don't know exactly where you're going with this one. I've never seen you do anything like it. But you're not giving up. Not again. How many half-finished canvases do you have at Dru's? A dozen? Two?"

"Even if your heart's not in it yet," Clair agreed, "give it some more time."

Time to find her heart . . .

Shaking off the notion, Bethany turned to Clair, contemplating what her friend's white jacket, white jeans, and trendy white silk top would look like smeared with throw-in-the-towel green.

"You two," she said, "were harassing me just now to quit."

"For the night." Nic slapped her arms to her sides. "Not the whole damn painting. Dru says you're giving up faster with every new piece you try."

"My sister needs to stay out of my studio. And what are you doing talking with her about my art anyway?"

"We're trying to help you," Clair said with uncharacteristic exasperation. She usually played the good cop when she and Nicole tag-teamed Bethany. "Your art is agitating you as much as everything else right now. Give it a rest until you figure out why."

"You think I don't know why?"

Bethany stared at her friends, haunted by the passion and need and flurry of her teenage brushstrokes. The restful, peaceful results she'd taken for granted. The excitement back then that had driven her to paint every second of the day, and to love every minute of it. The sense, finally, that anything in her life was possible.

Painting had helped her stay. In Chandlerville and with the Dixons, and with the two best friends she'd made at Chandler High. Painting had been a clean, easy space where she could hide all the hurt and pain, and where she could turn her fear into something beautiful. Back then, she'd believed her art would never hurt her. And then it had betrayed her, right along with Benjie.

Bethany tossed her brush down.

She rushed into her friends' arms, so glad they'd come. That they were still in her life, even though she'd left them behind, too, when she'd run away.

She hadn't been there for Clair's father's funeral. She hadn't consoled Nic through her parents' very public divorce. But her friends had shown up when Bethany moved back to Chandlerville. They continued to show up for her, hunting her down whenever she started to wander too far. They were holding on to her as fiercely as her family, believing Bethany was fighting with everything inside her to stay for good this time.

"I just . . ." She clung to Nic and Clair, easing away eventually and dashing at her tears with the sleeve of the T-shirt she'd layered under her sundress. "I keep telling myself that if I can just get my art back . . . I guess I thought it would mean everything else would be okay, too. I don't know what I'm going to do if it's not."

She wiped at her eyes again.

Her friends were staring at her, looking more worried than before.

"Then don't give up," Nic insisted. "On your painting or your parents or Mike or anything else you want."

"Things are just crazy right now," Clair responded. "Everything will settle down. So will you. So will your painting. You'll make it work."

"Just maybe not tonight." Nicole picked green paint out of Bethany's hair. "Not before you shower and sleep and chill out. And while you're at it, do some low-maintenance chillin' with your hunky cowboy. Let the rest take care of itself for a little while. It's *all* going to get okay, Bethany. It will turn out even better than your dreams."

Bethany stared into the wispy, filmy image she'd captured on canvas—her foster family's world, looking like something fantastical out of a children's picture book. It was exactly how she'd wanted coming home to feel . . . and she couldn't finish it.

"Let this canvas dry," Nicole reasoned. "Don't destroy it. Start something else tonight, if you just have to. But don't give up on this one. We'll help."

Bethany checked her watch. "You two don't want to hang here with me for the rest of the night. Go to your club. Meet hot guys who'll buy you drinks. Report back with details."

"Or we can bring the party to you," Clair quipped.

Nicole dug into her larger-than-normal purse and produced a small bottle of cabernet. Clair liberated three Dixie cups from her bag. They set their bounty on Bethany's worktable. Nicole unscrewed the cap on the bottle and poured generous servings, handing Clair and Bethany theirs before holding her cup up.

"To another painting," she toasted. "Do whatever you need to do tonight. We've got your back."

Bethany toasted but drank only a sip. Gratitude was clogging her throat. "You both have businesses to run tomorrow."

"If you're pulling an all-nighter"—Clair held her cup out to Nic for a refill—"we're pulling an all-nighter."

Nic scanned Bethany's clutter of paints and rags and brushes and thinner. "What do you need to get this show back on the road?"

Bethany sighed at the two best, most stubborn girlfriends in the world. She'd love them to her dying breath. She sipped her wine.

"If I'm not getting rid of you two—"

"You're not," Clair assured her.

"Then I need to start something else before I leave. It'll just be another hour or two, I swear. There are some prestretched canvases down the hall. Maybe a larger one this time." Bethany pantomimed how large, then threw her hands in the air. She was too distracted, exhausted, to describe what she meant. "I'll be right back."

"We've got it." Clair set her wine down, grabbed Bethany by the shoulders, and pushed her into the folding chair that came with the cubicle—the only other furniture provided, besides a basic worktable. "Large. Canvas. We'll find something. Then you've got two hours before we're revoking your painting privileges. If we have to strap you to one of the cots down the hall and hook you up to a cabernet IV, you're going to get some sleep."

"Two hours." Bethany sank into the chair and took another sip.

Her arms and hands throbbed from the work she'd already done. Her brain was mush from the things her friends had forced her to think through. Things that she found herself wondering whether Mike would want to hear. Her other boyfriends since Benjie hadn't minded her being quirky and sometimes moody. As long they didn't have to listen to her talk about why she couldn't seem to settle down and just have fun, like normal people her age.

Don't make me wait too long for that date now, darlin'.

"We'll be right back," Clair said.

Bethany nodded. As her friends headed out in search of the supply room, she turned to her worktable to sort through the pile of oil paints she'd selected, consumed with thoughts of tall, dark-eyed, smiling cowboys.

"Wowza," Nicole said from down the hall. "This is amazing."

Bethany set her wine down and dragged herself to her feet. She discovered her friends with the door open to what she'd been told was the co-op manager's office, not the supply closet. Nicole and Clair, who'd been peering from the hallway at whatever they'd seen, headed inside.

"Don't." Bethany hurried after them. The artists who'd given her a brief tour of the place had mentioned that the office was kept locked. That the area beyond was the owner's private space. "The supplies are next door. I . . ."

She stalled out beside her friends, just past the threshold.

The vast, open rectangular space was dominated by a massive desk that boasted an equally enormous flat-screen monitor, perched on top of its black lacquered surface. A large leather chair, weathered and beaten up as if had been carted from place to place forever, was the only other piece of furniture other than two equally battered leather guest chairs and a low bookcase behind the desk. The walls were a shade of gray close to steel, only lighter. And covering practically every inch of them were massive prints of mesmerizing landscape photography.

Each black-and-white photo was of a different location: panoramas of expansive vistas; and closer, more intimate shots of settings so rich in texture and contrast you could look for hours and not absorb every detail. Mountainscapes, oceans, fields and streams, waterfalls, gardens, historic homes, busy city streets . . .

"They're amazing," Clair said. She and Nic were staring at the walls, too, turning in slow circles. "Look at them. They're pictures, right? But they look like they're on canvas."

"They're giclées." Bethany stopped before a narrow, floor-to-ceiling vertical canvas of a sparkling waterfall bursting from a granite cliff, rushing from a forest of thriving foliage to plummet below into a crash of boulders. "High-resolution photography printed on canvas."

A splash of color on the rocks beneath a waterfall drew her eye. She leaned closer. It was a Western hat that, glancing around, she realized had been placed in the rest of the photos, too.

"I think I've seen these before." She turned to a series on one of the shorter walls—coastal beach scenes at sunrise and sunset. The hat was positioned on the sand near the surf, out of place but somehow giving the sense that it belonged there. "They're part of a series. *Rise & Fall.* The Art and Design section of the *New York Times* spotlighted this artist a few years back."

She remembered being struck by the photographs' effortless beauty and the description of the artist's process. He'd been experimenting with large-format photography for the first time, to capture landscapes that the smaller camera lenses he'd worked with before couldn't. The resulting pictures were even more striking in person.

"Sunsets and sunrises only," she told her friends, the three of them moving closer to one particular grouping. "These are of the same stretch of beach, shot at opposite times of the day, capturing different tides and weather and cloud patterns. He focused on sky and clouds, with just a touch of the water and sand to ground viewers to what they're seeing. Look at the lines he's captured with the edges of the dunes and tidal pools. He won all kinds of awards for them. And . . . nobody knows who he is. He works in complete anonymity, releasing new sets of photographs without fanfare, and donating the proceeds from his sales to charities all over the world. He's never given an in-person interview, doesn't have a bio pic or social media presence. He goes by only his initials and lets his art speak for itself."

She peered closer to the nearest print and read the signature.

"HMT. He's never said what it stands for, and it kind of adds to the mystery behind his art. No one . . ." She looked around them in wonder. "No one even knows where he works."

Just like, according to the resident who'd shown Bethany around the Artist Co-op, no one there had met the owner of the space. Only the business manager. The owner had started similar nonprofits in other cities, but he hadn't interacted directly with those artists either.

"He can keep his secret identity." Nicole had zeroed in on her own favorite photograph. Another ocean scene. "As long as I find out where this was taken and can book the next available flight. I'm so there."

"Nab me a cabana boy," Clair agreed, "and I'm *so* with you."

"One who doesn't mind getting naked in all that gorgeous surf."

"And out of that surf."

"I'm thinking right here"—Nicole pointed to the pristine white towel laid out in the sand just shy of the water, the hat positioned beside it—"is where we'll work on our tan lines."

"And let us all say, 'Amen.'" Clair raised her hand heavenward.

Bethany left her friends to their Caribbean fantasies and studied the rest of the images. There were an astonishing number of them, worth an absolute fortune to a collector. Or the artist himself?

Curious, snooping now, she worked her way to the giclées on the wall behind the desk. She fell instantly in love with a stark image of the interior of a dilapidated, falling-down Victorian home. Paint was peeling. The staircase was crumbling. A broken window in the distance allowed sunlight to pour into the scene, illuminating the same hat, placed this time on the scarred floorboards.

"Amazing . . ." She turned toward the monitor on the desk and froze—at the photos grouped on the screen and the Stetson sitting beside the keyboard. The monitor had kept her from seeing it when she'd walked in.

"Oh my God." Nicole stepped beside her. "Is that . . . ?"

"It's the hat in the photos." Bethany stared at it, recognizing it now that she saw it in person. She pointed at the monitor, her hand shaking. "And that's . . ."

"Marsha and Joe's house?" Clair rounded the desk, too.

Bethany and her friends stared at the beautiful photographs of a beautiful place, capturing the loving world Bethany hadn't been able to bring to life with her paints.

"How did pictures of your parents' house get in here?" Clair picked up the hat. Her jaw dropped. She held it up to Bethany and Nicole. "What is this doing here?"

"It's here because it's mine," a deep voice said from behind them.

Bethany, Nic, and Clair turned, gawking in unison at the tall man standing in the now open doorway across from the one they'd used. He wore a faded chambray shirt, worn jeans, and scruffy hiking boots.

"You shouldn't be in here," Mike said.

Chapter Eight

Bethany wasn't on the co-op's August schedule.

Mike had double-checked George's email to be sure. Which was why he hadn't thought twice about coming back to his studio to tinker with the collection of prints that he'd promised his mother—after he'd asked George to, grudgingly, decamp to her own office at her apartment.

He'd needed his part of the loft to himself in between his sessions with Joe, to get lost in the last series of photos he'd captured for Jeremy. And to mull over how he was going to explain to Bethany and her family—assuming Bethany ever gave him the chance—exactly who and what he was.

"*I'm* not supposed to be here?" Bethany sputtered.

Mike watched her girlfriends silently ease out of the office. "I was going to tell you about all of this as soon as we went on our date."

Bethany looked ready to bolt herself.

"Please." He inched closer. Today she had green paint splattered all over her vintage-looking sundress and the white men's

T-shirt she'd worn beneath it. She looked exhausted. "Let me explain before you assume the worst."

"The worst?"

"I know how this looks."

"Like you've been lying about who you are? To me and my whole family. *While* we've all been trusting you to help my father."

"None of my therapy patients know about this part of my life. There's no need for them to. But as soon as I found out Joe was your father, I knew I had to tell you."

"Except you didn't."

"We were going to get together to talk, remember? I've tried to reach you."

She gazed around at his work.

"I'm sorry for how all this looks," he apologized again. "But I'm glad you know."

Bethany stared at him as if she wanted to burst into the kind of laughter that ripped you apart. He'd hurt her, not trying to and not really understanding how he could have avoided it. She picked up his hat from the desk and held it out to him, saying nothing.

He slipped on the faded, worn Stetson. "This is—was—my brother's. Jeremy was the cowboy, not me. At least, he always wanted to be one."

Like the money clip their father had given Jeremy his last Christmas—even though Jeremy had been confined to a hospital bed for over a year and had no way to spend money—Mike now took his brother's hat with him everywhere he went. He looked around and smiled at the lovingly selected photographs covering every wall of his studio. He felt Jeremy's memory draw closer.

"These are my personal favorites," he said. "I did a half dozen series after Jeremy died. Photographing his hat for a year, taking it all over the world on trips he'd helped me map out. These were his bucket-list places that he knew he'd never get to see. He was too sick by then. His last year or so . . . my photographs were how my big brother traveled. I guess"—Mike motioned to the images around them—"even after Jeremy was gone, I was trying to keep him from missing out on the life he should have lived."

Bethany nodded, compassion softening her shock.

She swallowed. "And the artist co-ops?"

"They're one of the ways I invest the income from my photography, funding grass-roots art communities in urban landscapes. Cultivating art awareness and participation by promising young talent—in a creative climate too often monopolized by high-end dealers and those who can afford to throw money away on trends. The residency programs encourage more organic artistic pursuits."

"You . . . funded my residency."

He nodded.

He knew how it made him sound—like he'd known who she was from the start.

"I'm the money around here, Bethany, that's all. My business manager—you've emailed back and forth with George—and the residents run the art centers I set up. They pretty much make all the decisions. I write the checks I'm told to write. Your application was reviewed by a committee of current residents. George pulls together a five-name short list whenever a slot opens up. She selects two of you based on the committee's recommendations, and I review digital portfolios of the finalists. My decision was based on your body of work. It was an impartial selection. I never meet any of the co-op residents. Each center evolves from the vision of artists who create there, and the communities they volunteer in. George helps me make sure who and what I am never get in the way."

Bethany was still as a statue, only inches away, making him want to hold her, physically reassure her, kiss her so she'd remember how good they could make each other feel.

"How many centers are you running?" she asked. "You know, in addition to traveling the globe taking fine-art photographs that people pay a fortune for. And tending bar part-time like a drifter who has nothing better to do with his life. Oh, and sidelining as a rogue physical therapist. Because why not, right?"

It sounded careless.

Irresponsible.

Reckless.

Mike sighed at the labels his parents had given his life since Jeremy.

He *was* a drifter. He had a purpose in life: doing his damnedest to honor his brother with each choice he made. But after ten years of searching for the next opportunity, the next artistic or business challenge, he'd started to wonder if there was something to what his parents were saying. If it wasn't time to rethink, dig in a little deeper, and not move on quite so fast or so far, with another adventure on the horizon and his latest success in his rearview.

"I've started four co-ops so far," he said, wondering if he could explain in a way that would help Bethany understand, without him sounding like a complete flake. "I've chosen larger cities that I've lived in long enough to get a read on the local landscape. Seattle, San Francisco, Chicago, and now Atlanta. The first one was just a crazy idea that George helped me bring to life. Then it took off, and I was hooked. Each new location has a strong enough local art climate to offer a steady influx of residents, and to allow the artists to share their craft and teach others how to find their own creative voices. Nothing fancy. Everything's grass-roots, steering clear of affiliations with fine-art galleries or investors who make decisions based on valuing art as a commodity."

"Nothing fancy?"

Bethany's monotone question made him want to shake her and tell her to go ahead and get angry. Instead, she felt like a calm, distant stranger. He could handle just about any other reaction from her but that.

"I purchase the buildings outright so there's no rent," he continued. "I front each center enough money to launch the nonprofit and keep it viable financially for at least a year. George swoops in and implements our business plan. And then I turn the day-to-day running of things over to her and the talent we pull in through the residencies. The artists dig into the community, create pieces for shows to generate exposure and sales and fund-raising contacts that bring in local business donations—from people interested in tax write-offs, and the ones who truly believe in what we're doing. Every single center has been self-sufficient within a year."

"Which is when you move on," Bethany summed up, as if he were making all kinds of good sense. "Wow. It's . . . impressive, everything you've done."

"I didn't want you to find out this way," he said, wary of her easy acceptance. "George must have left the office door unlocked last night. When I told her I was coming down, she was doing inventory in the supply room. I have a project I'm working on. When I'm here, I come and go through the side entrance in the alley that only George and I have the combination to. And I swear, Bethany, I was going to—"

"Let me get this straight," she interrupted. "You're HMT."

"Harrison Michael Taylor."

"A world-renowned fine-art photographer, who's been taking snapshots of my family home and gabbing about them with my niece. Because you're the physical therapist whom my dad's depending on to save his job and make sure he's strong enough not to collapse at my sister's wedding. And you're the owner of the nonprofit that's giving me a chance to find my way back into painting, *and* you're the bartender who's been flirting with me—kissing me—to the point that my entire hometown is talking about us."

"Yes." Mike stepped closer, feeling like he was on trial.

Emotion finally sparked in Bethany's eyes. Distrust. Disappointment, maybe. Most definitely hurt.

"Is that it?" she asked.

A part of him wished he were the kind of louse who could lie to her—a mongrel like Benjie. But there was only one way to do this and have a shot at convincing her that he was a good guy, caught in a bind he'd never seen coming. He was genuinely interested in Bethany, in the artistic voice she was struggling to bring back to life, *and* in her father's recovery. He wanted a chance, somehow, to stay connected to all of it.

"There's one more thing." He slid open the top drawer in his desk and picked up the packet of paper he'd left there.

It was the fax George had received from the director of the JHTF Developing Artist grant. Mike turned to the final page of the scholarship application from five years ago. The full-color photograph of the landscape that had been submitted as a sample of the artist's best work was an image of a country meadow near a pond at sunset. It was so realistic, so lifelike even copied in a facsimile, it could have been a photograph.

The work was joyous, the artist's love for her subject and her craft clear. Each time Mike looked at it, the clarity and creative vision of what she'd accomplished sucked him in. The same as when he'd first seen it—as part of the portfolio of work Bethany had submitted with her residency application.

He handed over the packet.

She glanced at the sheet on top, her eyes rounding. After a double take his way, she flipped through the rest.

"How . . . did you get this?" she asked. "Why do you have this?"

"My parents chair the Jeremy Harrison Taylor Foundation."

Bethany swallowed. "Jeremy . . ."

Mike nodded. "My brother. Our parents are philanthropists. When Jeremy was diagnosed with cystic fibrosis, we were told his disease was progressing so quickly he wouldn't live to see his thirtieth birthday. Our parents launched—"

"JHTF." Bethany backed closer to the door to the artists' portion of the loft. "The foundation that sponsored my full-ride scholarship to Pratt's fine-art program?"

Mike nodded.

The annual art grant had been created in Jeremy's honor, posthumously, at Mike's insistence. He anonymously—to his mother's perpetual dismay—contributed a sizable portion of his income from HMT gallery sales each year to fund art scholarships to a dozen graduating high school seniors. The income from the family money he'd invested in a trust supported even more art-related projects, through the foundation's long-reaching non-profit arm.

"Wow," Bethany repeated. "You're JHTF."

"My parents are JHTF." The foundation that had consumed their lives for the last twenty years. "I have nothing to do with the day-to-day business."

"Of course you don't." Bethany's anger flared. "Do you have anything to do with *any* of the things that are going on in your life?"

"Wait. What?" That's what she had to say? "I've done a lot of good with my life, for a lot of people."

And a part of him had been excited when he'd discovered Bethany in his office, anticipating her admiration for his photography and the things that the money from his business made possible. Instead, it felt as if he'd slipped into a warped, Freudian replay of his mother's running commentary on him wasting his potential.

"You're dabbling in things and people and places," Bethany said, "until you get bored and move on. Or am I missing something?"

If she'd thrown a bucket of ice water at Mike, he couldn't have been more shocked.

"I don't get bored." And he hated feeling defensive. It made him furious. Even now, when furious was the last thing he wanted to be with Bethany. "But I do move on a lot. Which I've made certain I don't have to answer to anyone for. Certainly not someone who keeps kissing me and then running from me, and then she decides she'll date me, and then she runs some more."

Bethany blinked, as if snapping out of a trance. She stepped closer. This time he jerked away.

"Mike," she said softly, sounding like the Bethany he'd thought he knew. "I—"

"My relationship with my family has been strained since I was nineteen and my older brother died," he bit out. "Jeremy was the last thing I had in common with my parents. I've accomplished a lot in the last ten years, whatever anyone thinks about how or why I've done it."

"You're right." She looked around them. "This is none of my business."

Another ice-cold blast.

"No." Mike inhaled, mentally kicking himself. "That's not what I meant. It's just . . . What I said just now is about my mess with my parents, not about you. I know this is a shock. I probably should have told you that day at Joe and Marsha's. But I didn't want your dad postponing rehab if things between us got rockier. I didn't want to risk . . ." Not seeing her again. "I'm sorry I didn't tell you everything at once, but I'm not sorry that you know now."

"We talked at Grapes & Beans," she reminded him.

"With Shandra and the entire dining room listening in. And we were agreeing that we weren't going to see each other anymore. Why tell you then, when it wouldn't have mattered?"

"You kissed me at my parents' house."

"You kissed me first."

She gestured toward the artists' portion of the loft. "You knew all this about my life, and I knew there was something up about the way you seemed so interested in my problems with my painting. And instead of coming clean about *your* life, you kissed me . . . because you didn't want to risk my dad's rehab?"

"That's not what I meant." Could he F this up any worse? "I wanted to kiss you—at McC's, at G&Bs, at your parents'. Right now, damn it! I've just never been certain that you knew what you wanted. Please give me a minute." A chance to take it all back and do it better so she'd stop looking at him the way she was. "I know this has caught you off guard."

"You don't know anything about me." She glanced at his monitor, displaying images of her life that he'd started tinkering with as a break from working on Jeremy's prints for the gala. "And vice versa."

"You already know a lot more than anyone outside my family, except for George."

It was alarming how radically Mike's life could change, depending on what Bethany chose to do next.

She could go public with what she'd discovered. Connect Mike Taylor to the artist HMT. Or the Artist Co-op to JHTF, the way his mother had been dying to for years, since his first center in Seattle had gotten its legs under it. It should have had Mike sweating buckets—the prospect of being outed to the world. Except . . . he trusted Bethany, the way he hadn't trusted anyone besides George in years.

"I'd like for you to know even more," he admitted, as stunned by the revelation as she looked.

"I . . ." She moved toward him, but with the same wounded expression as when she'd been staring at her no-good ex. "Why do I keep falling for guys, thinking they're being straight with me? And every single time they turn out to be strangers I don't understand at all."

Mike was the one looking at a stranger now as Bethany pressed onto the tips of her toes. She smelled like paint and a deeper scent that might have been red wine. And bubble gum. She pressed closer, his body responding with an instant need to love, cherish, and be more to someone than he'd thought he'd want to be again. But he could tell. She was saying goodbye.

Crazy.

This was crazy.

"I want to help you understand," he said. "You said you'd give us that chance."

"That was when you were just some nice guy I met." Her bottom lip trembled. "And I was thinking maybe I could enjoy myself, and not take it all so seriously for once. Now it's all tangled up, and we're . . . I don't know what my dad will do about his rehab. But I can't do this with you. I'm already having a hard enough time figuring out my life. I can't handle this, too."

"You can't handle caring about me?"

She pressed her lips to his.

She shook her head, her anger gone. "I've cared about a lot of men. That doesn't mean they were right for me. Or that they were going to stick around long enough to try and make it right. You're not an easygoing cowboy bartender with a heart of gold, Mike. You're a professional wanderer who's made a life out of not attaching to anyone—it sounds like since your brother died."

"And you hide in plain sight, with your camouflage truck and crazy clothes, overdosing on painting when you're not exhausting yourself helping out your family or other people's kids. It's like you've decided which parts of your heart you can trust, Bethany. And you're locking the rest of you away, thinking you can live without it."

"I'm trying to stick this time where I'm already loved. Instead of wasting more of my life thinking there's something better for me somewhere else."

"And I'm not going anywhere," he pledged, even if he didn't completely understand why. "Not like this."

"Exactly like this." She sounded resigned. "It's nice to finally meet you, Mr. Harrison Michael Taylor. The real you. If you keep working with my father, if I ever paint in the loft again and you're here in your studio, please stay away from me. I just . . . I can't."

And then she left him without a backward glance, heading through the door after her girlfriends.

Dru popped her head into the Dream Whip's kitchen Wednesday morning. She waited silently.

Silently made Bethany crazy. Especially when someone clearly had something to say at the butt crack of dawn. She stopped pretending she was ignoring her sister and looked up from prepping for the Whip's eleven-o'clock open. She'd been hand-forming hamburger patties using the ground beef the butcher counter at Sweetie's delivered fresh twice a week.

"You have a visitor," Dru said.

It had been over a week since Bethany and her sister had really talked—except for hellos and goodbyes in passing at the Douglas house. Bethany had filled in Marsha and Joe Saturday about what had happened at the Artist Co-op. She'd asked them to let her siblings know. She'd made it clear she was done talking about Mike. But she'd asked her parents to keep his identity in the family. Whatever else the guy was, however much Bethany needed *not* to be part of it, Mike seemed to genuinely be trying to do something with his life. Bethany didn't want to cause him problems. She'd never wanted to be anyone's problem.

Dru and the rest of her adult siblings had no doubt heard it all by now, and had been talking it to death. Joe had had another session with Mike on Sunday. Bethany had made a point not to ask her mother about it. And not to contact Mike, the way he hadn't tried to reach her. Everyone had been giving her even more space than before to sort things out. To hide in plain sight.

Until now.

"Who's here at this time of morning?" Bethany checked her watch, her breath catching at the thought that it might be Mike. She used the back of her hand to wipe her bangs out of her eyes. "It's not even seven yet."

"I guess," her sister said, "you're not the only one who can't sleep these days. I'll finish the burgers."

Bethany stripped off her gloves while Dru donned her own pair and took Bethany's place at one of the stainless-steel work counters where Bethany had put in as many hours as she could the last few days. She'd needed to work. She'd needed to keep busy, to stick in Chandlerville where she belonged, and to stay out of Midtown Atlanta. She'd even asked one of the other youth center volunteers to cover her art classes on Sunday and yesterday. Meanwhile, Bethany hadn't been able to touch her brushes and paints in her studio at the Douglas house. Instead, she'd stared each night till dawn at a room full of half-finished canvases.

"You know," Dru said as Bethany headed for the door that led to the Dream Whip's front counter and dining room, "maybe he really is sorry about how things played out."

Bethany stopped, her hand pressed to the still-closed door, not bothering to ask whom her sister was talking about.

"It doesn't matter," she said.

"Sure it does." Dru formed a ball of fresh hamburger and pounded it flat with the palm of her hand. "If avoiding Mike means the rest of us have to watch you avoid how you feel about everything else, it matters a lot."

Bethany watched her sister apply too much force, squashing a patty that would never make the kind of juicy, meaty burger the Whip was famous for. She deserved Dru's frustration. Clair's and Nic's, too. Since she'd driven back to Chandlerville Saturday night, she hadn't returned her girlfriends' calls or stopped by G&Bs. She'd barely spoken to them when she'd grabbed her backpack and all but sprinted from the co-op loft—asking only that they leave her be for real this time, until she was ready to talk.

"You're not alone, remember?" Dru rerolled the ground beef into a ball. "You never will be. We're not letting you go again, Bethany. You mean everything to us. We're your family."

Bethany blinked, angry tears pushing at the corners of her eyes. And the anger was at herself. Not at Mike. Not at her sister's well-intentioned meddling.

For days she'd stared at her art at Dru and Brad's house, trying to figure out what was missing in each canvas. But her painting of her foster home had been all she could see—the canvas that she'd left at the loft, because she'd been too much of a coward to go back for it and risk another possible run-in with Mike. And then what? He'd be the same great guy who'd inspired the maddening, ethereal landscape that was keeping her from working on something new. And she'd still want him, when he was an even bigger wild card now than before.

"I want to be exactly where I am," she insisted to her sister.

"Exactly where you were five years ago, you mean." Dru kept her eyes on her work. "You still don't know what to do with the rest of us. Only now there's some new guy making you feel things you don't want to feel, while everyone else watches from a distance to see if you'll bolt."

"I'm not going to—"

"You told Mom and Dad that you're thinking about giving up your residency at that art place. Because Mike's turning out to be too good to be true?"

Dru cut Bethany with an exasperated expression.

"Dump the guy," Dru said, "if tall, dark, handsome, and successful is a turnoff. But don't give up your chance to figure out what's going on with a gift like your art, when not being able to paint is tearing you up inside." She went back to making burgers.

"I don't understand how you do what you do, or why you can't do it anymore. But I'm pretty sure those people at your co-op could help you figure something out. Maybe even Mike could."

"I'm handling it on my own," Bethany insisted.

"Aren't you always?"

"It's . . . complicated."

"It shouldn't be. Didn't used to be. You loved painting. You *were* your paintings in high school. It's the only time I've seen you really happy. But then Benjie happened, and you hit the road. And now it's almost like you hate painting—while the family's losing you to it again."

"I'm right here."

Bethany had come straight back to Chandlerville after leaving the loft. Each morning, she convinced herself to stay with her friends and family. She might not be able to talk to any of them yet about what she was going through. But this community was where she wanted to belong. Didn't that count for something?

"Yes, you're still here," her sister agreed. "But . . . you're also a million miles away. And I wish I understood. I wish I could help. It's just . . ."

"It's just what? I'm fine."

Dru smiled, but it wasn't really a smile. She walked to Bethany and pulled her into a hug using her upper arms and elbows, her glove-encased hands covered in hamburger.

"Tell that to your visitor," she said. "You'd better get out there. She has to get to school by eight."

Shandra?

Bethany hugged Dru back, absorbing her sister's support. Bethany had apologized to Shandra over the phone Sunday, when she'd nixed their trip to Midtown for their youth center art class.

But she'd felt lousy about it ever since, even though Shandra had sounded fine.

Dru nudged Bethany toward the swinging door that would take her to the dining room.

"Go," Dru said. "I'll take care of things in here until Willie shows up to fire the grill. At which point you'd better be long gone or he'll sweet-talk you into working the rest of the day."

Bethany nodded; she couldn't remember ever feeling this exhausted. She pushed through the door and headed around the front counter. Her younger sister was waiting at the front of the dining room, looking at the painting Dru had proudly hung there. It was the one that had helped Bethany earn both her four-year JHTF grant to Pratt and her residency.

"Hey, girl." She gave her sister a side hug.

Shandra tensed but kept staring at the canvas of a meadow just outside of town, one of Bethany's favorite places in the world. Bethany looked, too, reliving the moment when Mike had handed her the fax of her scholarship application.

"I'm sorry again about skipping Sunday's class," she said. "We'll make it to Midtown this weekend for sure."

"Sure." Shandra shrugged.

She was wearing an emerald-green tunic top she'd hemmed to mid-thigh length, over a pair of checkerboard-patterned tights she'd bought on a thrift-store shopping binge with Bethany. She'd tied a bright-pink, paisley-printed bandanna over her hair. When Bethany had attempted Shandra's portrait, she'd used similar colors, wanting to capture her sister's exuberance and the passion for living Shandra shared with the world, simply by entering a room and brightening the day of everyone inside.

"Or you'll cancel again," Shandra said.

"I won't." The funk Bethany had let herself slip into was hurting her sister. Her family. Herself. "I swear. I'm going to get my act together."

Shandra sighed away the promise. "I hear people. I know more than everyone thinks I do. You're spooked. You'll stop pretending you're not one day, and you'll be gone. That's why I came to tell you I don't want to go down to the youth center this weekend, either. So don't worry about it."

"What? No." *We're not letting you go again, Bethany . . . We're your family.* "I am going back Sunday, and it wouldn't be the same without you."

How many foster homes had let Shandra down in some way before she'd been placed in Chandlerville? Now Bethany was becoming a part of that legacy.

She followed as her sister tried to leave. "Don't go."

"Why not?" Shandra whirled around, looking ready to explode. "You don't want to be anywhere the rest of us are. You're hardly ever at the house anymore. I heard you tell Mom and Dad you're not going back to your residency, not while Mike's there . . . It's just like before, people keep saying. Just like when you quit painting and quit the family and quit everything else after high school. So, fine. Dump the youth center, too. Like I care."

Of course she cared.

"Give me a chance to fix things." Bethany's knees wobbled as she remembered Mike begging her for the exact same thing.

But this was why Bethany had to steer clear of him. There was too much else at stake. She couldn't let falling apart over a guy ruin things with her family again.

"I'm not quitting painting."

Shandra looked at the tank top and jeans Bethany had worn to the Whip. Bethany knew there wasn't a speck of fresh paint on her. There hadn't been since Saturday. She ran a hand down the flared sleeve of Shandra's perfectly tailored tunic.

"I won't miss our youth center class Sunday," she promised. "I've just needed some time to myself. I'm sorry I let that get in the way of what we're doing together."

Precious moments that she'd lost with her sister, her students, and the life in Chandlerville Bethany wanted so badly to be real.

She sat in the nearest booth. She ran her hand over the coolness of the red leather seats. She'd always loved the look of the Whip, with its vintage upholstery and chrome-rimmed tables. It was retro, but it was classy somehow. The Douglas family had kept things the same from the moment they'd opened their doors when Brad's mother was a little girl. The permanence of a legacy like that had always mystified Bethany—how people could hold on and fight for something forever, no matter the obstacles. Never completely letting go.

"You're really scared of him," Shandra said, "aren't you?"

"What?" Bethany blinked and realized her sister was sitting across the booth from her.

"Mike. Is it really that bad, that he's famous and has money and wants to help artists like you and people like Dad?"

"No."

It wasn't bad.

Bethany rubbed at her tired eyes. It was wonderful, the things he'd done with his life. She'd come to terms with that while she'd lain awake the last four nights. It was sad, what had happened to his brother and whatever his parents had or hadn't done to help their sons get through it.

But . . .

"Bethie?" Shandra asked, deserving an explanation.

"He's just . . ." Bethany dropped her hands to the table.

He was too much like her. She'd sensed it that first night at McC's, when something about him had made her feel so safe, she'd trusted a total stranger to help her.

"It's scary, right?" Her sister slid a hand across the table and held Bethany's. "People acting like they like you. And you never know if it's real, or if it's going to last, or if you want it to."

Bethany inhaled, the air catching in the back of her throat. "All you know is that it hurts. It shouldn't, but it does."

"So you stop it from hurting." Her sister nodded, wise and angry and brutally honest beyond her years. "However you have to."

Bethany squeezed her sister's hand, feeling closer to Shandra than ever. "You always have the right to say stop."

They'd gotten to this place a time or two, as their friendship had deepened. On their long drives into Midtown, or when they'd grabbed something to eat before or after the classes they taught together. When they talked about one of their students Shandra had grown particularly close to—Darby, a little girl who seemed to be quietly hurting in her own six-year-old way.

"It's okay to hurt," Bethany said. "We all do sometimes. But you don't have to keep hurting. Your life starts getting better as soon as you accept that."

Shandra had never talked about what she'd endured in her biological home and maybe some of her earlier foster experiences. But the pain was there, just below the surface, the damage done.

"Fighting back is never a bad thing," Bethany insisted, "even when we sometimes make self-destructive choices thinking we'll feel better."

"Like when you walked away from Mom and Dad after high school?" Shandra asked, Bethany's long-ago decision hovering between them like a shadowy path that she might follow again. "Because they said they liked you. And Benjie treated you like he liked you, and then treated you so bad. And you didn't want to be treated bad anymore, so you left . . ."

Shandra pulled her touch away, a brave young woman who'd run from several homes of her own. Thanks to Marsha and Joe, she lost herself in fabric now, and designing crazy-cool clothes, the way their parents had helped Bethany find her paints and brushes and canvases, so she'd have something beautiful, something totally her own, to believe in, too.

"I'm back for good," Bethany promised her sister. "I want my life here, with you and Mom and Dad and everyone. I know I'm being flaky, and I'm sorry about Sunday, and that I'm scaring you. I'm trying to fix this scary thing I'm going through. But I'm not going to run just because I'm scared." She sat up straighter. "That's no way to live life. Neither is you nixing the youth center and Darby and the other kids because of me."

"You're fixing yourself?" Her sister slumped into the booth's plush cushion, arms crossed. "By ditching another guy, a *good* guy this time who's been good to you? And now you're ditching everyone else you *want* to be with, because you feel like shit without him around?"

Language, Marsha would have said.

Damn straight, Nic would have responded.

"No," Bethany said. "Mike's just . . . too much for me right now."

"Fighting back can be a bad thing, too. Right? If there's no real reason to fight?"

Shandra sounded so young and scared. And so not the funny, strong, determined teenager Bethany had watched blossom. She was a kid, after all. A lost, scared kid who desperately needed someone to tell her that everything would work out okay.

"Right," Bethany agreed, hating that her insecurities were backing up on the sister she'd wanted so badly to inspire.

Except how did Bethany convince Shandra that things would be fine . . . when Bethany kept shying away from the people who loved them both to distraction, and kept fighting how perfectly at home she felt in a wandering cowboy's arms?

Chapter Nine

Mike opened the door to one of his favorite smells.

A bell tinkled overhead. One baked aroma after another welcomed him. Bread and cake and something with cinnamon and butter. And best of all, chocolate. The Wednesday-afternoon air was frosted with the scent of cream cheese and powdered sugar. Dan's Doughnuts was so much more than its humble name suggested. The pastry shop exceeded every thumbs-up description Chandlerville locals had given it, and Mike had barely made it through the door.

He took in the scene and smiled. Someone should bottle and sell the fragrance seeping from every pore of the place. His brother would have loved it here.

Jeremy had never met a dessert he wouldn't devour—eating more than his share, he'd insisted, to make up for what Mike couldn't have. Twice a week when they were boys, his and Mike's nanny would take them to a corner bakery not far from their Upper East Side apartment. Mike hadn't minded that there wouldn't be something sweet for him on the other end. Their nanny would always bring him an orange to snack on. And besides, the things he couldn't have were nothing compared to Jeremy's problems. And being outside and goofing around with his big brother, without their mother telling them to settle down and behave like young gentlemen, had been the real treat.

Visiting Dan's brightly lit space felt like the same kind of extravagance. Kids were munching on afternoon treats. Grown-ups grouped and chatted near the register, waiting to buy or order or pick up whatever they'd come for. Everyone, regardless of age, was all smiles. The photographer in Mike wanted to capture each carefree moment, every expression. Then his attention snagged on a familiar young smile.

Camille Bowman's cheeks were smeared with chocolate. Her eyes were closed in pure joy while she licked frosting off the top of a cupcake. Mike already had his smartphone out and was kneeling when he made eye contact with the beautiful woman standing next to the little girl. He gestured silently, to see if it was okay. She nodded, grinning her approval.

He zoomed in with his camera app and snapped a shot of Camille, mentally titling it *Rapture*. The little girl's eyes popped open, and he snapped another shot before standing. She rushed toward him.

"Hey, Mike!" She held out her treat. "Do you like cupcakes? Uncle Dan and Aunt Leigh make the best. Even the ones like mine that most people don't know how to make right. Want to try? It's red velvet with cream cheese frosting . . ." She frowned down at the almost completely gone icing, shrugged, and offered the well-licked treat again. "There's enough left for you to taste. And you won't miss the stuff that's missing in mine. I can't have dairy and nuts, and Uncle Dan makes sure they're gone. But you'll love them anyway, promise."

"I'd love to try one." Mike chuckled at her excited chatter. So did the natural beauty he presumed was Camille's mother. "But there'd have to be no sugar in them. That's what has to be missing for me."

"I'll let Leigh know," said the tall brunette, curling Camille to her side. "I'm sure she and her husband could come up with something you'll be able to eat if you snag an invite to Dru's wedding. Dan is magic with specialty desserts. I'm Selena Bowman, by the way." She held out her hand. "And you're Michael Taylor, the cowboy my husband's fuming about for getting grabby with Bethany. Or is it Harrison Michael Taylor?" She'd lowered her voice as she said his full name. "The man my sister-in-law is fuming about, for . . . Well, I'm not exactly sure why yet. But you seem to be helping Joe, so that makes you okay in my book."

"It's Mike." He shook Selena's hand, genuinely happy to meet more of Bethany's family. "If you've heard all that, I'm sure you know I was never really supposed to be coming to the wedding. I guess remaining Joe's therapist is touch and go, too, unless I settle things with your sister-in-law."

Mike kept showing up to work with Joe. And the other man kept cordially welcoming Mike into his home each time. But Joe continued to have a hard time committing to his rehab plan—during therapy, and with the solo exercises he was supposed to do between sessions. And Mike was concerned that some of his patient's resistance might be stemming from Mike's ongoing issues with Bethany.

"The Dixons are a volatile bunch," Selena conceded. "But they're fair. Even my Oliver. And everyone's crazy distracted right now. I was just checking with Dan about the cupcake bar for Dru's reception. We're already doing a special order for Camille. It's no trouble to add something for you, just in case."

"I'd say to order plenty of whatever this is"—Mike showed her his photo of Camille's bliss—"and you're golden."

"Let me see!" Camille nabbed his phone. "Cool! Mommy, I wanna show him the pictures I took of Grammy's flowers, and Bear and the quilt on my bed and Hello Kitty."

Selena plucked her smartphone out of her tote. She traded with her daughter.

"Would you mind texting me a copy of this?" She handed over Mike's phone. "I googled you, you know. You have an amazing gift."

"No problem sending you the photo," Mike said. "Or any of the other ones . . ." He scrolled to the images in his gallery of the kids playing outside the Dixon house. He passed Selena his phone.

She studied each picture. "Wow."

"Add your name and number to my contacts. I'll text you the lot. And I . . ." How did he say it without sounding full of himself? "I would appreciate it if your family would keep the details about the rest of my life private for now."

"Bethany's already asked us to. Didn't she tell you?"

Mike simply shook his head, leaving how much Bethany's family knew about his and Bethany's last conversation up to Bethany to tell them.

Selena's attention returned to his photos. "I didn't think the cameras in these things could take pictures like this."

"The newer ones have advanced a lot. They read light and handle exposure more effectively. You have better choices about how and where to focus. You can wrangle the lens into seeing what you want it to, like any other camera."

"Look what I did last night at my Grammy Belinda's." Camille tugged his arm until he knelt to look over her shoulder at Selena's phone. It was smeared with chocolate from Camille's cupcake.

"Like I said"—he scrolled through, taking his time, enjoying her wonder and excitement and pride—"you're a natural. How does your grammy keep her flowers looking so beautiful?"

"She has the best garden ever," Camille said. "And she says I'm the best helper ever." She glanced to Selena. "My mommy and me help her together, now that we live down the street."

"And this must be Bear." A floppy-eared, bedraggled-looking stuffed bunny had been plopped onto a blanket on the grass in front of a bush full of bright pink blossoms.

"And my favorite quilt. My grammy's got lots of quilts. And last night she said I could take pictures of all of them."

"You're telling me a story with each photo," Mike praised. "Keep doing that. You have a great eye."

"A what?"

"The way you show us the things you love." He tweaked her nose. "Your pictures make me love them too, Camille. That's what photography's supposed to do. Would you mind if your mom texts me some of these, after I send her the pictures from my phone?"

"Can we?" Camille begged Selena.

Selena had leaned over Camille's shoulder, too, to study her daughter's photos. She smoothed a kiss to the top of Camille's head. She took her phone back and handed Mike his.

"We'll send Mr. Taylor whatever photos you like." Selena met Mike's gaze as he stood. "And don't worry about my family. They'll protect your identity if that's what you want, even if your helping Joe doesn't work out. Now," she said to Camille, "let's say goodbye to Mr. Taylor." To him Selena added, "I hope we get the chance to talk more soon."

"Call me Mike," he told her.

He hoped they spoke again, too. And that his therapy sessions with her father-in-law *did* continue. And not just because they gave Mike an excuse to stick around Chandlerville longer.

You're dabbling in things and people and places, until you get bored and move on.

Selena grabbed a handful of napkins from a nearby dispenser and tackled the cupcake residue on her daughter's face. "Let's let *Mike* get on with whatever he came here for."

"'Kay," Camille said. "Bye, Mike."

She scampered off, making a beeline for another little girl who'd just walked in with her parents.

"You've really started something with her taking pictures," Selena said. "Your excitement for what you do is contagious."

"It's my pleasure, seeing someone your daughter's age having fun being creative."

"That's exactly how Bethany describes the classes she teaches in the city." Selena smiled. "So, sugar free?"

He pocketed his phone and pushed up his shirt sleeve, revealing his MedicAlert bracelet. "I'm better off avoiding cakes and sweets entirely."

Selena nodded. "How long?"

"Since I was a kid. It's no big deal. These days I hardly notice the things I can't indulge in."

"Yet here you are, about to order something truly decadent. To bribe my sister-in-law, perhaps?"

He tipped back the brim of his Stetson, appreciating Selena's to-the-point vibe that no doubt kept Oliver on his toes. "Does Bethany really like strawberry cupcakes as much as I've heard?"

"Loves," Selena corrected. "Bethany loves Dan's strawberry cupcakes."

"A half dozen?" All he knew was what he'd heard the girls say at McC's.

Selena hesitated. "As soon as you place your order, Chandlerville will be buzzing about who they're for."

"I can live with that."

"Until you wander off to wherever you're going next?"

"I guess you could call me a professional wanderer," he admitted, not liking the sound of it these days any better than Selena seemed to. "But I'm in town for as long as I can help Joe. And I'd like to start over with your sister-in-law. And at least make sure she keeps painting in Midtown. I want . . ."

He wanted more than he should.

He wanted more than Bethany did. She'd made that clear. The cupcakes were only a gesture, he told himself, a peace offering. He'd make amends and move on, as free and easy as ever, leaving as much good as possible in his wake.

"If you're planning on showing up at her front door uninvited"—Selena dug her keys from her tote bag—"take some blueberry scones, too. Bethany's been a sucker for them since Dan Jr.'s dad ran the place and she spent all her allowance here as a teenager. Hey, Dan!"

"Yo!" The heavyset guy behind the counter sported a white apron over his belly and a perpetual smile for his customers.

Selena turned toward the baker. "Have Leigh add sugar-free treats to our reception menu. I'll let Nic know. She's going to hyperventilate when she sees our next order summary."

"You bet."

Dan waved Selena's and Mike's way. Curious customers turned from the counter and the tables scattered around the bakery. Their curious stares locked onto Mike.

"Just in case you finagle yourself a re-invite to the wedding." Selena patted Mike's arm and headed after her daughter. "Good luck."

"Thanks." The door's bell jingled happily as the Bowmans left. "I think I'm gonna need it."

Dan stepped around the counter. He and Mike watched Selena pull out of the lot in a beat-up car Mike couldn't believe was being driven by Armani's wife.

"They're a great family," Dan offered. "After everything Joe and Marsha have done for their kids, what they've all been through lately, the whole town would do just about anything for the lot of them." He clapped Mike on the shoulder. "We really appreciate you helping get Joe back on his feet. And it was high time someone put that Benjie Carrington in his place. Wish I could have been there to see you and the Dixon boys take him down. Now, how can I help you?"

It felt as if the entire bakery had paused to hear Mike's answer.

"I need some strawberry cupcakes," he said. "And blueberry scones, I guess."

Dan nodded and headed around the counter.

"If you're wanting to win Bethany Darling over," he said, voice booming, "then—"

"No," Mike corrected. "This is just—"

"A half dozen of each, I'm thinking." Dan folded a bakery box together, filling it with pastries. "That girl deserves a good man in her life for a change."

"Bethany," Brad called from the front of the Douglas house. "It's for you."

Bethany's brother-in-law had stopped painting the living room with a fresh coat of taupe to answer the doorbell. The living room was the last project on Brad and Dru's must-do-before-the-wedding home improvement list. Bethany was bent over, still taping trim. Without standing up, she looked behind her toward the door.

Which left her practically standing on her head, butt in the air, gaping between her legs at the cowboy stepping into the Douglas foyer. Mike's smile was even more gorgeous upside down.

"Um . . ." she said. "Hey?"

"Hey, yourself," he answered.

She righted herself, blood rushing and making her dizzy. Wiping her bangs from her eyes seemed like as good a way as any to stall for time. Until the wetness on her cheek reminded her that a few minutes ago she'd brushed the sleeve of one of Brad's faded plaid shirts against a freshly painted wall.

"Shoot!" She scowled at Mike's chuckle.

"Need this?" Dru handed over the rag she'd been using to wipe up spills on the drop cloth protecting Vivian Douglas's rug.

Bethany snatched the hole-riddled kitchen towel and dabbed at her face. She threw it back at her grinning sister.

"Can I get you something to drink?" Dru asked Mike.

Bethany shook her head at him.

She'd planned to hunt him down herself, to deal with what she'd run from at the loft. And with what she and Shandra had talked about. But now that he was there, it was getting all mixed up again. What she needed to do, what she wanted to do, and the crazy things he made her feel. All while she had no idea he wanted anything more with her than to have a little fun for a few weeks.

"I'd love some water," Mike said. "And some milk for Bethany, to go along with these."

Bethany's attention zoomed to the signature pink box Mike held. "From Dan's?"

Her mouth had already been watering at how good he looked:

cowboy hat again, long-sleeved shirt, lovingly fitted jeans. He stepped closer and opened the pastry carton. She swallowed, barely keeping herself from attacking its contents.

"Strawberry cupcakes *and* blueberry scones." Dru whistled, nodding her approval. "Excellent groveling."

"Guy's got chops." Brad wiped his hands on his own paint rag and relieved Mike of the box. "We'll take these into the kitchen and give you two some privacy."

"What?" Bethany stared at her Benedict Arnold sister and soon-to-be brother-in-law, who were walking away. "No, I—"

"It's great to see you, Mike," Dru said as the kitchen door swooshed shut behind them.

Bethany stared after her family, loving them desperately. There'd certainly be no other reason for putting up with them.

She glanced back to the front of the house and found herself alone. She rushed into what had once been Vi Douglas's formal sitting room. Mike—HMT—was standing before her easel, beside an ancient folding table loaded down with her disarray of oil paints and cloths and brushes.

"You shouldn't be in here," she said, repeating his words when he'd found her in his loft, gawking at his high-priced photographs.

Surrounding him now, leaning against all four walls, were her cast-aside canvases. Dozens of them. Natural light sparkled through the bay windows, washing everything in a gentle golden glow. While an intensely focused, world-class artist, the brim of his Stetson pulled low, took his time scanning the disappointing results from each frustrating attempt to create something meaningful and lasting for her parents.

Bethany held her breath, waited, needing him to understand—when she didn't know how to be comfortable needing anything from him.

"They're amazing." He slowly made his way around the room. "Realistic, but surreal somehow. This isn't how you painted in the samples you submitted for your residency. These are almost . . . dreamlike."

"The landscapes in my scholarship and residency submissions were from high school. I can't paint that way anymore." She stepped to his side. She couldn't seem to be anywhere else when he was around. "This keeps happening now, even if I'm working from photos of people and places I've known for years. They're all failures."

He shook his head, browsing through several canvases that had been set aside together. "They're your heart. And they're terrifying you."

She tried to step back, and realized she and Mike were holding hands. "Please stop."

"You're not ready to give them everything," he said, not looking up from her pieces. "You're angry at what's happening. But you keep trying. That's courage, Bethany, not failure." He let her go. The concern and . . . wonder in his tone kept her close. "Unless you keep deciding to give up."

"I . . ." The truth was even closer with him there, than when she'd talked with Shandra. "I've quit so many times. I've already told my parents I might give up my residency."

She finally had his attention. "Because of me?"

She shook her head. "Because of me. Because it's what I do, when I think something's over anyway. And my art's been over since high school. I want to paint something for my parents, for people I love. But I can't."

"You are."

"For a while, when I first start each new project. And it feels like before, when I could spend hours and hours on a canvas and never even notice. But then it stops. Or I stop. Or it doesn't feel safe anymore, so I make it stop. I don't know. I don't know what I'm doing. But I shouldn't have applied for the residency. Another artist who can actually produce something should have that spot."

"So you're just going to walk away from your art? From us?"

"Us?"

"I told myself I wasn't going to make coming here about us. We haven't even figured out if there is an *us*. But you've flat-out decided I'm no good for you. Now your residency isn't good for you. Don't do that. You're too talented, Bethany. If nothing else, I can help you with your creative process."

"But you want more than that, right?" She squared her shoulders, aware of her deplorable appearance. "And I want more than that."

A relieved smile softened his features. "Then let me in. Let me help. Let me show you what I see when I look at all you've done."

"When you look at what?"

She waved at the cluster of the landscapes she'd attempted when she'd first picked up a brush again. She'd been living in her tiny place above Dan's and thinking it would be so easy to just dive back into painting now that she was ready.

"These are of the same meadow in your fax," she said, staring with him at her dozen or so attempts to re-create the oil that hung near the entrance to the Whip. Different times of the year, different seasons. She hadn't come close to finishing a single one of them. "There's no life in them, no light. It's not working."

"Do you mind if I take some pictures?"

The idea made her sick to her stomach. "Why?"

"Because they're your first love."

"What?" Something inside Bethany clicked, like a piece of a puzzle locking into place.

"Art was your first love in high school, not that mongrel Benjie. And I can see how maybe you lost it for a while when he hurt you."

"Painting started hurting, too." Anger flooded her along with the memory. "I couldn't create anymore. I couldn't go to art school. While Benjie moved on, at least partially because of work that I'd done. And after that I couldn't stay here with my family and friends, wanting to fight back against all of them, because . . ."

"You thought you'd lost the one thing you needed most?"

Mike scanned her canvases as if they were treasures—the same way he'd looked at her just now, when he'd arrived and found her sweaty and covered in paint.

"Your love for painting is in every one of these," he said. "You're struggling with your creativity, just like you're struggling to stay with your family. But believe me, you haven't lost anything. You'll get your art back, better than ever."

The world-renowned HMT had his phone out, looking like a kid in a candy store, eager to photograph the unfinished attempts she'd never meant for anyone to see. He waited to make certain it was okay. Bethany hesitated, then nodded, trusting him while she clung to his confidence in her ability. He worked quickly, businesslike in his intensity. But his smile never dimmed. He was having a blast.

He started with her landscapes. He crouched in front of another grouping, sifting through and shooting each unframed piece with equal care. They were some of her more recent work, since she'd moved in with Dru and Brad.

"What made you so indecisive about these?" he asked.

Indecisive?

He was kneeling in front of the first portrait she'd attempted. It was of Camille. Bethany rode out a wave of disappointment.

"I'm looking for something special for my parents. Dru and Brad are getting married on Marsha and Joe's wedding anniversary. I want to present a painting to my parents at the reception. And Camille's been such a special surprise for all of us . . ."

Bethany knelt, too, and studied the work she hadn't been able to look at in weeks.

"What stopped you from finishing her?" Mike asked.

"I . . ." Bethany flashed back to her talk with Shandra. "I think sometimes you fight the hardest against the things you want to care about the most."

She was suddenly eye-to-eye with Mike, his gaze warming at her admission.

He was a too-good-to-be-true man who'd taken his first pictures so he could bring the world back to his sick brother. He was a man who'd then spent a year photographing Jeremy's bucket list, and had donated the money he'd made from the sales of the prints to help other kids and families and struggling artists like Bethany.

He was a man who was kissing her. Or was she kissing him again? All she knew was how right it felt to touch Mike, even as she ducked her head away.

"I wish . . ." She brushed her fingertips across Camille's half-finished image.

Mike hugged her to his side and pressed his lips to her temple. "What do you wish?"

"That I could show my family how it feels to belong to them. Just once, even if it's the last thing I paint."

"Show your family, or show yourself?"

Bethany shook her head, not questioning anymore the way he seemed to understand.

"What about when you were in high school?" he asked as she inched away.

"I guess it was easier to pretend then." She stared out the bay window's gauzy curtains at the muted world beyond.

"Before that asshat Carrington got into your head?"

"I'd started believing things were going to finally work out in my life." Bethany leaned her weight against Mike. "And my paintings were getting better and better. They were dreams I could make happen with merely a brush in my hand. Then it all just fell apart when Benjie and I did. Or I ripped it apart. I ripped up every painting I'd ever done, except for that one of the meadow Dru has at the Whip. The images I submitted for the residency were the photographs my dad took of my work when I was a teenager. I was pissed at the world back then and needed to destroy something, I guess."

"I understand."

Bethany laughed. "Well, I don't. Benjie was nothing. I know that now. I wish I had then. Before I did the kind of damage to my life that maybe it's impossible to undo."

Her knees gave out and she landed on her butt.

Mike sat beside her, crossing his legs, the two of them surrounded by her attempts to capture the very best of the home she was finally determined to keep. He curved her into the warmth of his body. She could sense him listening, when she didn't know how to say more. She didn't know how she'd managed to get what she had out. Or maybe she did.

"I keep forgetting who you are."

"Who am I, darlin'?"

She sighed. "An easy-come, easy-go cowboy. A part-time, drifting bartender. A grieving little brother. A healer who's helping my dad, even if Joe's not so good at being helped. A celebrated, philanthropic artist who sees way more than the rest of us can. A man who wants to help and be needed, but never long enough to need anything or anyone himself."

Mike chuckled.

"You and your family make easy-come, easy-go damn near impossible," he said. "And you see plenty yourself. A lot more now, I'm betting, than when you were a teenager, when you first started dreaming while you painted. And maybe that's part of the problem."

"What problem?" she asked, the answer bubbling inside her, just out of reach.

"That you can't pretend anymore. Painting was your escape when you were a kid. But your first love knows how hard life can be, too. And now, if you want your art back, you have to deal with reality as you create."

While Bethany watched Dru and Brad start their lives together. And Oliver and Selena make their future with Camille a dream come true. And Marsha and Joe—beating the odds and fighting back after Joe's heart attack and surgery, refusing to consider that it was time to maybe scale down their foster home full of kids like Shandra, who'd be lost without them. Everywhere Bethany looked, there was love. The kind that never gave up, and never backed down from a challenge.

And she kept trying to paint it all. Even though, when she was being totally honest with herself, just her and her brushes and paints, what she'd kept finding herself thinking about was . . . leaving it all behind again.

She looked at her recent attempts, at the colors she'd mixed and layered and applied. She'd poured her feelings into each stroke, hoping something beautiful would emerge. Something that wouldn't hurt when she looked at it. Something she could see through to the end.

"I was glad it was gone for a while." The awful truth came tumbling out before she could catch it. "My art. The escape it had been. It all seemed like such a lie."

Mike gave her a supportive nod. "So you ran from it, when you left your foster family."

She shook her head at the years she'd wasted. "I didn't make it far. And I never belonged anywhere else. Wherever I went, I was desperate to get away from there, too. I was always searching for a home to come back to."

His gaze jerked to hers, their connection stronger than ever. Their pasts and present and more colliding.

"And now?" he asked.

"Now?" She swept her arms wide, encompassing her new pieces, one failure after another. "This is all I've been able to do since I promised my family I wanted to stay."

Mike captured her arms and crossed them over her chest, hugging her close.

"Then stay," he said. "So your life and your art are different now. So what? Figure out what staying means now—to you and your paintings. Let them take you in a new direction. It'll be the adventure of a lifetime, I promise you. I know it's scary, but you can do it. What you create is always about where you are. And right now, you're not sure about your place with your family. I get how hard that can be."

His drifter's gaze made her think of the stormy sunset images on his office wall.

"But trust me," Mike said. "You can create beyond your anger and your fear and any other emotion blocking you. You already proved that to yourself when you were a teenager. You'll get your light back. Your dreams. You'll be able to show how you see the world and want to change things for the better. The only thing your paintings can't be about anymore is—"

"Pretending," she said, swept along by the passion in his voice. His heart. This stranger. This generous artist who understood. A man who saw and seemed to cherish even the stormy parts of her.

"Once you break through," he said, "you'll create the most beautiful things you've ever painted."

"The way your brother's illness inspired your photography?" She was thinking of the priceless photographs Mike had taken of Jeremy's hat—his brother's memory—posed in wondrous places Mike had traveled to alone.

He ran a hand down her arm.

His fingers tangled with hers.

"Jeremy's life changed mine. As hard as it was to watch him keep fighting and grow weaker and sicker and finally lose his battle with CF . . . it was inspiring. He made whatever time he had a good thing. He made me promise to make a difference, the way he couldn't."

"You do. And because of you, so many other artists get to make that difference, too." While Mike kept to himself. "Through your co-ops, and the volunteer work the resident artists do, and the money you donate . . . Jeremy's why you work with people like Joe, too, right?"

Mike nodded. "I can't . . ."

"Not help people?"

"Don't romanticize my life. I've been furious with my own childhood for a long time. I've made my own mistakes. I've wandered the globe for years—"

"Disappearing from everywhere you've been before you could get too attached?"

Mike caressed her face. "See? We're not so different after all."

"No," she agreed, "we're not."

He'd never been a stranger. Not really. Not when he could talk about her art so honestly, and about escaping and coming home for real. Not when he could promise her she'd create again, and she found herself believing him. Not when every time they touched, the same recklessness took over, making her want more, even if Chandlerville was just a temporary stop on the way to his next adventure.

"That's what's scaring me," she said as she kissed him.

Mike returned Bethany's kiss, letting her take the lead. This was her show, her choice. But, God, he hoped she didn't slam the door on them again.

He'd reminded himself on the drive over that he was coming to talk about him continuing to work with Joe, and about her continuing with her residency. He'd made it clear that he didn't expect anything more. Then while Bethany's sister had been distracting her, he'd slipped into her studio after glimpsing it when he'd walked inside. And once Bethany had followed him in here—and stayed, talking to him about her art and her past and her fears for the future—there'd been no way he could keep his distance, short of Bethany tossing him out on his ear.

When she stopped kissing him and stood and moved out of his reach, he let her go, watching her stare at her paintings. She wore baggy overall shorts and a neon-pink tank top layered under a man's flannel shirt that had been ripped in several places. Everything was too big on her, except for the tank, which looked shrink-wrapped to every tantalizing inch of her upper body. She'd gotten taupe wall paint all over herself.

He wanted to capture her with his camera so he could show her how amazing she was to him, even scattered and disheveled and looking lost as she frowned at her niece's half-painted face.

"I dreamed the other night," Bethany said, "about washing soft pastels over this. A rainbow of them. Like the colors in one of Camille's quilts, the ones she and Selena's mother are so into. This is the first portrait I tried to paint. I've been looking at it for months. But I can't . . . get it right."

"And more color would make it right?"

He'd seen Camille's pictures of her quilts. He was intrigued by the challenge of merging something like one of their patterns with the little girl's image.

"I have no idea." Bethany moved on to a barely begun group portrait of what looked to be her and Dru and Oliver when they were teens.

Mike joined her. It always surprised him how tiny she was—despite her over-the-top personality and determination to bulldoze through every challenge.

"Maybe you're not supposed to know yet," he suggested. "Maybe it's time to play, instead of worrying about things being right. Playing is different from pretending, Bethany. It can get you through a lot when you're blocked. Whatever you end up doing with all of this will be unexpected, but it will wow people the same as your teenage paintings. Even more. Because there will be more of you in your work now. Trust that, and just play for a while."

"Because being afraid is no way to live your life?" She kept searching her canvases. "That's what I told Shandra."

"It's no way to live your art, either."

"I'm afraid of you." Bethany peeked sideways at him. "You came from out of nowhere, and now you're a part of all of this somehow. My father's recovery. My painting. My . . . feelings. It's way too much, too fast."

"The fear is mutual, love." She had him quaking in his hiking boots.

"But you're still here."

"And you keep letting me in."

"So far."

"Fair enough." He motioned to her treasure trove of new beginnings. "Let me spend some more time with you and your work. I think I can help."

"Just my work?" She stared into his eyes, challenging him. "My art's why you brought me strawberry cupcakes?"

"I got the scones, too."

"Because . . ."

He shook his head. "Because I want to get to know you, Bethany, for real this time."

"But only for as long as you're in town?"

Mike wished he had a different answer to give. "I don't expect you to trust me. I'm a work in progress, too," he warned. "I liked things the way they were before I came to Chandlerville. But now . . ."

The sensitive fingers of an artist glided over his cheek, the way he'd caressed her earlier. "No more pretending for you, either?"

"I don't seem to have a choice. Not with you. I see all you have, and how fiercely you're fighting to hold on to it. And it makes me think I don't really know anything about myself anymore. Except that I need more of you in my life."

She studied him with the same intensity as she had her paintings. "And once Joe is better?"

"My photography can take me anywhere in the world when I'm doing a new series. But I'm here now. And I'd like to spend that time with you."

Her gray eyes narrowed. "How long has it been since you've been honest with someone this way, about who and what you are?"

"Too long," he admitted. "Thank you, by the way, for asking your family to keep the details of my professional life to themselves."

"It seemed important to you."

"*You're* important to me, too." Something he hadn't let happen with any of the women he'd briefly dated since his engagement.

"Another dream to play with?" She led him back into the living room, walking lighter with each step, smiling brighter.

"Another adventure not to quit," he countered, "until we see where this can take us. I get how that's not your comfort zone."

"Evidently, no matter how hard I try to sometimes, I'm not a quitter either. Just like my foster father."

She opened the front door and motioned Mike out with a sweep of her arm.

"Is . . . that a yes?" He joined her, accepting that he had to go, even if he'd dream tonight of bubble-gum-pink lips and strawberry cupcakes.

"You'd better saddle up, cowboy," Bethany said as she shoved him out the door. "That's a yes."

Chapter Ten

“Only your part of the mural is uncovered,” Bethany said to her and Shandra’s Sunday youth center class. “Let your creativity go.”

She smiled, thinking of all the glorious work that had gone into the wall-sized project, the rest of the painting already completed by her other classes. A community canvas was emerging, with just one more section to go.

“The floor’s covered, too,” Shandra added. “So don’t worry.” She grabbed a brush and smeared paint on the transparent poncho she wore, identical to the kids’. “You can’t mess up your clothes. You have the images you’ve practiced. Now all you have to do is paint them on the wall.”

“This is your day,” Bethany said. “Show us what means the most to you in your life, your neighborhood, your family. Ready. Set . . .”

“Go!” screamed the kids in her youngest class, ages six through eight.

Their eardrum-splitting enthusiasm rang through the Midtown Youth Center’s common area, where Bethany had commandeered a wall for this quarter’s curriculum. She let herself take a few moments to enjoy the mayhem that followed. It was exactly what she'd hoped for. Kids enjoying being kids and enjoying art the way they did other games. The project was her brainchild, and what she'd written her Artist Co-op residency essay about.

She'd give anything for Mike to be there, seeing it come to life. A reality that was still possible, since as far as she knew the mural would stay up indefinitely for the kids and their parents to marvel at each time they came to the center. She could bring him by, assuming that she and Mike kept seeing each other. Their first date was tonight, once he finished working with Joe and she dropped Shandra off at her foster parents'.

But Bethany had another pressing matter to attend to first, as she watched Shandra kneel beside Darby Parker. One of their youngest painters, Darby had been an enthusiastic, budding artist the first few weeks of class. And she'd quickly attached to Shandra as her teacher of choice.

She hadn't wanted to paint, though, the last Sunday Bethany and Shandra had taught together. And when she eventually had picked up a brush, the images she'd created as she'd practiced for her piece of the mural had concerned Shandra enough to show them to Bethany before they'd headed home. The volunteers who'd subbed for Bethany and Shandra last weekend had said Darby didn't come to that class at all. And today, as the kids had practiced one more time, Darby had painted the same thing as two weeks ago.

Now she was sitting at a worktable instead of rushing to the wall with her friends. She didn't look up when Shandra slipped off her poncho and sat next to her. Bethany inched closer, easing out of the vinyl protecting her own clothes.

"Can you tell me what you're going to paint?" Shandra asked, her voice low and soothing, the way she and Bethany had discussed.

Each of the kids had been allowed to select three cups of paint to work with—most of them opting for bright primary hues like green and red and blue. Darby had wanted only red and black the last time, and she'd asked for the same today.

"Is this where you live?" Shandra asked. She smiled at Darby's nod, even though the girl hadn't looked up from her work.

The outline of the room was red. Big brushstrokes. Layers of the same color swiped on with a natural eye toward texture and dimension and depth. It could have made for a cheery result, if it weren't for the black.

Black outside the window. Black to represent the taller stick people inside. A black caption cloud beside the tallest of the adults. Black, angry-looking swirls inside the cloud, presumably depicting whatever one grown-up was saying to the other—a smaller adult figure wearing a skirt, her arm in a sling while the taller one held a stick or something else raised as if he were going to hit her.

It could have meant almost anything or possibly nothing at all. Except Shandra had watched Darby labor over the same image two Sundays ago. And just before the little girl had run across the room to leave with her single mom as soon as Ms. Parker arrived, Shandra had said she'd seen Darby slash a huge black *X* across the tall, angry figure, as if erasing it from the picture.

"You said . . ." Darby threw her brush on the table. "You said to paint what we wanted."

Shandra nodded. "Whatever you like best about your family."

"I don't," Darby insisted. "I don't like my family anymore."

"That must be really hard," Shandra reflected back to her young friend. "I remember not liking a lot of the families I've been with."

Darby finally looked up. The students had been told Shandra was a foster child and what it meant. Darby crawled into Shandra's lap now, hugging her, the noise and craziness around them fading for Bethany as she watched her little sister, who'd needed love so badly when she'd come to the Dixon family, become another child's hero.

"Did people ever get . . . hurt in your families?" Darby asked.

"Sometimes." Shandra stared at Bethany, wide-eyed and a little scared, but she held on so Darby wouldn't know. "And it was hard for me to talk about. For a really long time. Until not talking about it got even harder. Is someone hurting you?"

"Not . . . me."

You are so wrong, my friend, Bethany thought. She caught the glint of tears in her foster sister's eyes, proof that a young child's pain could last forever—even in the strong, brave, beautiful adult they could become.

"Who's getting hurt, Darby?" Shandra asked.

"He said not to tell. Me and my mom don't tell anyone. He'll get mad. That'll make it worse. But he's so mad again anyway, and he said he wouldn't be anymore, when my mom said he could come back."

Shandra turned Darby until they were looking at her painting together. She pointed at the taller stick figures.

"Who hurt your mommy?" Shandra asked.

Shawn Carlyle, the youth center's activities director, stepped to Bethany's side.

Other volunteers were seeing to the now madly painting kids, while Shandra and Bethany and Shawn created a protective semicircle around Darby. Shandra and Bethany had shared their concerns with him. He'd told them to keep a close eye on Darby, but that he couldn't speak with her mother in an official capacity, or contact the police or family services, unless there were visible signs of abuse, or Darby gave them more details.

"My mom . . ." Darby turned her face into Shandra's shoulder. "Her arm hurts. He doesn't mean to, but he gets so mad."

"Is he a friend of your mom's?" Shandra looked like she was going to cry or scream or hit someone herself, while she gently stroked Darby's baby-soft brown hair.

Darby didn't answer, quietly rocking in Shandra's arms. Bethany knelt next to them, so proud of her sister's courage, of the volunteer work Shandra was doing with her free time. She checked with her sister to see if she was okay. Shandra nodded.

"Are you afraid of him?" Bethany glared up at Shawn. No way was he keeping her from talking with Ms. Parker now, whether or not Darby said another word. "Are you worried that if you tell, he might hurt you?"

Darby nodded, practically curling into a ball in Shandra's arms.

"Your mom is scared, too?" Bethany asked.

Another nod.

"Adults can be scary sometimes," Shandra said, imparting teenage wisdom that Bethany wished to God her sister didn't have. "And it can feel like there's no way we can stop them, when you're small and everyone else is big and no one knows what's happening. But I'm big now. So is Bethany. We can help if someone's hurting your mom."

Shawn knelt and rubbed a comforting hand down Darby's back. "We'd all like to help."

Darby stared at him, quiet and serious, looking so lost the rest of them fought even harder to keep their rage from showing.

"Tell us how to help you and your mom," Bethany said, realizing anew how lucky she was to have had the love Marsha and Joe had thrust into her life. "We'll do everything we can, Darby. You're not alone in this."

"Can you help . . ." The last of Darby's control crumbled, making her words hard to hear as her tears fell like cleansing rain. "Can you help my brother stop being so mad?"

"Like we discussed." Mike was wrapping up his latest ninety-minute session with his frustrated therapy patient. "Your best bet at this stage is to walk as much as you can. Twice a day is the ultimate goal."

"I've been walking." Joe struggled to a sitting position on Mike's portable massage table. He swung his legs over the side.

"Twice a day? Every day?"

"Is that really the expert advice my insurance premiums are paying you to give me? It's been two weeks, and you're still mostly taking my pulse and pressure, when you're not twisting me into a pretzel."

"Yoga, floor exercises, light weights, massage . . ." Mike looked up from the clipboard, where he recorded Joe's steady but slow progress. "Your flexibility and range of motion are improving."

"Because you've got me doing the same damn exercises in between our sessions, too. What do I need you for, if this is all we're ever going to do?"

"Once we improve your core strength, we'll up your cardio work. It'll be less of a challenge to your balance then. You'll get more benefit for your respiration and stamina. Walking more will help that process along faster. Walking also works a different set of muscles than the more contained exercises we do together. And fresh air can be a miracle drug for some people."

"Are you telling me if I walk, I can nix the blood pressure

meds and the other scripts that are making me feel like I'm moving in slow motion?"

Joe mopped at his forehead with a towel, sweating profusely despite the air conditioner running constantly, its thermostat set to arctic. He walked to the antique bed in the Dixons' master bedroom and sat on the edge of the mattress, workout clothes soaked through with exertion.

"Then I'm in," the man sniped. "The side effects of the drugs they're giving me are worse than the symptoms. How am I supposed to work and live like a normal person while I'm taking them?"

"You're determined not to take an extended leave of absence?" Mike folded the massage table.

Voluntarily taking time off work to focus on his recovery remained a non-option for Joe. Just as, despite Mike's recommendation, his patient had insisted on having their sessions indoors. Mike's eye was on the back patio for future workouts—assuming Joe kept at his recovery. And assuming his embarrassment ever eased at the thought of his family watching him struggle.

"I'm already missing more days than I'm showing up to do my job," Joe said while Mike packed his exercise bands in his duffel, along with the foam brick he'd shown his patient how to use to modify basic yoga poses. "When I am at the office, I'm heading home early in the afternoons. I'm tired, grumpy. I can't focus on anything. I need you to help me stop that from happening. Instead, you keep telling me to take my meds and take leave until I get better."

Mike nodded. "The symptoms you're describing could be from the drugs."

"So this is just the price I pay," groused the gentle, patient man everyone in Chandlerville adored, "for following my doctor's orders so I won't have another heart attack?"

Mike sat on a vanity bench—its fabric upholstered in an ultrafeminine floral pattern—careful not to jostle the dainty table behind him. A rainbow of pastel perfume bottles perched on top, plus a deeply patinaed silver brush, comb, and mirror set. The entire thing reminded him of something from a classic movie.

"The problem is," he said, "your doctor can't reduce your medication until your vitals improve."

"Or maybe you're all just making excuses. Things are getting worse, not better. I'm even more tired since you and I started. More sore. My HR manager at work keeps popping in to check on how I'm doing, like she's afraid I'm going to collapse. She started talking about early retirement the other day—which isn't something I can take and be able to support my family."

Mike consulted his records of Joe's progress.

"Your pressure's too high," he said. "Your oxygen levels and lung capacity are low. Your body's not processing fluid properly, hence the diuretics. Your balance issues and the tremor in your hands and legs are likely a result of both of those factors. And you're right. The medication could be a contributing factor to the lack of concentration, fatigue, and loss of muscle mass. But those symptoms are also likely due to your overdoing it, trying to get back to your old life."

Joe's hands dug trenches in the edge of the mattress. "If I take long-term disability, my position will be filled while I'm away. My responsibilities transitioned to someone else. There'll be no job to return to, even if I do get better."

"Then your best option is to accept your current limitations, take a few weeks of leave while it's still a choice, and really focus on the things that will improve your chances of a better recovery."

"Things?" Joe bit out.

His chronic anger was out of character, according to his friends and family. He was worried about his loved ones, like many of Mike's patients, wanting to provide for them, protect them, love them, and not let them down.

"Things," Mike said, determined to help his patient get where he needed to go, "like working with me during our sessions and between them, instead of resisting my recommendations."

Mike and Joe had gone as far as they could, until Joe came to grips with his limitations. Mike laid his clipboard on top of his duffel and braced his forearms on his thighs.

"Your life is different from the one you knew before," he continued. "You're fighting the body you have now, instead of accepting it. That's where your energy's going. You might not be able to get back everything you had, but we can make sure you have a full, active life. Assuming"—Mike knew it was past time to confront the elephant in the room—"you believe that I'm the right physical therapist to help you."

"Why don't you tell me, son?" Joe slapped his towel over his shoulder. "Why are you, of all people, the right therapist for me?"

Mike scratched the side of his head. He thought of Bethany and the date they'd set for tonight. The risk it felt like they were still taking, opening their hearts and lives to each other because neither of them were able to stop.

He and Joe hadn't discussed any of it.

Mike had kept showing up for their sessions, after his and Bethany's run-in at the loft, and after his showing up at Dru and Brad's and spending time with Bethany and her art in her studio. And Joe had kept grousing about aches and pains and pointless exercises, and never letting on what he knew about his daughter and Mike.

"I'm good at what I do, Mr. Dixon. I've been run over by life a few times myself. I know what it's like to feel powerless to stop the fallout. And . . . I've seen how worried your daughter and the rest of your family are. I'd like to help Bethany and all of the people you care about, by doing everything I can to help you."

"And exactly how is Bethany feeling about you helping me? You've evidently won Selena and Camille over. Oliver's loving that, by the way. Watching him bristle whenever your name comes up is the most fun I've had in months."

"I've enjoyed getting to know your granddaughter and daughter-in-law." Mike grinned. "Riling up Armani is a nice bonus. As for your daughter and me . . ."

"Spit it out, son." Joe sopped more sweat from his face and neck and arms. "I'm melting here."

"Bethany blew me away," Mike admitted. "The first moment I saw her, I lost my head. I've stumbled around ever since, messing things up. But she's . . . amazing. I want her in my life, I can't seem to steer clear of it, and I'll do my very best by her, too. Still, that shouldn't be adding to the strain of your recovery."

Joe raised an eyebrow. "Do you love my daughter?"

A part of Mike wished he could say yes.

The Dixons, watching them these last few weeks, had come to mean more to him than just another patient and recovery support network. He admired everything they stood for. He envied them, the way only a man with his dysfunctional family history could. And he wished he could put Joe at ease now and say what the man wanted to hear for his daughter's sake.

But Mike hadn't been able to make sense of love in a very long time.

"I care about Bethany," he said. "Very much."

Joe frowned, a concerned father contemplating a man who could potentially break his little girl's heart. Then something about him eased, the grim set of his mouth softening.

"When Marsha and I first met at the University of Georgia," he said, "I practically ran her over, not watching where I was going. I knocked her schoolbooks everywhere. She should have been pissed, but she smiled at me instead. She laughed at the goofy grin on my face. And I was just standing there staring at her, brain-dead, with my mouth open . . . I'm not entirely sure I've had a coherent thought since, without Marsha by my side helping me figure things out. So I know a little something about grabbing hold of a woman and not being able to let go, even when you're not sure what to do with her."

Mike kept his silence. This moment had been coming since he'd hunted the man's daughter down after their run-in at Mike's studio. He and Joe needed to settle things.

"But I also know my daughter," Joe said. "She needs to be home for good. She needs to feel at home. And she's never let herself do that with us, not completely. Seems like maybe she's ready now. Problems between you two can't mess that up for her. I'm worried more about that than I am my recovery. My kids are more important to me than anything."

"Your daughter's happiness is important to me, too, Mr. Dixon."

"Joe," the other man said. "Please."

"You have my word, Joe." Mike gave a quick nod. "I'll be good for Bethany and her life here, or I'll remove myself from the situation. Just like my work with you is either going to be a productive solution, or you need someone else to guide you through your recovery."

Joe exhaled, rubbing his eyes with the base of each palm. He frowned at Mike's clipboard.

"I don't suppose there's anything in your bag of tricks that's a silver bullet for fixing my recovery."

"No, sir." Mike sat forward, relieved that the conversation was veering back toward Joe's therapy. "I tell my clients that I'm only going to give them about a tenth of what they need. The rest they already have inside them. Our time together is meant to show you how to pull the pieces of your life together yourself."

Joe's shoulders sagged. "Pieces?"

"Mind and body, working together. The mind is the key at your stage. I can show you how to safely strengthen your body within the limitations of your condition. But you'll undermine everything we try if you push too hard or continue ignoring my advice—and your doctor's."

"I've been working my ass off."

"You've been exhausting yourself, because your instinct is to keep going as hard as you can, or you worry you'll stop being able to go at all. I can get you working smarter, not harder. How long has it been since you were released from the rehab center?" Mike asked. "You've been pushing your system ever since, weakening it even more. Your resistance to your recovery plan is your biggest liability, Mr. Dixon. Joe. It's the threat to you regaining your quality of life. Not your meds. Not the physical limitations I can help you deal with."

"You think I'm depressed."

"I think you're in pain. And you're overdoing it at work and at home, putting your game face on, thinking no one will notice. You're a fighter, sir, just like your daughter. And that's admirable. But you're making risky decisions about your recovery. You need to stop, before you permanently damage your ability to be there for your family the way you want to."

Joe's panic was palpable. "I'd do anything for them."

"Depression can be a tricky thing. The denial. The need *not* to need help." Mike could remember his brother's bouts with it, and being there by Jeremy's side each time. "A strong man with your responsibilities thinks he shouldn't have to deal with that kind of hopelessness. It's a destructive cycle."

"I . . ." Joe's hands were shaking. He rubbed them over his face. "I can't lose them. Any of them. What Marsha and I are doing here is too important. And my Dru's wedding . . . You have no idea how hard she's fought for the happiness she has with Brad."

"Then let's work together and make sure you're a part of all of it. We'll get you stronger. You'll be there for your family, as long as you can accept the time that it's going to take for you to truly heal."

"Dad?"

Joe and Mike looked toward Bethany. She stood in the bedroom doorway, light from the hallway windows framing her with the same glow that seemed to follow her everywhere.

She wore a gauzy dress today. For once there were no splashes of paint covering it. She said she'd be coming straight from working with her kids in Midtown. Mike wondered how she'd managed to remain unscathed. On her feet were delicate sandals. And her hair . . . She'd pulled it back in a glittering, princess-worthy headband, tiny gems catching the light and casting rainbows of sparkling color.

"Is everything okay?" she asked.

Joe pushed to his feet. He limped to her side in a slow-motion hurry and drew Bethany into a hug. Her attention tracked to Mike as he stood, too.

"Is everything okay?" she asked again.

"It will be." Joe kissed her cheek. "Your fella here's getting me straightened out."

"My fella?" Her grin wobbled, squeezing at Mike's heart.

Joe let go. "I'm going to tell Marsha we've got a walk to take tonight." He glanced back at Mike. "*Every* night. And that Mike and I will be working out back on the patio next time, no matter who's around."

"Tomorrow at one," Mike reminded him, keeping his relief to himself. "We'll start with stretching and therapeutic massage. You're going to be sore, but we'll get you moving."

"Wouldn't miss it for the world." Joe made it sound like he was agreeing to be waterboarded.

He patted Bethany's shoulder on his way out the door.

She watched his slow progress down the hall and then the stairs.

"It's so hard for him," she said. "Nothing's ever stopped my dad before. Now . . ."

She turned to Mike, her fear making him wish he could tell her she had nothing to worry about.

"My mom says he's barely dragging himself out of bed before noon on the weekends. His manager at work said not to worry about coming to the office until Joe feels better. That's making him even more determined to be there every day."

"He's angry and frustrated, and he should be. His determination will become an asset, once he focuses it on the right things. We'll work it out."

Bethany smiled, taking Mike at his word and making him feel as if he'd won the lottery. She moved closer until she was within reach.

"Hey," she said.

"Hey, yourself," he responded, flashing back to their first meeting, their first kiss. "Is everything okay?"

Dark circles shadowed the fragile bone structure of her face. "It was a long afternoon at the youth center. But a really good one."

He caressed her cheek with the back of his hand, a little in awe as she leaned into his touch. "What happened?"

She began telling him how proud she was of her sister, the art program at the center, and how it was making an amazing difference in one special student's life. And that while it was happening, she'd realized whom she wanted to share the story with first.

"Me?" he asked.

"Helping kids discover art really can make magical things happen in these communities." Her eyes shone up at him. "You must hear stories like Darby's all the time, in your residents' reports about their volunteer hours."

He did. "But it never gets old. Is the family getting help?"

"We talked with the mother. Sat with her and Darby while family services took their statement. The brother's had a lot of emotional problems. The family hasn't had the money to get him the counseling he needs. The state's going to assign a family therapist. A caseworker followed Darby and her mom home, to talk with everyone together. Hopefully the brother will agree to it. If not, the caseworker will make sure the home is safe for the night, even if the brother has to be removed. I hope it doesn't come to that . . ."

"You did the right thing." Mike was proud to know her. Proud that she and other talented, caring artists were reaching out into the Atlanta community on behalf of the co-op. "You have an amazing heart, Bethany Darling."

"I'm not the only one."

She looked around the bedroom at the equipment Mike hadn't yet packed up. Her attention landed on a bedside table and a grouping of children's photos, like the ones hanging on the wall at the base of the stairs. Images of the vulnerable lives that Marsha and Joe's love had forever made better.

"Thank you for helping my family." Her lips found Mike's, where he'd wanted them since her dad left. "I know I haven't made it easy."

Mike kissed her back. He lifted her to her toes, sweet-smelling softness gliding across every unbearably hard inch of him. He molded her toned body closer, her filmy dress like a cloud beneath his hands. Then he made himself let go and put several inches of space between them.

"Every time." He plucked his hat from his duffel and jammed it onto his head. "This happens every time. I forget who and where I am. You go to my head, and suddenly I'm doing crazy things."

She ran a fingertip down the T-shirt that was damp from his and Joe's session. Mike had a fresh set of clothes in his bag to change into before their date. "Lucky for you, I'm the kind of girl who likes crazy things."

He eased her hand away with a groan. "Your parents know we're up here. If we don't do something about that soon, I won't be responsible for my behavior." He kissed her. Soundly. Torturing them both. "Assuming you haven't changed your mind about going out tonight."

Bright gray eyes sassed him. "You're not getting off that easily. I'm starving, Mr. Taylor. And I'm dying to see where a rambling cowboy takes a girl on their first date."

He tipped his hat. "Nothing but the best for a pretty little filly like you. We're dining in the finest eating establishment in Midtown."

Chapter Eleven

"What'll ya have? What'll ya have?" shouted the server taking Mike and Bethany's order.

They'd finally reached the front of their line at the Varsity.

"What'll ya have? What'll ya have?"

The iconic question continued to be repeated up and down the vast counter. At least a half dozen other lines were teeming with customers, ten or more people deep, patiently waiting for their chance to devour the Southeast's best burgers, hot dogs, fries, and rings. Perpetually moving and shouting servers took and filled orders in front of the divider that separated the counter staff from the Varsity's kitchen. Behind it, kitchen staff worked feverishly, producing the savory, tangy food unique to the historic, no-frills Midtown eatery.

Bethany would never forget her teenage excursions to the Varsity with Marsha and Joe and her brothers and sisters. Saturday mornings or Sunday afternoons, kids piling into Marsha's minivan, everyone splurging on their favorite, nothing-fancy food that was always fabulous. Everyone sitting at whatever tables they wanted to. Hanging out, having a blast, sharing their fries and rings and ketchup and mustard and milkshakes like a family.

She'd finally been part of a real family.

The multistoried interior had changed very little since its 1940s renovations. Complete with the view of the car-hop beyond the kitchen where runners hustled out food to what was touted as the world's largest drive-in. The Varsity was an official Atlanta landmark, daily attracting hordes of hungry locals, tourists, and celebrities, all jonesing for the experience as much as the cuisine.

"What'll ya have? What'll ya have?" Bethany and Mike's server prompted again.

"One of everything?" Bethany teased Mike.

"A slaw dog and onion rings," he said to the lady behind the register, his voice carrying over the Sunday dinner crush. "A pimiento cheese dog with fries. A Diet Coke and ice water." He propped his arm on the counter and grinned at Bethany. On the drive into the city they'd vigorously debated the merits of slaw versus cheese on their hot dogs, and rings over fries. "What else?"

"And an FO," Bethany said.

"A Frosted Orange girl?" Mike nodded his approval.

"It wouldn't be a trip to the Varsity without one." The vanilla-and-orange concoction was a decadently rich cross between a Dreamsicle and a milkshake.

Their server shouted Bethany's request down the counter to where ice cream and shakes were prepared. Mike handed over a twenty to cover their meal. The woman made change and shouted the rest of their order toward the kitchen, then began pulling their drinks from the fountain beside the register.

Another server produced a tray, filling it with heaping portions of onion rings and french fries—Varsity staples continuously being supplied from the kitchen. While Mike and Bethany waited for her shake and their dogs, the server at their register moved on to the family of four waiting behind them.

"What'll ya have? What'll ya have?" she shouted.

The young couple's two kids jumped up and down and squealed, excited to finally be ordering. Mike plugged his ears. Bethany swiped a fry from her and Mike's tray and popped it into her mouth. Closing her eyes, she let the memories swamp her.

Marsha driving the family van to Piedmont Park before or after those long-ago lunches. The friendly competition of touch football games. Swing sets and slides so high you felt like you were flying. Ducks to feed and chase after. And Bethany . . . sitting on a grassy, sloping hill watching the happy mayhem from a distance, sketching, dreaming under rolling clouds, being part of the day by drawing herself into each perfect scene.

She'd never known family could be that simple. Feel that safe. Make you want to experience every drop of it, even though she'd been too scared to really try at first. Those special trips into the city, to the Varsity and other wondrous places, had been the beginning. Her foster parents had opened her heart a tiny bit more with every beam of sunshine, each hug and smile and patient moment of understanding. They'd been coaxing her into belonging from the very start.

She opened her eyes and found Mike studying her.

"A penny for your thoughts," he said.

She grimaced. Kissed him softly. "This is a lovely treat. Thank you."

He kissed her back, his gaze swirling with awareness of how nervous she continued to be with him. "*You're* a lovely treat."

The kids next to them pounced on their own tray of fries and rings, stuffing their mouths. Their parents tried to slow them down. The boy and girl took off, the brother saying he'd get ketchup and mustard for everyone, the sister announcing that she'd scout tables in one of the three rooms of booths near the front, each with a wall-mounted TV preset to a different channel. The parents shook their heads, hugging, and waited patiently for the remainder of their meal.

Mike and Bethany's dogs arrived, along with her shake. Mike hefted their overflowing tray, and they set off. Stopping for their own condiments, they chose to sit at one of the smaller tables in a narrow, open walkway that had windows on both sides. They had a city view on the right and an overlook of the interstate connector on the left—where Interstates 85 and 75 merged and split Midtown in half, separating landmarks like Georgia Tech and the Coca-Cola headquarters from historic Peachtree Street.

Sunlight showered everything in its late-afternoon sparkle. People bustled past, coming or going. Rowdy conversations echoed from nearby booths. Groups tromped up and down the stairs leading to the parking deck outside. It was a sprawling, distracting, not in the least bit romantic setting. Bethany couldn't have imagined a better first date.

"Seeing you smile like that"—Mike fed her a fry—"does dangerous things to a man's best intentions."

"Intentions to let me eat first, before you try to have your way with me?"

The pull between them was more combustible each time they met. And Bethany had been schooling herself that tonight was just about getting to know each other. With maybe a little bit of flirting on the side. Okay, a *lot* of flirting.

"My intention," he corrected, "was to not ask so many personal questions that I scare you off." He took a bite of his slaw dog and watched her swipe a finger through her pimiento cheese. "*Before* I try to have my way with you."

"Maybe I'm not that easily scared." Despite the ambrosia of aromas wafting up from their orders, Bethany only managed to nibble at her food as longing thrilled inside her.

"I think you're scared pretty much all the time," Mike said. "But you're also one of the bravest people I've ever met."

"Says the man who wears an insulin pump, has to test his blood sugar before and after meals, and scales dangerous mountains to take photographs only a handful of people in the world could reach."

He'd explained about his diabetes testing after he'd parked the Jeep. He'd shown her the insulin pump at his hip and made it sound like no big deal that he'd worn one since he was a kid. He grew larger than life with every new thing she learned about him. While he seemed hell-bent on keeping the conversation focused on her.

"Battling your fears," he said, "whatever they are, makes you a fighter in my book. Scaling mountains, sticking needles into your finger, are no big deal compared to what a lot of people face every day."

She sipped her shake, surprised—though maybe she shouldn't have been—at how quickly things were turning serious. They'd come at everything backward. Kissing first, their physical connection flashing to full life, while who and what they were as people had been left to be discovered more slowly, one drip, one drop at a time, until a flood of catching up was inevitable.

"People like your brother?" she asked.

Mike shrugged. "Jeremy. Joe. Your student at the youth center. You and your foster brothers and sisters? You're all remarkable. Compared to that, I've got nothing much to complain about." He motioned toward where the small insulin pump was holstered to the waist of his jeans, beneath his shirt. "I have medicine that makes me good as new. I've always had whatever I've needed."

Whatever money could buy, at least.

"Having things," she reasoned, "being lucky enough to be healthy, doesn't make you feel safe. Otherwise I'd have settled in with Marsha and Joe and never looked back."

"Back at your first home?"

"With my mother, yeah. And all her loser boyfriends. Some of them liked little girls . . ."

Mike stopped eating, but his expression remained steady, as solid as when she'd walked in on him talking with Joe. She either told this remarkable man the rest now, risking him knowing it all, or she never would.

"So that was a problem," she continued, "because I'd run, and my mom wouldn't bother to come looking for me, and eventually the county caught on. I wound up with my grandmother. Not exactly a picnic. She was pissed at me and my mom because of the bother of it all. Then my mother took off with her latest guy. My grand liked the money the county gave her to take care of me, so we made it work. Stayed out of each other's way until she died and Joe and Marsha took me in."

Mike's gaze had hardened while he'd heard her out. Now she was done and waiting, wanting back the happy feelings of just a few moments ago. Guys hit the road once they discovered she couldn't pretend every second of every day to be the happy, fun girl she'd first let them meet.

Then Mike smiled, his easy acceptance of who and what she was like the sun brightening a bank of clouds.

"Look at how far you've come since then," he said. "The Dixons' home must have been a great place to finish growing up."

She nodded, the rest of what she usually kept to herself rushing out.

"Except I ran from them, too. When Benjie turned out to be using me just like my grand did. When I couldn't paint or stand to look at anything that used to make me feel good. So instead, I fell for even more men who didn't want me, the way none of the men my mom chased after turned out to want her, either."

Bethany stared across the booth, her hands clenched in her lap, knowing she was making a mess of their date. But this was who she was. Who she'd never hide again, no matter how much she wanted a man to love even the scary, lonely parts of her.

"You're back with Marsha and Joe now," Mike said, quietly studying her the way he had her paintings. "That's got to mean something."

It meant everything.

So did his acting as if he still thought of her as brave, and nothing could change that.

"Why did you leave your family?" she asked, her stomach settling enough for her to take her first bite of hot dog.

Mike picked at his onion rings.

"I didn't have any real family left," he said, "after I lost my big brother and my fiancée. That was ten years ago this month."

They both ate in silence.

"How old were you?" Bethany tried to picture Mike roaming the world aimlessly, taking phenomenal pictures, grieving alone—leaving even the woman he'd wanted to marry behind.

"Nineteen. I think my parents were glad to see me go. Abby, too."

"I'm sure they weren't."

"We'd all been through a lot. The last few years of Jeremy's life . . . took a toll. My parents had disappeared already into their New York world and their foundation. Abby fit in there, like the daughter they never had. But I wanted no part of it anymore. She seemed relieved, actually, when I asked her to come with me. We both knew she wouldn't. I gave her the out she'd been looking for."

"Good riddance?" Bethany would have reached for him, but he seemed so far away.

"We were young. I'd changed. I was lost and no good for anyone. My parents were more upset about our breakup than Abby and I were. They wrote me off. I guess they figured I'd come home when I got tired of roughing it. That's what my mother called it when I went exploring for Jeremy. They kept in touch by phone. It was years later before they pressured me to come home, after my photographs popped onto the radar of a few galleries they were connected with. I'd finally done something worthwhile with my life that they could brag about at their cocktail parties and foundation events."

"Is that why you've kept your identity in the art world anonymous, so they couldn't?"

Mike nodded. "I know that makes me sound like a vindictive bastard. But by then I'd settled down enough to be studying physical therapy in college. George had stuck with me. She took my idea for the bones of the first co-op and ran with it. I was putting the money I was making to good use, thinking I was making Jeremy proud somehow."

"I'm sure you were."

"I was happy being Mike Taylor, a guy working on a degree so he could help people when he got the chance. My parents could talk to their friends about that all they wanted."

"You've inspired people and communities all over the country to love creating art as much as you do." Bethany absorbed all that he'd revealed, trying to understand. "But none of them know who you really are. Your story. Jeremy's story. The real meaning behind your photography. That it all makes you feel closer to your brother."

"Closer than my parents ever wanted to be."

Mike looked at her, letting her see how lost a part of him still felt.

"There it is again." He reached out his hand, waited for her to cover it with hers. "Another part of us that just . . ."

"Fits?"

"We're both drifters."

"Feeling safer wandering than staying in one place. At least I did, until one morning I woke up, broken up with my latest guy, dead broke and fired from my latest dead-end job. And I realized who I was becoming."

Her mother.

That was what Bethany had seen when she'd stared, horrified, at her exhausted, defiant reflection in the bathroom mirror. She'd become a caricature of everything she remembered hating most about her mother.

"I was lucky," she said. "Everyone, my friends and family, welcomed me back."

"They're lucky, too, that you were strong enough to come home and accept their help."

She'd never thought of it that way. "It took Dad's heart attack to get me to face making things right for real. Maybe not being able to paint anymore is the price I'm paying for staying away so long."

Mike relaxed into his side of the booth and finished his last bite of hot dog. "Or maybe your art is like your family. It never really let you go at all. It understands that you just needed time."

He pushed his onion rings closer to her and filched some of her fries. She ate and sipped at her FO and distracted herself with his mouth while he took a long draw through his ice water's straw.

She could feel the things they'd shared sinking in. Closing the gaps that could have been excuses for not trusting each other. Now those spaces were connected. Stories about their lives that were so different were fitting together perfectly, the way their bodies did each time they touched.

While he finished eating, she busied herself stacking their plates, until his hand caught hers. Startled, she found his expression hardening—with passion this time, not anger.

"You're perfect just the way you are, Bethany," he said, "*because* of everything you've been through. Don't ever forget that. Even if your ex hadn't been such an ass that night at the bar, there's a light in you I needed to be next to. I'd have found a way, somehow. It's that powerful. Time and mistakes and hurting matter. What you've been through matters. But none of that diminishes who you really are. Not to your family or your art. Or to me."

Mike found himself locked into Bethany's questioning gaze. And for the love of all that was holy he wanted to stay there, listening to her open up, telling her personal things he hadn't discussed with anyone besides George.

While Bethany thought her secrets would make her *less* to him, not more.

"You survived," he said, and nothing was sexier to him. "You're this amazing, vibrant, creative bundle of positive energy that I felt drawn to, long before I glimpsed it in your paintings."

She ran her fingers through her brightly colored bangs, embarrassed. “I can’t even paint my meadow anymore.”

“That’s just you getting in your own way, telling yourself what you’re doing isn’t good enough. One day, when you least expect it, you’ll be—”

“Free?” She exhaled. “I used to feel free when I painted. And then not for a long time. And now . . . I only feel it when I’m close to you.”

Silence punctuated her admission, the commotion of the people around them fading completely. Mike’s hand shook a little. Or was it hers? Their fingers were too intertwined to tell.

“I’m scared of this, too,” he admitted. “It’s real. And neither one of us was looking for that.”

“Because the more real feelings get, the harder it is to let go when you have to.”

Mike nodded.

“I want . . .” she whispered. “I want to show you my meadow.”

“You do?”

She seemed surprised, too, as if the thought just occurred to her.

“I went there one of my first nights in Chandlerville.” She smiled. “It’s this perfect, peaceful place. The first place I can remember wanting just for myself.”

“I’d give anything to have been there for that.” Getting to glimpse the beginning of her happiness and the healing and belonging she was just now embracing.

“Come see it then. It’s just outside town, not far from my parents’. You should feel it. Take pictures of it. That way it can be yours, too. Always. Even after . . .”

Even after he left.

“It’ll be the same as when you captured the world you saw for Jeremy.” Excited, she rushed to her feet, not giving herself or him a chance to change her mind. She checked her watch. "If we hurry, we'll get there by sunset."

She tossed out their trash. Then she grabbed his hand and led him down the stairs to their spot in the parking deck. But that was where he stopped her. Kissed her. Pressed her against the side of his Jeep, his mouth and hands and the weight of his body leaving nothing to the imagination about what he was fantasizing would happen once they reached her meadow.

"I'll take my pictures until the light is gone," he said when they came up for air. "But I'll want more. When I look back at tonight, I know I'll want to remember it being so much more. And we agreed to play this slow."

She'd been hurt as a young child. God knew how much, and Mike would never ask unless she wanted to share the details. Her experience with her grandmother had been lonely at best. Criminally negligent, more likely. Which had finished shaping how difficult it must be for Bethany to accept that anyone could truly care about her.

Of course she'd struggled, chased the wrong attention from the wrong people, and run from those who would have, from the start, given her the love she craved. He'd never judge her for that. He'd never feel anything but the burning desire to cherish her for what she'd become, despite all the hurt. But he'd never lie to her, either, about who and what he was.

He'd be good for Bethany, like he'd promised Joe. Or he'd find the strength to either change what he had to, or walk away.

"I'd never do anything to rush you," he promised.

"I want more, too," she admitted, shaking in his arms, excited and off balance the same as him. "It's been a long time since I've let myself fall like this for someone. You probably don't believe that after what I just told you, but—"

He pressed a finger to her lips. "I believe you. We'll take it slow."

"We don't do slow," she whispered into his ear. And then, God help him, she nipped his earlobe.

"This time we will. You'll tell me what feels good to you. And that's all we'll do."

"We feel good." She eased back, her smile firmly in place. "Even if you can't stay. Even if it's going to be hard to let you go when it's time, I want tonight to be whatever it's supposed to be. You're right. We're real. We're the same in all the ways that are important. I don't care anymore how little time it's been. We belong together for as long as we have. I can't imagine being with you and it feeling anything but good."

Chapter Twelve

"Late-summer sunsets are remarkable," Mike said.

He was setting up the camera and tripod he'd produced from his Jeep, positioning them near the pond that held court at the far corner of the meadow. There'd be no settling for quick iPhone images this time, Bethany mused, mesmerized by his precise, practiced movements.

"This far south, especially." He stared at the sky in between fiddling with his equipment. "The oranges and yellows and pinks bleed differently. Their lavenders, navies, and blacks are more intense."

He adjusted the height and angle of the tripod's legs and attached the camera. His motions were confident. Unhurried, despite the waning light. He talked to her as he worked, answering her questions here and there, completely absorbed otherwise in what he was doing. She was watching a man in love with his art.

His passion for sharing with her what he usually did alone drew Bethany closer to the pond's edge. The sun was showing off in a magnificent display, charming the water's reflection into an equally grand spectacle. Mike had scouted the meadow and decided on the exact angle he wanted to photograph sunset and dusk, based on how he thought the light would drop behind the tree line.

"When I try to take photos this time of night"—she watched as he peered through the camera's lens and made adjustments on the digital display's touch screen—"all I get are shadows and washed-out gray."

"The colors come when you adjust for the light, where it's weakest or strongest, and for how vibrant or dark you want the exposure to be. It also depends on where you focus the lens. You have to work with the camera to get it to see what you want it to, even the newer ones. You compensate for its limitations and adjust for your environment—otherwise the lens won't see what your eye does. You can work with shutter speed and adjust aperture. This camera is digital. Film is a different medium with another set of tools to manipulate."

"It sounds . . ." Absolutely fascinating. "Complicated."

Mike looked at her, his gaze soft as velvet. "I'm being a total geek. Sorry. Your meadow is beautiful." He looked around them at the tall grass and the sprinkling of ancient oak trees here and there, then at the woods full of pines beyond the pond. "I can see what drew you to paint it. I'll want to capture it at dawn one day, on a cloudy morning with the sun burning through. That kind of diffused light would be incredible here."

While he made final adjustments to the camera, he snagged Bethany with a one-armed grab that plastered her to his side. She pushed up on her toes and wrapped her arms around his neck. Capturing his attention completely, she kissed him to distraction. He lifted her until her feet were practically dangling and whistled once his lips slipped away. He licked the corner of his mouth, making her feel like the dessert he'd denied himself at the Varsity.

"You make it hard for a man to concentrate." He sounded as desperate as she felt.

"Good." For tonight, for as long as they had, it was going to be so good. She finally knew that. Trusted that. Trusted him?

He eased her down his body. She rested her head on the delicious warmth of his chest. The sky and clouds over the water were magnificent, creating fantasy patterns of color and shadow. Each moment was an ever-changing celebration.

Mike watched her taking it all in. His large palm rubbed down her back. "I can always shoot this another night."

"Not gonna happen, cowboy." She backed away. She wasn't missing her chance to watch him work. "Make me a picture I won't be able to stop myself from painting."

She walked back to the Jeep and leaned on the bumper while he worked with his camera, quickly now as the light and colors in the sky—their reflections on the pond—shifted. His legs were braced for balance as he shot, muscles bunching beneath his whisper-soft cotton shirt. His slightly too long hair brushed his collar, making her mouth water to kiss the skin beneath. Nibble it. Make him shiver the way she knew he would.

He snapped frame after frame, the horizon vivid, vibrant, the late-summer sun slanting away. His adjustments to the camera were relentless, grabbing every glimpse of the world deepening around them. The day's afterlife emerged with the sound of night creatures: crickets and frogs and softly singing birds, their rhythms a soothing hymn. All the things she liked best about this place were now better because Mike was there.

The trees and the grass lost their dimension. The pond faded to shadow. Only fifteen minutes, maybe twenty, had passed. But it might have been hours, and he'd have stayed just as absorbed in his work, and Bethany in him.

He was motionless now. She stepped closer, wrapping her arms around him from behind and pressing her cheek to his back. A vast blanket of stars emerged, infinite, fragile, spreading above them. He sighed into their quiet spell.

"Thank you," he said. "For sharing this with me."

"I'll never be here again without thinking of tonight."

He drew her around him and kissed her. He removed the sparkly headband that Camille had helped her pick out at the dollar store, and he ran his hand through her hair and kissed her again. And again, as if he'd be satisfied to do nothing more until dawn.

"Don't go away." He left long enough to walk to the Jeep and store his equipment.

Long enough for him to grab a blanket and return and spread it at the water's edge. Long enough for her to change her mind. Except she couldn't. Not now. Not with this man. She was taking a huge risk. But how could she have thought *just friends* was possible with Mike? It turned out that this was a night *she* wanted to always look back on, too.

It was the night she'd remember giving her cowboy her heart.

Mike reached out his hand, relaxing only when Bethany joined him by the pond after watching him so calmly from her meadow's moonlit shadows.

He welcomed her body closer, her breath teasing his neck, every inch of them aligning. She smiled, her hands smoothing across his chest. They drew each other down to the blanket. He wanted them skin-to-skin, hearts pounding, need driving them until they couldn't think about anything else. But he kept telling himself to give her time, to make sure she was okay.

And then she kissed him, her body flowing into his lap, reckless and needing and out of control. He groaned and helped her drag his shirt free from his jeans. He'd already gotten his insulin pump out of the way at the Jeep, not wanting to worry her with the process, leaving her free rein now. When her hands moved to his belt, he stalled them.

"I'm trying to be careful with you," he said.

She hesitated for the first time. "Tonight I don't want careful."

He gave a short laugh, his body straining against his control, desperate to pounce. Consume. Dive into the pleasure he knew they'd find. "That makes two of us."

He kissed her long, hard, soft, easing her back to the blanket, testing his control.

She began unbuttoning the front of her dress, revealing fragile, feminine lace beneath. "You've already shown me more of your heart, wanted to know more of mine, than any man I've ever been with."

"It's not enough." He kissed the soft skin of her collarbone. Nuzzled the valley between her breasts. "I know I'm not nearly enough for you."

"It's everything." She smiled as he finished unbuttoning, all the way down to her matching panties. "Trust me. I've done the legwork."

His mouth worshiped her belly while he dragged off his shirt, her dress and sandals, and the jeans that got stuck on his boots. She giggled at his curse and helped him discard the offending footwear and clothes. Then he kissed his way back up her body. The last thing he removed was the beautiful lingerie he'd had no idea lay hidden beneath all her crazy outfits.

"You're one surprise after another." He took in the sight of her. "I should have dragged you out to the woods and shown off with my camera sooner."

She gave him another giggle and took care of his briefs, sliding them down, smiling her approval, easing back as he kicked them off. Her eyes were soft gray clouds. Her skin, satin. She returned his kisses endlessly, letting him slow them down and anchor her wrists on either side of her head, where he needed them so her inquisitive fingers didn't end things before they could really begin.

He lifted away to catch his breath and memorize her awestruck expression. Her sweet, trusting smile humbled him, as if this were her first time. He fished a condom from the pocket of his jeans and slid on the protection.

And then she was moving beneath him, her legs wrapping around his waist, sending him soaring into the night, into her, like a dissolving sunset bursting into a sky full of fireworks. Her body welcomed him, and Mike was lost. Found. Flying apart. Becoming whole. Making his way home in her heat, in their passion. The combination was nearly unbearable, bewitchingly intense.

Her hands clenched on his body as he moved faster, her nails biting just deep enough to make him crave more.

"How can you feel so good?" she gasped as she took him, and he took her, and they gave each other more.

"How can you be so beautiful?" He tried to remember to take his time, to make it last. But there was no slow. Not tonight. Not with Bethany.

"Too . . . too fast." She tugged at his hair, urging him on. "I'm going to . . ."

"Yes," he groaned. "I want it all."

All of her. All that Bethany had never given away to anyone else. Not this completely. The thought was intoxicating.

"Mike?"

"I'm here. Let me love you."

Her body clenched at his words, surging, making him curse, move over her, within her, faster, lifting them both higher, holding on. Clinging now.

"Too fast," he panted.

"I need you so much."

He pressed his forehead to hers. He closed his eyes against the brightness, the emotions, the . . . love consuming them.

Real.

Passionate.

Everything.

"I need you, too," he whispered. "Mine. Can't believe you're mine."

"Mine . . ." she gasped back, her pleasure sharpening his. Until release was rolling between them, their bodies straining for more.

"All mine . . ."

Chapter Thirteen

"Details," Clair insisted two mornings later. "We need details. And we're not moving from this spot until we get them."

Bethany was hand-pressing potatoes into fries in the Dream Whip kitchen.

"You *need* to get your butt off the counter," she said, "before Dru gets here and moves it for you."

Bethany had originally asked not to work today unless it was an emergency. Partly because she and Shandra were due at the youth center that afternoon for the official presentation of the mural to their students' families. And partially because Bethany had hoped to be back in her painting groove. She wasn't. Which wasn't exactly a novelty.

But not being able to sleep because she couldn't get a guy off her mind—*that* was a non-novelty that had propelled her from her bed, desperate for a diversion. Even if prepping fifty pounds of potatoes was the only available distraction. Too bad she'd had a brain fart when Nicole had called on Bethany's drive over. Bethany had answered the phone, when she'd let the rest of the world roll to voice mail since Mike dropped her off Sunday night. Nicole had pinpointed her location and destination with the speed of a federal agent tracking a hot lead.

Bethany's time to straighten herself out before she dealt with her friends and family was up.

"There aren't any details worth sharing," she told her friends. She might be in over her head with Mike. But unless he felt the same . . . "It was just one night. It didn't mean anything. And even if it did, it doesn't have to mean everything. I already knew it wouldn't for him."

"Because why?" Clair was munching on a dill pickle she'd snagged from the enormous jar in the Whip's walk-in refrigerator.

"Because Mike made it clear he's still leaving."

"After he slept with you?"

"Before."

I know I'm not nearly enough for you . . .

And then they'd made love. And it had been wonderful. And it would be wonderful again. Bethany couldn't wait to see him, talk to him, understand more about what made him the man she'd needed to meet, to know for sure that there was love in the world for her. *Once* she had herself under control enough not to hope for more than Mike was capable of giving—no matter what she wanted it all to mean.

Each time she closed her eyes, she saw his near rapture while he'd worked with his camera and the sun's light. The same expression had softened his features while he'd loved her, cherished her body, and cared for her while they'd driven each other crazy. But that was no reason to backslide into her compulsion to make every relationship with every guy the love affair that would end all others.

She'd blown her *just date for fun* experiment and fallen in love with him. But that was on her. Going in, they'd both been clear on the ground rules.

"You're full of it," Nic said, "and you know it."

"You're totally into the guy." Clair pointed her pickle for emphasis.

"And I'd bet money," Nic added, "that Harrison Michael Taylor is totally into you."

"And he"—Bethany pressed the lever home, shooting another potato through—"has just as many relationship hang-ups as I do."

He'd been so careful, making certain that making love was what she wanted. And she'd told him it was. She'd been so sure it was. Only, the one time Mike had phoned her cell after Sunday, she hadn't taken the call.

Mine.

All mine . . .

"He'll be working with your dad for a while longer, right?" Clair polished off the buttered hamburger bun she'd made in lieu of breakfast, insisting she needed the carbs. Her morning client had four Labs she didn't like to kennel when she traveled for business. And unless Clair wanted to spend half her day walking each one individually, she'd be wrestling all four pampered pooches at once around Chandler Park's jogging path. "There's plenty of time."

Bethany stopped pressing fries and gave her friends her undivided attention.

"Time to what?" she snapped.

Nic leaned a hip against the counter. "Lasso the one-eyed snake again?"

Clair snorted. "Strap on that Stetson for another ride?"

At Bethany's glare, Nicole sobered. "Talk to him."

"And say what?" What was Bethany going to say?

She wiped her forehead with the sleeve of the green-and-white men's rugby shirt she'd thrown on over orange checkerboard tights.

Clair looped her arm around Bethany's shoulder. "Tell him what you want. Do you even know?"

"I know it was just supposed to be dinner." Bethany caved at Nicole's snicker. "Okay, I figured it would end up as more than dinner. But not *that* much more."

"How much more?" Clair asked.

"He was . . . so into it. Lost in what we were doing, just like me. Like he couldn't stop, either."

"I can see how that could be a turnoff," Nic commiserated.

"And he held me afterward."

"The jerk!" Clair smiled.

"For hours." Bethany closed her eyes, picturing it, wanting every second of it back. "We just lay there, wrapped in a blanket under the stars, staring at each other and the sky and listening to each other breathe like it was the best sound, the best place in the world . . ."

"Oh, honey." There were tears in Nicole's eyes. "You're falling in love with him."

"No," Bethany lied, "I'm not."

"And Mr. Harrison Michael Taylor, wealthy, well-connected, Yankee cowboy photographer," Clair added, "is falling for you."

"No," Bethany told herself and her friends, "he's not."

"Because most men just looking to scratch an itch," Nic said, "take a girl to dinner, romance her, and then after the wham, bam, thank you, ma'am, curl up with her for hours."

No, they didn't.

"And most relationship-phobic women," Clair added, "spend every waking moment avoiding a guy, then thinking about the guy, and then talking *to* the guy, even though she doesn't want him. And *then* she goes out with the guy and makes love with the guy, and still tries to convince herself that she's not hopelessly in love."

"He's not staying!" Bethany shouted.

At least she'd meant to shout. But the words had come out strangled. She bit the corner of her lip.

I need you, Mike.

"It doesn't matter how fast I fell for him," she said. "Or if he's feeling something more than he expected, too. He's going to leave once he's finished working with Joe."

"And you're okay with that?" Nic asked.

"Does she look okay with it?" Clair said.

"He's a nice guy," Bethany reasoned. "He cares about me. I'm not going to pitch a fit and treat him like he's using me, when we both know that's not what happened. I'll be fine as soon as he needs it to stop."

That's the way it went in her mind, over and over as she'd tried and failed a half dozen times to return Mike's call. How many guys had she watched walk away from her? She should be a pro at it by now.

"As soon as *he* needs it to stop?" Clair grabbed Bethany by the shoulders and prevented her from pacing across the kitchen. "Or as soon as you do?"

Bethany shook her head at her friend and at the hours she'd spent staring at her paintings in her studio at Dru's—lost in her attempts to re-create the landscape of the meadow and finish her beginning portraits of her parents and siblings and niece. Her heart pounding, she'd flashed back over and over to Mike's total absorption in his photography. She'd told herself she could be like that again, loving her art the way he clearly did his. Like him she could be free in the moment, swept away by discovery, lost to the magic of being perfectly out of control.

Make me a picture I won't be able to stop myself from painting . . .

But she still couldn't pick up her brushes, not even to start a new piece.

"It doesn't have to hurt." Nicole was hugging her now. "Your family, your art, falling in love. None of it's supposed to hurt."

Bethany nodded.

But it did. Even loving a wonderful man like Mike hurt. *Especially* loving him. And love, like her art, was supposed to be the adventure of a lifetime. Instead, the fear of everything that could go wrong was paralyzing her.

She covered the enormous bin of prepped potatoes with plastic wrap and lugged it to the industrial cooler where she'd already stored another one. She returned to clean up the fry cutter so Dru's crew wouldn't have to.

"It feels like I'm hanging off a cliff by my fingernails," she admitted, confiding in her friends something that she could barely face herself.

Nic looked misty again. A little afraid for Bethany, and a little proud. "Love usually does."

"I've been running from it for so long. So has Mike. Even if he decided to stay after finishing with Joe . . . What are the chances two people like us could make something work long term?"

Mike had kissed her softly beside the pond, after they'd packed the blanket and everything else away. He'd driven her home in silence that had grown increasingly strained, and he'd kissed her on the front porch, the brim of his Stetson shielding them from the glare of the lamp Dru had left on. He'd lifted Bethany's hand and brushed her palm with his lips. He'd said he'd call her, and he had.

So what was wrong with her?

Why couldn't she be grateful for that moment, and every new one they had, and let it be enough? Why was she already worrying about how badly it was going to end?

"He left me a message Monday." She'd listened to it at least once an hour since. "He said he understood if I needed space. To take my time. He'd be waiting. But for what?"

Trying to answer that question had been like staring at her paintings, trying to feel something she couldn't.

I'm here. Let me love you.

"You're never going to know what's over that cliff you're clinging to," Clair finally answered, "until you trust someone enough to let go and fall."

"Hey, honey," Joe said on his cell.

He was gulping down air after Mike's latest round of *light* stretching. The guy had been true to his word. Once Joe had gotten with the program, their routines had become more intense every time they met.

"Make it quick," he panted. "My sadist of a physical therapist is on a bio break. He's got a full half hour left with me, and Lord knows what your fella has up his sleeve next. Yoga's supposed to be relaxing, right? Therapeutic? I think my heart's sprung another leak."

"He's not my fella, Dad."

"Uh-huh." Joe swiped at the sweat on his face, standing beside the backyard patio's picnic table, just outside the kitchen. "Then what is he?"

Mike hadn't straight-out asked after Bethany. And Joe had made a point not to mention the date he'd heard the two of them had gone on Sunday night. He and his PT specialist had been tiptoeing around the subject of Joe's daughter for close to an hour.

"How's your session going?" Bethany asked, suspiciously bright and cheerful for someone whom no one in the family but Dru had spoken with in days.

"What's wrong, honey?"

"Nothing."

Joe sighed. *Nothing* was going to be the death of him, if his daughter and her cowboy didn't figure themselves out.

"Mike's pushing me," he answered. "I'm finally pushing myself. I'm sleeping better, have more energy. I'm doing my exercises between therapy sessions, and I'm taking a two-month leave of absence from work so I'll have the best shot at a full recovery."

He and Marsha would have to make a serious dent in their savings to cover the drop in his take-home pay. There might be problems with his position at the office when he went back. And he might have to strangle Oliver if the boy kept offering to handle any of the expenses Joe couldn't in the meantime. But those were just details to sort out, when the details didn't matter now.

Joe was making the most of this chance to pull his life back together.

And maybe his daughter was, too.

"Now that we're all caught up on me," he said, "tell me what's wrong, honey." He could hear muffled conversation on her end of the connection. "Where are you?"

"Midtown, with Shandra."

"Right. Your mural's done. Congratulations. Shandra's so excited to catch up with Darby. She couldn't stop talking about what happened after the two of you got back Sunday. She really opened up with your mother and me. That was the first for her."

"That's great, Dad. She's the one who first guessed there was a problem. She's the reason that family has the chance to get better. We'll talk to Darby and her mom when Ms. Parker comes by later. But from what I can tell since the after-school bus dropped Darby off, she's doing much better."

Bethany paused, hanging on the line when he could hear how busy things were around her. And he knew she hadn't called him—when she always called her mother about family things—just to talk about his therapy and Shandra.

"Mike'll be heading back outside in a minute," Joe offered.

"Oh. Then I should let you go."

"Should you?"

Joe eased onto the bench Mike had shown him how to lean on for support while they worked through standing stretching poses. He gazed around the backyard, at the swing set he'd built, the old volleyball net that always needed repairing, and the secondhand playhouse that the younger kids dragged him and Marsha into for tea parties with their imaginary friends.

"Actually . . ." Bethany exhaled into the phone. "Mike left me a message the other day, and I—"

"Thought you'd call me to talk about it?"

"No. But when I picked Shandra up she mentioned your next session with him was this afternoon, so I—"

"Called me to check up on him, too?" Joe heard a noise and glanced over his shoulder. Travis, not Mike, walked out of the kitchen through the sliding doors. "So you didn't have to talk to Mike yourself?"

Bethany cleared her throat. "No, Dad. I—"

"Your mother and I don't ask. But that doesn't stop folks from keeping us in the loop about you kids. Sounds to me like you and Mike have plenty to talk about these days."

"I know we do."

Joe had heard Bethany sound lost like this before. When she'd been a hurting teenager. Then an angry one. And then a scared young woman working hard to make her way back to everything she was meant to be.

"Then why are you talking to me," he asked, "instead of Mike?"

"I've tried calling him a few times." There was a new tremor in her voice. This was a different, excited-sounding kind of lost that made Joe smile. "I dial the phone, and then I hang up. I just . . . can't. I thought maybe you could tell him something for me."

"Mike'll be right out. Tell him yourself."

"Actually, I've got to go, Dad. More parents are showing up."

"Then call back." Joe peered past Travis—and the worry on his son's face—to the clock on the kitchen wall. "We'll be done in a half hour."

"I'm sorry I'm interrupting your therapy. It's no big deal."

"What's no big deal?"

Something was definitely wrong with his child. Or, definitely right. Either way, Joe had no intention of planting himself in the middle of it. Marsha was the matchmaker, not him. He'd already meddled enough, working with Mike when sparks had been flying from the start between the young man and Bethany.

"Will you at least tell him that I called?" Bethany asked.

"I'll give him the message. But whatever you two have to talk about, honey, it's only going to get harder the longer you put it off."

Mike appeared on the patio, stopping next to Travis, both of them listening.

"I've got to go," Bethany said after a long pause. "I love you, Dad."

"Bethie—"

She'd already hung up.

I love you, Dad.

Such a simple, four-word sentence. One Joe lived to hear from each of his kids. But only when they were ready to say it. Which meant he never took a single day like today for granted—when all the hard work and financial strain and challenges of fostering kids paid off, and one of them turned to him when they needed something. Anything. Even if all he could do was get out of the way and insist that they did for themselves.

"I love you, too," he said under his breath, plunking his phone onto the picnic table.

"I have a message from Bethany?" Mike crouched to roll up the yoga mat he'd laid out on the grass.

"So it seems." Joe traded a long look with Travis.

Mike pulled his own phone from his oversized duffel bag. He checked the phone's display and frowned.

"Did she say what it was?" he asked Joe.

"Not exactly."

Travis confronted the guy. "You wanna tell me why my sister hasn't wanted anything to do with you or the rest of us for days?"

"Oh . . ." Joe leaned back against the picnic table, smiling at the sound of a bunch of the kids playing next door with Bud, Camille's forever barking puppy. "I think Bethany wants plenty. She just hasn't decided what to do about it yet."

Travis glowered at Mike. "Have you?"

Mike pushed to his feet, his bag of exercise tricks forgotten.

"Not exactly," he said, as if the noncommittal answer bugged him almost as much as it did Travis.

They watched the kids and the cocker spaniel race through the back hedges and head toward the front of the house, the warm August afternoon drenched with happy barks and laughter. Joe thought back to that morning's walk with Marsha, and how it could have been his lowest moment. This was his first official day of leave. But he'd been with his bride of thirty-five years. And instead of rushing to work, he'd admitted that he was too weak to keep up the charade that he didn't need more time to heal.

And for the first time since his heart attack, instead of his hating the dawn, it had felt like a new day. A fresh start. Because Marsha had been there, no matter what. Even if everything else in their lives had to change now, they were facing this next chapter together. Their love would be there to see them through.

His gaze turned to the insightful young man who seemed so reluctant to be forming the same soul-deep connection with Bethany.

"She's back in the city this afternoon," Joe said, meddling after all. "Some big to-do at the youth center she volunteers at with one of my other daughters."

Mike smiled. "Her mural. It must be time to unveil it for the parents."

"Might be a good opportunity for you to get that message from her in person." Joe promised himself he was done. This was the end of it. Except none of the rest of what he thought was happening mattered, unless he was right about one other thing. "That is, if you love the girl."

Mike dropped to the bench on the other side of the table. Travis sat beside Joe, forearms braced on the scarred wood, staring at Mike.

"Do you?" Joe's boy asked. At the flash of almost misery on Mike's face, Travis swiped a hand over his mouth. "Oh my God. You do."

Mike kept his focus on Joe, the panic in his gaze saying that he was only now realizing the truth himself. "You really think I should go down there? I left her a message. She hasn't called me back."

Travis crossed his arms. "What the hell? Go after her!"

Mike snorted. "Says the guy who not so long ago wanted to rearrange my face because you caught me kissing her."

"That was different."

Joe held up his hand. "Do you love her?"

"Yes, sir." Mike's response was halting. He sounded as rattled as Bethany had over the phone. "Sunday night . . . We talked about things I don't think either one of us expected to. I didn't at least . . ."

Joe nodded. He'd worked with enough troubled young men searching for answers to understand how hard those kinds of words could be to say.

"She talked about her past?" Joe asked.

"Bethie doesn't talk about her childhood," his son said.

"Well, she did." Fury flashed across Mike's face. "Some of it. Enough of it."

"Damn," Travis said. "No wonder she's spooked."

Joe smiled at the exchange that was like listening to his two oldest boys bickering. "She hasn't given many people a chance to know that part of her."

"Can you blame her?" Travis asked. "Especially after all those losers she's dated, like Carrington."

Joe patted his son's shoulder, leaving his palm there for support. Travis and Oliver had been overprotective of Bethany from the get-go. "She started guarding that heart of hers when she was only a little thing. She's gotten damn good at it over the years."

"Until Cowboy Bob here came along."

Joe squeezed Travis's arm and let go. He watched Mike from across the table that had been the site of countless Dixon family meals and conversations, and priceless, life-changing confrontations just like this one.

"I do love her," Mike said to himself, as if he were the only one there. "I want to love her and help her and be with her for as long as I can."

"And how long would that be?" Travis wanted to know.

Joe pushed himself slowly to his feet.

"That falls firmly into the *none of our business* column. Assuming . . ." he said to Mike, "that you're going to get yourself showered and changed and into Atlanta to see after my daughter. That's all I'm going to insist on. Don't leave her alone in this, no matter how much she thinks she wants to be. Whatever happens next, you two owe it to each other to figure it out together."

Travis and Mike stood, too.

Travis held out his hand to Mike, almost begrudgingly. "Don't mess with her heart, and you won't have any more problems with me."

Mike hesitated.

"Thank you," he said as he shook.

"Marsha's been after me to invite you for dinner." Joe had told his wife that morning that maybe it wasn't a good idea. Now his physical therapist sounded like a man who needed the support of family around him, almost as much as Joe's daughter did. "We're having everyone over Friday night. It'll be a zoo. You should join us."

"For family dinner?" Mike asked.

And Joe had thought the guy sounded nervous before. He steered Mike toward the sliding door to the kitchen. Travis followed them inside.

"Assuming Bethie hasn't kicked you to the curb by then," Joe's boy added with a laugh.

Chapter Fourteen

By the time Mike arrived at the Midtown Youth Center, the last of the crowd from Bethany's mural presentation had been making their way down the granite steps of the two-story redbrick building. A volunteer heading out to her car had directed Mike to the center's common area, saying that Bethany and Shandra were in the activity director's office with one of their students. He'd found his way, his footsteps echoing through the quickly quieting building.

Bethany and Shandra and the man the volunteer had called Shawn were in a tiny room composed mostly of windows, hunkered down, quietly talking with a mid-thirties-looking mother and her little girl. Bethany's student from her last class, Mike gathered. Shandra sat on the floor, Darby in her lap, quietly sharing a picture book. The adult conversation going on around them seemed intense, but something about it told Mike that good things were happening for the family Bethany and her sister had championed.

He could see it in the way Bethany was hugging her arms around herself. In the smile she and Shandra exchanged when

Darby laughed at something in the book and ran to show her mother. Mike was witnessing a normal, happy, safe moment. Thanks to the community art program Bethany had been instrumental in bringing to life.

He checked out the floor-to-ceiling mural that dominated an entire wall of the common area. It was the cumulative work of four different classes, Bethany's residency essay had said. Done by kids ranging in ages from five to thirteen, it was the culmination of months of volunteer hours.

It comprised images from all over Atlanta, enthusiastically painted in a crayon box of colors. Trees and buildings and sidewalks and cars. Pets and families and friends. They were miniature masterpieces, some little more than blobs of hastily applied paint, others crafted with more precision. Rendered with passion and excitement, each tiny tableau was a reflection of the fun and exuberance and the imagination of childhood. Mike pulled out his phone to capture a few pictures. Several boys and a girl ran up to show off their squares to their parents.

Bethany finally noticed him from inside the office. Her instant smile erased his doubts that maybe he'd made a mistake in coming. The mother was standing and taking her little girl's hand to leave. Darby gave Shandra a huge grin. She turned to Bethany, who smothered her in a hug.

The director opened the office door. The little girl waved and followed her mom out. Bethany and her sister watched them go, looking worried but happy and more than a little relieved. And then Shandra caught sight of Mike.

"Hey!" She rushed over. "My mom texted and said she was coming to pick me up tonight."

"What?" Bethany approached more slowly. "When?"

"Dad told her Mike was coming." Shandra rummaged in her backpack for her smartphone. "She just texted. She's out front at the curb. See ya later, Mike."

"Wait a minute." Bethany would have headed after her.

Mike caught her arm.

"Your mom left Chandlerville right after I did," he explained, "after your dad talked me into coming. Your family seems to have warmed up to the idea of us spending time together."

Bethany hustled him away from Shawn. The man had leaned against his office's door to watch, along with two other adults who'd joined Shawn after straggling in to collect their offspring.

"What do you mean, Joe asked you to come?" Bethany demanded when she and Mike reached the hallway.

"He gave me your message."

"What message?"

Mike ducked his head. "He seemed pretty sure that you don't know what to do with what you're feeling about us, any more than I do."

"Oh."

"I should have come and found you sooner." Mike smiled. "But I'm glad I got to see all of this. You're in your element here. Helping kids discover their love of art. Making sure another child isn't being hurt the way you were."

"It's . . ." His compliment seemed to make her uneasy instead of proud. "It's not the same thing."

"It's always the same thing."

He remembered feeling powerless to help Jeremy, and furious with their parents for not realizing that doctors and hospital rooms and the best equipment and medicine money could buy were only a small part of what their son—both their sons—needed.

"Making troubled children feel safe," he said, "can change their world. So can inspiring them. I saw your mural. Your project's a success."

Bethany eased closer, into his arms. "The kids did all the work."

"You know better than that." He kissed her. "I know better than that."

She smiled.

And then she punched him in the arm.

"Ow!" He rubbed the spot. "What was that for?"

"You. Inviting my family to meddle in our business."

"I can't picture your family ever waiting for an invitation. Besides . . ."

He thought of his own art project. The one he'd worked on nonstop the last two days, until he'd had to bug out for his session with Joe.

"Besides?" The flash of doubt in her eyes had him kissing her sweetly.

And then with more heat as her tongue feathered across his lips. Sampling. Needing. Promising. Flashing him back to their meadow. Her soft skin. Her sweet sighs of surprise. Their shared excitement and discovery and total abandon. He realized he was raising her onto her toes. He made himself ease off.

"I should have come and found you sooner," he repeated.

She shook her head. "You were giving me time."

"I was giving myself time," he admitted. "I—"

"You don't have to explain," she rushed out. "We both wanted more, remember? And I totally get why you live your life the way you do. But I . . . I don't think I can do this."

"This?"

"No more pretending, remember? And I can't keep pretending that I'm going to be okay once you're gone. I thought I could be. I really did. But I can't, Mike. Not after Sunday."

He could feel his pulse racing, his heart hanging on every word.

"I want more," she blurted out, inhaling before continuing. "More of tonight, helping Darby and her mom get her brother the counseling he needs, so they can stay together as a family. More working with my kids here with Shandra. More time with my family and friends in Chandlerville. More of my painting. Even if I never finish another canvas, I'm going to keep trying. And all of that's hard enough for me to imagine sticking with, without wondering if you'll be around, when you'll go, or even if you . . . realize how much I need you to stay. It's terrifying, Mike, how much I want you to stay, even though I said I wouldn't expect you to."

Mike dug his hands into his pockets, staring at the boots that had taken him away from so many moments of his life that he hadn't minded letting go of.

"And what if I told you I wanted more, too?" he admitted. "Would that make this easier, or more terrifying for you?"

"What if I . . ." Wrinkles of confusion formed between her eyebrows. "What if I told you that I loved you?"

Mike brushed back a lock of her bangs that had escaped the same sparkly headband she'd worn for their date. She was so sweet. Too sweet to have endured so much and still be this strong. Too sweet for the likes of him.

"Then I'd feel brave enough," he said, "to admit that I haven't known a lot of love, not the kind you deserve. But whatever there is of it inside me, it's already yours."

Bethany followed Mike through the side entrance to the loft, up his private stairs, and into his studio. He led her past his enormous desk, deeper into the outrageously masculine space until they'd reached the far end of the room—where her unfinished landscape of the Dixon house stood on an easel. Beside it was a worktable littered with the paints and supplies she'd gathered for her first session in the loft.

"Wh . . . when did you do this?" she asked.

"That night you stormed out of here. When you were ready, I wanted you to have something to come back to."

"But . . ." A piece of Bethany had been here with him all this time. "I wasn't sure I was ever going to speak to you again."

"Neither was I."

But he'd moved her into his workspace anyway.

Track lighting had been redirected, creating a perfect pool of illumination around the easel, bright enough to spotlight color and texture and detail. Not so harsh that her eyes would strain as she worked. She scanned the craziness of her supplies, screaming their disarray at the minimalism of his creative space.

She stared at her painting. The ethereal brushwork, the wash of color, deepening and softening in seemingly unplanned seeps of green on cream on white and the palest of grays. Frustration rushed back, at everything the piece could be, and everything it wasn't yet.

Her first love had been her art, he'd said, and she almost hated it now.

Mike studied her work with a critical eye. "It's an amazing perspective."

"It's empty." She saw only the ghostly heart of the near-transparent house. "Like no one lives there."

"But you want to." His hand rubbed down her spine. "I can feel how much you want to—"

"Belong," she finished for him. She wanted to belong completely to the life and passion and love of her foster parents' world. "But this? I look at it, and it feels . . ."

"Lonely?"

She curled an arm around him, a little numb from the things they'd said at the youth center.

Love wasn't a new thing for either of them. But fighting to hold on to it was. And she'd had a head start—the time she'd spent back with her family the last few months, letting her need for them in, in spurts and starts. Hearing Mike say he wanted to try the same thing with her . . .

Risky was too weak a word to describe them now.

He dug his phone from his pocket and scrolled through his photo app, arriving at his picture of her portrait of Camille.

"Did you feel lonely when you painted her?" He handed over the phone.

Even unfinished, her niece's beauty shone through. Camille's impish smile, her sparkling green eyes, her dark curls bouncing.

"Every time I look at her," Bethany whispered, "I feel like I'm home." She stared at her attempt to capture the Dixon house. "But then it's like I can't breathe when I think of how much I need all of them."

"So exhale, and let yourself need them." Mike turned her away from the easel, into his arms. "Need them and me and whatever you have to while you're here. Get lost in it, get comfortable with it, until you finish one of your paintings. Until you know that you're home."

"Here?" She blinked. "In your studio?"

"I have some work to do in the darkroom on my project for the next JHTF gala. I'll stay out of your way. I'll give you the codes to the doors. Come and go as you please. Or"—he led her toward the desk—"we could work together on making sure your art stops feeling lonely."

Bethany followed. "Together?"

Working with Harrison Michael Taylor.

"On something different for both of us," he said with that charming, easy smile. "Without you tossing away everything you've already done, and without me continuing to do my thing alone, like I'm nursing some damn grudge against the world. It could be fun."

"Fun?"

"Sit." He settled her behind the desk, in his chair.

He stood behind her, reaching around to drive the keyboard and mouse. A digital art program sprang to life on his enormous monitor.

"Close your eyes." He waited until she did, and then he clicked away with the mouse. "It's only a rough start. I did a lot of it in the middle of the night, so use your imagination." He sounded as nervous as she'd felt following him around her studio at Dru and Brad's. "But for a first attempt, I think the results are promising."

She felt him kneel beside her.

"Open up," he said.

She did, dying to see what he'd done. And then she stared, until her eyes insisted on blinking.

"It's . . ."

She couldn't finish her sentence.

Her thought.

Any thought.

He'd transformed his iPhone shots of her stop-and-start paintings from her studio into something unexpected and confusing and exciting—just like everything else about the man.

She took over the mouse and scrolled through each series of photos, some black and white, others full color. He'd cut and cropped and matted the pictures of her paintings together, layered them on top of one another in one collection, side-by-side in another. In the next, he'd worked in photos that he'd taken of the kids outside Marsha and Joe's house the day he'd arrived to meet Joe for the first time.

In another set he'd used images from around Chandlerville—overlaid, filmy, opaque, barely a whisper of them at times—combined with her various attempts at landscapes of the meadow and pond. She recognized the interior of Dan's. Grapes & Beans. McC's. Familiar people and places and shapes, filling up the empty spaces of her half-finished work, her halting visions of the life in Chandlerville.

And then she switched to a final collage of images and froze.

"Camille," she said. "Oh, Mike . . ."

"What do you see?" Mike took off his hat, tossing it onto the desk, feeling like a little boy showing off his new toy, wanting Bethany to love it as much as he did.

He'd grouped one final, very special collection of photos. Bethany's half-finished portrait of her niece, matched with a sampling of Camille's exuberant photographs. Selena had been happy to contribute, once he'd explained what he was hoping to do and why. He'd borrowed from images of Camille's grammy's flowers and quilts, a bedraggled blue bunny, her new puppy. Cookies that she'd baked with Marsha. A shot of her snuggling with Joe in his recliner in the Dixon living room.

Some of the shots Mike had cropped into pieces, forming a border for Bethany's barely begun portrait. Some were interwoven into a near-transparent background. He'd layered and overlaid and filtered, accenting Bethany's beautiful work with the washes of color she'd dreamed of, enhancing the open spaces and the emotion she'd shied away from capturing completely. He'd hoped to obliterate the isolation she'd seemed to have felt each time he'd watched her gaze at what she'd created. He'd finished it just that morning, thinking he'd maybe never get the chance to show her.

He eased Bethany's hand away from the mouse. "What are you seeing?"

Her fingers laced around his. "My niece looks so happy."

"So do you," he said, "smiling at her now, the way you weren't before when you looked at your portrait."

"Because I couldn't do this on my own. You've made her so beautiful." She turned to Mike, flowing into his arms, holding on to him like a lifeline. "Thank you. My parents will love it."

He helped Bethany to her feet, claimed the desk chair himself, and settled her in his lap, both of them facing the monitor. He ignored the sweet friction of her soft backside nestling against him. Anticipation flared, but not for more sex. He wanted more of her excitement for what she was seeing, what she could do with it, and what they could do together.

Maybe in her art he could show her the kind of love he didn't know how to shower her with in real life.

"*We* made something beautiful," he said.

Whatever happens next, you two owe it to each other to figure it out together.

"And it's just a start," he added, "if you want to work on your parents' present together. Camille's quilts were my inspiration, and your residency application about your mural project at the youth center. Merging beautiful, disjointed pieces of things to make them a stronger whole than they could be on your own."

"Together?"

"Let me walk you through the art software. You'll be up and running in a flash."

"With what?"

"Whatever you want. Sky's the limit. This will be a totally free creative space. No expectations or boundaries. No worries about getting anything wrong or right or even finished."

He kissed the side of Bethany's neck. Minimized Camille's collection and all the others, making them smaller and smaller until they were a vibrant pattern of thumbnails within the art package's workspace, displayed together on his oversized screen as if they were a palette of oil paints. He moved them around, deftly working with contrast and texture, using the shading of one grouping to offset the vibrancy of another.

"Think about all that history, everything you love about your home and your family and your life in Chandlerville," he said, waiting for Bethany to see it, too. "How each piece of your world fits. Exactly the way your parents have made sure each of you kids have fit, no matter where you came from before."

Mike continued rearranging the photo collections, minimizing some of them more, shifting others to create new shapes, interlocking them into a design that drew the eye to see an overall image, instead of each individual piece.

"Do you see?" he asked.

Bethany concentrated, her eyes squinting. "It's . . . like a mural."

He accessed the menu and reduced the opacity and saturation of the pattern he'd created, making it nearly transparent. And then he opened one final image that he'd saved for last, vibrant and full of light. Feeling Bethany tense, he rolled the new digital photo over the rest.

"My painting of the house." Her hand covered his, sliding it away from the mouse. "My parents' entire life, their town, their history."

"*Your* history," he reminded her. "Your family. Your paintings. It's your life, too. Your art."

He kissed the side of her neck again.

"Work with me here, Bethany. It's been a long time since I've had this much fun playing with something. Let me show you. I know you'll love it, too. Work with me, here in my studio. Let's see what we can do together."

You're never going to know what's over that cliff you're clinging to . . .

"I can't believe you did all of this."

Bethany was still trying to grasp that Mike was so close and offering her so much, with need in his voice as he asked her to work with him, to create beautiful things with him and let whatever love he could give her be enough.

"*You* did this," he insisted. "I was going to send you copies of all of it, even if you decided you couldn't see me anymore. So you'd know just how good your newer work is. How much of the life you want back is already there, inspiring you to paint. You just need to mix things up a little so you can see the potential of what you're doing."

"Mix things up a little with you?"

She relaxed into Mike's body, his praise and excitement, feeling a creative door open wider, along with her heart. The mixed-media approach he'd taken with her work fascinated her. Several of the co-op's artists were doing similar things with digital photography techniques. But it had never occurred to Bethany to try something like this herself.

Mike kissed her cheek. "Tell me you're in."

She wanted to be. She wanted all of it. She wanted all of *them* she could get. But everything would remain shimmering just out of her reach, unless she let go and let herself fall.

"You're not playing fair," she said.

"Life isn't fair." His hands roamed up her body, her sides, until strong, talented fingers caressed the contours of her breasts with phantom-like strokes. "But whatever I have, whatever I can give you, is yours if you want it."

"*If* I want it?"

She turned in the chair, straddling his lap and wrapping her arms around his neck. He kissed both her eyes.

"For now?" she asked.

"For as long as you tell me I'm good for you."

It was such a solemn promise. And a telling one. There was a part of Mike that believed his best would never be good enough, either.

"You're very, very good for me." She glanced at her painting on the easel. At the beautiful images he'd made for her on his computer. "You're so good, I don't know how to say no. You're the one who needs to be sure this time, that this is what you want."

She kissed him, his taste and hungry groan unraveling the last of her control. She began unbuttoning his shirt, pulled it away from his chest. She needed his skin beneath her hands.

"Because I'm warning you." She moved on to the buckle of his belt, and then the fastenings of his jeans. "I can be impossible to deal with when I'm painting."

He grinned. "I certainly hope so."

His hands relieved her of her blouse and long skirt, her underthings—far less sexy things than she'd worn Sunday night. Rough fingers excited, distracted, made her ravenous.

"Be as difficult as you want," he said. "But work with me. Stay with me. Let me help you feel as good as I do, every time I see this beautiful face."

He caressed her cheeks with his thumbs. It was such a sweet, familiar gesture. A rainbow of color burst through Bethany, happiness and joy and a tenuous sense of belonging that she promised herself they could nurture.

"You really want this?" she asked.

He drew her closer, skin to skin, his fingers threading through her hair, removing her headband. He tilted her face and fed from her lips, drowning her in the escape, the fall.

"I really want this," he said, his gaze stormy.

He carried her toward a tiny room on the other side of the office. It contained a bed, a nightstand, a four-drawer chest, and a wall-mounted TV. And beyond that, another door to what looked like his darkroom. He eased her down to the covers, his smile wickedly carnal.

"Hi," he said, his body pressing close, his jeans half-unfastened, his hiking boots still on.

"Hi, yourself," she answered back.

Chapter Fifteen

Bethany surfaced, buried in Mike's strong arms.

She was sprawled on top of him, actually, in his bed in the loft. They'd made love a second time before he'd tucked her into the curve of his body, and she'd drifted off for hours—sleeping through the night for the first time since she could remember.

Predawn light pinkened the sky beyond his bedroom's closed blinds. She was scheduled for prep at the Whip. Which meant a walk of shame was in her near future, slithering into Dru and Brad's to change for the new day. And after a morning at the Whip, there was wedding stuff planned. Girl stuff that she couldn't miss, didn't want to miss, *wouldn't* miss.

But first things first.

She snuggled back into the comfort of Mike's deep breathing. The peaceful smile on his face made her want to do a victory dance. To hell with the instincts cautioning her to slow down, be more careful, and hold just a little bit of her heart back, just in case. She'd dreamed last night about her painting of her parents' house. About the work Mike had done with his photos of her canvases, meshed with the people and places she loved in

Chandlerville. Her kids at the youth center had made an appearance, too, as she slept. Along with their mural.

Bethany's connection to all of it had felt so real. Solid. Everything she'd always wanted had been hers to create with, to be a part of. Because Mike had been there, helping her see that she already belonged—entrusting his enormous heart to her, and needing her love in return.

A blast of electronic music sounded from the general direction of his desk. Mike startled awake to the accompaniment of the Darth Vader theme from *Star Wars*. She laughed. She pressed her hands to his chest to push herself up. One of his palms stroked her bottom. The other swiped across his beard stubble.

He popped a single eye open, read his watch, and groaned at the time. His phone went silent. The buzzer that game shows used when you got an answer wrong sounded next, announcing either a voice mail or a text. And then Vader began again.

"Damn." Mike beat his head against the pillows. "The woman needs a mute button."

Bethany slid away and watched him sit on the edge of the bed, staring at his feet. A chill speared through her at the solitary figure he cut.

"Woman?" She rubbed her arms to warm them.

He snorted. "My mother."

"Oh." Bethany stood next to the bed while he stared into his dimly lit office. His mother's ringtone ended, followed by another message alert. "I'm going to excuse myself in here."

Bethany disappeared into the tiny bathroom. He'd told her enough about his own troubled childhood and his strained relationship with his parents to let her know he'd want his privacy while he dealt with his mother. She heard his phone sound off again, and the bed creak as he stood. She ran water in the sink, letting it warm.

His toothbrush and toothpaste were on the counter. Medical supplies, too, that she assumed were for his insulin pump. He'd been so nonchalant about it last night, disconnecting it so deftly she'd barely noticed, and then checking his glucose and reconnecting it, using a leg band, before going to sleep. Easy, smiling, kissing her, he'd reminded Bethany not to worry about him before he'd snuggled her close.

How long had it been since Mike had let someone worry about him?

She checked her reflection in the mirror and bit back a squeal. Her eyes widened. Her spiky haircut was smashed to the side of her head, stray pieces jutting out in every direction like a cartoon character's.

"Life most definitely isn't fair," she told her image, sticking out her tongue and using her hands to wet her bangs and restore order.

She washed her face, swiped toothpaste on her finger, and did the best she could with her teeth. She dried off on a bath towel that smelled like Mike's cologne. Wrapping it around her body, the sexy odor lingering, she found the bedroom empty and Mike in his office, dressed in yesterday's wrinkled shirt and jeans. He'd leaned his hip against the edge of the desk. Her rumpled skirt and blouse were neatly folded beside him, bra and panties on top.

Arms crossed, his expression guarded, he saw Bethany and smiled. She rushed into his arms, kissing him, loving the feel of him savoring her, his fingers skimming her bottom beneath the towel, fanning her need to have him one more time before she hustled back to Chandlerville.

Then he inched her away with a grimace.

"She's downstairs," he said.

It took Bethany a moment to follow. She was instantly, excruciatingly aware of her near-nakedness.

"Your mother?"

"She has the timing of a black-ops strike team." He laughed, like for a minute he'd forgotten how to. Then he winked. "You never see Livy Taylor coming, until you've taken the bullet between your eyes."

"I should . . . get dressed." Bethany reached for her things, jumping when his touch stalled her.

"We've done nothing wrong."

"I know that."

He pulled her against his body and kissed her.

Her heart caught a little. She snatched up her clothes. "Go see what your mother wants, before she barges in and catches me like this."

Mike nodded, something about him, in his eyes, his energy, different. Distant.

Chalking it up to his mom-vasion, Bethany headed toward the bedroom. She turned back and caught his slow smile, his attention rising from her backside to her face. He slipped his hat on.

"Be right back, darlin'," he teased before heading out.

"Mother." Mike peered through the closed, shadowed windows of the Lincoln Town Car parked at the curb outside the loft. Every cell in his body wanted to be back upstairs with Bethany. "What are you doing here?"

Ignoring Livy's call the way he'd wanted to, and her suspiciously timed visit, would have made his mother even more determined to have his attention. Otherwise, he would still be upstairs in bed with Bethany.

The window rolled down. One perfectly manicured hand reached through it for his, a stream of tobacco smoke wafting through the opening like something sinister in a Disney cartoon.

"You invited your father and me down for a visit," said the beautiful woman within, brittle smile beckoning. "Why don't you join me. I have coffee. We can catch up."

"I don't think so."

He'd worked in countless smoke-filled bars and it never fazed him. But being in an enclosed space with his mother and the habit that was slowly killing her was a deal breaker for Mike.

With a sophisticated pout, Livy disappeared into the luxury car. The door finally unlocked. He opened it and helped her step out gracefully. She was dressed head-to-toe in lightweight cashmere. Black, of course. She was a stylish New York woman displaying her affluence to its best advantage at all times. Conservative, elegant, bland. Topped off with stiletto heels and the high-end bag of the season.

He'd never known her to wear anything else. No one had. A few years back a rumor had made it all the way to page six that Olivia Taylor's will contained a wardrobe clause, instructing that she be buried in her one-of-a-kind, gold-embossed Alexander McQueen platforms.

"George will let you know when your prints for the gala have gone to the framers," he said.

"Yes." His mother studied him through the dark lenses of sunglasses she didn't need. It would be another hour before the sun rose high enough to clear the tops of the Atlanta skyline. "Your business manager and I exchanged emails. Georgina is the one who told me you were holed up at the office again instead of her. She sounds terribly busy. I wish you hadn't delegated the gala to her, too. It's a family matter you should be handling yourself. It must be such a terrible imposition."

"George is family to me," Mike reminded her. "Jeremy thought so, too. Plus I pay her a king's ransom for the luxury of imposing on her. And she's enjoying thinking the gala prints through with me. She misses Jeremy as much as I do."

His mother sighed at Mike's reasonable response to her opening guilt salvo. She reached into her Hermès Birkin for another cigarette and lit up.

"Aren't you going to invite me up?" She released an exasperated stream of smoke into the morning breeze. "You can tell me more about the good you keep insisting you two are doing in these places of yours. Besides, it's not polite to leave your mother loitering at the curb."

Mike stared at his boots. "I'm not alone, Mom."

"Oh?" His mother didn't have the poker face for feigning surprise. "Is that so?"

"Yes, it's so. Why do I have the sinking suspicion you already knew that?" And why did his mother suddenly care?

"I suppose when I spoke with Georgina yesterday and she mentioned you were in the city instead of immersing yourself in your small-town escape, I might have wondered at the reason."

"What I've been doing and with whom isn't something you've bothered wondering about for years." His mother was up to no good. And he didn't want it anywhere near Bethany. "Let me see my friend off, and then we can—"

"Hey," a soft voice said from behind him.

Mike's mother stared over his shoulder and smiled her emptiest smile.

Mike turned toward Bethany and her vibrant, unflinching authenticity. Of course she hadn't waited upstairs or tried to sneak to her truck without being seen. She glanced between him and Livy. She hesitated. When he didn't say anything, she focused on his mother.

"I don't mean to interrupt." Bethany smiled. "I'm on my way out. But it's a pleasure to meet you. I'm Bethany Darling."

"Of course you are, dear." Livy drew in another lungful of toxins and exhaled in Bethany's direction.

"I'm . . . I'm sorry?" Bethany asked.

Livy slid her attention toward Mike. "When the Developing Artist grant director told me what, and whom, you were rooting around in our scholarship archives asking questions about, I asked him to do a little legwork for me. He checked George's latest reports from your co-op here, to see if there were any connections I needed to be aware of."

Mike shoved his hat higher on his head. "When was the last time you felt the need to be aware of anything relating to my art centers?"

"Foundation grant money helps seed your nonprofits," his mother said. "Your business manager sends our legal department monthly updates on the artists whose work is being supported by those donations. For tax purposes, of course. I have to hand it to you, my dear"—Livy directed another stream of smoke at Bethany—"you do fast work. Receiving your residency here less than a month ago, and you're already moving up the food chain."

"What?" Bethany's hand slid into Mike's, almost protectively, as if he were the one his mother was attacking.

"That's not what happened." Mike tried to draw Bethany behind him. She stayed right where she was, facing Livy on her own. "Bethany's father is my physical therapy patient in a town not far from here. I recognized her name. That's when I looked into her connection to the Artist Co-op and the JHTF scholarship."

Livy dropped her cigarette to the curb and ground it out with the toe of her Vuitton. "So I can reassure the foundation's board that it's purely by chance that the latest recipient of your largesse at this center is also a new . . . *friend*, whom you're taking a personal interest in?"

"I earned my residency," Bethany told her. "The same way I earned my scholarship."

"She secured her spot to work at the Artist Co-op entirely on her own, Mother. And she and I have become more than friends."

Livy took stock of their wrinkled clothing. "Obviously."

Bethany shifted her backpack higher on her shoulder. "I had no idea who your son was when we met, Mrs. Taylor."

"And yet here you are, first thing in the morning, stumbling out of his studio. One wonders what comes next. My son's personal influence with your career? His professional support at a show? He has so many contacts, and he adores helping people"—Livy turned to Mike—"even though his father and I can't get him to own up to his identity on behalf of his brother's memory. Or to help with the work Harrison and I have devoted our lives to, trying to eradicate the disease that took Jeremy from us."

"I'm sorry." Mike blocked his mother from Bethany's view, stepping between them and turning to face Bethany. "Let me—"

She kissed him softly.

"*I'm* sorry," she said, ignoring Livy. "But I promised Dru I'd get to the Whip early."

He grazed her cheek with his lips. "Go. I'll see you tonight."

"Mrs. Taylor." Bethany nodded at his mother and headed around the building toward her truck.

"It was lovely to meet you," Livy called after her.

Livy watched until Bethany was out of sight. Then she sighed. "Really, Michael?"

He braced himself to let his mother have it. Then he noticed Mateo and his entourage on the sidewalk across the street. They were out for their morning constitutional and had stopped to gawk.

"Either get in your car and head back to the airport," Mike told his mother, "or come upstairs. I'm not doing the rest of whatever this is on the street."

"Such a heartfelt invitation. How can I refuse?"

Livy bent to the partially open front passenger window.

"Wait for me here," she said to her driver.

"This way." Mike headed down the alley.

He could have waited to see if she followed. He could have taken her through the co-op studio space, which had an elevator. But there were artists scheduled to work that morning, and some of them liked to get an early start. And even if keeping his identity separate from their work weren't the cornerstone of his ability to do what he did for them, he wouldn't dream of disrupting the creative energy of the space with the confrontation his mother seemed determined to instigate.

He punched in his code and opened the street-level door to his space, holding it wide, waiting.

His mother balked at the stairs. "In these shoes?"

"Take them off."

She sighed and slipped out of her man-eater heels. "I guess I should have packed my prairie skirt and sandals."

Mike didn't respond to her dig at Bethany. He followed his mother up and listened to her breathing become alarmingly labored before they neared the top. She ignored it, of course, expecting him to as well. He keyed in his code again and opened the door to the studio.

She hovered on the threshold of his private world, his photographs ultimately drawing her inside. She inspected each one with the critical, dispassionate eye of a collector.

“Have you really donated every penny you’ve earned from these?” was her only comment. “Is that some publicity agent’s brainchild?”

“I don’t do publicity.” Mike followed her, not liking how much he longed for her expert opinion of his work—if only her judgment could somehow be separated from the fact that the art was his. “Money was never what they were about.”

“No.” She’d reached the far corner of the studio. She could see into his bedroom and the disarray he and Bethany had made of his sheets and comforter. “They’re about you not wanting any part of your father and me.”

“They’re about searching for what I need in life.” Searching for the kind of love he’d lost with Jeremy, Mike realized, and was beginning to connect with in Chandlerville.

“And installing yourself in places like this Podunk you’re working in now? Is it really necessary for you to flaunt how little chance your family has of you ever coming home for good? People need help in New York, too, Michael. The city’s full of artists and the sick and people with no money. Imagine how much good you could accomplish there.”

“I’m not moving back to New York.” Manhattan was where Jeremy had died. Where their family had fallen apart. New York was done for Mike forever, no matter how upsetting his decision was for his parents.

Livy shook her head. “I keep waiting for you to get all of this out of your system. To accept the life you were meant to live.”

"This"—he looked around his studio, his gaze resting on Bethany's easel and painting—"is the life I'm meant to live. Wherever I can help. Wherever I can discover something that inspires me to create."

"And what exactly have you discovered here?"

Livy confronted Bethany's canvas, then moved to the desk where his work with the image of Bethany's half-finished painting of the Dixon house was displayed. It was such an intimate, poignant reflection of the family and community Bethany loved, he wanted to click it closed. Protect her somehow from Livy's jaded reaction.

"Very inspiring." His mother studied the collage, then the original canvas. "Your new protégé's good."

"Bethany's not my protégé."

"Then what is she?"

"She's . . . unexpected. Honest." Bethany had been showing him how to be honest from the very start, though she'd been running from her own truth, too. "She's the strongest woman I've ever met."

Livy eked out a tight nod, a sliver of a smile. "Is the sex really that good?"

"Leave it alone, Mother." He wasn't doing this with her. "I don't know why you've dug yourself out of your *very* busy life and thought you'd be welcome to meddle in mine. But you're going to leave Bethany alone."

Real emotion passed between them for the first time since her arrival.

Livy's lingering hurt at his years-ago rejection pulled at the hard edges of her sophisticated mask. Her reaction reignited Mike's pain at her abandonment—when his parents hadn't come after him when he'd fled New York. Her showing an interest in his choices right after Jeremy's death might have made a difference. It left Mike feeling violent now.

"Because this girl is your true love?" she asked. "Because you feel some responsibility toward bettering her sad life? Or is this something to do with the anniversary of your brother's death? Is it possible you've made your own existence so lonely, you'd latch on to any stranger who came along, for as long as you needed her to feel better."

"Lonely?"

"You made your entire teenage world about your brother. And then when he was gone and your father and I, your family, needed you most, you wanted nothing to do with us. Loneliness is the price you pay for that kind of selfishness."

"My *family* could have been a part of my life anytime you and Dad wanted. Just not *the way* you wanted. So you let me go. You were glad to see me go, and the feeling was mutual. I've known exactly what I've been doing all this time, and so have you."

And it hadn't felt lonely—at least not to Mike, not until he'd met Bethany.

"And what exactly are you doing now?" his mother demanded to know. "You could certainly offer this girl and her family a great deal. But how long is it going to last until you're glad to see them go, too?"

"A woman like Bethany's not looking for anyone to offer her anything. She's fought for whatever she has. She gives away more than she keeps. And her family already has a lot."

A lot that they were offering Mike, as if he had every right to be a part of them.

The collage he'd built around Bethany's painting of the Dixon home told her foster family's remarkable story. Creating it and the other collections had consumed Mike, when he could have spent the last few days finalizing Jeremy's series of prints for the foundation gala.

His photographs of Chandlerville were pretty. But they were a stranger's idealized perspective of a close-knit community. It had taken Bethany's art to make them personal and give them heart. It was her work that showcased the unbreakable bond that could form between people who knew how to love deeply and forever.

"The Dixons already have everything they need."

"And everything you need?" Livy stared at him. Beautiful. Polished. Smart. Intuitive. "What is all of this, Michael?"

She was hurt. Genuinely hurt, beneath her perfect makeup and clothes and Upper East Side calm. She wore the same wounded expression as when Mike had chosen to live his own life and honor his brother's last wishes—instead of embracing the emotional shambles of a family that would have shackled him to his parents' glitzy existence.

"Mom . . ."

He put his arm around her. Whatever they'd been through, she was his mother. He tried to find something to say that would help Livy understand what she hadn't been able to when he'd been nineteen.

That he needed more. That he always had. More than his parents had needed from life and from his brother's death. Mike had needed more from living than their money and privilege defining everything he would ever be. He'd needed to go and give and feel something besides loss. He'd needed to move.

And now, after a decade, he didn't anymore.

Bethany and her light and her world were there now. Her Chandlerville. Her journey, so very different but so strangely similar. Her creative energy had inspired him. Her imagination, her passion, was a second chance filling his empty arms. Her love was grounding him for the first time since he was a kid. All that Bethany had become in his life left him aching for more, each moment they were apart.

"Whatever all this is," he said to his mother, "I need you to stay out of it. I need you to trust that I know what's best for my life. I don't expect you to understand. I'm not sure I do yet, not completely. But I'm closer to being happy than I have been in a long time. And I need *you* to be happy about that. Not suspicious or jealous or tracking me down to make trouble."

"So now my visiting you is making trouble?" Livy sifted through her purse for her cigarettes. "Like your father and I were making trouble when you and your brother shut us out, even the last months of Jeremy's life, spending all your time together, wanting nothing to do with us."

"You had the foundation marketing team filming his final treatments." The memory of it made Mike sick. "Even when Jeremy was referred to hospice, you were dead set on turning it into a media circus."

"So Jeremy gave his baby brother his healthcare power of attorney, and you barred me from my son's room." Livy's eyes shimmered with tears that she didn't let fall. "Harrison and I wanted your brother's suffering to mean something. To show the world the devastating effects of cystic fibrosis, so we can one day wipe it off the face of the earth and save other families from the loss we suffered."

It was a noble speech, totally glossing over the worst moments of his family's rock-bottom.

"What you should have been doing," Mike said, "was sharing the last weeks of your son's life the way Jeremy wanted to live them."

"Which you prevented, by making me out to be a villain instead of a concerned mother. Just like you are now. How could you be so cruel?"

"I learned from the master, I suppose."

The unwelcome thought made Mike queasy. The fact that he could say it out loud to his mother reminded him exactly who and what he'd come from. He thought of Joe and Marsha Dixon and their blind devotion to raising at-risk kids, many of whom had learned the hard way that they couldn't trust anyone. He thought of the selfless example Bethany's foster parents had set—so that Bethany and Shandra and their other kids would grow up wanting to help others themselves.

Livy went to light a cigarette.

He hitched a thumb toward the stairway door. "Outside, if you want to smoke. I'll walk you back down and make sure your driver knows the way back to the airport."

"Don't be silly." She sounded genuinely surprised. "Take your mother to breakfast."

So they could have another charming heart-to-heart? And since when did Livy put anything in her body before noon besides Marlboro Lights and cappuccino?

She waved away his obvious skepticism. "There must be at least one decent place to eat nearby. Of course, you'd need to change."

She wrinkled her nose at his day-old attire, and then his computer monitor and his work with Bethany's canvas.

"You could make her a star," Livy conceded. An attempt, perhaps, to extend an olive branch? "Is that what you want?"

"I want whatever Bethany wants from her art." And Bethany wanted to love freely, and be loved, and through her art to share the world that meant everything to her. "I don't think being a star has anything to do with it."

"How quaint."

"Enough," Mike snapped. "I don't know why you're really here, but none of this is any of your business. And I have work to do."

"I'm sorry." Livy returned her cigarettes to her purse, her complexion paling beneath her carefully applied makeup. "Really. I didn't fly all the way down here to quarrel. I don't want things between us to be this way. I'm just asking for breakfast. A few hours of your time, Michael, wherever you'd like to go. Let's call a truce."

Mike sighed. Truces with his parents had the shelf life of unrefrigerated milk. But something was definitely off with his mother. Maybe it was the anniversary of losing Jeremy. Maybe Livy really was reaching for something with Mike that she hadn't before. After all, she could have continued snooping into his personal life long-distance, and sharing her running disappointment with his choices over the phone.

He told himself not to care what she thought or where any of this was coming from. But a part of him always would. And if he wanted to avoid more circular conversations like this one, he'd have a better shot of dragging whatever was going on out of his mother in person.

It was just breakfast. And maybe it was a beginning. And maybe . . . while he was sorting out being with Bethany and becoming a part of her life in Chandlerville, he should give his own family another shot at becoming something besides the world that he'd run from.

"Let your driver go." He steered his mother toward the stairs.

He locked up and helped her down the steps this time, looping her arm through his and counterbalancing her skyscraper heels.

"We'll walk to the diner around the corner," he offered. "I'll drop you at the airport when we're through."

"A diner?" Livy sounded as if he'd suggested they eat out of one of the alley's garbage bins. "Wouldn't the Ritz be so much nicer?"

"Where's Cowboy Bob when you need to kiss him?" Shandra scowled out the passenger-side window of Bethany's uber conspicuous truck—at the display Benjie and Norma Carrington were making coming out of Sweetie's Fairway.

"Mike is busy handling his own horror of a mother." Bethany cut the truck's engine, inappropriately mesmerized by the scene unfolding across the street from the Little White Dress Bridal Boutique. She and Shandra were meeting Dru and the rest of Dru's bridal party at LWD for their final dress fittings.

Bethany hadn't decided yet how to tell her family about how quickly her and Mike's relationship was deepening. Or about his help with her art. Or his mother's sudden, less than friendly appearance.

"You gotta feel a little sorry for the guy." Shandra propped her feet on the dash, silver toenail polish sparkling in the afternoon sun as she gawked at Benjie, as if she were watching the scene unfold on the big screen.

He juggled four paper grocery sacks and followed in his mother's wake. When they reached the trunk of Norma's Caddie, she slapped her purse toward her son, leaving Benjie grappling desperately to hold on to its straps while she rooted inside for her keys. The woman kept talking all the while. Complaining or nagging or whatever she was doing to Benjie in high-pitched, rapid-fire angry tones. His features were frozen in the same furious, resentful mask as when he'd gotten so angry at McC's.

"I don't know if *sorry* is what I'm feeling." Bethany released a sigh that felt like stepping back after one of her painting marathons and trying to understand what had appeared on her canvas. "But it's hard to keep hating a guy who's never been taught any better than to despise himself and the world around him."

The way it was easy to love a man like Mike, who'd known so little lasting love in his life but couldn't stop wanting to help and heal other people. His mother had seemed so heartless. While Mike's artistic soul discovered something remarkable every time he looked through the lens of his camera, and he wanted to share whatever he'd found with the world.

"Has she always been that way?" Shandra watched Norma leave Benjie to deal with the trunk, while she marched to the driver's side of the Seville, complaining loudly enough to turn heads up and down the street.

"Not toward Benjie," Bethany said after thinking back about it. "But she and his dad used to bicker all the time. Now there's no one else left, I guess."

And Benjie had evidently convinced himself that putting up with his toxic mother and running the family business into the ground was easier than finding something of his own in life that might finally make him genuinely happy.

He slammed the trunk closed, hung his head, and glanced around to see who had witnessed his latest humiliation. His attention snagged on Bethany. All of a sudden he seemed more lost than angry. And maybe for the first time, as the warm August breeze eased through her truck's open windows, he looked just a little bit sorry.

"Do you hate him?" Shandra asked.

Bethany turned toward her sister, leaving Benjie to stare or go, she couldn't have cared less.

She shook her head. "Everybody has problems. Every family has hard times. Hating people and places for that is what breaks things, not the problems themselves. Look at how Darby's mom is fighting for her family." And how Mike had stayed in touch with his parents, no matter how hard they'd made it or how much distance he'd needed. "I turned my back on Marsha and Joe when I wasn't much older than you, because I didn't understand yet."

Shandra picked at the polish on her little toe. "Understand what?"

"That I was angry at myself, not at them. I was hating the changes I needed to make in me, so my life could finally get better." Changes that could have spared Bethany from crashing through even more bad relationships after Benjie, hooking up with guys who could never have given her what she needed. "I was convinced that everything was happening *to* me, instead of realizing that I had a choice."

Shandra adjusted the bandanna she'd once more wrapped around her head. "A choice about what?"

"To make my world whatever I wanted it to be." Her art. Her family. Her need to love and be loved. "And then I finally chose to come home. So I could change whatever I had to, to stay."

Shandra nodded, looking across the street where Norma was pulling away from the curb. She whipped into the steady stream of traffic and cut off another car. She was talking away, gesturing with both hands instead of holding the wheel, while Benjie stared out his window as if looking for an escape route.

"You never really loved him," Shandra asked, "did you?"

"I thought I did." Bethany remembered Mike's wonder each time he'd stared into her eyes. His admiration for her work with the youth center kids, and her art, and her dedication to her family. "But when I was your age, I didn't feel like I belonged in Chandlerville. And back then, being with Benjie made that fear go away, so I could believe I was going to be okay."

"But we already had a reason to believe that," her sister said. "We have our family."

We.

Our family.

Bethany nodded, smiling with pride, honored that she'd had a small part in Shandra coming so far.

"We're lucky," she agreed.

And she could feel that now, thanks in no small part to the man who kept assuring her that she was amazing to him, just the way she was. And that even though he wanted to help her, she already had within herself everything she needed to help herself.

"I'm thinking," she said to Shandra, "that we're just about the luckiest two girls in the world."

Chapter Sixteen

"Mike's mother?" Selena helped Dru slip into the vintage wedding gown Bethany and her sister had discovered in a high-end Atlanta resale shop.

They'd just finished up their final fittings for the wedding: Dru and her matron of honor, Selena; her bridesmaids, Bethany and Shandra; and Camille, the most excited flower girl *ever.* When they'd arrived at Marsha and Joe's, garment bags in tow and early for dinner, their mother had demanded a fashion show before everyone else arrived.

Marsha and Camille had disappeared into one of the girls' upstairs bedrooms to get Camille into her *fairy princess* dress. From the laughter and squeals that had followed, Camille was enjoying showing off for her audience, while the rest of the bridal party dressed in Marsha and Joe's bedroom.

Bethany and Selena and Shandra were already in their gauzy creations. Dru had chosen her attendants' dresses from the sale catalog of a well-known chain store. The style had been the last of the line's Easter stock. With off-the-shoulder cap sleeves and an empire waist, the design complemented Dru's dress to perfection.

And each attendant had chosen her own color—lavender for Bethany, Easter-egg blue for Selena, and a buttercup yellow that glowed against Shandra's deeper skin tones.

Their head seamstress at Little White Dress was a family friend who'd offered, free of charge, to tailor the length of the skirts to suit each of them. Shandra had designed a trendy high-low effect for hers that had taken the longest to render. Selena's tea-length skirt made her legs look like they went on forever. Bethany had laughed at first when Camille insisted her dress should be like a fairy princess's, too.

And then Bethany had seen her niece's short, flirty, and above-the-knee skirt. She'd fallen in love with it, asking to have even more volume added to hers. Dru had wanted them each to pick whatever shoes they felt comfortable wearing all day to the outdoor ceremony and reception at Chandler Park. When Bethany had joked that she would polish her red cowboy boots before the big day, Dru replied that she wouldn't have it any other way. So that, as they said, had been that.

While they dressed and waited for Marsha and Camille to return, Dru kept pushing for details about that morning's scene outside the Artist Co-op. She'd been pushing since she'd homed in on something being different with Bethany when she'd arrived at the Whip that morning to help with prep. Bethany had side-stepped the subject then. But Dru had gotten it out of her at LWD—the high points about last night, and Mike's offer to collaborate with Bethany's art, *and* about his mother showing up.

"Mike's mother was waiting outside this morning," Bethany repeated. "When I . . ."

She glanced at Shandra, who was studying her reflection in the full-length mirror in the corner.

Shandra twirled in the three-inch heels she'd borrowed from Selena. "When you were heading home after getting busy with Cowboy Bob?"

"Yeah," Bethany said, "that."

"Awkward?" Selena asked.

"Aggressive," Bethany countered. "Passive-aggressive. She'd just met me. But she clearly knew enough about me that she thought . . ."

"What?" Dru stepped to the mirror. She turned sideways and ran a hand down her dress, contouring the fabric to her baby bump.

"Girls"—Bethany took a bow—"I'm officially a gold-digger. For dating a guy who wears jeans and threadbare shirts and hiking boots every day."

Selena looked stupefied. "She accused you of being after Mike's money?"

Bethany cringed at the first impression she'd made. "You should have seen the woman's clothes. She looked like she'd just walked out of a Fifth Avenue showroom."

"One look at you," Shandra said, "and she should have known money isn't your thing."

"Ouch." Dru nudged their sister with her elbow.

Bethany snorted. "Thanks."

Shandra's eyes widened at her misfire. "I didn't mean it that way. It's just that other things are more important to you, like painting."

"Well, my residency came up, too. Maybe I've attached myself to Mike to jump-start my nonexistent art career."

Shandra had picked up Dru's veil. She tucked its comb into her own braids and twirled. "So basically, the woman showed up to throw you shade?"

Dru sat on the edge of the bed and toed off her wedding shoes. Shandra plopped down next to her and transferred the veil from her head to the bride-to-be's.

"I don't know why she was there." Bethany knelt to massage Dru's swollen feet. Her sister groaned her appreciation. "Mike went downstairs first while I . . ."

"Searched for your panties?" Shandra rolled her eyes at Bethany's pained stare. "I'm not going to go on a teen mom sex bender, just because you're finally hooking up with the hot guy you've been drooling all over."

Selena chuckled. She and Dru and Bethany traded secret smiles at the bond Bethany and Shandra had formed. "What did Mike say?"

"He tried to defend me."

"Tried?" Dru asked.

"His mother's not wrong about how it looks."

"Who cares how it looks?" Selena looked pointedly at Bethany.

"I don't." But it had been a bad scene.

And something about Mike's reaction had been worrying her ever since. She'd felt lousy leaving him to deal with his mom on his own. But he'd almost seemed relieved to have Bethany go. And she hadn't heard from him yet. Not that they'd said they'd call.

But still . . .

"I'm just being oversensitive," she said. "It sounds like things with his parents have been bad for a long time. If his mother doesn't like him seeing me, Mike will deal with it."

"Seeing you?" Selena asked. "Is that what you call last night?"

"Last night, the last few weeks, have been . . ." Bethany didn't have the words.

"Magical?" Dru said for her, adding a dreamy smile. "Exactly the way storybooks say love is supposed to be?"

Bethany recalled those chilly moments with Mike's mother. And her meltdown yesterday morning, with Clair and Nicole.

"It's a little terrifying, actually," she confessed.

She helped her sister to her feet and led Dru to the mirror to view the full effect of her dress and veil. A radiant bride, Dru hadn't always had the most magical of love stories, either. She and Brad had never given up on each other, though, never completely. And now she was glowing with happiness over her pregnancy, and exchanging vows of forever and ever with her one true love in just two short weeks. Bethany wanted to believe that was possible for her. Maybe even for her and Mike—a man whose loving heart had been wandering for years, too.

Selena stepped to Dru's other side. Both women smiled at Bethany's reflection, concerned, understanding, reassuring.

"Love knows when the time is right," Dru said, "whether you think you're ready or not."

Shandra pushed off the bed and hugged Bethany's waist. Their over-the-top dresses made them look like one of the confections Leigh and Dan created to top the Easter cakes people special ordered each spring.

"You love Mike, don't you?" Shandra asked.

"I do." Bethany wiped at her eyes.

She loved him deep, all the way in, even if her heart were racing while she wondered where he was and what was going on with his mother and whether for some reason—or maybe for any reason he could find—he might be regretting the wonderful dream he'd given her.

I haven't known a lot of love . . . but whatever there is of it inside me, it's already yours.

"It's just all happening so fast," she admitted. "And he . . ."

"Scares you to death?" Marsha said from the doorway.

Camille rushed in from the hall and straight to the mirror.

"You're so beautiful." Dru lifted Camille into her arms.

"I know." Camille preened at her reflection, then gasped when she glimpsed Dru's dress. "You're a fairy princess, too. I want to take pictures. Mom said I could."

Bethany's niece dashed to her mom's purse for Selena's phone. Camille chatted away as she took her photos, confident that she belonged right where she was, even though a year ago no one would have believed Selena and Oliver would reconcile.

Everyone modeled and posed and hugged, letting Camille direct them. Bethany checked on Marsha. Her foster mother was watching over the colorful, exuberant scene as if it were the most precious moment of her life. She smiled fiercely when she caught Bethany's attention. She walked to the mirror, motioning for Bethany and Shandra to come with her. Selena and Dru, with Camille once more in her arms, joined them.

Wearing khakis and a crisply ironed shirt, Marsha stood like a queen amid a bouquet of pastel tulle and bridal white.

"I know how scary love can feel." She gazed at their reflection. "But when it's meant to be, there's no use fighting it. And absolutely no reason you should."

She took Camille into her arms.

"The first time I set eyes on Joe," she said, "my first day on the UGA campus my freshman year, it was over for me. I knew there was no other guy who'd ever make me feel that way. Which was pretty inconvenient, since I was planning on a social work degree and a career helping kids and families, and I didn't have time for nonsense like a whirlwind romance and getting married after Joe graduated that spring. I was scared to death of all of it. Him walking up to me that day, me telling my parents I was marrying him.

Me walking down that aisle having absolutely no idea why, except I loved Joe with everything inside me . . ."

Marsha smiled proudly at the three generations of women standing with her with their hearts in their eyes. Even Camille had grown silent, waiting to hear what her new grandma would say next.

"But I trusted the man I loved," Marsha said, "more than I trusted the fear. I dreamed of the amazing future ahead of us, and I steered straight into it, every time something impossible came along wanting to steal away what we had. I've never let being afraid get its claws into us." She covered Dru's hands, where Dru had linked her arm through Marsha's. Her watery smile into the mirror was for them all. "We've worked every single trouble out together. Family takes care of family, no matter what. And just look at what I got in return."

"Hi." Bethany leaned against the Dixon front door, smiling at Mike as if he'd made everything right in her world by simply showing up.

"Hi, yourself." He checked his watch. He had five minutes to spare.

"You made it."

He eased by her, hanging in the entryway while she closed the door. "I'm sorry it took me so long. You have no idea how much."

"No worries," she assured him.

She was wearing a silky peacock-blue blouse and faded jeans. Her feet were bare. And her smile was exactly the antidote he needed to recover from the hours they'd spent apart. So were the sounds of her family milling about, their voices emanating from what seemed like every corner of the sprawling house.

Mike wrapped an arm around Bethany. "Dealing with my mother can be . . . intense."

"But she seemed so pleasant and down-to-earth." Bethany's giggle eased more of the pressure in his chest.

"She wanted to have breakfast"—he let Bethany step back, when every instinct screamed for him to hold on—"which turned into brunch, which turned into spending half the day in the dining room at the Ritz, where she charmed the hostess into letting us hold court in a secluded corner, despite my"—he air quoted—"deplorable refusal to change out of yesterday's clothes. I told her I'd dressed for the diner down the block. The Ritz could just lump it. I dropped her at the airport for her flight back to New York with barely enough time to shower and get ready to come here."

Mike winced at the terrible way he and Livy had left things when he'd dropped her at the curb, his mother refusing to accept his offer to help her check in for her return flight.

"That bad?" Bethany asked.

Mike pulled her into another hug. "I thought maybe since she came to me this time, it would be easier. But something new is going on. I'd hoped I could get whatever it is out of her, and that we could resolve something for a change. But we just ended up fighting."

"Because of who I am?"

"Because of who *I* am." Mike stroked Bethany's back, wishing they were alone and there were no questions and there was only the feel of her heart beating next to his, and the night stretching out before them. "Because I wouldn't get on a plane and follow her home. I'm sorry she gave you such a hard time. But I don't think any of this is about you."

"This?"

"She apologized. Said she wanted a truce. She strung me along all day, catching me up on things in New York and listening to my update on the co-op and my ideas for a photography donation I'm making to a gala fundraiser my parents are doing. And then when I told her I had to get back out here, and I wasn't changing my plans even if she took a hotel room for the night . . . I expected anger, but this was on another level, even for her. She started in on every mistake I've ever made, and how all of it has been a personal attack on her and my father."

Bethany kissed him, stretching on her tiptoes to take off his hat.

"It sounds like they left you and your brother to fend for yourselves," she told him, "a long time before Jeremy died."

Mike soaked in her understanding. "I let myself wonder for just a little while today if maybe this was a chance to start fixing things with my parents."

Bethany studied him more closely. "You look really worried. Has her flight left yet? Go find her if it's that important. My family will understand."

"Tonight, here, is important."

Not bailing on Bethany or her parents' generous invitation was important. Not rewarding Livy's childish tantrums. Not being away from Bethany for another minute, until his world had righted itself completely.

"I'm exactly where I need to be right now," he insisted. "And later tonight"—he gathered her into his arms—"I want you all to myself, working on our art together, and then—"

"Sit down, everyone," Marsha said from down the hall. "Kids in the kitchen. Adults in here. Bethany, you and that man of yours get a move on before the food gets cold."

Bethany eased out of Mike's arms. "Come on, Cowboy Bob. Remember, you said you wanted this."

When they reached the dining room, Marsha rushed over.

"Michael"—she smothered him with a smile, hugging and holding tight and beaming up at him as she stepped away—"I'm so glad you made it. Hope you like lasagna. This is a treat, having you with us for the first time. Prepare yourself for being the center of attention."

She steered him deeper into the swarm of people and the mouthwatering aromas filling the room.

Bethany followed in their wake. "Mom . . ."

"The only thing this family likes better than Friday dinners," Marsha continued, "is talking with their mouths full while they're eating. And we're all dying to get to know you better."

The room was packed with Dixons settling into their seats. Joe and his boys, Dru with Brad, and Selena with Oliver. Travis sat next to Bethany's friend, Clair. And all of them were looking expectantly Mike's way while he and Bethany eased into their chairs, as if the night's entertainment had just arrived.

Joe and Marsha were the last to sit, at opposite ends of the dining room.

Marsha waved her hands at the room at large. "Let's eat, everyone."

Beneath the table, Bethany's hand squeezed Mike's in support. People began to pass serving dishes, piling food onto plates and filling water glasses from pitchers. Mike followed their lead, feeling a little shell-shocked by the wholesome scene after the bitch-slap of a day he'd just had with Livy.

"I'd intended to bring flowers for the table," he told Marsha. He'd also worn a blazer with his jeans, traded his hiking boots for a pair of loafers that he'd slipped on over dress socks, and he'd tucked his hat under his chair just now before he sat. "I'm sorry, the day kind of got away from me."

"How lovely." Marsha smiled at his intended thoughtfulness. "But don't worry. Bethany explained that your mother stopped by for a surprise visit. Of course you'd want to spend as much time with her as you could. We're glad you could make it."

"Is this the same mother who chairs the foundation that gave Bethany her scholarship to art school?" Oliver asked with a healthy undercurrent, still, of Mike not being good enough for his baby sister. "Funny how that connection never came up, until Bethie figured it out for herself."

"He's exactly who he's always said he was," Bethany insisted.

Mike swallowed his first bite of lasagna, wiped his mouth, and sipped from his water glass. "My family is responsible for the JHTF scholarship grants and other philanthropic ventures. Their contributions and mine have seeded community art programs all over the country."

"Like Bethany's Artist Co-op?" Clair asked. "Even though no one knows you're also HMT?"

"Something else," Armani added, "that my sister had to uncover on her own."

Mike set aside his fork. The clatter of everyone else's silverware on dishes continued, plus the sound of the kids goofing around in the kitchen. It felt as if he'd spent the entire day defending the way he lived his life. But this was Bethany's family. They didn't deserve the resentment surging inside him from having endured his mother's relentless disapproval.

He met the steady gaze of his therapy client. Joe was finally making the progress he needed to. Bethany's father had faced his own difficult crossroads and pushed past it. Yesterday, the man had challenged Mike to show the same grit in his relationship with Bethany.

"You don't have to talk about anything you don't want to, son," Joe assured him.

"Yes, I do." If for no other reason than how good it felt to hear Joe call him *son*. "Because I'm a stranger. And that's going to keep causing problems and make me being in your daughter's life harder than it should be, until we settle this. She's too important to all of you for me to let that happen."

Joe nodded, tearing off a piece of garlic bread and popping it into his mouth.

Mike propped his arm on the back of Bethany's chair. "I give back to the art community. I donate the proceeds from the sale of my art and a great deal of my investment income to various charities. Photography helped me feel closer to my brother when Jeremy was alive. It helps me keep his memory close now. And the rest . . . If I can spend my day honoring his memory somehow, then that's been a good enough day to keep me going for a long time."

Marsha's hand covered the one Mike had fisted beside his plate. "Your brother died of cystic fibrosis?"

Mike glanced at Bethany.

"I only told them your name," she said.

"We may be small-town," Travis offered, "but these days Google's reached even the sticks."

"And we know how to take care of our own," Joe added. "So as far as anyone else in Chandlerville is concerned, you're Mike Taylor until you want people to know about the rest."

"We'd like to understand, if we can." Marsha patted Mike's hand. Everyone else kept eating, as if they were discussing the weather, or if the Braves would make it to the World Series. "Is Jeremy why you became a physical therapist?"

Mike forked in his next bite and made himself chew.

"I couldn't help my brother anymore," he finally said. "And I couldn't be a part of the dog-and-pony show my parents were making out of searching for a cure for CF."

"So you went to school to learn how to help people who were hurting." Joe pushed back in his chair. "But only part-time?"

"Yes, sir."

"As much as we all appreciate how good you are at your job, me especially, it seems like part-time is what you've mostly been about for years."

"Joseph." Marsha's warning tone suggested she and her husband had already had some version of this discussion and weren't exactly of the same mind.

"He's right," Mike admitted. "I've moved around a lot. Between a lot of places and things and people."

Marsha propped her chin on her folded hands. "Maybe you haven't found the right place to tempt you to stop moving yet. That must have been very difficult for you, after losing so much so young."

Mike took another slow drink.

"Jeremy . . ." He cleared his throat, his palm sweating when Bethany slipped her hand back into his. "My brother wanted to go everywhere and never could. Bringing the world back to him, when I was old enough, was the only thing I could do to help."

"Through your photography?" Selena wiped the corners of her eyes with her napkin. Her husband rubbed a soothing hand down her back.

"That's how he got started," Bethany answered.

Mike nodded, the memory pulling at him. "And Jeremy made me promise to keep going. To keep enjoying life. I used that as an excuse to move from one place to another almost constantly for a while. Then I realized there was more for me to do, even if I still couldn't settle in one place."

"And look at what you've accomplished," Marsha praised. "You should be very proud of that, Michael."

"Even the bartending?" he teased, floundering. What would it have been like to have a parent like Bethany's mom in his corner years ago? "I've been a drifter for a long time, Mrs. Dixon. I know what everyone sees when they look at me."

"Marsha, please," she corrected. "And you're much more than what you let yourself appear at first glance, or you never would have caught Bethany's heart."

"I hope you're right." Mike nodded, the sting of Livy's criticism still fresh.

Bethany turned his face toward her. "Look at what you're doing for Dad, and your photographs, the art centers, and how you're inspiring me to paint—"

Mike kissed her, not wanting her to spoil her surprise for her parents' anniversary.

"I am looking," he told her. "I haven't been able to take my eyes off you since we met."

A wave of smiles circled the table. Even Oliver wasn't immune. Marsha lifted her glass of tea.

"To Bethany and Mike," she toasted, everyone joining in.

While they were all drinking, Bethany's phone and then Clair's sounded off. Clair pulled hers from the purse she'd hung over the back of her chair. Her eyes widened as she read whatever text or email had come through. She motioned to Bethany to read hers. Before Bethany could, Mike's cell began to vibrate.

Travis took Clair's phone and began to scan its display.

"It's from Nic," Clair said. "She got some social media alert about Bethany."

"About what?" Bethany slipped her phone from the pocket of her jeans.

Mike dug his out, too. There was a brief 911 text from George. He pushed back his chair with a deafening shriek. "I'm sorry. I need to deal with this."

He kissed Bethany's cheek and beat a path away from the Dixons' family dinner.

He gave himself credit for not swearing a blue streak while he dialed his petulant mother on the phone—with the intention of this being the very last conversation they had, if she didn't step way the hell back behind the line he'd told his parents to never cross.

Chapter Seventeen

"She wouldn't have done this," Bethany said.

She'd joined Mike in her parents' living room after he'd hung up on a brief and what had sounded like a very angry phone call with his mother.

"Nicole texted a link to something on the Internet." She stepped closer. He was staring at his phone. "About me—"

"Stalking and bedding the reclusive photographer HMT," Mike finished, "and using your Southern charms to get me to collaborate with you."

"And your foundation auctioning off a piece from our work together at the JHTF holiday gala. But your mother couldn't have done all of that since you left her at the airport, right? Why would she?"

"It's done. George sent me the link, too. It hit the social media pages she follows because of my photography about a half hour ago. She's talked with the gala director. My mother—" He held up his phone, his fist clenched around it. "Livy is demanding my presence in New York. She'll consider retracting her statement—if I present myself at my parents' town house to discuss it.

Otherwise she'll keep it up with the press. Continue to rake you over the coals. Reveal who and what I am, my work with your father, my connections with the art co-ops."

Bethany sat on the edge of Joe's recliner.

Mike went to rip off his hat and seemed startled that it wasn't there.

"But . . ." She handed him the Stetson he'd left in the dining room. He sat next to her. "Why?"

"My mother wants my attention. Badly enough for some reason to pull a stunt she knows I can't ignore."

"Because she's threatening to reveal your identity? You said never to do that, or you'd cut off all ties. Why would you cave to her blackmail now and fly home?"

"Because she's using me to hurt you." Mike slipped his hat on. The brim shaded his furious expression. "It's out of character, even for my mother. I can't tell you how sorry I am. I'll take care of it."

Bethany grabbed his arm and waited for him to look at her. "She's that jealous of seeing someone else love you?"

"No. She hates seeing me trying to love someone with everything I am, the way I loved my brother." Mike kissed Bethany. "The way she's never let me get close enough to love her."

Bethany clung to the words Mike had said and the rightness of being in his arms. She fought the panicked sense that he was disappearing.

He eased them apart. "I have to deal with whatever this is."

"*We* have to deal with it. I'm a part of it."

"You met my mother. You can't begin to understand my family's baggage." He grimaced at his memories.

"Let me be with you while you talk to your parents."

"Livy would only hurt you again, and I'm not letting that happen."

Bethany felt his bone-deep sadness. She battled her own impulse to run away from the way he seemed to be brushing her off. Instead she followed Mike to the door—steering straight into his troubles. *Their* troubles.

"I can wait wherever you want while you speak with them," she insisted. "Get a hotel room. Be there for you afterward if things get as bad as you think they will."

"If? This trip will end things between my parents and me. My mother seems to have decided that should happen, in an even uglier way than when I left after Jeremy. There's no reason for you to put yourself through that."

"You're the reason I'd put myself through it. Because I love you."

Mike crushed her to him. "I love you, too, Bethany."

His voice was a gravelly, raw thing.

Her heart filled at them exchanging those three powerful words for the first time.

"But you have your own family," he said. "Your surprise to finish for your parents. When is the wedding?"

"Two weeks."

"Focus on that. Work in my studio, on your parents' painting or our digital collections. George will give you the codes and help you set up whatever you need. I'll settle things and be back in a couple of days, once I'm sure Livy won't take more potshots at the life you're building here."

Bethany threw her arms around him, giving a watery laugh when he hauled her onto her toes. She wasn't losing him, she told herself. He wasn't every other guy she'd been with. This was Mike, and he was coming back. He wanted to stay with her and see what they could do together.

"You belong in Chandlerville, too," she reminded him. "You

said for as long as I wanted. And I'm always going to want you with me."

"I'll cover whatever I can myself," Bethany heard George say, as Bethany let herself into Mike's studio Monday morning. "I'll cancel the rest. You need to stay there, Mike. See this through. If you want, I could . . . Yeah, I'm pretty sure I'm the last person your parents want to see, too. No, I won't. She said she'd be here sometime this morning. She should hear it from you."

"Hear what?" Bethany asked, assuming she was the *she* in question. Her heart clenched at the implications of what she'd just heard.

George sat behind Mike's desk, which was covered in an even more mind-boggling flood of papers and folders and files than Bethany was used to. She and George had gotten along in mostly companionable silence since Mike had left Friday night, sharing the studio space but keeping to their own work. Focused on their own projects. Waiting to hear from him.

Displayed on Mike's monitor was the calendar software used to track and log resident artists' schedules. Though at the moment, the program was showing a more simplified view—from the sound of it, Mike's personal commitments. George smiled thinly at Bethany, while listening to the barely discernible masculine voice on the other end of the line.

"Yes," George said. "She's here. I'll tell her. Yes, we'll discuss it, but you need to—" She paused, listening. "Okay, let me know as soon as you can."

She hung up and jotted a brief note on a Post-it pad.

"How is he?" Bethany asked, holding in the worry and disappointment that Mike hadn't called since he'd left. He hadn't texted or made contact with either her or his business manager in the two days since leaving for New York, only to reach out to George first once he did.

"He's not great." George tossed her pen onto the desk. "I'm going to make a few calls while I run errands. He said he'd reach you on your cell in a few minutes."

"Because I should hear *what* from him?"

Bethany had been trying not to jump to conclusions, or to fall back down the rabbit hole of her doubts and fears about emotionally unavailable men—or *anyone* in general who said they cared and then disappeared like they'd never been in her life at all. She'd tried to stay focused on her concern for Mike and what he must be going through, and his declaration of love for her.

George stood and swiped her denim jacket from the back of the desk chair. She'd worn what looked like a vintage cocktail dress to work—embellished with sequins and possibly feathers, dating it from sometime in the sixties. There were a few threadbare spots, some of the sparkles were missing. But, the same as Bethany, George didn't seem inclined to care what anyone else thought about what she wore and why.

What George *did* care about, clearly—from what Bethany had gleaned as George had taught her Mike's photography software and then disappeared back into her own mountain of work—was Mike. And the look on George's face as she studied Bethany now was more worried, more troubled, than the calm she'd kept in her voice while she'd spoken on the phone.

"Mike should tell you himself." George sighed. "He should have told you the other night, about half an hour after he landed at La Guardia. Sometimes I think that man goes out of his way to make the world as lonely as it possibly can be for him, because he . . ."

"He thinks that's the only way he can get through things?" Bethany finished. "Because that's the way he got through losing Jeremy?"

"He doesn't do it consciously. I know he's been glad to have me close, the times we've been around each other. I know for sure this isn't the way he wants things to be with you. From day one, you've had that wanderlust of his on the ropes. But . . ."

"He's not coming back to Atlanta?"

I'll settle things and be back in a couple of days.

Instead, Mike had been talking with George just now about clearing his schedule. Bethany was sure of it.

There'd been no other rumors on the Internet about the two of them, no follow-through on his mother's threats to out his identity, reveal his connection with the co-op, or further harass Bethany online about her connection with the elusive photographer HMT. It was as if Bethany were no longer a factor at all. While she'd spent most of the last two days in Mike's studio, sleeping in his bed, working on her and their art, and missing him so badly she could barely breathe.

She'd imagined Mike wanting to be there with her, too, needing her in his life, holding her through the night, creating amazing dreams with her.

"He would rather be back with you," George assured her. "Try to remember that. Try to get him to remember it."

"You're scaring me." Bethany sank onto the edge of the desk, meeting the other woman's troubled gaze. "You sound scared."

"I am." George slipped into her jacket. "But anything I could do to change Mike's mind about how he lives his life died along with Jeremy. I make sure he always has someplace, anyplace, to come back to. I clean up after him when he bugs out. I help him put all that money that makes him feel too much like his parents to good use. But that's all he's let himself need from me in a long time. You, on the other hand . . ."

"Me, what? He hasn't talked to me in days."

"Because that's what he does when he's freaked." George huffed out a frustrated breath. She glanced to the landscape of Marsha and Joe's house that Bethany had finished a little before dawn that morning. "He's a mess, Bethany. But you're inside that mess now, a lot deeper than I've ever gotten. Thanks to you, I think he's really started sorting himself out. Enough for it to take another chunk out of his heart now if he tried to back away from you."

"Is he backing away?"

Bethany couldn't take it if he was.

How was she supposed to handle Mike calling her next—*after* he'd sorted out his business situation with George—to say that he needed to *cancel* her, too? Because dealing with his family meant Mike once more needed to move on from everything he knew.

"It's not that simple," George told her. "It never has been with Mike and his parents."

When Bethany's cell phone rang, Mike's business manager and lifelong friend moved toward the stairs. She turned back at the door.

"I'm not going to lie to you," George said. "I haven't heard him like this in a long time. Don't let him off the hook the way I did right after we lost Jeremy. If you love Mike, if you want him not to give up on loving you, call him on his shit before he walls his heart off again."

Chapter Eighteen

"How are you?" Mike asked the second Bethany answered her cell. "I'm sorry I haven't called."

God, he was sorry.

He needed to see her, feel her, hear her voice in person. He needed to breathe. And he couldn't anymore, not deeply enough, not while Bethany was so far away. He hadn't slept since he'd been home. He'd barely had time to think beyond the next minute, the next conversation with his parents, the next decision that had to be made.

"What's going on, Mike?" Bethany's voice was steady, but the control was costing her. He could hear the same defiant fragility in her voice as when she'd faced down Benjie at McC's.

"It's a long story."

"It's a two-day story that George says I should hear from you. Why haven't you called?" She was angry, and she had every right to be. "You got your mother to back off whatever she was doing. Nothing else has been posted on the Internet about you and me. But you're not back here. It doesn't sound like you're coming back. Tell me what's happening."

He sat in a plush leather chair in one of JHTF's four conference rooms. He rubbed a hand over his eyes, forcing the words out, knowing they'd hurt—both Bethany and him.

"I told my parents I'd stay in New York until my mother dies."

The cell line crackled, a full thirty seconds passing.

"What?" Bethany finally asked, her temper gone. "Your mother's sick?"

"Cancer. And it's . . . She's . . ."

He'd been able to tell George. He'd talked the grim details through with his dad, when Livy had done nothing more than blurt out her prognosis and then refuse to discuss it further. But saying it to Bethany made it real.

"It's end-stage," he said. "My mother's dying. That's why she's been pushing so hard to have me come back for the holidays. She couldn't come right out and say why, of course, or that she needed me home so we could deal with this like a family. She'll be demanding to have everything her way till the end, just because that's the way things should be. Meanwhile . . ."

Mike closed his eyes, seeing Jeremy wasting away in a hospital bed, while he'd dreamed of exploring the world with Mike. And then Mike pictured their mother facing the same fate soon, only she'd want Mike chained to her side like one of her priceless handbags, or a piece of jewelry that only mattered when she could show it off to someone else.

"I'm so sorry," Bethany whispered into the chasm that had opened inside of him.

"She's known for a while, evidently. She didn't tell anyone, not even my dad. And now there's nothing anyone can do."

"Except be there for her."

"I've been gone for ten years." And he regretted that now, no matter his reasons.

"Which was more her doing than yours."

Bethany's understanding was the hug Mike had needed for two days, only there'd been no one in New York for him to turn to.

"I'm glad you're staying," she said. "Really. I could come up there, if—"

"No," Mike said too quickly, too harshly. "Livy's still off-the-charts pissed at me. Though she's changed her tactics now that I'm here, and she and my father are working on me together."

"About what?"

"It doesn't matter." None of his and his parents' differences mattered now. Why couldn't Livy see that? "But I'm not giving her another crack at you."

"Me? I'm worried about you. You're giving your mother another crack at *you*, because you love her, and she knows it. I admire you for being there for your family, even after what they've put you through. But let me—"

"Jesus, I can't, Bethany!"

He heard himself barking at the woman he loved. He heard the worst of who he could be coming out—parts of himself that he'd never wanted Bethany to see.

"I'm sorry," he said. "But I can barely stand being here as it is. My parents are relentless, the both of them coming at me about how long I've been gone, and what they want from me now that I'm back. And all the while, all I can think about is—"

"Jeremy." Bethany sounded like she was crying. "I get it."

"No, you don't."

Mike winced, blocking out the image of his brother's bedroom in their parents' penthouse apartment, with every single one of Jeremy's things still there. Livy hadn't changed an inch of the space in ten years. It was the last of her firstborn's life that she could cling to and say was hers.

"This is a toxic place for me," Mike said. "I'm a different person when I'm here. That's why I hardly ever come. And now . . ."

"You can't leave."

"And I can't have you in the middle of it."

He couldn't watch any of this touch Bethany. He couldn't watch her turn away from him because of the things he couldn't keep from changing in himself. In what he'd wanted for them.

"I'm not Cowboy Bob when I'm in New York, Bethany. I'm not Mike Taylor or HMT. I'm Harrison and Olivia Taylor's son, which comes with a shit ton of baggage that's going to weigh me down for God knows how long."

"The son who's going to run far and wide as soon as he's free of his parents' world?"

Bethany's anger was back as she jumped to the obvious conclusion. She felt suddenly like a dream that had been slipping away since the moment Mike had first taken her into his arms.

"Is that why you haven't called?" she asked. "Is that what you're trying to protect me from, while you tell me your family is the problem? When it's *you* who thinks I shouldn't be with you while you go through something this unimaginable. When it's you who's talking yourself into not being with me anymore—because it's easier for you with me hundreds of miles away."

"You're the best thing that's ever happened to me." He knew it wasn't what she needed to hear, but he hoped she could understand. "I want you with me every second of every day."

"Just not while you're hurting. I'm so good for you that for two days you've shut me out. And now I'm supposed to do what? Wait and see if you'll want me back a few months from now?"

Mike rubbed his eyes with the heels of his hand. "Six months, her doctors are saying."

"And after that? With me out of the picture, that clears the decks nicely for you to wander off somewhere else and lick your wounds. Anywhere you can tend bar or take pictures or help another stranger like Joe, and no one will expect you to stick around."

Bethany's voice was a whisper, her fear sucking away the last of the denial that had protected Mike since he'd lost his brother.

He'd been a coward for ten years, not hunkering down and making some kind of peace with his parents. With his own mistakes. With the shreds of his heart that he'd wanted to give to Bethany, and with her find a way to love again. He'd wanted to make her his home. Now he could feel the pressure building inside him—to break free and get as far away from everything as he could.

"I don't want to hurt you," he said. "I don't want to ruin us. I swear I don't. But I need time to work some things out."

"By yourself."

He tried to believe he wasn't slamming the door shut on them completely. But he *wasn't* certain where he'd wind up on the other side of his mother's illness. And Bethany deserved better than that. Better than him—one more man promising to love her and then letting her down.

"I have to be here for my family," he said. "And you need to be there, reconnecting with yours. But George will make sure you have everything you need at the loft."

"Everything but you."

And Mike wouldn't have anything without Bethany.

"I'll think about you every day," he promised, when he knew he had no right to say something like that to her now. "I'll wish I could see you with your family at your sister's wedding. Or watch you paint. Or have you in my arms, smiling and making me feel more loved than I ever have. I really am sorry about this."

"So sorry that you're putting us on hold," she said, "while you work out, all by yourself, whether there's even going to be an *us* anymore."

Bethany ended the call before he could tell her that he loved her.

Thursday afternoon, Bethany watched her dad's new physical therapist work with Joe on the backyard patio.

"MedCare made it clear he's just a substitute." Marsha was watching, too, gazing through the kitchen window.

"An *indefinite* substitute," Bethany corrected, her hand covering her heart as if she could hold back the hurt. "Because Mike hasn't given them a return date."

"This must be very hard for him." Her mother rinsed the last of the dishes from the kids' after-school snacks. The brood was in the living room or the dining room or upstairs now, doing homework. "Going through losing his mother, after what his family endured with his brother's illness."

"It is."

And Bethany's heart hurt for him, even though she hadn't tried to reach him since Monday, and Mike hadn't called her again.

"That man loves you." Marsha started the dishwasher and dried her hands on an ancient dish towel. "I understand how the way he's handling things is hard for you both. But—"

"I should hang in there?" Bethany shook her head. She snorted, furious with him. Scared for him. "He's been talking to George about business practically every day."

"The co-op's manager?"

"She's been great about me working in the studio. But I don't think I can keep going down there, knowing she's still in touch with him."

"But you could be in touch with him, right? Call him, Bethany, if talking to Mike is what you really want."

"So he can tell me again that staying away from me is in everyone's best interest?" While all the things he'd promised they could be for each other disappeared, like so many other promises she'd let herself believe.

"You've spent a lot of time away from this family the last five years," Marsha reminded her. "No one here believed that being on your own was what you really wanted."

Bethany turned to the foster mother who'd never judged her for the mistakes she'd made. "I didn't know what I wanted for a long time."

Marsha folded the towel, smoothing out every wrinkle. "We were willing to wait for you to decide."

"I worried you all so much." Bethany had never realized *how* much, until she'd experienced Mike doing the same thing to her. "I treated you like an accessory I could just throw away because I didn't want it anymore."

"We trusted you to figure out what was important. And here you are."

Bethany nodded, reliving the moment when the man she'd trusted had told her to stay away from him and his problems.

"How's your painting coming?" Marsha asked. "The one you're giving your dad and me for our anniversary."

Bethany rolled her eyes. "Who told you?"

"It's a small family." Her mother smiled. "Actually, it's a large family, which makes secrets even tougher to keep. We're all dying to know what you're doing in Mike's studio."

"Which is exactly why I'm not talking about it—with any of you."

Her plans for the wedding had grown now, far beyond a single present for her parents. Thanks to Mike's inspiration for how to kick-start her imagination, hours flew by each time she booted up his photography software. She couldn't be with him, so she lost herself in the excitement of combining their work, nudging and cajoling and coaxing their collaborative pieces into reflecting how beautifully their lives could fit together. And when she wasn't on the computer, she was painting. *Really* painting. And then taking photos of whatever progress she'd made, thinking . . .

Thinking that one day soon she'd show Mike the light and energy and passion for creating that he'd helped her rediscover. George had even downloaded Mike's shots from his and Bethany's night at the meadow. Their sunset over the pond. Each image was a vivid reminder of their worlds and hearts and dreams colliding, stunning them, forever changing things. Forever changing Bethany.

Her creative mojo was back, the excitement, the freedom of liking what she was doing and trusting that her art had its own mind and knew where it needed to go. She'd barely slept since Mike left. And when she did, she dreamed of him being there, creating beside her. Only to wake up to the reality that he might never return.

She smiled, hoping her mother would ignore her unshed tears.

"My art's never felt more alive." Her first love was back. "Mike made that possible. Why won't he let me help him the same way?"

"Why are you waiting for him to *let* you?" a man's voice asked from the doorway leading to the family room.

"Grammy!" Camille flew around her dad and straight for Marsha. "I made a picture book for show-and-tell at school.

It's a whole story about me and Bud and Grammy Belinda and Mommy and Daddy and you and Grandpa. Mommy helped me add the words on her computer and print it out. And my teacher says it's great. Wanna see?"

"Of course I do." Marsha took the stapled-together booklet of eight-by-ten paper. She took Camille's hand and led her away from Bethany and Oliver, toward the dining room. "You take the most beautiful pictures. Come tell me your story from page one."

Oliver's attention shifted to Bethany once they were gone. "Mike's shutting you out?"

Bethany nodded. "It's how he deals with things."

Alone.

Something Bethany couldn't stand the thought of Mike resigning himself to.

"Then kick the door down," her brother said. "Show him how our family deals with things when we know someone's in trouble."

"We?" Bethany scoffed.

She knew she'd heard her brother right. But what self-respecting kid sister would pass up the chance to rub it in? She crossed the kitchen and punched him in the arm.

"Don't tell me you like the guy now," she said.

"You love the guy." Oliver, dressed in his business suit from working downtown, teasingly punched her back. Then he pulled her close. "And I love you. And I don't want you to have any regrets about how you played this."

Bethany jerked away, confused and angry at Mike, annoyed at the endless advice swirling around her. "Mom was just telling me to give him time. That I can't change his mind."

"You can't. Not about staying there or coming back here or going somewhere else where no one knows him. Trust me, I've been there. I couldn't keep Selena from leaving when we were kids."

"So what's the point?" Why did people do this to themselves? Falling in love. Giving someone else their heart to keep safe—knowing full well how much it was going to hurt if things wound up broken instead.

"The point is," her brother said, "that I should have made damn sure I knew what I really wanted—and what Selena wanted—before I let her go."

"Mike knows that I want to be there for him."

"He knows you *said* you wanted to be there. There's a difference. For Selena and me, that difference was the seven years it took me to show her that I would always be there for her and our daughter, no matter what."

Like Mike and Jeremy had been there for each other until the very end. Just as Mike was determined to be there for his difficult, disapproving, controlling parents. Because *that's* the kind of man he was. When someone really needed him, the Mike she loved couldn't turn away. No matter what it cost him.

Bethany shook her head at her brother, her tears finally falling. Oliver wiped them away, worried but confident, calmly waiting for her to work through what she had to.

"I love him so much," she said. "What if I go after him, fight for him, and lose it all anyway?"

"What if you go after him and end up with the love of your life, just like I have?"

Bethany stared at Oliver, her old doubts swarming, biting, and stinging away at her terrified heart.

What if she wasn't enough for Mike? What if no woman ever would be? What if they weren't as connected as they'd thought, outside the dreamlike bubble of Chandlerville and the few precious weeks they'd had together here?

"What if he'll never let me all the way in?" she asked her brother.

Oliver shook his head.

"I don't believe in never anymore, Bethie. There's always another chance to live life the way you want it. That's what Marsha and Joe are about. Look at Dad out there, fighting for whatever he can still have. Look at the way you're painting again, and back with us again, and loving again no matter what happened with your first family, or how many guys like Benjie haven't been there for you. You don't believe in never anymore, either. Is Mike what you really want?"

Bethany nodded.

Her brother held up his smartphone. "Then there's a flight to Manhattan at seven. I've booked you a seat with my miles, and a car service to take care of you on the other end. Go after your heart, Bethany. Give Mike what you know he needs, even if he's not ready to accept it. Don't ever stop fighting for love."

Chapter Nineteen

Bethany stepped off the ninth-floor elevator of Manhattan's Lenox Hill Memorial Hospital.

She'd waited until she was at the gate for her flight leaving Atlanta, to call George and tell her what she was doing. She'd made it clear she was hunting Mike down, whether George helped her or not. Not that she'd needed to worry about having the other woman in her corner. A text had been waiting for Bethany when she landed at La Guardia, telling her where to go, that Olivia Taylor was with her oncologist for the day having tests run, and that Mike would be expecting Bethany.

George had signed off, saying simply, *"Go get 'im, girl!"*

An older gentleman met Bethany outside the hospital room the volunteer downstairs had directed her to. He looked like a more distinguished, more buttoned-down version of Mike. He wore a suit that appeared to be even more expensive than Oliver's finest. Bracketing the man's mouth were lines Bethany couldn't imagine had been forged by smiling.

But his eyes were the same brown as his son's. And there was a sadness softening Harrison Taylor's forbidding features. A weariness, too, that would have told Bethany he'd been in this very place before, even if she hadn't already known how he'd lost his son.

"You must be Mr. Taylor," she said, offering him her hand.

"Please call me Harrison." He shook politely, his tone formal. "My son's told his mother and me about you, Ms. Darling. May I call you Bethany?"

"Of course." She smiled, even though his greeting had sounded more practiced than friendly.

Bethany doubted he approved of her relationship with Mike any more than Mike's mother had.

"Georgina alerted us that you were on the way." A glimmer of suspicion shadowed Harrison's expression. "She failed to mention why."

"I hope I'm not imposing," Bethany said, sidestepping his question and wondering if the man had purposely intercepted her before she and Mike could speak.

"Of course you're not imposing," Mike's father assured her. "Although this is a private matter for my family, and I must ask that you not upset my wife or son any further."

She cleared her throat. "I'm not here to cause trouble, if that's what you're worried about. How is your wife?"

"She's dying. Not today, perhaps not even this year. But we have our second and third opinions and recommendations for invasive treatments. And Livy's decided not to put herself through the torture of any of them. She'd rather make the most of the time she has left. Plan her last gala. Make it a bigger success than all the others, with her son by her side. I hope you can understand what a comfort that will be for her."

"I do." Bethany shivered.

Did Mike's parents understand how difficult it was going to be for him to do what they were asking of him?

"I hope you can also understand how vital it is that Michael take his place now where he's always belonged."

Bethany blinked. "And that place would be?"

The door opened to the hospital room Harrison had been waiting beside. Mike emerged looking as different as he could from the easy-smiling man she knew.

"Bethany," he said. The grim set of his unsmiling mouth—so similar to his father's—softened at the sight of her.

He was dressed in a tailored golf shirt and ruthlessly pressed khakis, with polished brown loafers on his feet. He'd found the time to cut his hair. His hat was gone. He was cleanly shaven. He looked so conservative, so pulled together, Bethany wanted to muss up his hair, just to have a taste of her cowboy back. She gently wrapped her arms around him instead, wishing she'd come sooner.

"I'm so sorry," she told him.

His body, stiff for several seconds, melted into her, his arms snagging her closer.

"Bethany," he repeated. The love in his voice beat back against her worries.

"I'll check on your mother." Harrison stepped away and entered the hospital room to Mike's right.

Mike held Bethany long after they were alone in the hallway, rocking with her as if they were slow dancing. He took a deep breath and exhaled, his hand cupping her head to his chest.

"I couldn't stay away," she said.

"I've missed you every second I've been back." He rested his forehead against hers.

The gesture was so familiar amid the other crazy changes she couldn't process, her eyes filled with tears. "Then why did you tell me not to come?"

He led her to the cluster of chairs grouped several feet away, an arrangement around a table boasting a single lamp.

"I don't want to hurt you," he said. "I already have, and I've been home less than a week. And I have to do this for my parents."

"Of course you do." He was a healer. A deeply feeling man with a bottomless heart. "You love them. You wouldn't have stayed in touch with them at all if you didn't. There's nowhere else you could be now, if there's a chance you can help."

"My mother doesn't want my help." He laughed, harsh, brittle, and dropped his head into his hands, his elbows braced on his knees.

"All I can think about, sitting in this hospital where we lost Jeremy, is watching my brother suffer. And not wanting my mother to . . ." Mike inhaled against a sob. "Meanwhile, all *she* can think about is me promising to take over the family legacy after she's gone."

Mike swallowed, sucking the emotion down while Bethany pulled his hands away from his face.

"Is that what you want?" she asked him, sounding hurt and worried—for both of them.

Instead of answering, he took her in his arms again.

God, he'd needed her. He'd needed to breathe, and he couldn't anymore—with his parents carrying on, business as usual, no one dealing with the emotional reality of his mother's condition and the aggressive cancer that had already spread to her bones and several organs.

"George said you were doing okay," he found enough of his voice to say to Bethany. "Tell me you're doing okay."

She shrugged. "I finished my painting. I wish you could have been there for it."

Mike lost himself in the love looking back at him from Bethany's crystal-gray eyes. She'd finished her foster parents' anniversary present. Her art was back. Stronger and more beautiful than ever, he'd bet. And he was missing it.

"Your mother wants you to take over at the foundation for her?" Bethany asked.

He nodded. "She's already bullied the other directors into letting me serve on the JHTF board, taking her seat alongside my father's."

Mike felt it consume him once more, the desperation to be gone once his mother was, and to never look back. Just as Bethany had predicted.

"Do the other directors know you're HMT?" she asked.

"Not yet."

"But your mother wants them to."

Mike stared at the floor. "It would make her so proud, she told me. To finally be able to let people know that I haven't been wasting my life all these years."

"You haven't been." Bethany took his hand. "You should be proud of everything you've done with your life."

But Livy wasn't, and now she was dying.

He couldn't process it. There was only numbness, while jagged emotion seethed just below the surface, ready to rip him apart with guilt and the compulsion to destroy.

He looked down at Bethany's hand in his. He was holding on tighter than he should, their fingers linked, his grip crushing. But she didn't seem to care, and he couldn't turn her loose.

"You need to go home," he told her. "I want to cover your flight. You shouldn't have to pay for—"

Bethany stood, pulling away from him.

"That's what you have to say to me?" she demanded. "Your heart is breaking because you love your mother and she's still being horrible to you. Your parents are asking you to make decisions about the rest of your life, and trying to use your mother's cancer to guilt you into doing what they want. And all you're worried about is me not having to pay for my return flight, while I race back to Chandlerville to get away from you and your family?"

She rummaged in her backpack and pulled out her phone, pointing it at him.

"I had George email this from your computer." Bethany had accessed a photo from her gallery app. "Look at it and tell me I should go away."

Mike studied the exposure he'd taken of their sunset at the meadow pond. But his capture was only part of the image. Overlaid with it was a digital photo of one of Bethany's newer landscape attempts. She'd done more work with the painting, adding shading and shadow, better reflecting the sky and clouds in the water, matching her brushstrokes to what his lens had seen—the remainder of the sundown effect coming from his photo.

Like two matching pieces—half her, half him—the collaborative result was an ethereal reflection of Bethany's favorite place in the world. And now Mike's.

"It's amazing." He shook his head, losing his heart to her all over again.

"You and I." Bethany knelt in front of him, her own eyes damp, her feelings open to him, honest and loving, when she'd so carefully protected her heart for years. "*We're* amazing. Together. Apart, we'd both get by. But life will never be what it should have been for either of us if you keep pushing me away. Don't you see?

You've shown me how to create—to be free and fearlessly follow my dreams the way you have."

"Bethany—"

"Now you need to let me show you what I know. And I can show you how to stay, Mike. How to come home. You didn't have anyone here for you when you lost Jeremy, and it nearly destroyed you. You're back in New York now for your mother anyway. That's how deeply you know how to love. But I bet you're already thinking about where you'll go next. And it's somewhere new and different that won't tempt you to stay the way coming to Chandlerville did. I know you're in pain, and that's bringing out parts of you that you don't want me to see. And you're thinking you have to protect both of us from that. But—"

"I don't want to hurt you any more than I already have." He brushed the backs of his fingers across her cheek.

"Then don't." She dropped her phone into her backpack and stood. "I'm going home. You need to decide what's best for you and your family—without worrying about me. Just know that I'm going to be okay now, no matter what. You helped me realize that. Now it's your turn to believe that I'll be there for you. Whatever you want to do with your life, Mike, I'll be right there, wanting to do it with you. To explore and paint and create, and to face times like this, no matter how hard they are. Being afraid is no way to live my art, remember? Or your life. You taught me that. Don't keep hurting *yourself*, thinking you have to keep going through this alone."

"It's good to see you in here finally," Mike's mother said a week later from the doorway of Jeremy's room.

Mike looked up from sitting on the edge of his brother's bed, at the beautiful woman who'd brought them both into the world.

She looked more tired by the day; meanwhile, she insisted on going in to her office at the foundation. It was more obvious how much weight she'd lost when she was in her silk nightgown and robe instead of the heavier clothes she hid in when she was outside of the house. The blue of the expensive material made her skin appear even more pale. She was in full makeup, when the hour was well past midnight. He was pretty sure she'd had her eyes and cheekbones done at some point in the last year. She'd always been determined to stay fresh, despite the passage of time.

Outwardly, she remained one of the loveliest women he'd known.

He thought of Bethany's natural beauty. How her generous, brave heart had been in her eyes as she'd told him to stay and take care of his family. And that she'd always be there, if he found his way back to her.

She was where she belonged now. Her own family and friends were no doubt circling the wagons and helping her through the pain he knew he'd caused her. The Dixons would be in the midst of the final crush of prepping for Dru's wedding, which was the day after tomorrow. But they'd make sure Bethany wasn't alone.

Livy joined him, sitting silently beside him on the bed. A wave of expensive perfume arrived with her. The scent took him back to the times as a young child when he and Jeremy had watched their glamorous parents leave for dinner or some other evening event. He and his brother would beg to be able to go, too, or for their parents to stay home and play with them. Only to inevitably spend the evening just the two of them, with their toys and games and their nanny.

"Thank you for coming to the hospital again today," his mother said, while Mike gazed at the image on his phone that Bethany had forwarded, of their combined rendering of the meadow and pond where they'd first made love.

He nodded. "I like several of the homeopathic options your oncologist recommended, if you're determined not to pursue traditional treatments."

More invasive treatments risked greater side effects while offering very little chance of significant results. And that would keep Livy from behaving as if nothing was wrong for as long as she wanted to. At least through the holiday gala, she'd insisted.

His mother looked around at Jeremy's things, perfectly preserved as if he'd only just stepped out of the room.

"I couldn't understand your brother's decision," she said, "or your determination to get your father and me to accept it. To go on living life as long as possible as if he weren't disabled. And then when he couldn't continue the ruse, to keep his focus on the world going on beyond these walls, instead of—"

"Devoting the time he had left to recording his death for the foundation's marketing team?"

Livy sighed at Mike's calling a spade a spade. Then she nodded.

"I was hoping," she said, "I could expect the same understanding you gave Jeremy. For my decision to keep making the most of my life, my way, for as long as I can."

"By working?"

He looked up from the unspoiled beauty he and Bethany had found together, into the exquisite features of a woman who'd built her entire life around impressing and influencing people, by trading on her looks and lifestyle.

"By working with *you*," she said, igniting the argument that got worse each time they resumed it. She never came at him the same way. "You and your father and I working together to make the gala a success, transitioning you onto the foundation board. Being a family finally at JHTF for as long as possible, instead of fighting the way we have the last two weeks."

"For the last decade, you mean?" Mike shook his head at the time they'd wasted over anger and accusations and blame and guilt.

His mother nodded stiffly, her attention snagging on Jeremy's Stetson where it lay on the bed next to Mike. Mike had placed it there and hadn't worn it, hadn't been back in this room, since he'd come home.

"You need to let this go, Mom."

"Or what? You'll leave again? More payback for the way you said your father and I abandoned Jeremy when we wanted something from the two of you that you refused to agree to?"

The fact that she could even think that of Mike finally pissed him off, when he'd been biting back wave after wave of frustration and anger since his first night home

"Damn it, Mom!"

He gently squeezed her hand to keep her from walking out, the way she had every other time things had gotten tense. They were going to have this out once and for all.

"I'm not going to leave you to go through this alone," he said. "If you'd ever stopped demanding that I love you exactly the way you wanted me to, you'd have known ten years ago that you didn't have to manipulate me to get me here. I love you. I've always loved you. I would have gotten on a plane as soon as you told me you really needed me. Done whatever I could for you. Don't you know me at all?"

It hurt to say the words, to feel them scraping, cutting, burning their way out of his chest.

It clearly hurt his mother to hear them. She stood, crossing to the window to stare at the dark night beyond. Hugging herself, she gazed at a brilliant half-moon.

"What about the rest?" she wanted to know. "The things your father and I have asked you to finally do for us?"

"You've demanded them," he reminded her. "Not asked. And if I say no, can you and Dad let it go while I'm here without making it a daily ordeal? Or leaking my identity to the press or to the JHTF board or whatever schemes you'll come up with next? Because if I won't do things your way, I don't really love you?"

"Yes," his father said from the doorway, securing both Mike's and his mother's attention. "She can."

But despite his father's assurances, it was already swirling inside Mike—the differences between his family and Bethany's in Chandlerville. In Bethany's world, he'd found the unconditional love and acceptance he'd been searching for. Only to toss it away when he'd asked Bethany to leave New York. Because a part of him had been afraid of having this moment with her one day, when she realized that who and what he was would never be enough for her, either.

Except he *had* been enough, as the stranger she'd met in a bar. As a cowboy drifting through town. As an artist whose photographs had inspired her long before she'd known it was his work. And as a lover, whose heart had touched hers as much as hers had begun to fill the loneliness in his. How could he have thought he could turn his back on that, knowing how empty his life would become without her?

"We'll respect whatever decision you make about living your life," his father said, "however we might continue to disagree. The foundation remains important to your mother and me. A man with your talent and professional networks and interest in helping people could do great good working within JHTF. But you have a right to make your own choices. And this separation between you and your mother and me has gone on long enough. And we . . . Our family can't waste any more time."

"But we—" Livy started to argue.

She stopped at Harrison's raised hand.

"All we ask is that you become an active part of this family for good." Despite his clipped, controlled delivery, the pain consuming Mike's father's expression as he looked around Jeremy's room spoke of deeply buried emotion. "However that has to happen."

Mike stood and faced his father, leery of believing that they could really put a stop to the tension that had been escalating since he came home. There was so much disappointment and resentment. There was his mother's need to forever be the victim. His parents' determination that Mike should shoulder the blame for their family's estrangement. And, yes, there was Mike's desperation to be done with all of it.

But his father was right. The pain they'd caused one another since long before losing Jeremy needed to stop. Mike staying for Livy's sake shouldn't be a toxic thing. It should be about what helping Jeremy had been about: support and caring and family. And *Mike* could change that, whatever his mother insisted on saying or doing. For *his own sake*, he needed to focus on making the most of the last of her life. Not on their lifetime of differences.

That's what he'd been mulling over for the week since Bethany had left, each time he'd looked at the photograph of their combined work. Together, they'd captured the timeless beauty of her meadow—and how a moment can be a lifetime, if you let it mean everything to you.

And Bethany meant everything to him.

Enough to finally do the work he should have long ago, to make things right with his parents.

He thought again about the remarkable chaos of the Dixon home. Of Joe and Marsha weaving their family from a tribe of children others had cast away. They'd created a tapestry of love and acceptance that was the envy of their entire community. And their welcome had begun a healing in Mike, far surpassing the help he'd given Joe. The Dixons were the kind of family Mike and Jeremy had dreamed of having. And it was Mike's to make his home in. Bethany had flown all the way to New York to make sure he knew that.

If Mike could come out the other side of this time with his own parents understanding how to belong—instead of knowing only how to run.

Being afraid is no way to live my art, Mike, Bethany had said. *Or your life. Don't keep hurting yourself, thinking you have to keep going through this alone.*

"I'll be here for you and Mom." He held out his hand to his father, shaking as if they were sealing a business deal. "We'll work together as a family to figure out the rest—assuming you really do finally want a cease-fire. I have only one condition, and it's nonnegotiable . . ."

Chapter Twenty

That Saturday afternoon, Rick Harper, Mike's former boss at McC's, steered Mike through the vendor area for Dru and Brad's wedding reception.

"I'm glad you decided not to let anyone tell her you were coming," Rick said. "Your surprise, whatever it is, will be more fun for folks now that the reception is in full swing. Since you didn't fly back with Bethany from New York, you've had tongues waggin' all over town that you weren't comin' at all—no matter what the Dixons have been saying 'bout why you've been gone. I'm really sorry to hear about your mama."

Mike nodded his thanks.

Livy had endured some final tests over the last week, none of them telling them anything they didn't already know. He'd been with his parents this morning to hear the last of the results. Hence his having to catch a later flight than he'd wanted, and the rearranging of the plans that he'd asked Dru and Brad's help with making, along with a select few of Bethany's other family and Chandlerville friends.

"Anyone in particular rooting against me?" Mike gazed around him.

The bulk of William B. Chandler Park, not far from the heart of town, had been turned over for the day to the Hampton-Douglas nuptials. Cars were parked at the curb and in every available lot. They were teeming from the driveways of nearby homes whose owners had agreed to accommodate the spillover. Mike had noticed the white bows on the mailboxes as he'd driven up, indicating to friends and family which driveways were available.

"I figure Benjie Carrington mighta put some money down on you crashing and burning," Rick said. "But you and the Dixons got nothing but friends and family around today. You do your thing."

"Thanks." Mike had been back in Chandlerville for less than an hour. It had taken less than a minute to fall back in love with the place. "Have you seen Bethany? How does she look?"

"The bridal party's prettier than a rainbow. The entire family's over the moon. I hear she's missing you. Worried about you. But you know she's going to make sure her sister and parents have the best wedding possible. She's rolling with it."

Rick was helping Mike skirt the perimeter of the park, keeping close to the grove of trees on the other side of the soccer fields from where guests had gathered after the ceremony for the reception. The sun was setting on a perfect day, stars and a full moon replacing blue skies and puffy white clouds. A DJ was working his way through Dru's playlist, and Rick had said the bride and groom had already had their first dance.

The sound of happy people beckoned, making Mike want to find Bethany immediately and make sure she was joining in the fun. But he didn't want to ruin Selena and Clair and Nic's plans to keep his arrival off Bethany's radar until the timing was right. Through the trees, he caught glimpses of the bandstand and dance floor and twinkling white lights strung all around. Linen-covered tables and chairs were sprinkled about so people could rest, eat, drink, and mingle.

"Nice threads," Rick said with a critical eye for Mike's suit.

"Dru said it would work with Bethany's dress." Mike straightened his lavender-patterned silk tie and smoothed a hand down his gray suit jacket.

Rick smirked. "No more Cowboy Bob?"

"Not tonight."

"Except for that mangy hat of yours."

"The hat's more important than you know."

Mike lifted a finger to Jeremy's Stetson in a mock salute. He hoped to have only happy memories when he looked back at pictures of tonight—knowing that Jeremy had somehow been a part of it. But along with thoughts of his brother came a twinge of longing.

It had been important to make this happen for Bethany while her community was there to share the moment with her. But Mike couldn't help but wish he had the same kind of family in his corner—a support system waiting to cheer if he could pull tonight off the way he'd hoped. Then again, perhaps he did, since he'd had plenty of help planning and executing his surprise.

He caught sight of Bethany near the dance floor and the laptop and projector she was using to display their image collages onto a white screen beside the DJ's table. While reception guests danced and the smiling bride and groom and wedding party either mingled with the crowd or ate at the head table, Bethany's slide show flashed poignant images of the Dixon family and the town they loved.

She'd crouched in the midst of the ongoing celebration, her lavender dress and its full tulle skirt flowing as she hugged an excited Camille. Both of them wore glittering headbands and matching ear-to-ear smiles. Bethany's pixie-cut auburn hair and gray eyes were shining. Her head was bent close to her niece's dark curls as the two of them blew bubbles from heart-shaped wands.

Mike stopped and stared, his heart pounding against his ribs.

"Keep moving." Rick steered Mike around the food tents that had been set up. "You don't want to catch anyone's eye too soon."

They ducked behind the temporary bar Rick had set up for his McC's staff. It was situated beside Dan and Leigh's tent, where guests were icing their own specialty cupcakes and indulging in other favorites from the bakery. Mouthwatering aromas wafted from the other vendor tents, an eclectic mix of local restaurants serving up their best. There was everything from pizza to gyros to a selection of dim sum from Hong Kong Gardens. Savory finger sandwiches were being served next to quiche and cappuccino, compliments of Grapes & Beans. There was even a milkshake bar, manned by the Dream Whip staff that was also turning out baskets of sliders and fries.

"Don't press your luck," Rick said. "Stay out of the way until one of Bethany's besties comes to get you when it's time. I've got to get to it. People are thirsty, and Law's going to have my ass for leaving him doing all the work. You and that girl of yours have a good time once you pop out of the cake or whatever you're doing next."

Mike nodded, only half listening, playing and replaying his plans in his head. He was determined to get this right, after the remarkable things Bethany had promised him in New York, and the life-changing decisions he'd made for himself since working out a truce with his parents.

"You look nervous, boy." Rick slapped him on the shoulder. "Relax. What the hell? Whatever you've got in the works, what could possibly go wrong with her family and half the town watching you do it?"

"Go enjoy yourself," Marsha told Bethany over the noise of the wedding reception rocking on well past sunset. "Your surprise is wonderful. Your father and I are so proud of what you've done with your paintings. Dru couldn't be more thrilled with our combined wedding and anniversary gifts. Your slide show has everyone mesmerized. Now get out there and enjoy your moment."

Bethany had hung close to her laptop during the reception, watching over the PowerPoint presentation George had helped her design. Bethany had wanted everything to be perfect—while she'd missed Mike more every minute, wishing he could be there to see everyone enjoying how he'd inspired her.

She'd kissed him goodbye at the hospital. On her car service ride back to La Guardia, she'd emailed him the copy of their meadow collage—to which he'd texted that it was beautiful, just like her. And that he was sorry. And that he'd be in touch. Bethany had been the one this time to say that she understood that he needed space. To take his time.

She'd be waiting, she'd reminded him, wishing there was something more she could do to somehow make what he was going through easier. And then she'd come home to her family and the last flurry of wedding plans.

She hadn't reached out to Mike since, and missing him had been driving her crazy.

Her family and friends had been patient, not asking too many questions. They'd accepted that Bethany didn't have the answers about what was going to happen with her and Mike. And that she was done talking about it, at least until after Dru's wedding. And above all else, they'd trusted her not to come completely unglued or disappear on them, even if Mike never came back to her.

She was stronger than that now.

Love could hurt. It could hurt badly sometimes. But her heart was finally wide open to her family—and every other good thing she could grab hold of in her life.

The wedding ceremony had been every beautiful thing Dru and Brad had wanted it to be. The reception was an ongoing, nonstop celebration of two friends and lovers beginning their lives together. And it had filled Bethany's heart that her and Mike's collages were contributing to the magic.

"I am enjoying myself." Bethany hugged her mom, gazing around them, her smile widening because she had one more presentation up her sleeve that her mom and dad didn't know about. "It's a magical night."

"And you've made it so much more special," Marsha said. They watched the slide show for a while, until the image of Camille that Mike had worked on filled the projection screen. "Is this what you've been doing in Mike's studio?"

"Partly." Bethany basked in her mother's radiant smile. "He helped me rediscover how free creating can be. Because of him, I'll never give up on my dreams again."

"Hearing that is an even better anniversary gift than your beautiful pictures." Marsha kissed her cheek.

"Actually . . ." Bethany hugged her mom closer. "The slide show was for Dru and Brad. You and Dad haven't seen your anniversary surprise yet."

"Is that right?" Marsha's eyes lit with excitement.

There was also the suspicious twinkle Bethany had seen in her mother's expression once or twice throughout the day. And on more than one of her siblings' and friends' faces since the reception started.

"I guess it's a night for surprises then," Marsha said.

"Mom?" Bethany asked. "What's going on?"

"Nothing, dear. Joe and I just want to see you having a good time. So whatever you have up your sleeve, come over and join the party instead of watching everyone dance without you. Joe's getting ready to have his turn with Dru. He's going to be looking for you after that. The man's on a mission to show off all the rehab work he's done. Don't make him hunt you down all the way over here."

"Go," Clair said, appearing from behind them and startling Bethany. "I'll keep an eye on the slide presentation."

"Where did you come from?" Bethany's friend had dropped out of sight nearly an hour ago.

"Around." Clair, when she faked innocence, was like a child with crumbs all over her face, acting as if she hadn't just devoured every cookie in the cookie jar.

"What's going on?" Bethany demanded.

Her nerves might be on edge because of the strained silence between her and the man she loved. But that didn't mean she was being completely neurotic. Something suspicious was definitely swirling in the gentle night breeze.

"I've been helping Nic take care of some last-minute reception things. Now go be with your family. I've got you covered here."

Clair all but shoved Bethany into trailing after her mother. While Bethany followed Marsha, she waved her hand toward Law and Rick, who were working in the tent McC's had set up to provide drinks for the guests. Law nodded at their agreed-upon signal and began pouring fresh glasses of champagne. He headed their way.

“Have a seat with Dad.” Bethany steered her mom to the head table and smiled once her parents were sitting together.

The DJ’s music stopped. Law arrived with her parents’ bubbly. Which hopefully meant Nic was somewhere nearby orchestrating things, even though Bethany couldn’t find her as her gaze skimmed over the crowd.

“I’d like to make a toast,” Bethany said, taking and lifting her glass of champagne.

She couldn’t catch her breath suddenly. It was like the very first time in high school, when she’d shown her parents her very first landscape and trusted them with her dreams.

Voices quieted as Marsha and Joe took their glasses from Law. Guests on the dance floor and around the reception turned to watch Bethany and her parents. Dru and Brad and Selena and Oliver and Travis and Shandra grouped around Bethany, holding their own glasses to toast with. They’d corralled their younger foster siblings and Camille to stand quietly with them, creating a family circle that silently spoke of love and time and each of their commitments to never forget the priceless gift of belonging that their foster parents had given them.

A couple of Nic’s serving staff arrived with Bethany’s easel. It and the framed landscape beneath were covered in a cloth that matched the bright white table linens. They set it down beside Oliver and Travis, exactly where Bethany had wanted it.

“Mom and Dad,” she said through her nerves. She raised her glass. “We all love you so much. We’re grateful that thirty-five years ago today, your love for each other started us all on a journey that’s made not just today possible for Dru and Brad, but so many other remarkable days for all of us. Unforgettable moments in our family’s life and the lives of many others in Chandlerville. To show you how much you’re loved and how much love you’ve given all of us, I've been working on something I hope will help you see . . . just how much you've blessed the lives of everyone lucky enough to be here with you today."

Joe kissed his wife as they listened to their daughter.

Marsha hugged his arm and leaned her head against his shoulder. They were eager to see whatever Bethany had saved to show them. It would be the icing on the cake of a perfect day—and the coming surprise for *Bethany* that the family had been waiting all evening to arrive.

Their Dru was married to a man who'd cherish her forever. Their kids and friends were grouped around them on a perfect fall night. Joe had made it through the ceremony and reception and all the pre-wedding photographs and fuss with enough energy in reserve to dance with the bride soon, and then with Bethany and hopefully Camille and Shandra before he called it quits and headed home to collapse into bed with his own bride.

But the look of confident joy on Bethany's face as she gazed at them, surrounded by her brothers and sisters, was the real victory for Joe and his wife. They'd watched their daughter thrive over the last few weeks, no matter how difficult the waiting to hear from Mike had been for her. Bethany was finally embracing who and what she was, both as a part of their family, and as a woman who could love with her whole heart. Even if that love came with worry and waiting and the chance of losing—as loving the most important things in life often did.

Their Bethany was finally home to stay.

"We'll make this quick," she said, "because there's more dancing and fun to get to. But, Mom and Dad, this day—so many days—would never have happened if it weren't for everything you've given us."

She looked to Oliver and Travis and the rectangular something hidden beneath the cloth that had been thrown over her easel. Joe had been blown away by the amazing images Bethany had created for the wedding's slide show, from work she'd done with her paintings and Mike's photography. The thought that there could be something more, just for him and Marsha, had his heart swelling with pride.

"Joe and Marsha Dixon," Bethany said with damp, smiling eyes, "this is what I've been trying to paint for you ever since I came back to Chandlerville. But I didn't understand what it needed to be, how to finish it, until recently. I hope you like it." She raised her glass higher, toasting as everyone joined in. "We all love you very much."

She sipped and then nodded to the boys. Oliver and Travis removed the cloth to reveal the most beautiful painting Joe was certain he'd ever see. He stood, slowly, his wife next to him, and they walked closer. His legs were tired, his entire body was aching, and he'd likely hurt all over tomorrow. But in that moment, he was certain he could run a marathon.

"It's amazing," he said.

"It's wonderful, honey," Marsha agreed tearfully. "It's so beautiful."

Bethany had painted their house in a way Joe had never seen her use color before. It was so light, transparent, but remarkably full of energy and motion and beauty.

The trees and the sun and the porch and each window of the home where he and Marsha had raised their family was recognizable, but only with hints of what the building looked like in real life. Brief touches of Bethany's brush had suggested the structure, rather than reflecting it in detail. But there was so much life and love and beauty in the dreamy way she'd captured their world. Hope and possibility, swirling in ghostly wisps of glorious green.

And on the matting that she'd used when she'd framed the piece were more of the photographs she and Mike had combined into the collages in her slide show. Faces and eyes and smiles and places so familiar and dear, a lifetime of them, surrounded Bethany's beautiful perspective of the house she'd been welcomed to and loved in. The collection seemed to capture every chance at the happy life she'd been given. And the happiness of the woman she'd become, now that she was finally, fully, loving them back.

Joe pulled his daughter into his arms. "I'm so proud of who you've become, Bethie. Thank you for letting us be your family."

Marsha joined their hug, then Shandra, holding Camille, and Oliver and Travis and Selena, too. And at their center, Joe could hear Bethany laughing softly. Or maybe she was crying. Maybe all of them were. But it was the happy kind of crying. The best kind of crying, with your family around you and the future ahead of you, and it felt as if there was nothing you couldn't conquer together.

"I have one more surprise for the evening, if I may," a familiar voice said from outside their family circle.

Joe turned, hugging his daughter to his side, until she could see that Mike Taylor stood at the edge of the crowd of spectators, dressed in an expensive suit, his hair cut short and conservative, wearing his Stetson and a smile for the woman he'd called Joe last night to say that he loved with all of his heart.

Mike glanced to Bethany's painting and then back to her.

"I hope you don't mind the interruption," he said as Bethany squealed and ran into his arms.

Chapter Twenty-One

"You're here!" Bethany couldn't believe it. She couldn't let Mike go.

"I've wanted to be here every day I've been gone." He lifted her onto the toes of her red cowboy boots. He kissed her beneath his Stetson until she couldn't breathe. And then he eased back.

Her cowboy was dressed like a banker in his beautiful suit and a silk tie that was the exact shade of her dress.

"How did you sneak in here?" Bethany asked.

A thousand questions raced through her mind about why he hadn't called and how things were with his family and what his showing up now meant. But there was only one answer that mattered. Mike had come back, and he was smiling down at her as if he'd never leave.

"Have you been here all day?" she asked.

"I had a little help. And no, there's no way I could have stayed away from you looking this beautiful if I'd been here all day." His next kiss was less ravenous. Sweet, even as instant heat sparked, promising much more to come.

"Help?" she asked, a day's worth of her family and friends'

suspicious smiles and half-answered questions coming back to her. "Help with what?"

"There was something important I wanted to talk with you about." He tilted her chin up.

Her breath caught at the serious tone that had crept into his voice. "Here? In front of everybody?"

"I wanted your family and friends to hear what I have to say. I've already checked with the bride and groom and your parents, to be sure they were okay with me intruding on your family's special day."

"Everyone wanted you here," she insisted, hoping he'd found a way to see them belonging together, loving together, sharing each other's good and bad times, no matter what life had in store for them next. "My family wanted you to be part of *our* special day."

He gazed at her painting.

A look of longing crossed his features that would have confused her once. He seemed so confident and easygoing most of the time. Then he'd let her see all of his heart. And she'd chased him to New York and witnessed firsthand the darkest and the bravest, most loyal parts of Mike that he'd never wanted her to know.

"You did a beautiful job with it," he said about her painting.

"*We* did a beautiful job. I would never have finished it if you hadn't helped me let go and play and dream."

She kissed him, loving him for everything he was and all they could be.

"Mine," she said softly, so the words were just for them.

"All mine," he whispered back. "You look like a princess and taste like bubble gum."

Then he reached into his pocket and pulled out a red velvet box.

"What . . ." She gasped as he took her hand and knelt, slipping his hat off so she could see all of his handsome, smiling face as he gazed up at her. "What are you doing?"

"Asking you to forgive me," he said, "for losing sight of the most important thing you've taught me. And—"

"You're forgiven." She tugged on his hand, her ears ringing as she glanced around at the sea of smiling faces staring at them. "Whatever it is, get up off your knees and we can talk about it later when—"

"I've already waited too long to ask you to marry me." He popped the top of the box open to reveal the most gorgeous ring she'd ever seen. A delicate band that could have been platinum or white gold or silver, or tin for all she cared, had been set with a sparkling, heart-shaped diamond.

A collective gasp sounded from the crowd.

"Mike . . ." She lifted her eyes to his face. "What have you done?"

"I've decided that I need you to be my home, wherever we are. And that whatever we have to face in this world, you're what's best for me. I know you'll be okay without me, Bethany. But I'll never be what I could be, without you in my life." He glanced at their art, flashing silently on the projection screen. He smiled at her, pride in his eyes for what she'd done with their images. "Please be my bride, Bethany Darling, and I promise I'll never forget that again."

Bethany looked up from the love on Mike's face, to the smiles and hugs being exchanged beneath the stars and twinkling lights of Dru's wedding. Her sister and Brad were holding each other close, not minding a bit that Bethany and Mike were hijacking their reception.

"Answer the man," Dru said, wrapped in her husband's arms. "We've been waiting all night for Mike to make his move."

"But . . ." Bethany tugged Mike's hand until he was on his feet beside her.

Oliver had Camille in his arms now. And Camille had her bottle of bubbles and was blowing through the tiny wand to shower Bethany and Mike in a cascade of iridescence. Marsha laughed, softly clapping and smiling as Dru and Brad and others began clapping, too. Softly at first and then with more enthusiasm, the rest of the reception guests joined in, encouraging Bethany, accepting Mike.

"But"—Bethany gazed into the bottomless brown eyes of her wandering soul mate—"what about your mother and your family's foundation and your fight with your parents over your place there?"

"You and I can do a lot of good at JHTF," he said, "if that's what we decide to do. We can do a lot of good at the Atlanta Artist Co-op, or starting more nonprofit centers, or making art and selling it to raise money to do whatever we decide is best to do next. We can do anything we want, make whatever we want work, Bethany, as long as we do this together."

We.

Together.

I was scared to death of all of it, Marsha had said about the risks she and Joe had taken over the years. *But I trusted the man I loved more than I trusted the fear.*

Bethany threw her arms around Mike, the tulle of her skirt bunching between them.

"And your parents?" she asked as Mike held her close. "It's not like either of them were thrilled to discover me in your life."

"I've settled things with Livy and Harrison. I told them that they're my family, and I love them, and I'm not going to let them down just because we don't see eye to eye. I'm going to be there for my mother for as long as she has left. And I'll find a way to have a better connection with my dad. But I told them that I love you, too. And they'll have to accept that, and you, without reservations. That I'll only be involved with the foundation in whatever way I think is best. And that I won't know what that will be"—he eased Bethany away—"until I've had the chance to discuss it with my fiancée. So, no more pretending, darlin'. It's you and me out in the open now, for both our families and the whole world to see."

Bethany heard someone sniffling, and she realized that it was Nicole, her unsentimental friend, melting at Mike's words.

"I love you, Bethany." He kissed the tip of her nose. "I need you. I'll always need you. Say you'll marry me."

"I need you, too," Bethany gushed out. "Wherever you are, Harrison Michael Taylor, wherever you go, that's where I'll always want to be."

An ear-splitting cheer went up from the crowd. Mike plucked the ring from its bed of velvet and tossed the box to Oliver, who snatched it from the air like a fly ball. Bethany's brother nodded his approval at her, his and everyone else's support meaning the world. And then Mike was slipping the representation of his heart over her finger and kissing her softly.

"Hi," he said as he held her gently.

"Hi, yourself," Bethany answered back, the peaceful beat of her heart pressed close to the strength of his. She pushed up to her toes to whisper into her cowboy's ear, "Let's take each other on the adventure of a lifetime."

Acknowledgments

An author cherishes each unexpected encounter that opens the door to possibility. Chance meetings on two recent trips became the inspiration that flourished into the journeys of *His Darling Bride* artists Bethany Darling and Mike Taylor.

I'd like to thank Steven Fey, of Steven Fey Fine Art Photography, Bainbridge Island, Washington (stevenfeyphotography.com), for more than his valuable insight into large-format photography. His uncompromising philosophy for sharing his view of the world as he does (rather than pursuing more contemporary digital techniques) became the core of Mike Taylor's commitment to his own unique perspective.

I'd like to thank Robert Lange and Megan Aline of Robert Lange Studios (RLS), Charleston, South Carolina (robertlangestudios.com), for their generosity and passionate pursuit of inspiration and community. The diversity of art in their studio helped me frame the progression of Bethany Darling's creative voice. Their residency program and desire to support artistic experimentation, networking, funding, and volunteering was the genesis of the art co-op and outreach programs depicted in this work of fiction.

Please support local artists in your community.

About the Author

Anna DeStefano is the award-winning, nationally bestselling author of more than twenty-five books, including the Mimosa Lane novels and the Atlanta Heroes series. Born in Charleston, South Carolina, she's lived in the South her entire life. Her background as a care provider and adult educator in the world of crisis and grief recovery lends itself to the deeper psychological themes of every story she writes. A wife and mother, she currently writes in a charming northeast suburb of Atlanta, Georgia, not all that different from her characters' beloved Chandlerville. She is also a workshop and keynote speaker, a writing coach, and a freelance editor.

Get to know Anna at annawrites.com/blog and the Anna DeStefano: Author page on Facebook, where she shares her inspirations, her challenges, a healthy dose of honest optimism, and tidbits about upcoming projects.

97724258R00202

Made in the USA
Columbia, SC
19 June 2018